ALSO BY RINA KENT

LEGACY OF GODS

God of Malice

God of Pain

God of Wrath

God of Ruin

God of Fury

God of War

VIPERS

Beautiful Venom

SWEET VENOM

RINA KENT

Bloom *books*

Published by Bloom Books, an imprint of Sourcebooks
1935 Brookdale RD, Naperville, IL 60563–2773
(630) 961-3900
sourcebooks.com

Cataloging-in-Publication Data is on file with the Library of Congress.

Printed and bound in the United States of America.
LSC 10 9 8 7 6 5 4 3 2 1

For the survivors with scars no one sees,
and the ones who choose the light
even while standing in the dark.

Author Note

Hello reader friend,

Sweet Venom can be enjoyed as a complete standalone, but for a better understanding of the world, it's recommended to read *Beautiful Venom* first.

If you're new to my books, you might not know that I write darker stories that can be intense, unsettling, and even disturbing. My characters and their journeys defy societal norms and aren't meant for everyone.

Sweet Venom contains references to mental illness, depression, suicidal ideation, and emotional abuse, including parental neglect and child abuse. It includes graphic violence, murder, torture, stalking, attempted child sexual abuse, the death of a family member, and mentions of multiple abortions and drug use/overdose involving non-main characters. Specific kinks in this book include consensual non-consent (CNC) and somnophilia. Reader discretion is advised.

For more things Rina Kent, visit rinakent.com

Playlist

Chokehold—Sleep Token
Granite—Sleep Token
Panoramic View—AWOLNATION
Right Here—Chase Atlantic
Cry Baby—The Neighbourhood
Rain—Sleep Token
Bad Omens—5 Seconds of Summer
Keeping You Around—Nothing But Thieves
It's Not Living (If It's Not With You)—The 1975
Tongue Tied—Grouplove
FUNERAL—Neoni
My Oh My (feat. DaBaby)—Camila Cabello, DaBaby
Landmines—BELLSAINT
Can't Pretend—Tom Odell
I don't wanna lose again—Munn
Poison or Patience—Friday Pilots Club & OSTON
Is it Love—Loreen

You can find the complete playlist on Spotify.

CHAPTER 1
Violet

SOMEONE'S WATCHING ME.

Constantly.

Overtly.

The attention prickles the back of my neck like a thin, tiny needle delving deep beneath my skin.

In the beginning, I thought it was one of the bar's patrons who had a tendency to make me feel uncomfortable with their lingering gazes and 'accidental' touches.

Or maybe it was one of the desolate souls from our sketchy neighborhood who looked at me as if I were a piece of meat.

For as long as I can remember, I've always been that.

A piece of meat.

An object.

A toy.

One that bounces and ping-pongs, no matter how hard it's kicked.

So this time shouldn't feel any different. Once again, I'm just another something to someone.

A fixation.

A twisted fascination.

As long as they don't come any closer, I'm safe.

I ignore the feel of those disturbing, creepy eyes like I do everything uncomfortable in my life.

Shove it in the closet. Close the door on it. Pretend it doesn't exist.

I wipe the bar counter after the last patron is escorted out by the manager, who laughs along with his drunken mumbling.

HAVEN is the main sports bar in Stantonville, a small run-down town in the Northeast whose entire personality revolves around an overt obsession with ice hockey.

Tonight, there was a replay of a game where the local college team—the Stanton Wolves—crushed it, according to all the happy faces I served.

If it had been a live game, I would've been nervous. Considering the men we get here, I don't know which is worse—when the Wolves win or when they lose.

In both cases, there are drunks who slur, shout, and don't keep their hands to themselves, but I guess maybe it's better when they win. Otherwise, we have to deal with ugly violence.

Hockey—and sports in general—doesn't really appeal to me. I was always bad at physical activities and was the class bookworm from a young age. However, since I go to Stanton River College, or SRC, where the Wolves are worshiped like gods, I have to keep up the pretense to care so I don't stand out in a bad light.

While others might be fine with saying they truly don't care for hockey and can take the malicious commentary that will most definitely follow, I'd rather remain in my own bubble and avoid confrontation.

The smell of alcohol saturates my senses, and I try to block it out as I wipe faster, my lower back aching, my arms screaming, and my head swimming in a fuzzy mess. I'm so sleep-deprived and tired, I can barely keep my eyes open.

Laura slides up to my side and helps put the glasses on the tray, her face worn out, her movements lethargic, and her gaze lost. She's in her thirties and had to take a second job to afford to raise her adorable daughter, Karly.

I have extreme respect for Laura for being able to juggle being a single mom and working multiple jobs. I can barely survive work, volunteering, and college.

And even though it's mid-July and vacation season is in full swing, I'm taking summer classes to improve my GPA.

As Laura starts to carry the tray of glasses, I pull it from her hands and smile. "You can go home. I'll finish up."

"Really?" Her expression lights up, but she bites her lower lip. "You always do this. I feel bad taking advantage of your kindness."

"You're good. I know you miss little Karly and you're worried since she hasn't been feeling well."

"Ahh, you're honestly the best, Violet." She side-hugs me, her face still tired, but a soft smile lights it up.

And that makes me feel better. The tension in my shoulders eases a little, and I take on her tasks with renewed energy.

I like lessening the burden on others, especially if it's someone like Laura who needs to work twice as hard to put food on the table for her little girl.

Maybe that's because I was also brought up by a single mom.

"Oh." Laura turns on her heel, then comes closer, casting a discreet glance at the security guys and the bartender, who are talking to the manager. "Did you see the huge motorcycle parked across the street when you came in?"

All the ease vanishes, and my body tenses up in that frozen response I have for everything. "There's…a motorcycle?"

"Yeah. It looked expensive. Kinda hot. Here, I took a picture."

She fishes her phone out of her back pocket and scrolls through her gallery.

My breath catches.

It's him.

The tall man cloaked in black—jacket, gloves, and helmet—leaning against the monstrous gleaming black bike, his legs crossed at the ankles. No part of his face is visible.

But I know that bike.

I've seen it near my neighborhood.

Why would he park it across from HAVEN? Why not hide like he always does?

My stomach twists.

This…this is an escalation.

He's done hiding.

He wants me to know.

I try to remain calm, but my insides war with anxiety and the need to throw up. My fingers instinctively find the small tattoo on my left wrist, and I trace it back and forth, back and forth, willing it to quiet the chaos.

But there's no calming my thoughts.

Am I…in danger?

"Can you send me the picture?" I ask Laura with a forced smile that she doesn't see, because she's zooming in on the man.

"Sure. He looks so hot, right? I've got a thing for biker guys in leather." She chuckles and I laugh along with her even as my fingers tremble when I retrieve my phone.

Laura leaves after she sends me the picture, and I add it

to the folder with some other discreet pictures I took from my apartment. Maybe this will be enough for the police to provide me with protection?

Though that's highly unlikely. Last week, when I showed them some of the ones I'd taken, they dismissed me and said I was being paranoid. Admittedly, the man is hard to make out since he was always in the shadows and never really in full frame like in the one Laura sent me.

This is the first time he's been standing there in person, and I can't help but think his actions are becoming dangerous. I can't get away with ignoring him, but I also know the police won't help me.

I zoom in on the picture Laura sent me, my wet fingers slipping on the screen.

Is that even him?

He looks…intimidating. All wrapped in black and danger.

I'll have to try harder with the police because this guy's presence is starting to mess with my head.

He's everywhere.

Like air.

And I've lived among enough creeps to know he probably won't be satisfied with just watching. He'll eventually take action and it'll end badly for me.

My head is full of macabre thoughts as I quietly finish my shift. It's around one thirty in the morning by the time I finally leave HAVEN, my back pain killing me and my thoughts swirling in a black pool.

I relax a little when I don't see the motorcycle or the guy.

The only silver lining is that he's not there all the time. He probably has a job or something, because his presence has been sporadic over the past few weeks or so.

With a sigh, I pull my hoodie tighter over my head, feeling more at ease now that I'm not dressed in the tight shirt and jeans we have to wear at work. But at least we're not forced to wear short skirts—I've quit many jobs because of that.

In my everyday life, jeans are fine as long as I get to wear baggy hoodies or sweatshirts that don't outline my body. I even wear light hoodies during the summer.

Thankfully, the apartment I share with my sister is only a twenty-five-minute walk from HAVEN, so I don't have to spend money on transportation. I pass by a twenty-four-hour fast-food place and go in to buy a few sandwiches, then walk out in the middle of a drunken brawl without even being noticed.

It's easy for me to be invisible as long as I have my hoodie on, my hair is hidden, and my eyes are covered by the thick-framed nonprescription glasses I'm currently wearing.

"Don't let me hear you breathing, Violet. If you lay low and shut your trap, you won't get into trouble."

Mama's words have been my mantra since I was a little girl. At twenty-two, I've mastered the art of moving around in an invisible cloak.

As long as no one notices me, I'll be fine.

The neighborhood where Dahlia and I have been living for the past couple of years reeks of desperation, a place where dreams come to die and vices fester like an open wound.

It's not far from Stantonville's town center, but it feels like another world entirely—a forgotten pocket where street-lights flicker on their last breath and shadows move with intentions best left undiscovered.

Small-time gangs linger on the corners, dealing drugs for quick cash, their hooded figures blending into the peeling painted brick walls. The sidewalks are littered with cigarette butts, discarded needles, and the occasional broken bottle.

As I walk, the air is thick with the acrid stench of stale beer and burnt rubber, mixing with the faint scent of rotting food from an overflowing dumpster. A couple fights down the street, their voices raw and venomous, laced with anger that comes from years of resentment. The man's growl is slurred, the woman's shriek sharp enough to slice through the humid night.

"You worthless piece of shit! You call yourself a man?" she spits, followed by a crash—a glass or a bottle meeting a wall or the ground.

"You're the fucking whore!" he roars, and more curses ensue.

The neighbors, who, like me, are accustomed to this nightly ritual, shout back from open windows, "Shut up already, for fuck's sake!"

Another voice, hoarse with exhaustion, yells something about calling the cops, but no one actually will. Not here. The cops don't come unless they have a reason, and even then, they look the other way for the right price.

It's why I don't trust them to keep whoever is stalking me at bay. I suppose they're just an imaginary safety net I hold on to so I won't go mad.

A gust of wind carries the scent of cheap perfume and sweat from a nearby alley where a woman leans against a car, her thigh peeking out from a torn fishnet stocking as she laughs at what a man is whispering in her ear.

I step over a fresh puddle of something dark—could be coffee, could be blood—and pull my hoodie tighter around me. This place is a landfill of humanity, a breeding ground for ghosts who are still alive, but just barely.

And I'm one of them.

My feet halt by Johnny and Bo, who are sleeping by a corner. They're covered with scraps that barely protect them from the night chill. I gave them my blanket when my sister Dahlia bought me a new one, but I think they sold it. It's summer anyway, so they probably don't need it.

"Night, guys," I whisper as I drop the sandwiches I usually buy them, then, because we got decent tips tonight, I slip a few bills under each of the wrappers.

Dahlia always tells me not to give them money, because they'll buy alcohol with it, and maybe they do, but the other day, Bo was grinning wide after he showed me the shoes he bought from the thrift shop with the money I gave him.

I walk through the alley that leads me straight to our street. The lone streetlight that's still working flickers with a buzz, highlighting the waste rotting on either side. I breathe through my mouth to avoid inhaling the stench of piss reeking alongside the walls.

Heavy steps echo behind me, slashing through the silence. My heart lunges and I grab my backpack tighter, my nails sinking into the straps as I quicken my pace.

The footsteps follow, bouncing off the alley's walls with a threatening caress.

My hoodie sticks to my back and sweat beads on my temples. Could it be…?

No. He's never approached me.

But then again, he's also never shown up in front of HAVEN before.

Is he escalating twice on the same day?

I just need to get home and hide—

A strong hand latches onto my elbow and pulls me back. I go into shock mode.

It's… I don't know what it is, but whenever I'm in danger, I just freeze completely, catatonically, almost. My limbs go numb and refuse to follow my brain's commands to move.

Run.

Do something.

Anything.

People have fight or flight, but I have freeze.

I stare back, expecting to see the black helmet of my grim reaper, but all that comes into view is balding shaggy blond hair and a stained sleeveless white shirt.

"D-Dave…" I exhale, my heart still beating loudly, but at least my muscles unlock.

It's the local alcoholic, Dave, who's been drinking himself to an early grave ever since his wife took the children and left.

"Heeey, beautiful…" He sways on his feet, his meaty fingers digging into my arm as he takes a swig from his bottle of whiskey.

I pull my arm, but he latches onto it tighter, so I feign a smile. "Let me go, please."

It's not the first time he's done this, and he lets go when I ask. Usually, that is. Right now, however, he looks terribly drunk. Flushed cheeks, beady eyes with bags underneath them, and he reeks so badly, I have to breathe through my mouth.

"Maria won the court case, and I can't see my kids." He slurs his words.

"I'm sorry to hear that." I speak softly, subtly pulling my arm.

"Stupid judge says I'm a bad influence. Why the fuck is that?" He growls, tightening his grip on my elbow, and I wince.

"I'm sure if you show you're improving, the judge will let you see them—"

"Shut your trap." He's in my face now, his alcohol-laced rotten breath skimming over my face. "All you women do is yap and fucking complain. You never appreciate a good man."

He's anything but a good man. Maria is the good woman who took a lot of abuse from him before she finally left, but I can't say that, because he looks irritated and I'd bear the brunt of his anger.

If anything, I'm instinctively cowering, withdrawing into the broken shell Mama built for me one lash at a time. I'm back to being the little girl she screamed at, kicked for being a nuisance, and locked in the closet.

My mere existence used to vex her.

Just my trying to help used to annoy her.

"Don't touch me!" she shouted and shoved me against the wall when I tried to rub ointment on her bruised face after a 'client' left. "You're the reason I'm like this, you goddamn leech. I wish I'd killed you! Stop fucking looking at me with those disgusting eyes!"

Dave didn't tell me not to look at him, but I lower my gaze anyway as I whisper, "Please let me go."

"Why?" he slurs, stepping closer. "I can show you a good time."

"No." I try to speak loudly, but my voice comes out small. I'm incapable of screaming, because my mom stripped that away from me—among other things.

"All you women want is money, fucking sluts. I said I'll show you a good time, so stop whining and thank me for it." He pushes me, his large, heavy body that reeks of alcohol and sweat trapping me against the wall.

A low buzz starts in my ears, but I shove at his chest with unsteady hands.

"Dave…please don't do this. Think of your little girl. You wouldn't want her to be hurt like this, right?"

He wavers a bit, and I try to slowly disengage, my heart hammering in my ears. As I'm about to slip away, he grabs my breast over my hoodie, and bile fills my throat.

"Where ya think you're going?" He fondles me as I push at his hand. "I wanna see your tits."

I should knee him. He's drunk, so he'd probably fall over—

Before I can do that, a gloved hand wraps around Dave's head and pulls him back so powerfully, he stumbles before he falls against the opposite wall.

I watch with complete horror as the tall, large man who's dressed entirely in black slams his fist into Dave's nose.

He flashes me a look over his shoulder, and I can finally see the face of the man who's been stalking me for weeks as he says in a deep, gruff voice, "How annoying."

CHAPTER 2
Violet

CONFRONTATION HAS NEVER BEEN MY STRONG SUIT.

If anything, I avoid it like the plague, but the thing I avoid most?

Violence.

I've been in too many bad situations where I was overpowered by people so much bigger than me that I couldn't have possibly taken them.

My mom. The men who visited her. My foster parents.

Dave just now.

All of them used their size to intimidate me, and I'm easily intimidated—a scaredy-cat through and through.

My favorite activities include reading, embroidering, and scribbling in my journal. Hell, even working is fine.

Anything is fine compared to being overpowered by another person.

Right now, however, I'm not the one being intimidated or thrown around.

It's Dave.

He's being held by the collar of his stained sleeveless shirt as a man drives his gloved fist into his face.

And it's not just *any* man.

It's the man who's been following me sporadically for over a month.

My stalker.

And this guy just called *me* annoying before he went back to pummeling Dave against the wall.

I'm the annoying one.

Me.

The crunching of bones tightens my stomach, raising the bile in my throat. Dave's blood splashes on his shirt and the wall, and the dots of red look black under the flickering light. Like an ancient curse.

My drunkard neighbor groans and tries to resist, but his uncoordinated movements do nothing to halt or even slow down the stranger's assault.

I'm transfixed by the view, trembling as I push further into the wall, the solid surface digging into my back as the air assaults my tightened throat.

Violence isn't anything new to me. I've witnessed it in spades and have been on the receiving end of it more times than I can count. But this is the first time I've seen anyone being so…*calm* while they're beating the shit out of someone.

Laser focused, even.

As if his sole purpose is to dismantle Dave limb from limb.

I can only see the stranger's back, but even that feels like a disturbance. He's tall, at least 6'4" or 6'5". I'm 5'6" and still feel like an ant behind him.

But it's not only the height.

He's broad and muscular, as if he's carved from stone, and his fists strike powerful punches.

I don't like overly tall or extravagantly big men.

Actually, I stay away from all men by using my invisibility tactic.

It's simple in my mind—dress shabbily, lower my gaze, don't speak too much or draw attention.

The formula Mama gave me has worked most of the time.

Not with this man, though.

Because not only has this one been following me, but he's also beating Dave because of me.

The ridges of his big muscles strain against the leather as he lifts his fist.

Thwack.

He lifts it again.

Thwack.

Blood drips from his glove, forming small pools on the dirty concrete as Dave squeals like a pig being slaughtered.

His fight and his voice wane, but the stranger is still punching and punching and *punching.*

A rush of apprehension ripples through me with each of his hits. The horrendous sound fills the turbulence in my head with red.

"Stop it," I say in a small voice, tracing my wrist tattoo. "You'll kill him."

The stranger doesn't pay me any attention. I doubt he even hears me.

I take a hesitant step forward, physically pushing off the wall with my palm because, all this time, I've been trying to become one with it.

Logically, I should go home. Leave both monsters to battle it out in the darkness, but I don't want to be the reason behind someone's murder.

I tap the stranger's arm that's still grabbing Dave by the collar. Blood trickles down, staining the white shirt crimson and coating the black glove in a dark, sticky mess.

"Stop," I whisper, unable to tear my eyes from Dave's shattered face. It's unrecognizable—blood, saliva, and snot distorting his features.

"Stop?" the stranger repeats in a low growl that crawls across my skin. His voice is so deep and startling, it makes me flinch.

He speaks like it's a chore to utter words. As if I'm wasting his time.

"Yeah…you'll kill him."

"Why would you care?"

I stare up at him.

Big mistake.

I've done everything in my might to avoid eye contact since that usually helps me go unnoticed, but here I am.

Looking at the most soulless eyes I've ever seen.

They're dark brown or black—I'm not sure which—but they're so utterly lifeless, I feel as if I'm in the presence of death.

But death has never scared me. If anything, the thought of it has comforted me. Whenever I'm kicked or thrown around and so damn tired, I think of death and how it'll free me from all of this.

This stranger, however, is a gruesome version of death, a dark, ruthless entity who I'm sure would snap my and Dave's necks without any form of remorse.

And it'll definitely not be the peaceful type of death I've always envisioned in my darkest hours.

It'll be merciless and bloody.

Staring at his face is akin to looking into a deep lake. Pretty from far away but frightening up close.

He's the kind of beautiful that feels like a trap—razor-sharp, calculated, and entirely lethal. His features are carved with cruel precision, from the defined cheekbones that cast harsh shadows under the dim light, to the precise cut of his jaw, as if sculpted from ice and tempered by fire.

His straight nose adds an aristocratic edge that speaks of lineage and old money, but there's nothing refined about the way he looks at me.

Almost as if...I *disgust* him.

"Answer me," he repeats when I say nothing. "Why would you care?"

"Why would I care if you kill someone?"

"Yes." He speaks the lone word with a gruff tone, as if he didn't want to say anything and was forced to.

"Maybe because that's wrong?"

"Wrong," he repeats with an edge.

His dark hair is styled back, slick and perfect, and my gaze is drawn to a few rebellious strands that have slipped free, curling over the thick line of his forehead. They don't soften him. If anything, they make him look more untamed, like a beast barely contained beneath a shell of restraint.

It's like I'm in the presence of a brewing storm or a pending disaster. My body is tight due to the awareness that he could erupt or blow up in my face at any second.

Like Mama.

"So, you know what's fucking wrong?" His lips press into a firm line, betraying no emotion, but his nostrils flare just enough to suggest irritation—almost as if my mere existence offends him.

"What?"

He says nothing, just continues to stare at me.

No. *Glare.*

There's a danger in his stillness, a quiet violence

simmering beneath the surface. His gaze is dark, unreadable, but it sinks into my skin, a slow, deliberate scrape that peels back layers that I want to remain hidden.

The stranger isn't just looking—he's dissecting, calculating, as if deciding whether I'm worth his attention or if he should simply erase me from the world.

I can't look away, even when every instinct screams at me to run.

And for a moment, he seems familiar. Like a face I've previously encountered.

Impossible.

There's no way I wouldn't remember someone as striking as he is if I'd met him before.

"If I let him go, will you take his place and be my punching bag?" he asks out of the blue, his eyes tapering to an uncomfortable calm.

"No...of course not."

He throws Dave aside and he falls against the wall, then stands and stumbles out of the alleyway, muttering something about how the stranger will pay for this.

I can't focus on him, though, because the stranger is now stepping into my space. His broad frame blocks my vision until he's all I can see or pay attention to.

The scent of something masculine and heady floods my senses as he towers over me, trapping me in his disturbing presence.

I have to crane my head to look up at him, once again making the eye contact I should avoid at all costs.

"Too late. I already let him go." He takes a step forward, and I instinctively step back, my beat-up sneakers scraping against the concrete.

"I didn't agree to that." I discreetly reach into my back

pocket. If I can call 911, if they could hear what's happening, maybe they'll send help—

A large hand latches onto my wrist, pulls my arm, then twists. My stomach coils at the view of the bloodstains at the palm of his glove.

"What do you think you're doing, hmm?" The rumble of his voice seeps into my skin.

I try to pull my hand, but he tightens his grip. It doesn't hurt, but it's firm enough to suggest that he'd make it painful if I struggle any further.

Someone like him who seems to escalate frequently in a short period of time is unpredictable and, therefore, dangerous, and in order to survive, I can't risk provoking him.

So I remain still. "Please let me go."

He shakes his head once, tsking as he pushes into me. "Don't beg yet. We'll get there…eventually."

My back hits the wall and I jump, my fingers clammy, my teeth grinding together with the force of the fear that slithers down my spine.

I've been cornered twice tonight, but what Dave did feels like child's play compared to this mountain of muscles and rage.

Because I can feel the anger in his touch and the way he looks at me—like a ticking time bomb, ready to explode.

I'm caught right in the eye of a turbulent storm.

"Now." He tilts his head to the side. "Shouldn't you thank me?"

"Thank you?"

"Yes."

"For…stalking me?"

"For saving your life." I hear a tinge of annoyance, and that shimmering anger grow in intensity, spilling into his words.

I swallow, and the gulp that gets caught in my throat can be heard in the oppressive silence. "I didn't ask you to."

It's subtle, but I see his free hand flex, sticky blood still dripping onto the concrete. "If I hadn't shown up, that pathetic waste of space would've violated you. And considering your meek, entirely washed-up, and boring personality, you would've let him."

I would've *never* let him. I was going to hit him.

But I don't need to explain myself to a literal stalker. Besides, explaining myself has never worked, and it's only gotten me into worse trouble.

So instead of slipping down that hopeless road, I tilt my head to the side. "What's it to you?"

He narrows his eyes, a hint of rage flashing through them. "The fuck you just say?"

"Nothing. Just…let me go."

"No, you said something. Repeat it. Now."

I let out a fractured exhale, causing my glasses to fog up.

Maybe it's the exhaustion or the throbbing pain in my back. Maybe I just want to go home, read my novel, then go to sleep so I can wake up early and study and then go to class.

Maybe I'm just suicidal.

Whatever the reason, I let the words I constantly police spill out in one go. "I said it has nothing to do with you. Whether I'm assaulted or killed or thrown into a dumpster is not your business. And honestly, if you believe me to be boring and washed-up, why not stalk someone else? Or maybe quit the whole despicable ordeal and do something better with your time?"

He remains motionless, probably as surprised by the statement as I am. I didn't mean to talk back, but I guess I now have no filter when I'm nervous. Add all the physical and mental pain, and I'm ready to just…go.

The stranger's face slips back into stark indifference, a blank, careful mask I can't read. "You think I want to follow you around? See your pathetic life in 3D?"

"I'm sure you don't. So why are you?"

"Why do you think?"

"I don't know. Why don't you tell me?"

He steps farther into my space, his chest a breath away from mine, his fingers tightening around my wrist. He's so close, his boots rub against my sneakers, and I'm assaulted by the smell of wood and leather, a potent masculine combination that fills me with apprehension.

I can't help it.

Having lived in a world where most men use and abuse women, I can only feel dread at the scent.

"Have you done something bad, Violet?"

I gulp. Sure, I thought he'd know my name if he'd put so much effort into watching me, but still, hearing it uttered in his voice causes goosebumps to erupt on my skin.

"No." The lone word leaves me in a strangled breath.

"Liar." He has a distinctive way of speaking—precise, deep, but also frighteningly monotone, as if talking is a true hindrance.

"Why would I lie?"

"Because you're no different than the rest of them. All of you are rotten to the core."

Who are 'all of us'?

Before I can ask, he strokes my wrist with his bloodied glove, and the hairs on the back of my neck stand on end. It seems sensual, but, in reality, it's no different than a veiled threat.

Both of us watch as he smears my tattoo with blood.

"Endure," he reads the word inked there. "Very fitting."

I try to pull my wrist free, but he tightens his grip. "You'll need to endure, Violet, for a long time."

He releases my wrist, and I think the nightmare is over, but then he traces a line on my cheek with the back of his bloodied hand, smearing the sticky mess from the edge of my glasses to the corner of my mouth. "When I'm done with you, there'll be nothing left."

My chin trembles, and I want to look away, to escape his black-hole-like orbit, but I don't.

"Why are you doing this?"

"You'll have to figure that out yourself." His lips hover near my cheek, and with every word he breathes against the blood, a chill spreads across my skin. "Reflect on your sins."

CHAPTER 3
Violet

"MORNING, VI!"

I flinch when slim arms hug me from behind, nearly making me spill the soup in the saucepan.

Masking my nervousness, I turn to face my sister, who's grinning wide.

Dahlia is about a year younger than me, and even though we're not related by blood—we met in my last foster home—she's the only family I have.

She's curvier than me, with golden olive-toned skin, long, wavy brown hair, and the kind of bold presence that makes people stay away. But it's her eyes that always strike me the most. Big, expressive hazel, sharp and bold, like they've seen more than they should and somehow refused to shatter.

Her smile drops. "What's up with the dark circles? You worked too late and barely got any sleep again, didn't you?"

"It's nothing." I pour the soup into a container and put on my practiced smile. "You know how it is at the bar."

"Yeah, not sure the tips are worth it. They're obviously exploiting you. How many hours did you even sleep?"

Three.

Despite the exhaustion, I couldn't fall asleep. I kept

tossing and turning in bed, my mind filled with that stalker and his threats.

"*Reflect on your sins*," he said.

What sins?

The only person I've committed a sin against is dead.

So why…?

I kept thinking about it all night, searching for the possible reasons he'd say something like that, but I still came up empty.

Since I couldn't fall asleep, I scribbled in my journal and sketched a few things, and then I was able to drift off, but my sleep was riddled with nightmares of dark eyes and a bloodied gloved hand squeezing my throat to death.

I woke up both terrorized and…disappointed.

It's not the first time I've dreamt of death, and I'm always left with this niggling sadness at the realization that it's not real.

That I didn't die like I should've.

"I slept enough," I answer Dahlia, who's still watching me with a slight frown. "Look, I made you soup and a few sandwiches so you won't eat junk food."

"It's not that I want to eat junk food. I don't have time and can't cook to save my life, remember?" She smiles sheepishly, opening the cabinet. "Cooking is overrated anyway."

I laugh and fix the collar of her jacket. It's leather.

My fingers twitch.

Why did it have to be leather?

I let her go, and she retrieves an instant coffee packet.

"Eat something. Don't just drink coffee first thing in the morning."

"Don't have time. I'll be late for work."

"You're a med student, Dahl. You should be mindful of

what you eat." I place a wrapped sandwich in front of her. "Here. Eat it on your way."

She side-hugs me, squeezing me tightly. "You're truly the best ever."

I hug her back, her warmth and carefree energy offering me a much-needed reprieve. Dahlia is nothing like me.

She's a firecracker through and through.

Several weeks ago, she caught Dave trying to harass me, and she pointed a gun at him. No kidding. It wasn't hers or loaded, but she still used it to scare him off.

She's always been like this, not hesitating to speak up, shout, and destroy anyone who comes at her or me. I've always been in awe of how she couldn't care less about confrontation or how social anxiety is scared of her.

Dahlia and I met when she was twelve, at a foster home where the parents used us for cash flow and repeatedly hit us—Dahlia more than me because she talked back.

As for me...well, I had a different encounter with the 'dad,' another man who only ever wanted my shell of a body.

We ran away and have kind of survived together ever since, leaning on each other, being the home we both didn't have.

I've never told her this, because she'd freak out, but if Dahlia weren't in my life, if I didn't have a self-imposed purpose to take care of her and make sure she thrives and reaches her goals, I would've killed myself a long time ago.

I would've stopped *floating* with nothing but pain tethering me to life.

She's my lifeline. Literally.

"Vi, honest, I mean it. You need to ask the manager for fewer shifts. You look out of it lately." She takes a sip of her coffee as she grabs some books she left on the kitchen table, where she usually studies.

We live in a run-down one-bedroom apartment that we moved into recently, after the guy who used to rent us his attic tried to drug us with his homemade wine. It's a couple of streets away from our previous place, and we were lucky to find it after the old man who lived here died and his son rented it out to us for a bargain. It's way better equipped than the attic and we pay almost the same rent.

Honestly, both Dahlia and I think we've hit the jackpot. It even has a balcony, can you believe it? I've never lived anywhere with a balcony, so these past few weeks have felt surreal.

I usually sleep in the living room, having insisted Dahlia take the other room so she can focus on her studies. She wanted us to share it, but it's small and I don't want to disturb her healthy sleeping schedule with my erratic, nightmare-filled one.

"I'm actually earning a bit more from my job now that I'm working extra shifts in the summer." She shoves the books into a tote bag. "I'll help out more."

"Spend that money on your studies or your expenses. I'm truly fine, Dahl."

She throws the bag over her shoulder and frowns. "No, you're not. You're just saying that so I won't worry. Your back pain is flaring up again. Don't think I didn't notice the heat patches you're using on the regular now."

"It's a chronic injury. It's bound to flare." I hand her the sandwich she left on the counter. "You'll be late."

She kisses my cheek. "I'm totally helping out more. See ya!"

And then she's off before I can reply.

Since she said she'll help out, I can't stop her. I guess I'll buy her some necessities in return. Starting with a new pair of her favorite white sneakers—her old ones are so beat up, they look gray.

Maybe I'll design and embroider her a medical-themed patch for one of her bags.

My classes start late today, so I spend an hour or so sketching some ideas in my journal while making food for Dahlia for the rest of the week. I haven't eaten anything since last night, but I'm used to this constant sense of starvation. I consider it intermittent fasting—apparently, it's good for you.

I would definitely rather Dahlia eat than me. Seeing her well-fed, well-dressed, and crushing it at school brings me joy and a sense of accomplishment of sorts.

I'm apprehensive as I leave the apartment, even though I'm dressed in my signature hoodie and jeans. My strawberry-blonde hair that reaches just below my shoulder blades is gathered in a bun and hidden by the hood.

I'm also wearing my thick-framed glasses and carrying one of Dahlia's tote bags.

Although it's daytime, I can't help glancing around corners, expecting the stranger to appear out of nowhere.

He doesn't usually, not during the day, but I'm panicking a bit about his threat.

I contemplated telling Dahlia about the whole thing earlier but decided against it. I didn't in the past, because I refused to put her in danger, and I wouldn't now, because knowing her, she'd definitely confront him, and I'd never survive if he were to beat her to a pulp like he did Dave.

Or maybe even kill her.

No. Dahlia can't know about this.

Thankfully, the stalker isn't around, and I spend an uneventful day in class, going through the motions until I have to leave for work.

My shift starts in the early afternoon today, and I still

release a breath when I don't see his motorcycle or large frame close to HAVEN.

The need to constantly be alert is starting to take a toll on me. I don't know how long I can survive looking over my shoulder, giving myself a pep talk every time I go to work or even step foot out of the apartment.

I'm organizing the bar when Laura comes over squealing. I plaster a smile. "Good news?"

"The best!" She shows me two hockey tickets. "Boss gave us these for the Wolves' first game next season. He can be so sweet when he's not getting on my last nerve."

"Nice. Who are you taking?"

"Um, you! Boss said it's one ticket each."

I line up the glasses on the shelves. "Can I tell you a secret?"

"Girl, spill."

I lean over and whisper, "I don't really like hockey."

"The blasphemy! We live in Wolves territory, where hockey is huge."

"I know, I know. How dare I?"

"Uh-huh. We need to have you checked and consult the priest for an exorcism and shit."

I laugh. "How about you take little Karly instead? She'd enjoy it much more than I would."

Her eyes round. "Oh my God, are you sure?"

"Absolutely. Don't waste a ticket on me."

"This will be her first live game. Oh my God, she'll love it!" She hugs me. "You don't know how much this means to me, truly, Vi. I don't know how I'll ever repay you."

"It's nothing. Don't worry about it, really."

She hugs me again and scurries away, calling her daughter

to tell her the news. I love how she squeals, nearly jumping in place at hearing Karly's reactions.

A while later, patrons start filtering in and the manager puts on another replay of a hockey game. He sometimes rotates other sports, but, really, he and the owner are hockey fanatics, so they always play it on at least one TV, even during the offseason. During the season, however? That's pretty much all that's shown.

This one is apparently the Wolves' fiercest game from last season against their archnemesis, according to one of the regulars.

I'm working at the bar, helping out the bartender, as the two guys sitting on the stools whistle at something happening on TV. I don't even pay attention to the game, mostly thinking about whether the stalker will show up again tonight and what I can do if he does.

The bar gets packed fast, the crowd smelling like beer, sweat, and cheap aftershave. The game plays on a few screens, the flicker of harsh arena lights casting a bluish tint over the faces of the regulars. Their voices rise and fall in drunken excitement, spouting curses and half-slurred commentary between gulps of beer.

I wipe the counter absentmindedly, my rag catching on a deep scratch in the wood, one of many scars from years of slamming glasses and flying fists. Their voices push their way in, seeping into the cracks of my mind like smoke.

A glass thuds against the counter, liquid sloshing over the rim, spilling beer where I just wiped. "Jesus Christ, Callahan's at it again."

"Cheap shot on the back-check?" another guy grunts.

"Nah, worse. Laid that poor bastard out with a reverse hit. Kid never saw it coming."

"That's Callahan for you," another man mutters, shaking his head. "Most violent bastard in the league aside from our own Osborn."

My ears perk up at Marcus Osborn's name. He's one of Dahlia's useless exes, and I'm glad she only stayed with him for two weeks before realizing he's a can of worms she shouldn't go near.

I've always wished I could be as assertive as Dahlia in the way she treats men. She loves danger and having fun, but she also doesn't hesitate to throw them away the moment she gets bored. Which is what she did to Marcus.

He's still a hockey god in this town, and even someone like me knows he's the Wolves' captain and Stantonville's pride. So to hear one of the regulars compare someone else to him in the form of praise is rare.

I glance up just as the instant replay rolls. The Callahan everyone's talking about plays for the Vipers, the team from the neighboring affluent town, Graystone Ridge.

No way.

My fingers clench around the rag as he stands there, his large physique and the glare I've had nightmares about on full display.

The replay shows him skating at supersonic speed, but he doesn't chase the puck—he's tailing the other player like a predator timing his strike. The other team's forward barely turns his head before Callahan plants his skates, shifts his weight, and slams into him with the force of a car crash. The guy crumples, chest first, against the boards, his stick clattering to the ice.

A collective wince ripples through everyone watching the game.

I can't stop staring at the screen, held captive by the scene as my heartbeat thuds against my rib cage.

Callahan—Jude, judging by the banner that appears on the screen—isn't celebrating or even looking back at the wreckage he left behind. He just skates away, his jaw tight, his eyes empty under the harsh lights of the rink.

The same dark eyes that peered into my soul last night and filled my nightmares.

My stalker has a name and it's Jude Callahan.

But that's not what sends bile up my throat, forcing me to rush to the toilet, my eyes watering, my knees shaking, and vomit filling my mouth.

He...couldn't have been related to Susie Callahan, right?

The woman who was killed right before my eyes, and I couldn't do anything to stop it.

CHAPTER 4

Jude

THE END OF THE UNOFFICIAL SUMMER SKATE LEAVES ME with…nothing.

Just another flare of violence.

Another burst of light.

But then it's all done.

And I'm back to square one.

Violent-less. With these goddamn urges still coursing through my veins with the blood.

Slipping beneath every ridge of tense muscle, every scar, tattoo, and godforsaken memory.

The shower is scalding, but it does nothing to burn off the adrenaline still thrumming in my veins. My muscles ache in that raw way that should imply I left everything on the ice.

But I didn't.

This rage is uncontainable. Indestructible.

No amount of hockey violence can rip me from its clutches.

I shut the water off and rake a hand through my hair, pushing it back as I step into the locker room, the thick scent of sweat, tape, and victory hanging in the air. The place is alive with noise—guys shoving each other, laughing, and talking about the game.

"Nice hit out there, Callahan." Ryder slaps me on the back as I pass, his grin sharp and his eyes still wild with post-game energy. "Thought you were gonna take Hunter's head clean off."

"Should've. Next time." I yank a towel off the bench, rolling my shoulders, not caring that everyone can see the map of scars on my back, partially concealed by tattoos.

Half of the guys here know the reason, and the other half wouldn't dare ask.

"Fucking savage," Drayton, our goalie, mutters, shaking his head as he laces up his dress shoes. "You play like you've got a personal vendetta against the ice itself."

"Ice started it." I reach into my locker.

A few guys chuckle. Others are chirping about a missed play. Even though it's summer, elite college hockey teams like the Vipers don't really take time off. We often do captain-led practices—whether they're skates, scrimmages, or drills.

The coaches are technically not involved—aside from conditioning and strength coaches during some sessions—but really, it's all due to a program created by our captain, Kane.

He's currently leaning against the lockers, already fully dressed, and going through his phone.

Unlike me, he doesn't like showcasing his scars. Not that I *love* it per se, but it's a fuck-you to the system, so everyone can see what type of monster my father truly is.

Not that I'm any better. Birds of a feather and all that.

"Davenport," I call Kane's last name, and he lifts his head, his expression calm, his face so welcoming, you'd think he was an angel. "I need a word."

"About your irresponsible play?" He lifts a brow. "Sure."

I pause after grabbing my deodorant. "I only got sent to the box twice."

"One is overkill."

"I was still the best player."

"Nah, that's me." Preston lifts his hand in my peripheral vision. He's sitting on the bench, a towel hanging low on his hips, one ankle resting on his knee like he owns the damn room.

He pauses taping his wrist, his usual smirk firmly in place. "Hell of a game, Callahan, but we all know I'm the fan favorite. Even though it was a practice game, there's already an article." He slides his hands in the air as if unveiling the title. "Armstrong, the league's undefeated left wing strikes again, even during the offseason."

I lift a brow. "Pay the reporter?"

"Stay jealous, big man. Now, more importantly, how's my hair?"

"Like roadkill on a humid day."

"I see you're still jealous." He pats his styled blond strands. "Don't listen to Jude's nonsense, my premium genetics."

"And yet those premium genetics still lost the puck battle against a guy built like a traffic cone," I remind him, just out of spite.

Pres, Kane, and I grew up together, but Pres is probably my best friend. Kane has always been self-contained in a way, never goes too high or too low, perfectly able to remain calm under duress, then shove himself back into a mold. He has the type of control Pres and I lack in spades.

So we inevitably grew closer. In a sense, Pres's sickness speaks to mine and his darkness mirrors my own.

We're the toxic duo everyone hates to see coming.

Preston tuts, unfazed. "That was strategy, Callahan. Gotta let the little guys think they have a chance before you yeet the whole damn carpet into next week."

"It's 'pull the rug out from under them,' not whatever crime against language you just committed."

"I meant to add my special twist."

I chuck a roll of tape at him, hitting him square in the chest. "Nah, you just don't know your idioms."

"I do." He catches the tape before it rolls onto the floor, then stands, squaring up to me with a taunting dimpled grin. "You're the boring prick who has not one ounce of creativity in his thick head."

"I'll knock your teeth out."

"Oooh, is that a threat?"

"Fuck around and find out, Armstrong."

"Oh my." He lifts a hand to his chest in mock disbelief. "You have the heart to hurt my beautiful face?"

"Is beautiful in the room with us?"

"Pfft. You jealous, petty bitch? One day you'll appreciate my genius more."

"Doubt it."

"That's what they all say before they realize they can't live without me. Oh, the horror. Imagine not having me in your life?"

I pause, my index finger tapping my lip as I pretend to be thinking. "Pretty peaceful, actually."

"Why do you lie?" He's about to punch me, but Kane steps in with the usual sigh of exasperation he gives when Pres and I bicker or start hitting each other for no reason whatsoever.

Actually, that reason is aggression. Something Kane can rise above but we can't.

"If you're done fighting like chickens, get dressed, Jude. I don't have all night."

Kane leaves first, and I throw on my sweatpants and shirt

in record time before following him to the coach's office down the hall of Vipers Arena—the pride and joy of Graystone University and, honestly, the entire town of Graystone Ridge.

We were born and bred here, raised in this pocket of wealth where centuries-old tradition collides with modern edge.

A place where old money doesn't fade—it evolves, sharpens, and makes sure everyone remembers who built this town.

I find Kane leaning against the desk, staring at his phone with a tilted head and a hooded expression.

Not sure who or what captured his attention, but it's bad news for the other party. While it's true that he's calm and collected, like all of us, he was born with a demon lurking inside him.

"Sorry I'm late!" Preston barges in behind me. "Not really sorry, but anyway. I'm here now. You're welcome, bitches."

"This has nothing to do with you," I grunt as I close the door he left wide open.

"Nonsense. Everything has to do with me." He grins, trudging to Kane's side and hitting his shoulder. "What's the plan? And don't be boring."

Kane doesn't acknowledge either of us for a while, still staring at his phone.

Even though Kane is the captain, he shouldn't have free access to the coach's office.

In theory, at least.

In practice, the three of us have unrestricted access—not just to Graystone University, or GU, but to the entire town of Graystone Ridge.

Our clearance comes in the form of the black ring on each of our index fingers.

They're more than just symbols of status. They're proof

that we belong—not only to the founding families of this town, but to the secret society that shadows it.

Vencor.

Callahan. Davenport. Armstrong. Osborn.

The four pillars of Graystone Ridge. The originators of Vencor. The ones who've held this place together—and in their grip—for generations.

The black rings mean we're Senior members.

The highest rank attainable for anyone outside of direct bloodlines.

Trial, Member, Senior, and Founder.

That's the order.

And while we currently hold Senior status, we're in the final stretch. After graduation, we'll face our last trial and ascend to the position we were always meant to inherit.

Founder.

Kane taps his index finger against the back of his phone. His ring bears the Davenport family crest—a compass rose. It's a symbol of control, steering direction, and navigating dominance. Fitting, considering the Davenports have monopolized the import and export industry.

I twirl my own ring slowly.

It's etched with the Callahan crest—a caduceus twisted in thorny vines.

A corrupted version of the medical symbol.

It represents our family's unrelenting grip on the pharmaceutical sector. Hell, ever since my brother, Julian, took over the Callahan empire, we've become unrivaled.

Pres wears the Armstrong crest—a sun and a crescent moon. A nod to his family's hold on energy, in all its forms.

Then there are the Osborns. They don't currently have a college-aged member—at least, not officially—but their crest is a lion's head framed with gears, reflecting their control over real estate, construction, and every inch of urban development in this town.

Over the centuries, the four families learned to carefully and calculatedly share power.

That uneasy balance eventually gave birth to Vencor, the society we now oversee.

It's through Vencor that we've built our empire—recruiting, shaping, and eliminating as needed. Ensuring that Graystone Ridge stays exactly the way it was always meant to be and that our legacy never dies.

"What the hell are you watching?" Pres peers over Kane's shoulder. "Is it porn? If yes, why am I not invited?"

Kane slips his phone into his pocket and shoves Pres away. "Why are you even here?"

Pres releases an exasperated sigh. "You keep asking that, and yet you can't live without me."

"Highly debatable."

"You little ungrateful cretin—"

"Anyway." Kane slides his attention to me. "What did you want to talk about?"

"I need another name from the list," I speak in a calm tone I don't feel.

He raises a brow. "You already took care of Violet?"

My throat constricts, and I feel the veins popping in my neck, my muscles tightening and sporadic fire spreading across my skin.

At just the mention of her name.

All their names.

And she *is* just another fucking *name*.

"It's time for the next name," I say, ignoring his question.

"What the fuck!" Preston jumps up. "Why haven't I been

on this Violet's hunt, big man? I thought we were bros, but then you go on killing sprees without inviting me?"

"There was no hunt." Kane tilts his head to the side. "Was there?"

"That's none of your business. Give me the next name."

"Whoa. Hold up." Pres stalks toward me, then circles me. "You mean to tell me you've had this Violet's name for a while, and it didn't result in a hunt? Blink once if you've been possessed."

"Kane," I growl, ignoring Pres's buzzing. "Don't make me repeat myself."

"I'm curious is all." He crosses his arms. "Is this a new pattern? Not finishing off your targets?"

"No. I just have a different plan for her. And stop asking questions."

"All right, I'll leave you to it." Kane pushes off the desk and comes closer, shoving Preston, who's been circling and poking me, out of the way, then whispers in my ear, "Remember, the sister stays out of whatever you're doing."

I stare down at him. "Depends on how fast you are with that name."

He narrows his eyes. "You know, your brother has been threatening me to stop enabling your violent sprees."

"My brother can go fuck himself. I expect a file in my inbox tomorrow at the latest."

He grunts out a reply and leaves.

"Heeey…" Preston whispers near my ear, resuming poking me. "Do you hear me? Will the real Jude please stand up?"

"Fuck off." I swat him away.

"Oh, you're back, big man." He grins. "I was on the verge of starting an exorcism side gig and shit. Might accidentally become a cult leader, though. Not that I'm against the idea per se, but those fanatics can be crazy, not that I'm less crazy, so maybe it's not a bad idea. Think Dad would finally disown me once I'm on the news...?"

I leave him blabbering and stride out of the office, but, of course, he falls in step beside me and wraps an arm around my shoulder. "Sooo, Violetta, huh? Are we stalking? Because I have the perfect hoodie."

My shoulders tense, but I feign indifference. "You are *not* stalking, Pres."

"Why not?"

"Because you start shouting 'This is stupid. Let's fuck them up instead!' ten minutes in."

"I mean, it kind of was. Your previous targets that I had the misfortune of stalking were more boring than monogamy, and we all know that's, like, my least favorite thing. *But—*" He headlocks me. "You're not killing this Veronica or hunting her after all this time, so she must not be boring. I want to see for myself."

"No." I punch him in the side. Hard.

"Fucking hell." He grunts, releasing me and bending over, then grins with a manic edge. "*That* interesting?"

I leave even as his unhinged laughter echoes in the air.

Well, fuck me sideways.

I think I just piqued Preston's interest in something neither he nor Kane should know about.

CHAPTER 5
Jude

A FEW HOURS LATER, I'M SOMEWHERE I SHOULDN'T BE.

I should be home, but I don't have one of those.

My only home—my mother—was ripped from between my fingers in a gruesome scene.

So here I am again.

Tilting on the edge of violence, rage, and…something else I can't quite pinpoint.

I lean against my bike, my arms crossed, the chilly night air curling around me like a ghost.

I barely feel it against my leather jacket slipping off me, like I'm made of something the cold can't touch. My helmet stays on, visor down, turning the world into a dim, distorted reflection. I prefer it this way—keeps the filth at arm's length.

Across from me, 'HAVEN' glows in flickering neon blue, casting a sickly light over the cracked sidewalk and the half-smoked cigarette butts crushed into the pavement.

The irony of the name isn't lost on me. This place is no fucking haven—just another Stantonville hole-in-the-wall where men rot from the inside out and women learn to smile through it.

The air is thick with the stench of old beer, fried grease, and sickening desperation.

Stantonville is a shithole, always has been. Its streets sag under the weight of rusted-out cars, busted streetlights, and people who stopped trying a long time ago. A far fucking cry from Graystone Ridge, where power drips from every surface and the world bends to the will of men like me.

But even in this dump, *she* stands out.

Through the bar's hazy windows, I catch a glimpse of her moving behind the counter, wiping down glasses, her mouth set in a small line.

She looks like she belongs here. And at the same time, like she doesn't.

Violet Winters is a contradiction of epic proportions.

Starting with her hair. It's not red, not blonde, but something in between, like fire and honey tangled together. It's a little messy, just past her shoulders, with strands that slip from behind her ear when she moves too fast.

Then her face. Too soft and full of disturbing innocence for a place like this. Heart-shaped, delicate, like something carved from porcelain and left in the hands of men who don't know how to handle fragile things.

I'm one of those men who keep just…wanting to break her fucking neck. See that face shattered to pieces right beneath my shoe.

But one of the biggest contradictions?

Her eyes, blue and troubled but not the type that fade into the background. No. They slice through shadows, searching, like she's always looking for something that's just out of reach.

Like right now.

She stares out the window and freezes. Her hand holding the glass shakes uncontrollably and she drops it on the counter.

I don't hear the shatter, but I see it. In the slight jump in her shoulders and the way her lips form an O. I can almost *feel* the tremors racking her body like when I cornered her in that filthy alley last night.

Violet Winters is scared of me. No. *Terrified*.

She should be.

Because Kane and Preston are right. All my previous targets are buried six feet under, and she'll join them.

Soon.

The bartender, a tall guy with a buzz cut, checks on her, and she flinches slightly, but then she forces her lips into this mechanical smile as she picks up the shards of glass.

With her bare fucking hands.

Naturally, she pricks her finger, and the bartender grabs her hand and presses a napkin on it, saying something to which she smiles.

Awkwardly.

I suppose her coworkers wouldn't know it's awkward, considering she always seems to be smiling as if her life is perfect and she's the happiest goddamn person alive.

She's not.

Subtly, too subtly, she pulls her hand from the guy's grip and bends over, but she's behind the counter now, so I can only see the bartender as he looks down.

I tilt my head to the side. What the fuck is happening behind that counter?

The moment lasts for a while before he moves at the raised hand of one of the customers.

Violet emerges soon after and scurries out of view.

My fist clenches and unclenches as I watch the place she disappeared to.

She's always…disappearing.

With a grunt, I hop onto my bike and drive it to a secure parking lot, then I walk back in time to see them leave.

I wait by the corner as Violet waves at the bartender and they go their separate ways.

She glances around, probably looking for me, and when she doesn't see me or the bike, her tense shoulders relax and she pulls the hoodie low on her face. That's what she always wears if she's not in her work shirt—baggy, unflattering hoodies that don't showcase her body.

I follow from a safe distance as she performs her usual ritual. She buys sandwiches from some greasy fast-food place, then walks back to her shithole of a neighborhood at a brisk pace, her eyes aimed at the ground.

Always.

She has no idea I'm watching.

Not when I make myself unnoticeable. She only sees me when I want her to see me.

Though she wasn't supposed to last night, but I couldn't just stand by and let another man play with my toy.

Only I get to break her.

I watch with a barely contained snarl as she gives the homeless people food and then cautiously approaches the alley in which I cornered her last night.

She glimpses behind her and then goes in, quickening her steps.

I stand in place.

If she looks back again, if she searches for me one more time, I'll finish her.

Kane and Pres are right. It's long overdue.

Maybe I'll just kill her without the hunt I make every target go through just so they'll feel the desperation.

See a light at the end of the tunnel, only for it to be me.

Their grim reaper.

But that wouldn't solve the mystery as to why I haven't ended Violet's miserable life up until now.

See, there's one more contradiction about Violet Winters.

The worst of all.

She's a girl who feeds the homeless while staying hungry, volunteers at multiple charities, and stops to play with kids and dogs. She also checks on people on the side of the road, even if they look forgotten, in pain, or simply done with life.

I know, not only because I've done my research—or Kane did—but also because I was on the receiving end a couple of years ago.

The rain pours down on me, plastering my torn shirt to my body, seeping into the cuts all over my face and chest.

I can't walk anymore, so I sit by the bridge, my bloodied knuckles hanging off my bent knees, the sting of raw skin drowning beneath the downpour.

My body throbs, every nerve alight in the aftermath of my latest trial for Vencor. Physical. Fists, boots, words—the founding members wielded them all like weapons, and they made damn sure I felt every single one.

I was tasked with fighting my way out of a literal violence fest, and I did. Because Mom needs me to be powerful so I can protect her from this world. Regis—the man who contributed in making me—sure isn't.

Julian has always said that the only way to protect those I love is to rise in the ranks, beat up those at the top, and take their place. It's to make sure those who look up or covet my position would end up with a chopped-off neck.

There's no room for weakness or second thoughts. A moment of hesitation can mean losing my mom—the only person who's ever loved me unconditionally.

So I aced the trial, left the men who went against me in worse shape than me, and finished before even Kane and Preston.

I have to check on them, see how they did, but for now, I'm just...so *fucking* tired.

As I stare at the horizon where the deep clouds meet the lake, I find solace in the small patch of orange that's trying to slip through. Despite the rain, despite the gloominess, there's that little smidge of brightness that just refuses to give in.

And it gives me hope that I'm the patch of orange for my mom. The reason she'll hold on to life.

But then it's snuffed.

The sliver of orange is suffocated by the dark clouds, murdering any sense of expectation.

The rain pours, soaking through my clothes, dripping down my lashes, filling the spaces between my fingers with cold. It doesn't let up, doesn't ease, just keeps pounding against my skull like a slow, relentless hammer.

On and on as if attempting to rinse the blood off of me.

And failing miserably.

I just sit there, letting it drown out everything, staring at the pavement slick with water and blood.

Red is still a color in the darkness. If it's the only hope I have, then so be it.

The rain stops.

No, it doesn't.

Something's blocked it.

A pair of beat-up sneakers come into view, water pooling around them, the edges darkened by the downpour. My gaze trails up, taking in the faded jeans clinging to slim legs, a black hoodie pulled low over a delicate face that's covered by thick-framed glasses.

But they don't manage to hide the deep-blue eyes.

Fuck. Those eyes.

I'm held hostage staring at them and the conflicted emotions they carry in the clear, bright blue—perturbed, soft, but also searching.

The girl holds an umbrella over our heads, the fabric sagging under the weight of the rain.

Blue. Just a shade lighter than her eyes.

She's angled it more at me, letting the downpour soak the shoulders of her hoodie, dripping on her worn-out backpack.

There's no flinching, no hesitation. Not at the sight of my busted lip, the split skin stretched tight over my cheekbone, or the blood smeared on my face and down my throat.

Not even at my clothes, torn and damp, clinging to me like the last evidence of a fight I barely walked away from.

No disgust.

No wariness.

Just concern.

Pure, unfiltered concern for a fucking stranger.

I say nothing, just drop my gaze, willing her to fucking go.

"Do you need help?" Her voice isn't pitying, isn't careful, but steady, assertive. Like she genuinely means it.

"Fuck off," I grunt low in my throat.

The sneakers slide back, just an inch, dragging against the concrete, but she doesn't leave.

Instead, she reaches into her backpack and presses something into my bloodied palm.

A chocolate caramel protein bar.

"Sorry, that's all I have. Stay strong."

Then, before I can tell her to shove her sympathy up her ass, she does something even dumber.

She places the umbrella in my hand and runs off.

Holding her backpack over her head as she disappears into the foggy rain.

That was my perception of Violet Winters. A Goody-Two-shoes who would stop and help as much as she could when others wouldn't even bother to look.

So why the fuck is her name and face on the list of people who stood by in a public square as my mother was stabbed to death twenty fucking times?

As I watch her scurrying through the alley, I want to grab and shake her. To kill her and avenge my mom.

But that would be too easy, wouldn't it?

As if feeling my gaze, Violet pauses, glances back, and freezes, her eyes widening and her shoulders shrinking.

She shouldn't have looked back.

Because I'm striding toward her, and this time, I will burn that first encounter out of my mind.

She's not the girl with the haunting eyes, blue umbrella, and chocolate caramel protein bar.

She's one of *them*.

CHAPTER 6

Violet

MY STALKER HAS A VENDETTA AGAINST ME.

In reality, he's not a stalker, but more like a man out for revenge.

Jude Callahan.

That's the name of the man who's been inserting himself into my unremarkable life lately.

I googled him earlier, after I threw up upon seeing him on-screen.

Jude Callahan is not only a hockey god, but one of the heirs to the Callahan pharmaceutical empire.

Someone who could buy Stantonville and everyone in it without batting an eye.

And he's related to Susie—her only son, actually.

After that night and being questioned by the police, I learned the name of the woman I failed, but I never thought I'd hear it again a few months later.

This time, coupled with her son's name.

It all made sense. The stalking, the 'reflect on your sins' declaration, and his harsh glares from outside the bar's window.

It's all...*my* fault.

My nails sink into the straps of my backpack, and I stand frozen in place by the coldness in his dark eyes.

I can't move.

I want to, but I'm unable to.

My body has a tendency to give up on me in these types of situations, as if it's just had enough and would like to rest.

For a moment.

The stench reeking through the alley does nothing to propel me into action. But then again, what's the point of running when he'll keep coming back again?

And again.

Until I'm finally no more.

I gulp past the sandpaper taste at the back of my throat as he strides toward me at a frightening fast pace.

He is frightening.

From the way he's built—broad and tall and muscular—to how he seems to wear a permanent scowl or how his eyes darken in increments. Like pools of deep brown that can only be found in the depths of hell.

It doesn't help that he's dressed all in black again. Though there are no gloves today. The veins on the backs of his hands tighten as he flexes them, and I make out a black ring with unintelligible symbols on his left hand's index finger as he kills the distance between us.

I instinctively stiffen my body and mentally prepare myself for the hit. Not sure why I expect him to shove me to the ground like Mama used to, with a palm to my face, because I disgusted her.

But his palm doesn't come.

And neither does his fist.

Both his hands are inert at his sides as he stops a few feet away from me.

Despite the lack of violence, I don't release a breath of relief, my body remaining tense because he's close.

I can breathe him in.

Leather and wood.

Danger and retribution.

All wrapped in a gorgeous exterior I can't look away from.

"Why did you look back?" Jude asks with a tinge of veiled infuriation.

As if I annoy him.

Like I used to annoy my mom.

I remain silent, not knowing what I should say that won't annoy him any further. Because that's how it starts—mild annoyance that escalates to shoves and curses, and then I'm beaten up and locked in a closet.

I can never go back to that closet. I…can't do closets.

Just the thought quickens my breathing and fills my turbulent headspace with smudges of red.

"Why the fuck aren't you running, Violet?" Jude's booming voice pulls me out of my sinister thoughts and I jump a bit.

I hate how I immediately slide to the edge whenever anyone yells.

I'm not an idiot. I know it has to do with the cocktail of traumas Mama gave me instead of affection, but I don't know how to fix it.

Or if I ever could.

"What's the point?" I whisper, looking down at my shoes, at the neatly tied laces and the scratched-up white fabric.

"What's the point?" he repeats with an edge, stepping forward until his black boots are in my field of vision. Big and intimidating like the rest of him.

"Yeah." I lift my shoulder. "It's not like I can outrun you."

"Look at me."

I lift my head because the firm tone suggests retribution if I don't.

I immediately regret it.

Eye contact with Jude is no different than being dragged into the depths of a somber forest with no way out.

Prickling hate and volcano-level rage shimmer behind his brown irises, and the hopeless part of me that feels others' pain before my own can actually see his.

It's convoluted, like it's become something darker and more vicious, but it's there.

And some stupid part of me would love to ease it a little, make him…feel better.

Somehow.

Someway.

I can help him, screams my naïve side, knowing my death would do him the greatest favor.

"If you think you can't outrun me, should that stop you from fucking trying, Violet?" He's speaking in that tone again, somewhat angry but also frustrated.

And I don't understand why he seems pissed off that I'm not running. Isn't that what he wants?

"It would be a waste of both our time," I say.

"With that mentality, it sure fucking would be."

"I don't know what you want me to say or do." I release a breath. "If I run today, so what? You'll be back tomorrow or the day after. It's not like I can run or hide forever."

"No, you can't. Not when that's your train of thought." He steps forward, and my leg twitches to step back as I look down at the shortened distance between our shoes.

"I said. Look at me." His order makes my body tense up with both discomfort and something else I can't quite pinpoint.

I halt, my nails digging harder into the backpack straps, the wound from when I picked up the shards of the glass I dropped when I saw him across the street earlier throbs in needlelike pain. All I want to do is touch my wrist, but I don't want to draw his attention to it again.

"How the fuck did you survive this long with that mentality, hmm?" He tilts his head, watching me like I'm something broken he's trying to dissect. "It's like you're asking to be killed."

"If that'll give you the revenge you so desperately seek, I don't mind."

Something shifts in the air.

His expression, always sharpened by rage, falters for a second. His eyes widen—not dramatically, but just enough to let me know he wasn't expecting that. Then, just as quickly, they narrow to slits, calculating and cold once again. "Is this some kind of reverse psychology tactic?"

"I wish I were that sophisticated." I let my lips curl in a small smile, but it dies quickly when he doesn't return it. I clear my throat, my nerves tightening around my windpipe. "I…I know who you are. I saw you earlier on TV. It was a replay of a hockey game, and I recognized your face, so I googled you. I was hoping you weren't related to Susie Callahan, but you are. And then everything started making sense."

I glance down briefly, swallowing hard.

"I know you're doing this to avenge your mother's death. I understand that kind of grief. And I get it, really. I do. Death doesn't scare me. There's no pain in it. No thoughts. No constant fight to stay alive. It's peace. So if that's what you're after, if killing me would bring you that peace, I'm okay with it. Just let me say goodbye to my sister first. Please. Don't hurt her. She has nothing to do with what happened."

My breaths come in long, fractured exhales after I finish talking, curling and dissipating in the chilly air.

Jude's been tilting his head the entire time, watching me as if I'm a freak show, and maybe I am.

"You're suicidal?" he asks with a slight squint in his eyes.

"Not really."

"You are. No one would accept death so easily if they haven't been constantly thinking about it."

I drop my hands from my backpack straps and trace my wrist tattoo back and forth, back and forth. "Why does that matter? I'm giving you a chance to exact your revenge, so why...don't you take it?"

Another step, this time his boots touch my shoes, and I step back, but he wraps his hand around my elbow, trapping me, holding me hostage until my senses flood with him.

His scent.

His size.

His rage.

His piercing disapproval.

It's all too...much.

"You want me to kill you because you didn't have the guts to end your own life?"

My lips part, and I'm shaking now, my whole body going into shock.

"Tell me, Violet. Do you think you deserve the easy way out?"

"Isn't your purpose to hurt me and make me pay?" My voice is on edge for the first time since I started speaking to this prick.

"Not if you welcome it. Where's the fun in that?"

I purse my lips, my heart thundering against my rib cage until I'm nearly panting.

Maybe I'm having a panic attack.

Or a rare rage fit.

I don't even know.

This man suffocates me. His words are like invisible hands around my throat that I can't breathe through.

"People like you who wear the robe of a saint to camouflage rotten insides don't deserve the finality of death." He leans in farther, and this time, my chest that's rising and falling in erratic breaths brushes against his solid muscles. "I have to figure out a better way to make you pay for your sins."

He's speaking so close to my mouth that his exhales rush along my lips, and I can taste mint and a hint of alcohol on his breath.

The overpowering smell saturates my senses, but I have no choice but to stare at those dead eyes and the blatant sadism shining through them.

This is a man who'd crush me beneath his boot without a second thought. He'd dismantle me just for his sick entertainment.

No, not entertainment.

Revenge.

I'd be able to feel more victimized and sorry for myself if he were just some run-of-the-mill stalker, but now that I know his motives, I can only hang my head in shame.

What am I even supposed to say?

That I'm a coward?

"You know." His chest rises and falls in a quicker rhythm, and it's contagious, making mine just as frantic. "I've killed six of the people who watched my mother being stabbed to death and did nothing. You're number seven on the list."

"I'm sorry—"

"Shut the fuck up." His face is closer now, peering into

me, and I'm scared to breathe. "Your apology means jack shit to me."

My lips tremble, sweat beading along my temples and down my back. "I really am. I…have been dreaming about her for months, and I know my actions are unforgivable, but I…"

I gulp, the words balling in my throat, refusing to be spit out.

"You what?"

"I know everything I say will sound like an excuse, and it probably is. But if I had a redo—"

"You don't. None of you do. It's why I'm slaughtering every single one of you, Violet." His voice is frighteningly low. "If my mother doesn't get to breathe anymore, why should you? You stood by while she was bleeding in the street, so I decided to be your personal grim reaper. One you'll never escape."

My jaw hurts from how tightly I'm locking it, but I remain silent. I don't think he wants to hear me talk.

His pain has transformed into hot rage, and all I can do is stand here as he burns me alive.

So what if I tell him my semi-dormant suicidal ideations have been a constant itch beneath my skin since that day?

Or that I freeze in times of danger, so if the man who stabbed Susie stabbed me, I'd still be frozen to the spot.

He wouldn't believe my excuses.

I don't think he even wants to hear them.

"But I won't be your grim reaper." Jude grabs my nape and my whole body stiffens. "At least, not yet. You see…"

He searches my eyes, peering down at me with an intensity that burns despite the chilly air.

"I would've killed the previous ones by now, after I

hunted them down and made them lose all hope, but you…" He runs his harsh gaze over me. "Death doesn't scare you, so you need appropriate torture. Hmm. What do you have to offer me, Violet?"

I swallow and hesitate, conscious that my lips could touch his full ones when I speak, then say, "I'm fine with whatever. Just don't bring Dahlia into this."

"You don't get to dictate the rules." He releases me with a shove, back to being disgusted with me. "Your role is to obey."

"Obey what?"

"Me." He slides his gaze from my shoes up my body, and it's like I'm being stripped naked.

It's that uncomfortable male gaze I'm used to, but this time, it's more…malicious rather than sexual.

"From now on, your life is mine. You don't get to die or hurt yourself as long as I don't allow it." His lips curl into a small smirk, something I've never seen on his face before. "I'll see you around, Violet."

CHAPTER 7
Violet

A CRUSHING WEIGHT SMOTHERS ME, PULLING ME DOWN so viciously, I gasp, my eyes flying open.

At first, I think it's sleep paralysis—that sickening awareness where my mind is awake but my body refuses to move.

But it's worse than that.

A woman sits perched on my ribs like a demon, her seemingly skinny frame impossibly heavy, suffocating the breaths from my lungs.

Her once soft and beautiful face is now a grotesque mockery of what I remember. Sunken cheekbones, eyes stretched wide, pupils swallowing the amber, lips curled into something between a grin and a snarl. Our hair is the same color, but hers is longer, reaching her lower back in silky strands.

Mama.

"You bitch." The bite in her cold, venomous voice slithers over my skin, seeping into me, crawling under my ribs and settling in my bones.

Like it belongs there.

Like it never left.

I try to move, to shift, but my limbs don't obey me, remaining as rigid and motionless as cement.

Despite the numbness, I want to reach a hand out and touch her. Beg for her forgiveness.

Ask, *Why can't you love me, Mama?*

That's what other mothers did. They loved their kids and spoiled them. I was fine with not being spoiled, but I desperately tried to make her like me. Since we moved all the time, I had no friends, and she was my only source of affection.

Affection she never gave me.

Right now, her fingers dig into my shoulders, nails as sharp as claws. "Useless."

She lifts her hand and slaps me, the sting reverberating in my cheek. "Your face is fucking disturbing! You're the mistake of my life and the weight around my neck, Violet. A *thing* that shouldn't have been born."

I shake my head. A small, weak motion. The only rebellion I can manage—or could've ever managed. I want to speak, but my lips remain sealed shut as if stitched together with an invisible thread.

I can't breathe.

I can't fight.

I can only listen as she spits her rancid words into my ears, the stench of something decaying curling around my face.

"You *killed* me, you worthless piece of shit."

Her hands tighten, her nails biting deeper, slicing through the fabric of reality, into my skin, cutting open the fragile pieces of myself that I try to keep together.

I didn't, I want to say. *I didn't do it, Mama.*

But there are no words in my throat, no sound except the way my pulse pounds and pounds and *pounds* against my skull.

She leans in, close enough that her lips brush my ear,

her breath thick and rotting. "You're a terminal disease who will kill anyone stupid enough to love you. Starting with Dahlia."

The weight intensifies. My ribs groan under the pressure, my heart a frantic animal trapped in a cage that's too small.

I scream.

And suddenly, I'm falling.

The world shatters.

And my shout reverberates in the small closet she shoves me into.

I jolt up, gasping, drenched in sweat, my pulse hammering against my ribs like it's trying to escape me. Faint light greets me, and I release a breath.

It's not the closet.

I'm not in the closet.

The air is still thick as my breaths come in ragged pulls. My unsteady fingers dig into the sheets, searching for something real. Something that isn't her.

But her voice lingers, coiled in my head like smoke, and I press my hands to my ears as if that will dilute the words I can still hear.

I know Mama's dead.

But, in reality, she never really is.

She lives on in my nightmares, always reminding me how useless I am. How I can never be…more.

My feet tangle in the sheets and I fall on my knees on the hardwood floor, groaning, but I jerk up and run to Dahlia's room.

My breathing slowly eases when I see her sleeping peacefully in bed. I walk on my tiptoes and pull up the sheet that's fallen off, then quietly close the door, leaning my back against it.

My fingers still shaking, I slide down to the floor, burying my face in my hands. It's times like these when I just want to…end it.

Once and for all.

Just stop everything.

The nightmares.

The dark closet.

Mama's cruel words.

My silly yearning for love and affection that I never received.

Except from Dahlia—she's always loved me unconditionally. She lost her parents to an accident and, like me, was pinballed in the foster care system.

Unlike me, however, she has no silly notions of hopeless romanticism or an unattainable need for affection.

Or any late-night secret meetings with Death, toying with the idea of it as a coping mechanism.

But now, I'm putting the only person who ever cared about me in jeopardy.

Because *he* is still there.

Death.

And I know if I continued to toy with the idea, Jude would use her to put me back in my place.

I stand on unsteady legs and walk to the living room window. Tremors still plague my hands as I pull back the muslin curtain slightly, squinting at one of the few working lampposts, its glare assaulting me.

It's four in the morning, so he should be gone by now.

But he's not.

Across the street, I spot a parked black car. I can't see who's inside, but I know it's not empty.

Over the past two weeks, ever since Jude declared that my life was his, I haven't seen him around, but I've felt him.

Everywhere.

At first, it was a feeling of being shadowed. At work, in the neighborhood, but also during my college summer classes.

You'd think he'd have summer training or something better to do with his time.

But then I realized he wasn't doing the stalking himself. About a week ago, I spotted a tall, buff guy near my place—a pseudo stalker of sorts.

That guy comes into HAVEN every day and walks me home.

I mean, not *walk* me, but sort of walks a safe distance behind me. The other day, he punched a drunk guy who tried to come close to me.

His name is Mario, which I only know because Laura has been talking—and flirting—with him. She thinks he's become a regular because of her, and I don't want to shatter her illusions.

Still, even though the whole thing has made me deeply uncomfortable, I'm glad I haven't had to see Jude. That man terrifies me. Not only because of his vendetta or his ability to beat people to a pulp without blinking, or his violent streak on the ice I keep hearing about, but something far more distressing.

He has a curious ability to see through the chunks of my soul that I thought I'd expertly wrapped up.

And last night, he did something that probably contributed to the nightmare.

He got into the apartment.

I know because of the last entry in my journal, where I mentioned that maybe I could convince Dahlia to move away from here or even possibly leave on my own since I don't have the heart to make her lose the scholarship she worked her ass off for.

Unlike her, I don't care much about mine and would consider dropping out of college altogether and continuing to work part-time and take odd jobs here and there.

Last night, after Dahlia and I binged some Netflix and she went to sleep, I opened my journal to write an entry.

That's when I saw it.

A sticky note with neat print handwriting.

Abandon any useless thoughts about escaping me. Don't act stupid and force me to show you what I'm truly capable of.

My body trembled so hard upon seeing that.

He came into my home.

Was it the first time?

Or maybe the first time he's made himself noticeable?

But why now of all times?

His unpredictable actions are messing with my head so badly, I looked around the apartment, searching for his ghost, terrified that Dahlia would see anything amiss or, worse, get involved.

Because Jude is right. I have no clue what rich, privileged, and violent people like him are truly capable of.

And I don't want to find out.

———

Later that night, I'm back at work after spending the afternoon embroidering one of Dahlia's shirts while listening to an audiobook.

"The usual." Mario's gruff words reach me from the other side of the counter.

Laura rushes to serve him his Guinness, grinning while

he talks steadily. He's older than me by a few years, maybe late twenties?

I think I need to warn Laura about him, but when I alluded to the fact that he might be untrustworthy the other day, she gave me a weird look.

So I keep those thoughts to myself.

The bar hums with low chatter, the thunk of glass against wood, the distant echo of laughter swallowed up by the bass-heavy music filtering through the speakers.

The usual crowd is gathered under the neon haze of 'HAVEN' like sinners seeking temporary absolution.

I work on autopilot, pouring drinks, wiping spills, and nodding along to slurred conversations that don't require real listening. But then—

Something shifts.

My skin prickles as if the air has been punctured, the oxygen thickening and darkening in increments.

I don't see him at first. I *feel* him.

Like a storm pressing in before the first crack of lightning.

Jude strides in, dressed in black, built like a wall.

No, a warning.

A threat.

The low amber glow from the bar lights drags over him, sharpening every edge, casting shadows where shadows shouldn't be. His black T-shirt stretches across his torso, and my eyes widen upon seeing what's on his half-exposed arms.

Full sleeves of unintelligible ink.

They stand out like marks of war, like a language only monsters speak.

He moves like he owns the place. Like he owns *everything*.

And I hate that my pulse stutters at the sight of him.

That my entire body tenses and my senses go on high alert.

I grip the bar towel tighter, pressing my fingers into the damp fabric, forcing myself to breathe.

Because he shouldn't be here.

He *never* comes inside.

He's only ever been outside, lurking like something too big, too sharp, too dangerous to step into the light.

But he's here now.

Like he was in my home last night.

Why...?

He sits beside Mario, but his presence carries a different kind of weight. Where Mario blends into the background, Jude shifts the entire atmosphere.

His arms rest on the bar, muscles coiled under the sleeves of black ink. Serpentine scales wrap around his forearm, climbing, coiling, each ridge and curve etched with such precise detail that I can almost feel the rough texture beneath my fingers.

A skull is inked on his wrist, cracked and hollow-eyed, as if it's seen too much and survived anyway. Thorn-covered vines twist through the gaps, weaving between bone and shadow, like something alive waiting to bite.

Jude doesn't glance at me. Not at first. He just taps his fingers against the counter in a slow, deliberate motion.

Then he speaks in a voice that snakes down my spine and settles in places it shouldn't. "Double bourbon. No ice."

His detached, dissecting gaze lifts toward me, and it's as if he's seeing straight through me, peeling me apart layer by layer.

I hate that Jude makes me feel this way.

I'm fully clothed, but I feel stark naked around him.

I swallow hard, my fingers twitching as I grab the glass.

There's no reason for my throat to feel dry or for my pulse to thud unevenly.

No reason at all.

After I pour his drink, my hands steadier than I feel, I slide it toward him. His fingers brush against mine when he reaches for the glass.

And for a moment, our eyes meet, mine frantic, his intense and unforgiving, like the grim reaper I used to fantasize about.

A spark of something dark and ancient courses through me at the feel of his long, rough fingers, and I jerk mine away, feeling heat creeping up my neck.

His eyes narrow slightly, but I'm already rushing to another customer at the other end of the bar.

Even though I spend the rest of my shift trying to ignore him, I can *feel* him.

His eyes.

His attention.

His sheer presence.

It's suffocating.

I'm teetering on the edge of a breakdown, trying to think about what the hell he plans to do next.

I've been jittery for weeks, and I don't think I can survive this for long.

Shaking my head, I choose to focus on work.

The tray wobbles in my hand as I move through the crowded back tables, balancing drinks with practiced ease, my mind staying three steps ahead.

That's when a sharp slap cracks against my ass.

I freeze.

The tray tilts dangerously, liquid sloshing over my fingers.

A sharp inhale burns my throat, but I swallow the yelp down, choke on it, and bury it where all the other moments like this go.

This isn't the first time; it won't be the last.

The cold, familiar feeling of disgust slithers through me, but I force a tight-lipped smile and step back before he can trap me—

It happens so fast.

One second, I'm pulling away. The next, a rough shove knocks me backward, and my balance falters as the tray tilts from my grip.

The world lurches.

The crash of breaking glass shatters the air.

Beer spills in sticky ribbons over my hands, soaking into my skin before the sharp scent of alcohol hits me. But that's not why my breath locks in my throat.

That's not why the whole bar falls silent for half a beat.

It's *him*.

Jude is no longer sitting at the bar.

He's now lifting the bald, heavyset man who just spanked me by the collar.

Then punches him in the face.

The impact is sickening. A crack, a gurgled gasp, a splatter of red. The man barely has time to react before Jude throws him onto the table.

The wood splinters under his weight, shattering into two uneven halves. His friends stumble to their feet, wide-eyed, like they don't know if they should fight or flee.

They should probably run.

Because there's no stopping him.

Jude moves like a force of nature, not a man, not even a monster—just a raw, uncontrollable force. He punches. And punches.

And *punches*.

Like the first time we 'met'—when he brutalized Dave until there was nothing left but blood and bone.

The look in his eye now is the same as then.

Blind rage.

No limits.

No conscience.

Mario blocks the other men, shoving them back like they're nothing, ensuring Jude's violent spree is left undisturbed.

I should leave. I should run.

Escape to the staff room, hide my face, pretend this never happened.

That's what I always do.

But for some stupid, reckless reason, I push through the chaos, through the people shouting, through the beer mugs pounding against wood as the crowd chants, "Fight! Fight! Fight!"

And then I do something I shouldn't.

I touch him.

A tentative hand on his inked arm.

His muscles bunch beneath my fingers, as tight as steel cords. He's still clutching the semi-conscious man by the collar, his knuckles dripping red, but at my touch, he swings around, his fist raised.

My breath catches and I flinch back, my hand burning where it touched him, as if his rage is contagious.

His pupils are blown wide, drowning the color in his irises in two pools of darkness.

Violence.

Rage.

It's always as if he's standing on the edge of something inhuman.

But then, for a moment, as his gaze locks on to mine, recognition flickers and his fist hangs in midair.

"Please stop." My voice is quieter than the storm around us, but he hears it.

Because his gaze drags down to my mouth, like he can read the words off my lips, which twitch uncontrollably, crumbling under his attention.

The way he looks at me with that quiet intensity ignites a disturbing feeling inside me, a deep discomfort laced with an invisible thread I can't quite cut.

The fight drains out of him.

Or maybe he just decides the man isn't worth any more effort.

Because Jude lets security take the bald guy from his grip.

Then, in a single, casual motion, he pulls a stack of cash from his jeans and tosses it at the manager. "For the damage."

And just like that—he turns and leaves.

Mario follows without a word.

I release a shaky breath, gripping the tattoo on my wrist as my knees threaten to buckle.

By the time my shift ends, I feel like I've been washed, wrung out, and hung to dry. Every inch of me aches—my back, my feet, my skull.

All I want to do is snuggle into my couch and fall asleep listening to an audiobook.

My backpack slung over my sore shoulder, I walk out of HAVEN, massaging it, already dreaming of patches, heat packs, and the blessed oblivion of sleep—

My eyes widen and my fist that I'm using to rub my shoulder is frozen.

Because Jude didn't leave.

He's still here.

Dressed in black from head to toe, he's leaning against his bike, his legs crossed at the ankles. His leather jacket and gloves radiate quiet menace as he toys with his helmet with controlled movements.

The streetlamp overhead flickers, its light flashing over the shadowed cut of his jaw and lips that are always set in a line.

I wonder if he ever smiles.

No.

I really shouldn't care whether or not my stalker smiles.

I lower my head, quickening my pace in the opposite direction.

In a fraction of a second, a large shadow steps in front of me.

My stomach drops as heavy boots and dark jeans come into my vision. "You're coming with me."

My fingers twitch against my wrist, tracing my tattoo out of instinct. "Why—"

"I'm over here." His voice is low, steady, and completely void of patience. "Look at me when you talk to me."

I lift my head, my pulse hammering. "I'd rather not go anywhere with you."

"Your preferences don't matter."

Before I can react, he slams the helmet onto my head. "Hop on the bike, Violet. We have a long night ahead of us."

CHAPTER 8
Violet

"DON'T MAKE ME REPEAT MYSELF."

The gruff edge of Jude's voice makes needlelike goosebumps erupt on my skin.

The heavy helmet on my head smells like him—leather, wood, and inescapable danger. It's suffocating, but I still look around, searching for someone.

Anyone who'd be able to save me.

"Violet."

I grow still, my gaze flashing to him. He's already on the monster of a bike, his legs on either side, and his gloved hands grabbing the handlebars. He has another helmet on, so I can't see his face, but with the slight tilt of his head, I can tell he's regarding me as if I'm an annoying insect beneath his boot.

Even though my heart hammers loudly, I lift my head. "I don't want to."

"Do you believe I give a fuck what you want?"

"No, but—"

"If you don't get on the bike, I'll change plans, drive to your place, and give your sister a little visit. Let's see if you'll regret your choices by then."

My body tightens up, the nightmare from last night and

Mama's words about killing whoever loves me playing in my head on a loop.

"Don't you dare," I whisper-yell, my hands balling into fists.

He tilts his head to the side farther, his domineering gaze sliding to my hands before he wrenches his attention back to my face. "Was that a threat? You're capable of those?"

"Don't go anywhere near Dahlia."

"That depends on your cooperation. Or lack thereof."

I let my fists relax and begrudgingly hop onto the bike. It takes me a few moments to get situated behind him.

I grab onto the back of the motorcycle with both hands as it revs beneath me, vibrating through my aching muscles. I'm conscious not to get too close or to touch him.

Only bad things happen whenever we touch.

"Where are we going?"

No reply.

Instead, he kicks the bike into gear, then stops, and I slam against his back, my hands grabbing onto both sides of his leather jacket at his waist for balance.

I'm about to pull back again, but he speeds away, the force of gravity not allowing me to move unless I'm in the mood to fall over.

My heartbeat escalates in frightening increments as he increases the speed until everything is a blur of light, faces, and the rotten town.

I lift my head and when the air slaps me from every side, I can breathe in the sharp tang. I sink my fingers deeper into his sides until I feel every ridge of his muscles, every contour, and every strong line.

The man is built like a weapon and he knows it.

"Can you please slow down?" I try to shout over the wind.

"Why? Does this scare you?" He goes faster, sliding between cars, and I slam my eyes shut as gravity shoves my head against his back muscles.

Even though the helmet separates us, I can feel how taut and rigid he's built.

Everything about him is.

And yet I can still feel his warmth and inhale the masculine scent emanating off of him and flooding my senses.

"Don't be scared yet. There'll be plenty of chances for that."

He goes even faster, as if testing those limits.

Seeing how far I can last before I fall.

I close my eyes half of the time, scared we'll crash or that he'll send us flying off a hill.

In my doomsday thoughts, I don't feel when we leave Stantonville and only realize we're in Graystone Ridge after seeing the sign between the grand angels and horses monument in the town center.

I'm dazzled by the lights, the chic restaurants, and the absolute absence of…well, the constant rotten smell lathering Stantonville's streets.

The cobbled pavements and the bright signs give me a fuzzy feeling, like the start of a fairy tale or a distant fantasy.

Dahlia has always said we should come here for our movie and dinner nights, but I shut it down. Not only because it's expensive, but I also don't like seeing a world I can never belong to.

Like a dream that will never come true. I'd rather stay exactly where I belong—in Stantonville.

We leave the town center behind too soon as Jude takes a few turns.

He stops in the driveway of a house on a suburban street. It's located on the hill, the highest of all the other streets.

My lips part upon seeing the rest of the town from up here, its glinting lights mesmerizing like a movie scene. The air smells of pine and nature, courtesy of the tall trees lining the neighborhood.

"Are you going to continue hugging me for long?"

I startle at Jude's gruff voice, letting him go and hopping off the bike. "I was only trying to stay alive. You drive like a madman."

My feet actually wobble when they touch the ground, probably from having my body fully pumped with adrenaline during that wild ride.

"A madman, huh?" He towers over me, peering down at me with menace.

I lower my eyes and start to remove the helmet. "I didn't mean to call you names."

"You did." His glove brushes against my hand as he pushes it away when he sees me struggling, and he removes the helmet and places it on the motorcycle.

Then his hand slides to the back of my neck, and the leather glove feels like burning fire even though he's not touching me directly.

I shouldn't have this reaction to his skin on mine.

Or his glove.

I shouldn't have this reaction to anyone touching me.

He bunches his fingers in my hair and drags my head back, and then his lips brush against mine.

The slightest graze.

Like a promise—or a threat.

His lips are softer than they look and they feel so full and all-consuming. Imploring, dizzying.

And I'm frozen again, my mouth trembling beneath his, and I'm consumed by the sensation.

The pull.

The heat.

I've had full-blown sex that didn't feel as intoxicating as his lips barely touching mine.

No.

I snap out of it and pull back, sliding a palm over my tingling lips. "W-what the hell do you think you're doing?"

"Look away from me again and I'll kiss you. And it'll escalate to something worse the more you indulge in that distasteful habit."

"You...wouldn't."

"Try me and see how far I'll go."

"You've lost your mind."

I drop my hand, and his rich brown eyes slide to my lips, darkening, peeling off my outer layer and settling beneath my clothes, my skin, into my bones.

He's...dangerous.

Because why am I reacting to him this way?

I've never been into physical touch or sex. Hell, I've avoided it like the plague and only succumbed to peer pressure in college because, apparently, if you keep your virginity after eighteen, society deems you a weirdo, and your classmates give you pitying looks.

The few times I let some frat boys fuck me were a disappointment.

No.

I actually disliked it.

Being exposed, touched intimately, and feeling ugly throughout it all.

I had body dysmorphia, no matter how much they praised me and told me I "feel so tight."

It didn't help that I had flashbacks of the noises I heard

when Mama was being fucked while I was cooped up in the closet.

Whenever I heard the guys breathing heavily on top of me or growling and moaning, I only had flashbacks of the men in Mama's life.

I even slammed both hands to my ears during the last time I had sex, because I could hear the one man who loved punching my mama and leaving her bleeding after he was done.

Because the guy I was having sex with smelled like him—cheap cologne and strong cigarettes.

I even started humming like I did back then while doodling sketches in my notebook in the near darkness to drown out the sounds.

Needless to say, the guy called me a weirdo for ruining the mood and left as if his ass were on fire.

I just lay in bed, stared at the ceiling, and laughed, but then started crying because that's what Mama did after they left.

Then I threw up. I usually do after sex, and since I barely find pleasure in it, I stopped it altogether after the "weirdo" episode, choosing not to poke a bear I didn't need to.

So, as a certified sex avoider, why the hell did my stalker's lips just now make me feel like *that*?

I don't know what *that* was, but it was different from my usual disgust, and I definitely have no bile gathering in my throat.

"Follow me." Jude's words snap me out of my thoughts, and I have no choice but to trudge behind him and toward the house.

He doesn't have to say the "Or else…" for me to understand that my actions will determine Dahlia's fate.

While I have little to no regard for my own life, Dahlia

is the only person who's ever cared about me, loved me, and made me feel like I'm important. I'd never let Jude or anyone else hurt her.

Ever.

No matter what I have to go through.

I follow him into the house, my steps careful, and I slide my glasses up my nose.

The air is laced with something clean and expensive, a faint trace of musk and cologne clinging to the walls.

The entrance spills into an open floor plan, warm lighting cascading over polished wood floors leading to an off-white staircase that disappears into darkness.

It's beautiful but odd.

This isn't the kind of mansion or penthouse I imagined someone like Jude would live in. Two stories, sleek and modern, like something out of a magazine. Muted grays and blacks, soft ambient lighting that doesn't feel harsh, and furniture that looks like it belongs in a high-end showroom.

And yet…as I glance around, my chest squeezes with unease.

Something feels off.

The house is too sterile and perfect, like no one really lives here.

Like it was put together with intention but has never actually been touched.

My footsteps are too loud as I trail behind Jude, gripping the straps of my backpack tighter. The thick silence presses against my ribs with each breath.

I don't know if he's doing it on purpose, but Jude has a way of integrating silence and using it to make me uncomfortable.

It doesn't help that the house feels wrong. There's no

lingering scent of home-cooked meals or any worn-in furniture. Just…nothing.

We walk toward the living room, and I take it in—a charcoal-colored sofa, a glass coffee table, and a massive flat-screen mounted on the wall.

Everything is pristine, not a pillow out of place, not a single mark on the floor, not a hint of the man who's taking over my life.

And my sanity.

Jude's silent, controlled strides are my only tether to reality. He removes his leather jacket and throws it on the chair. His T-shirt stretches across his back, ink curls down his arms, the shadows animating the symbols and designs.

He faces me and I stop dead, swaying in place, then look down. His boots come into view, and I jerk my head up, covering my mouth with my palm.

I certainly don't want to give the prick a chance to kiss me again.

His lips twitch, just the slightest bit as he flicks a glance to the sofa.

Sit.

No words. Just a single motion.

I hesitate, clutching my backpack tighter, then my shoulders hunch and I sit. On the edge.

Still gripping the straps.

Jude doesn't join me, just stands in front of me, looking like a wall. He's already tall when I'm upright, but at the moment, he's ten times more intimidating.

"Now what?" I ask, remembering to look at him.

He doesn't reply, just continues to stare at me, his eyes slightly narrowed, as if he's trying to figure out what I'm thinking about.

"You brought me here for a reason, right? If we can reach it soon, that would be great."

Jude tilts his head to the side. "In a hurry to go back to your unremarkable life?"

"Yes, actually. It might be unremarkable, but it's mine and I'm happy with it."

"Happy enough to write about how much you've thought about dying every other day?"

My throat dries, the emotions getting clogged in there. "You had no right to read my journal."

"I think we've established that I don't give a fuck what you think."

"Fine." I release a breath, feeling exhausted by just looking into his unfeeling eyes. "Can you tell me why I'm here? I'm tired and could use some sleep before my early classes tomorrow, so if you don't mind…"

I start to stand up, but the look he gives me pins me in place.

Finally, however, he turns around and flips on the TV. "Don't move."

Before I can ask what's going on, he pulls out his phone and sidesteps me.

My eyes trail after him, but he disappears around the corner.

Even with his absence, I don't feel relaxed, not in the least. If anything, my shoulders are crowded with tension as I stare at the screen. I'm not in the mood to watch TV—

My lips fall open.

The scene playing before me is familiar.

The video is cut, set to vertical mode, showing only two people.

A man and a woman I'll never forget for as long as I live.

My breathing comes out in harsh pants as the man stabs the woman.

Then he does it again.

And again.

And *again*.

Her blood spills on the pavement, on her beautiful white-and-yellow sundress, her blonde hair, and her eyes turn lifeless.

Bile gathers in my throat, and my heart nearly rips out of my chest, but I remain frozen. Just like the time I saw this same scene play out right before my eyes.

And just like then, Mama's words play in my head like a mantra.

"Don't meddle, you little bitch."

"Do you think anyone would need the help of an ugly whore like you?"

"Who do you think you are?"

"Useless."

"Useless."

"Fucking useless."

Tears stream down my cheeks and my fingers twitch, my entire body trembling so hard, I'm wheezing.

That's when I hear it.

A muffled moan of pain.

A groan.

A bang.

It's not coming from the TV since there's no audio, and the woman, Susie Callahan, is lying in a puddle of her own blood, her empty eyes staring at nothing.

No, the sounds are closer.

Somewhere in the house.

I consider leaving, maybe…maybe calling the police.

But the police didn't save Susie when I called them that day. Ever since then, I've regretted my cowardice and the way I let Mama's voice freeze me in place.

I'm paying for my silence by being assigned an angel of death in the form of Jude.

So, I'll never be a bystander again.

Standing on wobbly feet, I cast one last glance at Susie, then wipe my eyes as I try to find the source of the sounds.

Muffled groans.

No, they're screams, I think.

My legs are still shaking as I go down the stairs, jumping a little when the lights switch on.

Damn. I really hate basements. I've watched enough true crime documentaries to know this is where the shit hits the fan.

I pull out my phone, gripping it tighter as the volume of the sounds increases.

I pass by an open door and stop.

A large blond-haired man with bulging eyes is strapped to a chair in the middle of a sterile basement room. The walls are white and there's a metal cabinet behind the chair.

His mouth is covered by silver duct tape, and his shirt and pants are torn in places, blood oozing from his multiple injuries. The worst part is his bare feet, where dirt and leaves are stuck to the dried blood.

"Mmmm!" he screams behind the duct tape, rocking back and forth in his chair upon seeing me.

I rush to his side, my legs barely carrying me, and I try to slowly remove the tape. "Are you okay?"

"Do I look okay, you stupid bitch!" he snarls, shouting. "Untie me before that sick motherfucker comes back."

"Oh, okay." I'm breathing harshly as I slide behind him and work on the tight knots. "Who did this to you?"

"Who else? It's that motherfucking crazy asshole!"

"J-Jude?"

"I don't know his name. Stop talking and hurry the fuck up!"

"These are special knots. It's hard to undo them."

"Useless stupid bitch."

I release the rope. "If you're going to call me names, I won't help you."

"You…" He exhales deeply. "Just please, okay? I've been under a lot of stress with that fucker chasing me with his friends and then drugging me. I just want to go home, so help me out, yeah?"

With a sigh, I work faster on the ropes. People can be really deranged when they're under a lot of stress, so I don't blame him.

More importantly, I keep thinking about why Jude and 'his friends' chased this man.

As soon as his hands are undone, he helps me untie his feet.

The moment he's free, he wobbles toward the exit, but a shadow appears at the door.

Large, imposing, and holding a knife in his hand that shines under the light.

I freeze and so does the man.

"Not so fast." Jude looks at him with that familiar aloofness.

"Fuck! Just let me go, you sick fucker."

"I can." Jude's gaze slides from the man to me. "But only one of you gets to leave this place alive."

I take a step back. "Please don't do that—"

"Her!" the man screams. "Kill that stupid bitch, not me."

I swallow, my heart shrinking. So much for helping him.

"What do you think?" Jude asks me, tilting his head to the side. "Will you be a saint and sacrifice your life for this waste of space? You're into all that despicable business, so it might be tempting."

I look down, whispering, "Death doesn't scare me."

"But I do scare you, and I already decided that you won't get the easy way out."

I gasp as Jude grabs the man, who was trying to squeeze past him, turns him around, and looks me in the eye as he slices his throat open.

CHAPTER 9
Jude

VIOLET GOES INTO SHOCK.

Her entire body locks, and she stares with wide eyes even as the waste of space's blood splashes on her face, her glasses, and her clothes.

Her fingers twitched when I held the knife to the man's throat, but she didn't move.

Couldn't move.

And she's remained in that frozen state since then.

The same shocked yet unmoving position, wearing the same expression she did the day my mother was killed.

I know because I've watched her reaction in the surveillance video Kane gave me a dozen times, trying to figure out how the 'Do you need help?' blue umbrella girl just stood still.

I see it again now—that motionless wide-eyed look—as I throw the dead weight aside, not bothering to spare one final glance at his horrified empty eyes, the gash splitting his neck, or the pool of blood on the floor.

He doesn't matter.

None of them do.

Stalking, capturing, and hunting them before taking their miserable lives offers a momentary reprieve from the suffocating darkness.

Only a brief moment of pure air and a feeling of grandiosity that I'm doing right by Mom, but it only lasts for
a while.

Then it's back to nothingness.

And I'm shoved down to where my demons fester and rot,
where no one and nothing would be able to extract me from
these sick fucking thoughts.

And yet...

As I look at Violet's body that's shaking in silence, at her
lips that are trembling, her teeth that are chattering, I find
myself stuck in a strange pull.

Like a magnet.

No. A moth.

Violet is a flame in its most delicate form. She's not a
raging and absolutely destructive orange, but she's blue.
Discreet, seemingly safe but actually dangerous.

Just like the fucking blue umbrella she put in my hands.

"Death doesn't scare me."

That's what she said, but now she's staring at the man's
corpse as if she personally killed him.

I've never understood people who...feel too much for
others. Could be due to my upbringing. Even Mom couldn't
have been accused of being emotional.

My father, Regis Callahan, made me kill a guard who'd
betrayed him execution style when I was nine years old.

That happened two months after he told me to kill
Mom's personal butler in the same style for leaking information about our medical empire to a rival company. I
refused and even shot a vase, making the glass fly and injure
his face.

Mom's personal butler wasn't only a great part of my
life but also Mom's only friend, who followed her after her

marriage to Regis. He was the one who listened to her and joined her on walks in the garden.

I didn't give a fuck about an empire I resented, because Regis gave it more attention than he gave Mom, no matter how much she tried to win him over. But I cared about Mom's friend because she loved him and he made her smile.

Still, Regis insisted I kill him, shoving the gun in my hand and saying in clipped words, "This man jeopardized your and our entire household's safety as well as the empire we spent centuries building, Jude. I need you to not hesitate when you pull the trigger on traitors. Do you hear me, son?"

"No!" I screamed and fought even after Mom begged me not to.

I actually wish I'd killed the butler. A bullet to the head would've given him a quick death, unlike the torture the butler had to go through while my mom and I were forced to watch, gagged and strapped to chairs until he spit his last breath.

And then Regis scolded Mom for bringing him in and for not raising me "right," for teaching me "bad habits" and allowing me to "throw tantrums to get what I want."

Later that night, my mom overdosed on sleeping pills and I found her foaming at the mouth. She almost died.

Because of me.

So after that, I mindlessly killed whoever Regis told me to, because he realized he could threaten me with Mom in order to put me in the lane he'd specifically carved out for me.

We also made a deal. If he'd stop threatening to divorce my mom and give her the date nights she's always begged him for, I'd become whatever he wanted me to be.

A weapon for power within Vencor.

The muscle who carried out his kills.

Top student.

Top athlete.

The Callahan empire's perfect robot and the spare to Julian's genius.

It didn't matter as long as I got to protect my mom.

Julian called me an idiot for offering our dad my weakness on a platter, but Julian didn't have a mom or a heart, or the feeling that he needed to protect someone with everything he had.

But that someone whom I shaped my whole life to shield from Regis's cold shoulder and the whole fucking world is gone now.

And I've been on this killing spree to avenge her.

Bring her justice.

Fucking *fill* the hole her death has dug deep in my chest.

And if it means death to every single fucking person who was in that square, so be it.

So why the fuck...does seeing Violet in this state enrage me?

A lot of things about this fucking girl do—from the very first time she gave me that blue umbrella.

And it's only gotten worse since.

I despise her naïveté, the way she just lies down and takes everything thrown her way, but most of all, I hate how she smiles even though her life is a mess and her journal is full of suicidal thoughts and a shit ton of trauma and low self-esteem that was caused by her mother.

And I shouldn't have all these damn thoughts or feelings about someone from that day.

Someone who chose to stand by as that scum took away my mom—and the only light in my life.

And yet...

As Violet shakes uncontrollably and falls to the floor, heaving and wheezing, I throw the knife aside. The clattering of the metal is drowned out by the choked sounds she's releasing as she bangs on her chest with her fist.

A panic attack, I realize, as I tower over her, looking down at her reddish hair that's also smudged with blood.

I should let her rot. Or, better yet, just end her miserable life once and for all.

But then again, that's what she wants, so that's not going to happen.

I lower myself in front of her. This close, I can see the tiny freckles dusting her nose and upper cheeks like dotted stars on a moonless night. "I thought death didn't scare you."

She's still wheezing, her other hand grasping at the floor for balance.

"Or is that only when your own life is on the line? Do other people's deaths disturb you?" I reach out my bloodied hand and grab her cheek, lifting her head.

Pools of deep blue are marred with tears as she stares up at me while I smudge her pale cheek with blood. "Or is it because you're squeamish?"

Her breathing is still sharp, irregular, but she's no longer banging on her chest. I slide my thumb over her upper lip. It's slightly bigger than the lower one, giving her a permanent little pout.

And I paint it in blood.

Her mouth. Her skin.

Even her soul should be red.

Her quivering lips part slightly, giving me the tiniest opening I shouldn't entertain taking, but I do. I slide my middle finger inside, until it's resting on her hot, wet tongue.

And I thrust it against the surface, going in as far as

possible, until she chokes, her eyes widening, but then I pull back and rub it against her tongue.

She swallows around my finger, her delicate throat working up and down with the motion.

My cock jumps in my jeans, and I suppress a groan, because why the fuck would that be a turn-on?

I don't even like oral. Or any foreplay.

All the girls I fuck know that I want someone who's game to being dicked down on the mattress, wall, floor, anywhere where I can fuck the aggression out of my system, and then off they go.

I don't care for blowjobs. At all.

So why the fuck is Violet's mouth around my finger making my usually picky cock act up?

Little by little, her breathing slows, her hand sliding from her chest to her lap as she stares up at me.

She looks a mess, blood from my hand on her cheek, her lips, some in her hair, but it's her eyes that hold me hostage.

The blue is so calm yet deep, a force of nature that's no different from the ocean. Something that's unassuming on the outside but bears secrets no one has dared to uncover.

And I want to dive into those depths, dismantle each of her secrets one by one.

But as her tongue moves the slightest bit, not even licking me, my entire body tenses up.

"Don't flirt, Violet."

It's her turn to tense, and she attempts to shake her head, but I hold my finger at the back of her throat. "You must be a natural at sucking cock with these impressive little-to-no gagging skills. Tell me, have you considered selling your services like your mother?"

She pulls back with a cough, her saliva and dried tears mixing with the blood in a beautiful mess.

I like the view.

The way her disgusting innocence is smudged with my darkness.

A realization slithers beneath my skin and spreads through my chest with haunting violence.

That's what I've always wanted to do to Violet. Erase her innocence and crush any of her feeble hopes of keeping her lowly life together.

And I don't need death to accomplish that.

Death is reserved for the scum who's lying on the ground staring at nothing.

Violet jumps up and glares down at me—she fucking *glares*. "People like my mom do what they do to survive. Something you have no knowledge of, considering the silver spoon you were born with and the privileged upbringing and wealth that force doors open in your face. So *excuse* us normal people, for working hard for our next meal and the roof over our heads. Whether we do that in shitholes or lying on our backs is none of your business."

While she's tense, she's standing in a wide stance, not the mouse-like posture she usually forces her body into.

Even with the blood, the dried tears, and the disheveled hair, she looks the prettiest I've ever seen her.

I stand up and even that doesn't make her recoil like she usually does. "Did you just snap at me?"

"I wouldn't have done it if you weren't disrespectful."

"I don't believe that's the real issue. I've never shown you respect, and that doesn't seem to faze you, but the moment I mention someone else, you transform into a kitten with claws. Ever thought of adopting the same energy to defend yourself?"

She purses her lips but says nothing.

"Ah, but you have such low self-esteem, it's almost impossible to see yourself past *the worthless, useless, waste-of-space little bitch who should've never been born,* right?"

Her eyes round, her pupils enlarging more by the second. "How...?"

"That's what you wrote in your journal. Your dear mama's words that you take way too seriously. Religiously, almost."

"You...you..."

"While you find a response, I want you to do something for me. From now on, you'll stand up for yourself like you do for Dahlia and others. If you fail to do so, I'll fuck you in my next target's blood."

Her lips fall open.

She takes a step back.

But stops.

"Fuck me, then."

It's my turn to stop, narrowing my eyes on her. "What?"

She lifts a shoulder casually—too fucking casually. "I don't care about sex, and we're already surrounded by blood."

I grab her chin, my fingers digging into the skin. "Do you have any fucking idea what you're saying?"

Her sad fucking eyes stare at mine, lingering, peering. I can tell she's uncomfortable, but she still keeps up the eye contact. "Isn't that what you want?"

"What about what you want?"

"Doesn't matter."

I wrap my other hand around her waist and slide it beneath her hoodie, on the small of her back, my fingers tracing the two dimples there.

"Do you believe you can fucking handle me? I'll break your cunt the fuck up."

She swallows, her throat bobbing up and down, but then she does the most Violet thing ever—she forces a smile. "If it makes you feel better, I don't care. Won't be my first disappointing sex."

What the fuck…?

Did she just call the possibility of sex with me a potential disappointment?

As in, she lumped me in with all the limp-dicked assholes she's had sex with?

I realize I've loosened my hold on her, because she steps away, hopping over the bloody mess. "Let me know when you want that so we can get it over with."

And then she leaves, all but running away while gripping the strap of her backpack.

Get it over with.

That's what she said, right?

Like it's a fucking chore?

I tilt my head to the side, staring at the man's dead eyes and wondering why the fuck I'm not countering Violet's insolence with the same actions.

CHAPTER 10
Jude

"FUCK YES!" PRESTON SHOUTS, STANDING UP AND DANC-
ing mockingly while waggling his brows.

The game controller dangles from his hand before he throws it on the table and lounges back on the sofa, taking a sip of beer.

We're chilling in my penthouse, on the farthest side of Ravenswood Hill—an exclusive gated community up the hill that overlooks Graystone Ridge, where founding members live.

It's shadowed by trees and has iron-clad security that forces anyone with a wish to survive to stay away.

The place I live in is sparse with little to no furniture. The only reason I have a sofa, TV, and gaming console is because Preston brought them over. Or the men he sent did. At seven in the fucking morning the day after I moved in.

That was a few months ago, following my mother's death. I had no plan to continue living with Regis in that large, unfeeling Callahan mansion he calls home.

"My Highness would be open to teaching you some skills, peasant." Preston leans back against the sofa, grinning at me with that provocative edge. "All you have to do is get on your knees, call me *Master*, and beg."

"Says the loser who demanded we keep playing until you win."

"Never happened. Don't know what you're talking about." He passes me the bottle of beer and I take a sip, throwing down my game controller as the score is displayed on the screen.

Pres has been here since last night. When I came back from a run, I found him sleeping on the couch, upside down, with the TV playing some *Tom and Jerry* cartoon. He loves crashing here most of the time since he has furniture and essentials here and can get a good night's sleep. Though we both prefer to barge into Kane's space and make him cook for us, that weirdo loves working out on his days off, while Preston and I love doing nothing.

Actually, we prefer maiming people to doing nothing.

"Besides—" He kicks my side. "—you should let me win after you took away my kill the other day."

"It wasn't your kill. He was my target."

"What's yours is mine, and what's mine is also mine." He snatches the bottle of beer. "Where the fuck did you take that loser anyway?"

"To one of the safe houses."

"Aw, and I wasn't invited? I'm so fucking offended right now."

Thinking about the mess from about a week ago, Preston would've just been the last straw of chaos.

I haven't been going to Violet's workplace or neighborhood, but Mario has, and he said everything looks 'normal.' That guy needs to be specific about what's considered *normal.*

Or I can go and watch personally, but even I realize I need to stop getting fucking distracted by a nobody.

A nobody who said I'd be a disappointing fuck.

Not entirely, but it was something along those lines.

"Hey, Pres?"

"Nah, I won't accept your apology."

"That's not it."

"Might consider it if you let me kill the next…five targets."

"No."

"I'm being generous here. Okay, four. Final offer. Cross my heart and never die."

"It's cross my heart and hope to die."

"I meant it the other way. Don't be boring."

"Just shut up for a second. I have a question." I tilt my head in his direction. "What vibes do I give when it comes to sex?"

"Eh…thought of asking your fuck buddies?"

"They say I'm hot and would let me bend them in two."

"Ew. Cringe."

What the fuck? "*I* am cringe?"

"Sometimes. But I was talking about the girls who are desperate to get your D. They should try mine. Just saying."

"So you wouldn't say the girls who want to fuck me expect disappointment?"

Preston stares at me with one narrowed eye. "Disappointment? Who have you been hanging out with? Need names, addresses, social security numbers, and actual phone numbers because, fuck me, you look offended. Shit's interesting."

"Fuck off." I shove his face away with a throw pillow, then stand up. "Let's go to Kane's for food."

It's supposed to be our day off, but he won't mind us pestering him to cook. Though he'll spend the whole time talking bullshit about strength training and all that jazz. The guy doesn't know how to just chill.

Not that I'm any better, but I don't need a lot of technicalities to prepare for the hockey season or win my games. I just do, with the help of some violence.

Okay, a lot.

Preston stands up as I head to the bedroom. "Such a killjoy. Totally paying a shit ton of Daddy dearest's money to advertisement agencies searching for new friends. The ones I have certainly don't appreciate my genius. Hmm. Where to start…"

His grumbles lower in volume, but he's still speaking. I halt a few steps away and look back to check if he's actually talking to me and not himself.

Thankfully, he's glaring at me, and his mumbles stop as he kicks the couch and goes back to drinking.

A long breath whooshes out of me. He's all right.

I *think*.

Ever since we were kids, Preston has been kind of… fucked up, thanks to his useless damn parents and the world we live in. After the three of us were shipped to an all-boys boarding school, Kane and I promised we'd never leave him alone. Especially after he was assaulted by a teacher and the three of us killed the motherfucker.

We've made it our mission to just…be there for Pres at all times. Kill his demons—whether they're physical or mental.

While Pres is built like a mountain now and is often preening about his 'perfect' physique, he had girly looks when we were younger. It didn't help that he used to have his blond hair long and was a scrawny little twerp whose biting words exceeded his size.

All the bullies picked on him, not only because of his

looks but also because he was—and still is—a provocateur who truly doesn't know when to shut up.

Always asking for trouble. Attention. Fights. Altercations. *Anything*.

And although we grew up in the same world, I at least had Mom, but Pres didn't have anyone.

Well, except me and Kane.

And now that Mom's gone, he's the only one I have who I'll protect with everything in me.

I groan when my phone on the table flashes with Julian's name.

Pres fetches it and waves it at me. "Aren't you going to get this?"

"No. He'll just nag."

"It's a horrible fucking idea to be on Julian's bad side, big man. Don't be an idiot. I don't include those in my close circle." He picks up with a singsong tone. "Julian! It's been a while, man."

"You fucking—" I rush toward him.

"Jude? Yeah, he's right here. Byyyye!"

Preston thrusts the phone in my face, and I kick him when I take it, leaving him groaning as he grabs his shin and grunts, causing more drama than needed.

He punches me before disappearing into the kitchen, probably to raid my fridge.

"What do you want?" I say to my brother.

"You didn't join us for dinner over the weekend. Father was livid."

"I know. He called and texted about his feelings."

"You need to show up to family dinners, Jude. Don't make me force you."

My free hand clenches and unclenches. "Don't know

about you, but I have no reason to see Regis's face anymore, and I certainly don't need to keep up appearances."

"You think I do?"

"You de facto had him step down from being the company's CEO to an honorary chairman, so I'm not sure why you're licking the old man's boots."

"You seem to be forgetting that his power with the Callahan empire and the organization remains the same." My brother's voice is crisp and firm. Every word is spoken with a meaning, sometimes hidden, sometimes clear.

Just like Pres, Mom always told me to be on his side, not against him, but he's the one who tried to bury her fucking death.

I stare at the darkness through the floor-to-ceiling window. "An organization I have little to no interest in."

"An organization your life is built around and that you'll never leave unless it's in a casket. Don't be ridiculous, Jude."

"You know what's ridiculous? The love my mom showed you before you ended up covering up for her murderer."

"For the thousandth time, he killed himself soon after Susie died. I gave you his body, didn't I?"

"And then erased all the footage?"

"Not fast enough since Kane has it and has been enabling your violent sprees." There's a pause that's followed by a long sigh. "Jude. I'm telling you this as your older brother who cares about your well-being as much as Susie. Stop these impulsive hunting games and using our safe houses and resources for murder."

I tap my fingers on my thigh.

He knows.

I mean, he's well aware of the hunts, but I wasn't so sure news about the safe houses would reach him.

Julian has a vast network of Vencor and non-Vencor people whose entire job is surveillance.

The last thing I need is for him to learn about Violet. If he knows she's a target that I didn't kill like the others, he'll be inclined to find out why.

Julian, of all people, knows I don't do things without a purpose or deviate from my usual course of action without external stimuli.

Not that I know the reason myself, but Julian's nose still needs to stay out of my goddamn business.

When I say nothing, he releases a sigh. "You think Susie would be happy to see you're spiraling because of her?"

"The dead don't have any opinions. Stop fucking meddling."

I hang up, breathing harshly.

As I stare at the phone, multiple notifications come from the chat I have with Kane and Pres, that the latter keeps renaming with stupid shit.

The most recent one is "Pres's Sidekicks."

Preston: So, Kane, got enough groceries? We're coming over for food.

Kane: I'm not a restaurant.

Preston: Restaurant? Who the fuck says that? You're a cook. 😄

Kane: Just let me chill for one fucking day, Pres.

Preston: Nah, you'll develop depression without my godly presence.

Kane: More like clownish.

Preston: Shush, don't be rude. Anyway, I have a lot of tea to spill about the big man. Apparently, a girl

called sex with him disappointing, and he's been
moping like a bored housewife.

Kane: Really?

Preston: Heck yeah. He's been asking about his sexual
performance and stuff. I'm telling you, he's going
through a crisis of epic proportions. That and he's
being scolded senseless by Julian, judging by his
extra-grumpy replies from the other room. He might
need a pick-me-up.

Me: I'm going to knock your teeth out, Pres. If you're
going to talk shit about me, shouldn't you do it in
private and not in the group chat I'm in?

Preston: Nah, I believe in inclusion. Anyway, we're on
our way, Kane! Prepare the popcorn. Big man is done
being chewed up by Julian.

I'm on my way to the kitchen to choke the fuck out of
him when my phone pings in my hand.

Mario: We have a situation.

CHAPTER 11

Violet

"PLEASE, VI."

I release a long exhale at Dahlia's pleading voice on the other end of the phone as I walk home from class.

It's about forty minutes on foot, but I don't mind. This is the only workout I get, and walking helps clear my head.

"Don't try to be adorable, Dahl."

"But tomorrow is the only day you don't have an early shift. I just want us to have some fun at the movies and then go to your favorite kebab place."

"Or we can watch something at home and I cook. I'd rather you spend that money on your expenses."

"Boo. Just because we don't have much to spare doesn't mean we shouldn't have fun once in a while." She releases a sigh. "I know you've been stressed by work lately. I'm also exhausted, so I want to cheer us up a little."

"Fine, but can you pick a family-friendly movie? I promised Laura I'd babysit Karly tomorrow. She's struggling with her daycare and is scared of her ex suing for custody. Do you mind if we have her around more often?"

"Not at all! She's a cutie."

"Thanks, Dahl. I'll pay for myself and Karly."

"Don't be silly, I'll buy the tickets. I've got to go. My break is over. See ya!"

She hangs up before I can insist on paying.

Shaking my head, I slide my phone into my back pocket as I juggle two of my human sciences books in one hand. Classes are kind of kicking my ass, mostly because I don't have much of an attention span, but I'll be able to keep my scholarship if I improve my GPA.

In my peripheral vision, I catch a glimpse of Mario, and for the thousandth time in the last couple of days, I consider talking to him. Or falling in step to walk beside him.

But something tells me he wouldn't like that.

A couple of days ago, after I gave him his usual drink at HAVEN, I asked how he was, but he just looked at me with that detached expression and ignored me.

And I didn't push, because, well, I'm pretty sure I caught the glint of a gun beneath his jacket.

Guess he's not interested in talking to the person he's pseudo stalking.

Shocker.

The actual stalker, however, was nowhere to be seen, having delegated the entirety of his work to Mario.

There were no notes left in my journal, nor was there a motorcycle in front of HAVEN.

Jude just…disappeared.

Not entirely, since Mario is literally tailing me right now, but Jude's physically not there.

Which is a relief. Even if it's only been a week.

Ever since he forced me to watch a cold-blooded murder, splashed me with a stranger's blood, then promised to fuck me if I didn't get my shit together, I'm glad I don't have to look at him.

I mean, yes, I told him to fuck me, but, really, I was just in a post-panic attack adrenaline high and kind of just talked nonsense to escape.

Because he's right. Jude looks like the type who fucks like he speaks. In angry spurts of violence that I definitely couldn't handle.

Hell, I think I was in some sort of a daze when he thrust his finger in my mouth and kind of made me suck it.

A bloody finger.

With the blood of a man he just killed.

The fact that I only thought of that *after* I left should be a bright red flag.

Because I don't find dangerous men attractive. At all.

I've met enough of them to know they're the scum of the earth.

Jude Callahan's stoic face, rigid personality, and weapon of a body shouldn't be at the forefront of my mind.

The afternoon air is cool against my skin, the hum of traffic merging with the rhythm of my footsteps against the cracked sidewalk. The streetlights' shadows cast long figures in the afternoon sun that stretch and curl like grasping hands as I walk past them, my mind focused on what I'm going to cook for dinner.

I have several hours before my shift, so maybe I'll make Dahlia lasagna. She always says it's my signature dish and usually finishes a few servings in one night.

I balance the weight of my backpack slung over one shoulder. I have to find fresh meat, even if it's a small quantity and…

The roar of an engine splits the quiet.

I barely register it when a black van speeds toward the sidewalk.

No—it's rushing toward me.

It surges forward, tires screeching against the asphalt coming fast. Too fast.

I'm frozen in place, waiting for the death I've often spoken to before bed.

In a blur of motion, something lunges toward me—Mario—slamming into my side. Hard.

I hit the ground, out of the van's path. Hot, burning pain lances through me as my knees scrape against concrete, my breath shattering in my lungs.

And I watch with my mouth agape as Mario spins, reaching for his gun—

Another roar cuts through the traffic. This time, from the opposite direction.

The van does a U-turn in the distance as a motorcycle tears down the street, a faceless figure clad in black behind the handlebars.

Crack!

The gunshot rings out, and I flinch, pulling away on unsteady knees toward the wall for cover.

Crack!

Mario jerks, his shoulder snapping backward, his balance faltering as the rider speeds past, disappearing down the street.

He's hit.

Mario's hit!

My breath comes in short, shallow bursts as I stand up and scramble forward, my legs trembling, blood dripping down my knees from where my skin met the asphalt.

Mario stumbles as the van speeds toward us again.

I don't think as I shove him out of the way and then slam against the wall and slide to the ground from the impact.

A rush of air whips past me as the van swerves, nearly hitting us.

The world slows.

Then speeds up all at once.

The tires shriek against the asphalt as it peels away, disappearing around the corner as fast as it came.

It's over.

Are they...gone?

My hands tremble as I push myself up, my chest heaving, the adrenaline leaving a metallic taste on my tongue. My knees sting, but my gaze snaps to Mario, who's standing with his eyes narrowed on where the van and motorcycle disappeared as he sheathes his gun.

"Oh my God—your arm."

It's bleeding, a deep, angry wound blossoming across his upper arm, staining his jacket. His face is set in stone as he presses a hand to it.

I dig into my bag, my hands shaking, rummaging, searching—

My fingers wrap around the bottle of pills, and I offer a couple to him. "They're not much, but they might help with the pain." My voice wavers, my pulse wild. "You should go to the hospital."

Mario stares at me, then at the pills.

For a second, I think he won't take them.

But he snatches them from my hand and swallows them dry.

A brief pause. A shift in the air.

Now that I'm looking closely at him, Mario seems younger than I initially assumed. His black hair is damp with sweat, and his lips are slightly pale.

"Thanks." His rough and unused voice rips through the air, speaking the only word he's ever said to me.

It's so unexpected that my lips twitch in a smile before I can stop them. "Don't mention it. You saved me as well."

He keeps staring, not saying anything.

"Do you need my help with going to the hospital...?"

He says nothing, just types on his phone with one hand.

"Are we back to silence now? Got it. So much for worrying." I bend over and grab my books.

When I straighten, Mario's staring at me through narrowed eyes. "You should be more worried about why professional killers shot at you."

"P-professional killers? Why?"

"That's what I'd like to know." He squints more. "Who have you pissed off so much that they'd hire professional killers to eliminate you?"

"Aside from your boss? No one." My nails dig into the books. "Isn't this one of his sick games?"

Mario says nothing. A few moments later, a car with tinted windows rolls to a halt beside us, and I jerk back, the remnants of the adrenaline buzzing in my blood.

But then Mario opens the back door, his arm still dripping with blood, and tells me, "Get in."

"No."

"Please get in so I can drop you off and go get treated, Violet."

"I can go home on my own—"

"Out of the question. Not when someone is out for your life. Jude would kill me if he knew I left you on the street after what just happened."

"Pretty sure he'd do the same, though, so it'd be as if someone cut his expenses." I try to joke with the only dark humor I know, but Mario isn't laughing, and the driver is tapping his finger on the wheel impatiently.

So I sigh and slide in.

I don't want Mario to get in trouble because of me. I'm

sure he'd rather be doing something better with his time than following a boring girl like me.

And he needs to have his arm checked.

I'm shaking the entire ride, though. Because who would hire someone to kill me?

I've gone out of my way not to offend anyone—aside from Jude.

He must be the one behind this. There's no one who wants me to suffer more than him.

———

My mind is still racing as I push the lasagna into the creaking oven. I really hope it doesn't break down. I'm scared that our current landlord will be like all the previous ones and not care about repairs. In the past, we had to fix things ourselves while being told, "You're lucky to find a cheap place so close to town."

I pull out the two remaining cans of ginger ale from the case and frown as I set them down on the counter. Dahlia buys these for me because I once said I liked the taste. Ever since then, she's stopped buying her favorite soft drink—Dr. Pepper—so I buy it for her.

But I forgot today because I can't stop thinking about the attack this afternoon and whether or not Mario is okay. He left as soon as he dropped me off, but I could tell he'd lost a lot of blood, judging by the mess on the car's carpet.

Not that I should be worried about him, but he did save my life and got shot protecting me, so I can't pretend not to care.

If anything, I feel guilty that he's hurt because of me, and I keep having flashbacks from all the times Mama called me a curse.

As soon as I got home, I took a shower, dressed in a dark blue shirt that reaches my knees, and got busy with cooking so I wouldn't allow those thoughts to take over.

But I find myself doing that anyway.

Overthinking. Overanalyzing.

Blaming myself.

I squat down to the last drawer beneath the counter that I use for extra storage. Rummaging through the worn-out tote bags and old, slightly chipped cups, I pull out a chocolate tin from when I was young.

My fingers slide over its scratched exterior as I recall the day Mama gave it to me. It was for my sixth birthday and one of the few presents I ever received from her.

I pull it open, the scrape of metal against metal loud in the silence. Inside, there are other things Mama gave me.

A blue clip with ribbons that she bought me from a thrift shop because I kept looking at it. A cheap pair of sunglasses that one of her customers left behind. Pearls I unclasped from around her neck after she died because the people came and took everything, and I didn't want them to have the necklace. Mama always said her mama gave them to her—a family heirloom of sorts.

My fingers wrap around the most prized possession she gave me. A gold bracelet. It's nothing much, just a slim gold chain with a flat rectangular plate in the center about the size of a dog tag but much thinner and sleeker.

"Maybe it'll do you some good," she said, throwing it at me when she was coughing up blood right before her death.

She'd been sick for a long time by then. Customers dwindled and she barely had anyone over. We had to move to a smaller place with no heating and black mold on the walls, and it made her coughing worse.

Her hatred for me as well.

Even weak and lifeless, even as I wiped her down, mimicking the stupid TV shows, thinking it would make her better, she said, "It's all your fault, you little whore. All my misfortune started when I became pregnant with you, and you sucked out all my good luck and opportunities. I was beautiful, *so* beautiful...the most beautiful...no one could resist me. *No one.*" She laughed as tears streamed down her face. "Look what I've become because of you."

"I'm sorry, Mama." I hugged her frail body, moisture staining my cheeks. "Please get well soon."

"Stupid bitch." She shoved me away, sending me against the wall, crying and coughing and laughing. "You ruined my life, but I ruined yours, too, so let's call it even. I hope you die in a shithole, all alone and miserable and ugly just like me."

"Mama..." I stood up and walked to her on unsteady feet. "I'll be good, so, please, can you love me?"

She stared at me for a long beat before she let out a hollow laugh. "No one loves the reason for their demise, demon."

When I woke up the following morning, it was silent.

There was no coughing or shouting or slamming doors shut.

And my mama was motionless, frothing at the mouth, her dead eyes staring at nothing.

Overdose, they said.

I was ten years old, but I could tell it was because of the white stuff she sniffed on the regular.

"*She was already dying anyway,*" the cops whispered to each other.

"*Poor girl,*" the neighbor who gave me food told her scum husband. "*Savannah wasn't much, but she was Violet's only family. Now, the girl will be abused in the system.*"

"That slut shouldn't have had kids," another neighbor said. *"Now, her daughter will be the same. With a face like that, there's no doubt."*

"Drug overdose. Tsk. That's what you get for sleeping with other women's men. Karma, I'm telling you. Poor girl, though."

"Poor girl."

"Poor girl."

Poor. Goddamn. Girl.

Another statistic.

Another name.

Another 'single-mom tragedy' as they called it.

No one asked me if I was okay after I lost my only family at ten years old. No one stopped to wonder why I wasn't crying and was in complete shock for days, sneaking into our house and calling Mama's name, only to be greeted by silence.

I wanted my mama. I wanted the only person I had.

Maybe it was Stockholm syndrome. Maybe I was too attached to my abuser, but she was the only person who was forced by biology to be there for me.

And the ten-year-old version of myself felt the world crumble around her.

I read once that 'abuse can sometimes feel like love' and it stuck with me. That maybe that's what I felt toward my mother.

Over ten years later, I still revisit this box and wonder why Mama hated me so much. I tried my best at school, despite having little to no support, and got good grades. I learned to cook and clean early on to help her out, and I always stayed quiet because my voice annoyed her.

I hid in the closet whenever she had customers over,

because we had one room, and I disturbed them. The older I got and the weirder they looked at me, the more she demanded I stay out of sight.

She often said she became a prostitute because of me, so is that why she hated me?

Shouldn't she have given me up for adoption or something? Sure, I might have had a horrible life as well or ended up in the broken system I was eventually shoved into, but at least I wouldn't have felt worthless because my mother and only family disliked me.

I don't know why I'm thinking about this now or pulling out the box. Maybe because I was so rattled this afternoon, and that triggered the memory of another trauma.

A deeper, bigger one I don't think I'll ever be able to face or the way it shaped my life.

I put the box back beneath the tote bags and stand up.

The moment I do, I feel a presence behind me.

My heart leaps into my throat as I attempt to turn around, but a gloved hand covers my mouth.

The smell of leather and wood fills my senses, and my body tenses up.

Jude?

His deep and velvety voice whispers in my ear, "Shh, not a word."

CHAPTER 12
Violet

IT'S JUDE.

Why is Jude inside my home?

I mean, he was here before, considering the note and that he read my journal and messed with my stuff, but he's never stepped foot inside while I was here.

It's that escalation again, isn't it? Like when Mario started to watch me twenty-four seven or when Jude came into the bar and started a fight, then forced me to go with him and made me watch the recording of his mom's murder.

Before he murdered someone in front of me.

I had to literally block that from my memory and shove it in with the skeletons in my closet so I wouldn't break down.

After he left me alone, I thought he might have lost interest.

Hoped so, even.

But he's here.

In the flesh.

Of course he's here when I chose to go braless after the shower. And now, I feel self-conscious.

My body, which usually locks up when facing danger, is disturbingly pliant as he pulls me against him with the hand on my mouth and the other around my stomach. His large, gloved hand flexes on my belly over the apron covering my shirt as my back presses against his rock-hard chest.

He feels like a wall behind me, towering, impenetrable.

I tilt my head slightly, catching a glimpse of his handsome face that, as usual, is set in a disapproving scowl.

A sheen of darkness.

An overload of violence.

And it's all directed at me now. As if I've offended him in some way.

I try to pull his hand away, but he tightens his grip. So I let my arm hang at my side, losing all will to fight—not that I have that.

Maybe he truly got bored, and he's now here to finish the job.

I shouldn't feel relief about the possibility of death, but I'd rather face that than being the subject of Jude's suffocating fixation.

He stares down at me with unhinged focus, as if he'll miss whatever he's reading on my face if I blink. "Who wants you dead, Violet?"

I mumble against the glove and shake my head, but he doesn't remove his hand.

"Who else did you do wrong with that innocent act and those hollow fucking smiles?"

"Mmm."

"But you can't die when I haven't allowed it yet. The only one who gets to cut your lifeline is me. Your fucking god."

I'm trembling, my ass rubbing uncomfortably against his jeans.

No, not uncomfortably.

I feel weird whenever he looks at me with that intensity, as if he's stripping me naked and looking at my unsightly body.

A chilling realization settles through me—the reason for my unease around Jude isn't only because of fear; it's the shards of something foreign beneath the fear.

"So next time you're being shot at, you don't stand up and try to be a savior. You fucking hide, do you hear me?"

My eyes widen.

"I've seen the footage from the security cameras and your feeble attempts at being a superhero." He releases my mouth, then slides his hand down and wraps it around my throat. Not enough to choke, but it's firm enough to not allow me to move. "Too late for that, don't you think?"

"Not really," I whisper, my voice slightly low.

"What?"

"Well, you might make me watch you torture and kill people if I let Mario die. You seem to think people are all courageous and can act when faced with danger, so superhero it is, I guess. Did my actions satisfy you? Or should I have been shot, too, to prove the nobility of my sacrifice?"

His upper lip lifts, and I recoil, but that pushes me farther into his hard, warm body. I don't know what comes over me whenever this man is around, but I kind of just blurt out all my unfiltered thoughts.

"You seem to have a death wish."

"You already read my journal, so you know that's true."

"Violet…"

"What? You blame me for not saving your mom but still blame me when I turn around and save Mario? Will you ever be satisfied by *anything* I do?"

His gloved fingers tighten around my throat, still not choking but a little constrictive, then he turns me around in a blur of motion and shoves me back toward the counter, leaning dangerously close to me as the cool edge of it meets my lower back. "You need to learn when to shut that mouth."

"I thought you said I need to learn how to defend myself? Provide a better manual to avoid confusion."

He pushes me farther until I'm sort of sitting, sort of slumping on the counter, my back up against the wall. My heart lurches in my throat when he steps between my legs, and something hard pokes my belly.

Did this guy get hard from...manhandling me?

That would be creepy as fuck if I weren't horrified by an entirely different thing.

At his touch, warmth spreads through my belly and flows down...

Down...

Oh God. What's happening?

I don't really get turned on. I've always been told I'm dry, and if they don't use lube, I bleed. There's no way—

"You seem to have mistaken the fact that I didn't kill you for tolerance. Wait. No." He grabs the largest knife from the washed dishes and places it flat against my face. "You're provoking me to kill you, aren't you? End this nightmare on your behalf and take the step you've always cowered away from."

"Not here. I don't...want to traumatize Dahlia, please."

The knife's cool side lifts and then it's at my apron, cutting the strap at my neck, making it hang around my waist.

"It's amazing how you think your dead body would traumatize her, but not your death." He cuts the tie at my waist, and the apron falls to the floor.

My T-shirt is bunched up now, reaching mid-thigh. And he's staring at them, my thighs, where the shirt stops.

I grow hotter and warmer beneath his gaze, fighting the urge to fling my legs open.

Jude reaches a hand to my bandaged knee, then stops.

His unforgiving gaze slides up the length of me before meeting my gaze. "You don't really care about her, do you?"

"That's not true!"

"Hmm. You know how to yell?" He pulls at the collar of my shirt and places the knife there. "Let's see if you also know how to scream."

A gasp rips out of me as he cuts the shirt right down the middle. Since I'm not wearing a bra, my round breasts bounce free, the tips hardening in an instant.

It's not only because of the air.

My palms, which are flat against the counter on either side of me, tremble, but I keep them there as I stare at an invisible point on the floor.

It'll be over soon.

They all finish up quickly and get it over with.

If I remain completely still, it'll be over faster—

Rough gloved fingers slide from my throat to my jaw, gripping it tightly as merciless lips slam against mine.

He bites my upper lip, then my lower one, sinking his teeth so deep, I think blood will gush out.

I have no choice but to open as he thrusts his tongue inside.

Jude kisses like he speaks, walks, talks, and plays hockey.

With violence.

Bright red, rough, and completely ruthless violence.

He slurps on my tongue, biting down and nibbling, but he doesn't break the skin as he consumes my mouth, kissing me harsh and deep, like I've never been kissed before.

Like I never thought I'd ever be kissed.

There's an unrefined edge to him, a darkness that seeps from his tongue that's devouring mine, or his unforgiving fingers at my jaw.

I'm trapped between the edge of violence and desire, with no choice but to submit to his invasion while willing my body to remain disconnected.

It's too late, though, because I'm already moaning in his mouth. In the beginning, I think it's a noise coming from outside, but I soon realize the shameless whimper is mine.

Jude pulls his lips from my bruised ones, and I stare, entirely dazed as he slides his thumb to the corner of my lip. "Seems you did that on purpose."

"W-what?"

"I told you I'd kiss you if you looked away from me." His gloved hand slides from my jaw to my throat, over my collarbone, then wraps tightly around my breast.

I gasp, my nipples aching at the feel of his large palm on the tender flesh.

"It's time for that something worse." He puts the knife on the counter and grabs the can of ginger ale.

I watch with held breath as he opens the can, the sound of the metal and the released fizz barely cutting through the buzz in my ears and the uncontrollable heat in my body.

I'm mentally trying not to push my chest farther into his palm or rub my legs together or something equally ridiculous.

Jude brings the can to his lips, and I gulp, expecting him to put his mouth where I always do. Right at the edge, licking the remnants of the drink.

But he stops, his eyes on me as he holds the can in front of my face. "I want to try your favorite drink."

"How do you know...right. Professional stalker."

A small twitch lifts the corner of his mouth, and my lips

part. It's the first time he's ever smiled and he...looks so beautiful and different.

I kind of feel sad that maybe he hasn't had the chance to smile throughout his life.

But too soon, his mouth sets in a line, and he releases my aching breast, then grips my jaw, his gloved thumb pulling on my lower lip. "This mouth truly doesn't know when to shut up. Open."

"Why—"

The words are stuck in my throat when he pours the soft drink into my mouth. I swallow some, but he won't stop, liquid splashing everywhere—down my chin, my neck, on my chest, and even below.

He empties the can on me until I'm soaked in ginger ale.

I'm panting in my attempts to swallow as much as possible. "How are you going to try it if you waste it like that?"

"You don't like the waste?"

"Of course not. My biggest pet peeve is those who waste stuff just because they can."

"I better not be your pet peeve, then." He leans closer and licks my lower lip, then the upper one, sucking it into his mouth.

I flinch, but it's not due to discomfort.

No, it's something much worse.

Because my skin tingles where he licks me, his tongue drawing out sensations I've never experienced before.

It moves down to my chin.

"W-wait. I didn't look away just now."

"We're at the much worse part now, remember?" He sucks on a sensitive spot on my neck as he looks up at me, his eyes darkening to a frightening edge. "Besides, you don't like to waste, correct?"

My back arches as his tongue glides down, licking every droplet of ginger ale off my skin, his mouth sucking and biting my neck and collarbone until a strangled noise escapes me.

My thighs tremble, my lips parting as I feel something I've never experienced during sex.

Animalistic need.

The dark, wild type that I only read about in novels.

And it's…because of Jude?

No, that can't be right.

"Mmm. I still can't form an opinion." He grunts, his lips so close to my wet nipples, I shiver at the feel of his breath, but he doesn't touch me.

And I refuse to thrust myself in his direction.

A dark gleam flashes in his eyes. "About the drink, I mean."

"You're messing with me," I say in a voice so hoarse, I barely recognize it.

"Am I?" His teeth sink into my nipple, and he tugs on the tip until I'm whimpering. As if that isn't enough, he twists my other nipple with his gloved fingers.

I cry out. Because it hurts.

But it's also so…strangely titillating.

My thighs clench around his, chasing something I can't quite reach. But since my legs are spread so wide, I can't get any friction.

Jude bites, twists, and pinches my nipple, and my thighs throb with every touch, my core tightening with something primal and ancient.

"You're shaking." He speaks against my nipple, his eyes meeting mine. "Sex with me isn't so disappointing after all."

He slides his tongue down, both hands pulling at my nipples, sending jolts of wild need through me with every twist.

But I can't stop looking at him.

At the confident and easy edge he touches me with as his tongue swipes over my belly and to my now-soaked panties.

He pulls at the hem with his teeth, sliding the fabric against my throbbing clit.

The moan that rips out of me is shaky and hoarse, as if I've never moaned before.

Because I haven't, not even for show.

If the men from my past weren't pleasing me, they knew it. Despite my people-pleasing habits, I'll never feign an orgasm for a man. I also rarely gave head. They could fuck me, but I wouldn't put in the effort if they weren't going to reciprocate.

I'm not my mama in that regard.

And they hated that about me, and because of their fragile egos, they made it known that I was the bad person in all of this.

There was a running joke that I was like Sleeping Beauty, because I was like a lifeless doll in bed. I made no sound or expression.

They must've seen it as weird, but for me, I was just questioning my life choices, really.

However, right now, I can't help the noises that fill the kitchen. Even when I sink my teeth into my lower lip.

Even when I try to not be affected.

Jude lowers himself and slides my panties to the side.

"There's still some ginger ale here." He glides his hot, wet tongue over my slit, and I slam both of my palms on the wall on either side of me as my head drops back.

"Holy shit…"

"Mmm." He nibbles on my clit with his teeth, and I arch my back as my pussy throbs in his mouth.

Damn. Goddamn.

One gloved hand pinches my nipple as the other smacks the side of my ass cheek.

Hard.

Did he just spank me?

Yes, yes, he did, I think as I all but thrust my pelvis into his mouth, chasing, searching, *needing* something.

"You react well to pain. I like that." He spanks me again and I lurch, my hands turning clammy against the wall.

"Your cunt is soaking my mouth. Interesting." He licks my clit, then bites again, and this time, I'm thrashing, wanting...

No, *needing* more.

"Looks like you can be a very good fucking girl, sweetheart."

My insides clench, a hot wave rushing over me at what he called me.

A good fucking girl *and* sweetheart?

From Jude?

This must be a dream.

But the way he touches me doesn't feel like a figment of my imagination. He devours me thoroughly, even more enthusiastically than he did my mouth.

I've never met a man who was so...passionate about eating pussy, let alone who did it so fucking well.

I'm shamelessly shoving my core in his face, grinding against his mouth, but he grabs both my legs and lifts his mouth from my pussy. "No. That's not how it works."

My lips press together, suppressing a sound of protest, and he goes back to eating me out, thrusting into my opening with his tongue.

This time, I can't urge him to do it faster or harder when

he's holding my legs wide apart so that only his tongue and lips offer me any form of friction.

Just when I think I'll die, he pulls me so hard against his tongue, I throw my head back and scream.

I actually scream as the pleasure rips through my bones, riding his face, mumbling something unintelligible as I come the hardest I ever have.

Not even my little vibrator has given me this, let alone a man.

As I stare down at his dark eyes, I realize with horror that I just came on my stalker's tongue.

The man who wants to kill me gave me pleasure I've never experienced before.

Jude licks his lips, making me observe my own arousal glistening on his mouth, as he says, "You only had disappointing sex before me, sweetheart."

CHAPTER 13
Jude

I SLAM INTO HUNTER WITH ENOUGH FORCE THAT IT topples both of us on the ice.

He groans like a bitch as I squash him beneath me, and whisper, "Target Armstrong's legs again and I'll make sure your hockey days are fucking over."

Before I can do more damage, my team members pull me off him.

A chaos of wild, loud cheering from the superfans ensues as I get sent to the box. Again.

I absorb it all, feeling each call of my name, every scream. They rush through my veins with intoxicating adrenaline. Like a damn drug. And even though the arena isn't as loud as during the season, many superfans attend any and all of our informal practices.

Kane shakes his head at me, clearly disapproving of my excessive violence. The other players, however, look at me with admiration, some patting me on the shoulder during my skate to the box as I remove my helmet.

Damp hair falls to my eyes, and I shake it back, making the crowd go wilder.

Preston skates by me, slamming his shoulder against mine, then grinning as he glides backward. "I owe you one, big man!"

"Will you stop antagonizing him now?" I ask as I'm about to go in.

"Nah. I'm already in his head. It'd be a waste to stop now."

Not surprised.

Preston is a shit stirrer of epic proportions. I know he must've said something extra outrageous for Hunter to target him so viciously, but I don't give a fuck.

No one hurts Preston when I'm around.

Just like Kane, Pres doesn't even like to fight or indulge in much violence on the ice, so one of us has to take care of that pesky problem.

Team A takes the lead during the two minutes I have to sit and watch, but I'm not worried about that. Once I'm back in there, I'll settle things once and for all.

My head's completely in the game tonight, and they have no chance against this version of me. Kane will nag about this penalty box visit, but it's not the first time, nor will it be the last.

The crowd goes wild when I'm released from the box. This time, I check cleanly, scoring what I'm sure is my record high.

It doesn't matter that I'm playing against my actual teammates—an opponent is an opponent.

It's not that I can't play without over-the-top violence, because I'm fully capable of that. It's that I don't want to.

For me, hockey is an outlet for pressing urges that constantly bubble at the surface. A way for me to get drunk on the power I can wield on the ice.

We end up beating Team A, the overwhelming cheers of the crowd echoing around us.

Vipers Arena is half full today—people from all over GU

and the town must've seen our unofficial practice dates and come to cheer for their favorite violent and sometimes bloody sport.

It's why Vencor has to have control over the team and the university through Kane, Preston, and me, as well as three more Members who play for the team.

The Vipers have too much influence to leave unsupervised. Therefore, throughout the three years we've been at GU, we've been tasked with keeping an eye on Members, many of whom are college or management team staff.

We'll put some in their place if need be, slice their throat for betrayal. Anything that ensures Vencor has absolute power within this town and beyond it, even.

After a shower—and an earful from Kane about my reckless play—I'm cheered on like a king in the locker room.

The guys want to go for drinks and fuck. We usually hang out at this club downtown where all the puck bunnies flock to score with the hockey gods of the town.

But I'd rather be someplace else. In a fucking shithole that reeks of piss and rot, if you can believe it.

The guys are talking nonsense in the background as I pull a black shirt over my head and check my phone.

I might have texted Violet last night. You know, after I licked ginger ale from all over her body and then thought why not taste her cunt as well.

Not my brightest idea.

I meant it as an intimidation tactic, a way for me to exert power and make her tremble with fear. But *somehow*, that ended up with me wanting her to tremble with desire.

I could tell she was a bit apprehensive about the whole thing, probably as much as I was.

And she stuck to her act for a bit, refusing to move her hands and biting her lip so no sound would come out.

But then I called her a good girl, and she detonated in my mouth, shaking and screaming.

Violet was *screaming*.

And, fuck me, my cock twitches at the memory.

Now, don't get me wrong. I've had screamers and theatrical moaners. I've had dirty talkers and silent girls, and they all felt so good. But none of them made me as rock fucking hard as when I was eating Violet's pussy.

I was turned on at the knowledge that I could trigger those reactions from the most silent little lamb who still can't look at me sometimes.

And I shouldn't have been *that* turned on.

Because I despise Violet Winters just as much as I despise all the other people who couldn't help Mom.

Maybe I despise her more because she's clearly able to save others—like she did with Mario.

Fucking girl slammed into him as if she were bulletproof.

Which brings me to my point that someone wants my prey killed. Probably Julian.

However, when I confronted him about it yesterday, he had the most impressive poker face. Besides, he doesn't usually intervene in my games.

But he does love meddling, so I don't know what the fuck he's planning. I did tell him I'd mess with his plans within the Callahan company if he dares to put his nose where it doesn't belong, though.

I don't give a fuck who has a vendetta against Violet. I'm the only one who'll slice her delicate neck open—but that doesn't mean I won't toy with her in the meantime.

Last night, she was in a daze after she came all over my

mouth, messing up my lips with her sweet fucking taste that I couldn't stop licking. Her cheeks were flushed the deepest shade of red, making the freckles stand out against her porcelain skin.

The ding of the oven was the only thing that snapped her out of her reverie, because she jumped from the counter, gathering the pieces of her shirt around her and grabbing another apron to hide her nakedness.

"Can you go?" There wasn't her usual *please* in the question as she pulled a plate of lasagna from the oven. "Dahlia will be here any minute."

I was in the mood to make her choke on my rock-hard cock that she was avoiding looking at—or maybe she was avoiding looking at me—but I got a text from Mario's replacement, Larson, informing me that her sister was indeed approaching the apartment. Before I left, however, I made Violet give me a slice of lasagna in exchange for my leaving.

She looked at me as if I was weird, but she did give me a slice in a plastic container, then practically shoved me out of the apartment.

It was the best lasagna I've ever had.

Which is why I texted her a few hours later.

Me: You're not a bad cook.

Violet: Who's this?

Me: Who else has the capacity to have your phone number?

Violet: Right. Thanks for the backhanded compliment. I guess.

Me: It wasn't backhanded. Your lasagna is the second-best thing I've ever tasted. The first is your cunt.

Violet: You're honestly crazy.

Me: Only just realizing that now? I thought the stalking and murder would've given me away.

Violet: Why are you texting me this late in the evening, Jude?

Me: As per my first text, to compliment your cooking.

Violet: Is the compliment in the room with us?

Me: What's with these spurts of sarcasm? Or are you more daring when typing? Like those keyboard warriors?

Violet: I would just appreciate it if you leave me alone.

Me: You should already know that won't be happening. Especially now that I know the feel of your cunt. Mmm. Might jump through your window for another taste and have you wrap those lips around my cock this time.

Violet: Is this your new method of tormenting me?

Me: Maybe.

Violet: You should go to sleep. It's not good to stay up late.

Me: My, is that concern?

Violet: Let's call it that if it makes you leave me alone.

Me: Careful, sweetheart. You're piquing my interest.

Violet: Oh no. I thought it was already piqued, considering all the stalking, breaking and entering, and everything in between.

Me: Hmm. You are more audacious in texts.

Violet: And you're the same in every version. Oh, how is Mario, by the way?

Me: Well.

Violet: Wow, okay. I guess he doesn't matter to you either if his being shot warrants a one-word reply.

Me: Or maybe you shouldn't bring up another man

when I'm talking to you. By the way, you should
come watch me practice tomorrow.

Violet: Not sure if your stalking sessions have come up
short, but I have no interest in hockey and even less
so since I know you play it.

Me: Why?

Violet: Because I kind of don't like you and would
rather stay away from anything related to you.

Me: You seemed to like me just fine when you were
riding my face earlier today, sweetheart.

Violet: I'm not sure if you heard, but there's this thing
called 'sex has nothing to do with feelings.' Or did
you believe only men are capable of that?

Me: Certainly not. But I'm also aware of your
disappointing sex streak. Tell you what, sweetheart. I
want you to watch the Vipers game replays from the
previous seasons.

Violet: No, thank you.

Me: I'm sorry if it seemed like you have a choice. If
you don't watch a replay every day and text me the
highlights right after, I'll slice Mario's throat because
he failed to do his job.

Violet: You're a monster.

Me: Your monster, sweetheart.

So that's what I'm looking at right now, my lips twitching
at the corner. A text from Violet that landed in my messages
not too long ago.

Violet: Highlights: you won your opening game of the
last season, and you hit more people than should
be allowed. At least you were penalized for it,

which made me feel better. Davenport is the only levelheaded player amongst you all, and I still dislike this game and you.

I narrow my eyes, rereading her words.

Davenport.

Fucking *Kane*?

People know I'm the most popular on the team, while Kane is just a stickler for techniques and rules. Never fights, never gets out of line, and could be labeled boring in hockey terms.

Anyone who knows hockey would pick *me* as the actual hockey god, *not* Kane.

"Yo, Callahan!" Preston slams his shoulder against mine, then wraps an arm around me. "Who are you in the mood to fuck later tonight?"

A certain thorn in my side who keeps pissing me the fuck off.

No.

My usual fuck shouldn't be dedicated to Violet, especially after what she texted. If I go see her, I might actually snap her neck for the insolence.

Though there haven't been any fucks lately. I like to think that I could take my pick, but the truth is, I haven't been enticed by any of the pretty girls around me.

Not since Kane took me to the shithole that is Stantonville and I saw Violet from the top of the roof.

It should be disturbing that I haven't looked at any girls since then. I like to think it's because I don't really fuck as much as the other guys on the team and I can go celibate for a long time.

It definitely has nothing to do with those mystic blue eyes that keep appearing in my dreams lately.

I push Pres away. "Regis wants to see me."

"Boo! Your dad can wait."

"Julian said it was an emergency."

He releases me with a roll of his eyes, then slides to Kane's side. "We have one man down, so let's have the best fun and rub it in his face later!"

I dress in record time. Then, on my way out, I slam my shoulder into Kane's.

Hard.

He steps back, clutching his shoulder, his eyes wide.

"What the fuck was that for?" he bellows.

But I'm already walking out.

———

A few hours later, I'm not with Regis.

Yes, he keeps 'insisting' that I should go see him and if I don't, there will be 'consequences,' but I've already suffered the worst of said consequences.

There's nothing he could do that has the potential to hurt me anymore.

And yes, Julian blew up my phone like a clingy ex, showcasing his massive control-freak tendencies, but I ignored him.

The last time I had dinner with Regis was when Mom was alive. She tried her best to keep up the feeble appearances of a happy family. She held on to it with bloody fingers, and I played my role, not even clashing with my father so she wouldn't frown or, worse, cry.

So now that she's gone, I hope Regis will rot.

All alone in his big mansion.

So, no, I'm not with Regis or Julian. I'm standing in Violet's tiny living room, where I can touch the ceiling if I reach up my arm.

And she's sleeping.

Today was her day off at the bar. I know because I followed her around earlier, from a safe distance. She went to the movies with Dahlia and a kid—her coworker's daughter.

Now, even I was wondering why the fuck I was sitting at the back of the movie theater while people were laughing at a cringe-fest animated movie.

Oh, right. Because the surge of adrenaline hadn't left my veins, and I had to see her.

Strangle her for the Kane comment.

But I got distracted because she was laughing in a carefree way I'd never witnessed before. During the entire movie, Violet would answer the kid's whispered questions, feeding her popcorn, wiping her mouth, and doing a shit ton of other things that didn't include watching the screen. Like checking her phone.

Twice.

Then the three of them went for dinner, and I was at the back again, ordering drinks and blending in with some tall motorcycle gang guys to avoid drawing attention to myself.

There are two things I noticed during that dinner. Dahlia is a chatterbox who doesn't shut the fuck up, and Violet seems to smile from just listening to her talk. She even had this bright look on her face as if she was proud of her.

My highlight, however, was when Violet wiped some sauce from the kid's chin and licked her fingers, her tongue peeking out the slightest bit.

I had a flashback of when she sucked on my finger. The sauce was blood, though.

I know I said there wouldn't be a post-practice fuck, but my cock protested profusely after I merely saw her lips wrapped around her fingers.

Let's just say I was so close to grabbing her by the throat and dragging her out of there so those lips could be around something a lot harder.

And bigger.

But the kid was asking for ice cream, so, of course, Violet got up and bought her some from a nearby ice cream truck. In front of which a creep kept close to her. So close, actually, that I'm pretty sure his limp erection brushed against her ass.

In pure Violet fashion, she tactfully backed away without any commotion, handing the ice cream to the grinning kid and walking back to Dahlia.

Did I pull the creep into an alley and bash his head against the wall? Maybe.

Listen, I'm a violent man. Someone touches what belongs to me, and I respond in the best way I know how. By inflicting pain.

Blame my father.

That's what he taught me and Julian—aside from never believing in those silly things called feelings.

That's been doing my brother's train wreck of a marriage wonders, by the way, so I'm also a firm nonbeliever. I don't know of a single happy marriage in my entourage.

At any rate, I don't think Violet saw me, and if she did, she's getting way better at wearing her favorite poker face, because she never once paid me any attention.

Not that I wanted her to. I was only there to observe because Mario needs a few more days to get back, and I don't fully trust his replacement.

Violet bought the kid an expensive thirty-dollar doll. And it is expensive in her financial clusterfuck, because she barely has any money in her account. Yes, I checked. She's constantly writing in the stupid journal that they're always short on money and she wishes Dahlia would stop buying her unnecessary shit.

Patches for back pain—that's what's unnecessary in Violet fucking Winters's book.

I'm glad Dahlia called her out on the doll after they dropped the kid off at her mom's and made it back to their place. I was outside on the balcony. Sue me.

"Karly doesn't really have toys, Dahl," Violet said, giving her sister a glass of milk—seriously, what? "And Laura is really struggling."

"You're struggling, too," Dahlia said what I was thinking.

"Yeah, but I'm not dealing with fighting an abusive ex in a child custody case. Besides, I never had any toys growing up, so I wanted to bring some happiness to Karly. That's all."

"Aw, Vi. All right, but don't strain yourself, okay?"

"Okay."

Liar.

Violet is the biggest fucking liar I've ever met.

I was ready to see what she wrote in her journal that night and if her true words would contradict what she said.

In the beginning, I started to read her journals to see what she actually thought, because Violet is an inward person who bottles everything inside. Then I wanted to see what she wrote about me.

There was nothing.

She only mentioned me there once—the day she recognized me from TV. Since then, she's never talked about me again.

She probably thinks that if she ignores me hard enough, I'll stop existing.

But she can't possibly ignore what happened last night.

I waited patiently until Dahlia fucked off to her room, falling asleep in five minutes flat, snoring a bit, actually.

And then Violet scribbled in her journal for a while, worked on a piece of embroidery she's been doing on and off for a few weeks, and then also went to sleep.

I waited until her breathing evened out and she fell into deep slumber, then I unlocked the balcony door and came in.

It was so easy, since, well, they live in a little-to-no-security area.

Violet's asleep on the sofa, the sheet barely covering her plain beige pajamas. She dresses in such an unflattering way, and yet I can't help but notice the stretch of her T-shirt over her perky breasts or the delicate curve of her throat.

She had a scarf on today, to hide the hickey on her neck. My mark.

Mine.

A wave of something unfamiliar grabs hold of me, but I rip my gaze from her and take the journal from her backpack.

Today, she wrote about how it felt good to be out and about with Dahlia and Karly.

I run my finger along the last line.

Dahlia said I shouldn't have bought the toy for little Karly, and maybe she's right, but I simply wanted to be for her what no one was for me.

I turn to the previous page, but there's a dot where her evening musings should be.

A fucking dot? What the fuck is that supposed to mean? Am I...a *dot*?

I narrow my eyes on her. This fucking—

My plans to shake the fuck out of her dissipate when I see her trembling.

She brings her hands to her chest and bends her knees. I realize she's making herself as small as possible as she balls herself into a fetal position, mumbling something unintelligible.

I lower my head toward her, and I still can't make out what she's saying.

But it's clear she's in pain, her teeth chattering, and sweat beading along her upper lip. I touch her arm and it's tight. No one should be tight while they're sleeping.

It's as if she's half awake, waiting for something to ambush her.

What are you afraid of? I think to myself as she tightens further, almost clenching her teeth.

Something about the whole scene sits wrong with me.

Maybe it's because I don't like the idea of my doll being afraid of anyone but me.

It *has* to be that.

Because when I feel her relaxing beneath my palm, I stay there until she's no longer scared.

And it disturbs me. This…strange feeling that keeps drawing me toward her.

It's not normal.

Or logical.

And I need to amputate her before she turns into a bigger problem.

CHAPTER 14
Violet

I'M WALKING OUT OF MY APARTMENT WHEN MARIO STEPS into view.

He came back about a week ago, his arm still wrapped in a sling. I kind of force him to walk with me now and allow me to share my food with him.

He tried to refuse at first, but I can be persistent. Whenever he attempts to keep a distance, I slow down and fall in step beside him. Whenever he refuses the food, I remind him that some people are hungry and he should appreciate the commodity of eating.

I stare at the sullied, gray streets. I used to quicken my steps, my anxiety on high alert, and my heart in my throat.

But that was before I realized there are worse monsters out there. Monsters who dress well, smell divine, and are richer than sin. Monsters who find it fun to mess with someone's life just because they can.

So I stopped worrying about what's lurking in the shadows. It also helps that Mario makes me feel safe for some reason. No one would dare come near me when I'm walking beside him, and I think it has to do with his 'fuck off' expression that mimics his dear boss's.

"How are you doing, Mario?" I smile, offering him a

mint candy. When he doesn't take it, I place it in his hand and take one for myself.

"You should've stayed home," he says in a firm voice.

"You heard me talking to Toby the other day. I agreed to go on a date."

"You shouldn't have." He releases an exasperated sigh. "You do know I have to report everything back to him, right?"

"I don't care." I suck on the candy harder, fighting the urge to crush it between my teeth. It's mind-boggling how my calm temperament can be easily ruffled at the mention of that bastard.

God, I hate him.

I truly do. I never thought myself capable of hatred, but I despise Jude Callahan.

First, he stalks me, then he says I can't die until he permits it, as if I'm some marionette, and then he makes me feel like shit every time I see his face, because I failed to save his mom.

But the biggest reason I hate him is because he gave me a taste of something forbidden and wrong but so damn delicious, I keep having dreams about it. His mouth on my pussy and my reaction to his touch, and I wake up with my hands between my legs.

And I hate that the most because I have a low sex drive and have been happily celibate for a while, not even feeling the need to masturbate that often, so I can't forgive myself for the reaction I had.

It feels…wrong.

And stupid because the truth is, the man I had that reaction with wants to kill me.

Thankfully, I haven't seen him since the night he ambushed me in the kitchen.

Two weeks ago.

But even though I don't see him, I feel his presence in the apartment sometimes. Oh, and he leaves a few bottles of ginger ale in the fridge every night. At first, I thought it was Dahlia, until she mentioned we have so many now. And now, I can't even have my favorite drink without thinking of his hot tongue all over me.

So it's not that he's finally left me alone—he just doesn't bother to show me his face anymore.

He still wants me to text him the stupid highlights after every Vipers replay I watch, though, or he threatens Mario and Dahlia.

As a result, I've been somehow forced into learning the game and can understand the decades-long rivalry between the Vipers and the Wolves.

I'd still cheer for the Wolves. At the end of the day, the Wolves players were born and bred in Stantonville, and they're like me—they came from nothing and worked hard to play something they love without trust funds buying their coaches and sophisticated training camps.

I don't think Jude liked those thoughts when I texted them.

Which is why I texted them in the first place.

He's obviously super popular and a fan favorite, which gives him too big of an ego for my liking, and someone needs to deflate his god complex. I just volunteered for the task.

And yes, maybe I do have more audacity when I'm texting. It's not like he can intimidate me through the phone.

"You should care," Mario says in a slightly softened tone. "You already know how violent he can get."

I lift a shoulder. "If he wants to kill me, he should do it already."

"The more you want that, the more he won't comply."

"I know that."

"Apparently not, because you're provoking a reaction with this date, Violet. Whether or not it's on purpose."

I stop and face him. "So I should...*what*? Stop living? Wait for his majesty to issue the death sentence? I just want to have something outside of school and work and constant overthinking and anxiety about what type of unpredictable action he'll take next. Is that wrong?"

"No. But I'm not sure if you're doing this for the right reasons."

"I shouldn't want a boyfriend?" I scoff. "Would you tell him the same?"

Mario frowns. "Jude's never had a girlfriend."

"Is that a joke?"

"I don't joke. He doesn't even have sex that often either. Don't believe the rumors you read online."

I can feel heat creeping up my neck because he's referring to that one time he caught me reading some social media posts about the Vipers.

And yes, there were girls gloating about sleeping with the Vipers' players, including Jude, which for some reason made my day worse.

"I don't care what he does with his private life," I whisper.

"Again, you should now that you're part of it."

"I'm not. I just want him to leave me alone."

"I'm telling you this as someone who's known him since he was born. He's not the type to be forced into doing anything by anyone. There's nothing you can do that will make him give up. That will only happen once he loses interest."

"You've...known him since he was born?"

"Yes. My mother is the Callahan family's chief of staff." Oh.

My steps slow, and I watch Mario under the half-broken lamps. "Have you always stalked for him?"

"No. I'm a bodyguard, actually." He sounds offended. "Special Forces trained."

"Sorry."

"Don't be. It's not your fault."

"Yeah. It's Jude's." I grin but clear my throat when he doesn't show a reaction. "How was he when he was young?"

"Quiet, withdrawn, and prone to bursts of violence."

"So just like he is now?"

"Pretty much."

"Was he close to his mom?"

"Yes and no."

"What…does that mean?"

Mario says nothing, signaling that the conversation has ended, and the rest of the long walk is spent in silence.

Once we reach the place in which I'm meeting my date, Mario retreats to the shadows.

The restaurant is one of those trendy, dimly lit places—low-hanging bulbs, sleek black tables, and the scent of rosemary and charred steak clinging to the air.

Soft jazz hums through invisible speakers, blending with the murmur of conversation and the occasional clink of wineglasses. The walls are lined with bottles of expensive liquor, polished to a shine, reflecting the golden glow of candlelight.

It's warm, inviting, just like my date Toby, who waves me over from a table near the window, grinning wide.

I slide my glasses up my nose, touch my wrist tattoo, then walk up to him.

I'm self-conscious when I remove my denim jacket, revealing the blue satin camisole Dahlia lent me. It stops right at the waist of my pants, its spaghetti straps barely holding it in place, and the lace at the collar doesn't do a great job of hiding my cleavage.

I don't do dates that much, mainly because I don't have the time or energy, but Toby is nice, and he's often helped me with school material.

He asked before if we should meet up for a movie or dinner sometime, but I brushed him off. A few days ago, however, I was annoyed, so when he asked again as we were leaving a summer class, I said yes without overthinking.

Toby is 6' tall with curly blond hair and soft features. He also wears glasses, though his are gold-rimmed, and he's dressed in a button-up shirt and smart casual slacks.

Today, his hair looks shiny, his hazel eyes brighter than usual as he swipes a look over me, pausing at my breasts before focusing on my face.

"I'm glad you made it, Vee. I ordered some wine. Would you like some?" Even his voice sounds mellow, welcoming, nothing like the gruff grumbles of a certain someone—

No.

This isn't about him in any shape or form.

I smile at Toby and think about ordering ginger ale, but then just go for wine as well so as not to seem rude.

As we wait for food, Toby slides both elbows on the table, leaning his chin on his interlaced fingers. "God. You look stunning."

"Um. Thanks." I tuck a strand of hair behind my ear. "You look great yourself."

They're just words. Empty words. On paper, someone like Toby is my type. Softer-spoken, smart as hell, and just… not threatening, whether in looks, voice, or personality.

On paper, that is.

"You always wear those hoodies, but I knew you were

beautiful beneath it all." He grins. "So, tell me more about yourself. I don't feel like I know you that well."

I take a sip of my wine. "What do you want to know?"

"Like what do you do for fun?"

"Reading, watching movies, or going out for walks with my sister. I'm not that adventurous. What about you?"

"I love skiing and hockey."

Yikes. I force a smile. "That's cool."

We talk about mundane things during dinner, and I have to take a break and go to the bathroom because I'm losing interest.

And I don't want to lose interest, because I plan to have sex with Toby, or do oral or something. I need to prove to myself that I'm not sick for coming all over my stalker/potential killer's mouth and that I would've reacted that way with any other man.

I glare at my reflection in the mirror, at the makeup and hair I let Dahlia do—brown eyeshadow, pink lipstick, and soft waves.

I even made an effort today, wearing a camisole that only reminds me of Mama being fucked while she sniffed cocaine. Because, at some point, she couldn't have sex without drugs coursing through her veins. I hate these sexy lingerie-looking things. They make me anxious and scared, as if I'm trapped in that closet with trembling hands over my ears.

It makes me think of my foster mother accusing me of dressing like a whore and tempting my stepfather. When I was eleven.

Really, took me a lot of effort to step out of my comfort zone tonight. My thoughts need to focus and stop drifting elsewhere—to black-inked forearms, cold brown eyes, and a gruff voice that wraps around my spine like barbed wire.

After skimming my fingers on my wrist a few more times, I'm about to leave the bathroom.

The door bursts open and a tall figure appears.

My heart lunges, and my lips part as Jude walks in.

No, he walks *me* back.

His hard chest slams against mine, and he's still striding in. I have no choice but to step back or he'll topple me over.

His gaze is dark, so dark under the ambient red restroom light, and my hands shake around the strap of my bag.

"What are you doing here?" I ask in a low tone as the door slams shut, locking me in with my worst nightmare.

"The question is, what are *you* doing here, Violet?" The rough timbre of his words steals my breath, my thoughts, my sanity.

Jude's deep voice, like all men with similar voices, puts me on edge. But his does something more. Something I refuse to acknowledge, no matter how violent the war in my stomach gets or how many goosebumps erupt on my skin.

I jump when my back hits the wall, and he looms over me like a threat, or maybe a curse—I'm not even sure anymore. But I'm once again hit by how tall and massive he is. He truly is the tallest man I've ever seen.

The most dangerous, too.

Jude lifts the spaghetti strap of my camisole with his index finger, and even though the contact with my skin is brief, I catch fire. And just like that, inappropriate images of these same lean fingers someplace else rush through me like an aphrodisiac.

"It seems you have the very wrong idea about how this works." He lifts the strap again, and the fabric rubs against my nipples, making them hard, or maybe it's his body against mine. "Just because I lengthened the leash doesn't mean you get to roam around as you please."

"I'm not a dog."

"You're whatever the fuck I want you to be." He places his arm above the top of my head and leans down, his brown eyes like orbs of violent intent. "Your life is mine, remember?"

"Then stop the empty threats and take it."

"I told you that won't be happening. At least, not yet."

"Then leave me alone! Whether I date or fuck or work or breathe has nothing to do with you."

I thought he was intense a moment ago, but now his face looks taut, and his hand lands on my shoulder as the strap falls to my arm. "Did you just say fuck?"

I gulp. His voice sounds so low, it tightens my stomach with that uncomfortable feeling again.

"Answer me. Did you wear makeup and this *thing*—" He tightens his grip on the strap. "—to seduce the four-eyed asshole so he'd fuck you?"

"So what if I did? I told you that's none of—"

His knee slides between my legs, pressing up against my core that's been aching since he showed up. I grab onto the wall with both hands, my bag slipping down to the floor, its contents clanking on the tiles.

"Do you believe that little fucker would give you what you want? What you need?" His lips hover so close to mine, if I just tilt forward—

No. What the hell am I thinking?

"He might not be filthy rich or a popular athlete, but at least he's not a murderous stalker," I say with a miniscule bravado. "He also happens to be my type."

He doesn't like that last bit, not even a little, because he's increasing the pressure against my core, and I'm spiraling.

Because should it feel so damn good?

"Your type, huh?"

"Yeah. I prefer nerdy, normal guys."

"You'll prefer whoever the fuck I tell you to."

"That's not how it works."

"Fuck how it works." He moves his hand to my nape and fists my hair, forcing my head back as he slides his knee back and forth, back and forth.

The friction is maddening, pulling at the same strings from the other night. Dark pleasure I don't want to give in to mounts and mounts until I'm delirious.

"You'll do as you're told." The low growl of his voice makes me shudder.

I glare at him. "Get a pet for that."

"I have you, so why bother?"

"Just get out of my life, Jude! You don't get to invade my space, then disappear and reappear as you wish. Just let me fucking be!"

"We're making progress if I'm disturbing you to the point that you're yelling." He rubs his knee against my pants and I purse my lips, fighting, trying my best not to succumb to these strange feelings.

I know he can feel how hot I am, even though clothes separate our skin.

And I don't want to give him the pleasure of seeing me like this.

But as the pressure mounts, my hips jerk uncontrollably, stirring a type of abandon I didn't know sex offered.

My feelings and perception of sex are skewed. Maybe because I witnessed it my whole childhood in a negative light, where men used a woman, not caring how she felt. Or because it was transactional. Or because the men I've had sex with have never made me feel worshiped.

But, at any rate, my first real pleasure was on that kitchen counter, and my body's felt awakened ever since, thirsting for...more.

After that time, darker fantasies I used to repress invaded my dreams and in all of them, there were these dark-brown eyes. I wanted to write about them so bad, but knowing Jude would find my most embarrassing thoughts and moments, I just kept them in my subconscious.

My dreams.

But it doesn't help when he corners me—it triggers those illicit fantasies.

The need for something.

Anything.

Jude lowers his mouth so that his hot breaths skim my ear. "Here's how it'll go, Violet. You go back to your sorry excuse for a date, thank him for his time, and fuck off home."

"You don't tell me what to do," I snap.

"Yes, I do."

"No, you don't."

"Do as you're told. Don't make me intervene."

And then he pulls away, releasing me completely and vanishing as silently as he appeared.

I slide down to the floor, my knees shaking and my heart nearly lunging into my throat, and my pussy still throbs with an unsatisfied ache.

My limbs barely hold me, but I stand up with a renewed sense of rebellion.

I was losing interest in Toby earlier, but I've found it now.

Screw Jude Callahan.

On a cactus.

Until he bleeds out.

Amen.

CHAPTER 15

Jude

VIOLET LEAVES THE RESTAURANT.

With the curly-haired asshole.

Contrary to what I told her.

My fist clenches and unclenches as I follow behind, leaving a safe distance between us as they talk.

And *laugh*.

And Violet trips slightly and falls against his side.

Is she…fucking *flirting*?

So not only did she meet some nobody for dinner and then let him help her put on her jacket as if she's a goddamn toddler who can't perform the task on her own, but she's also *throwing* herself at him?

I have to calm the fuck down before I bash his face against the concrete.

Just kidding. I'll still do that, but there are a lot of pesky people around that would hinder that plan.

The guy slides an arm—that will be broken—around her shoulder to steady her. She smiles at him.

She fucking *smiles*, her eyes closing a bit as she looks at him.

I was so sure she was uncomfortable with being touched by a man. She fucking *flinches* whenever a customer touches her, and she did with me as well.

Not when she was coming all over my mouth, though. No, she was riding my face then.

But why the *fuck* is she touching the motherfucker?

He put something in her drink, didn't he?

That's the only explanation.

Or maybe she's more comfortable with him than she is with you.

I ignore that small voice that should be fucking gagged.

There's no way in hell she's fucking that guy tonight. Call it absurd or illogical or fucking territorial, but Violet's off-limits to all other men.

She's mine until I slice her goddamn throat open.

And I'm done watching from the shadows.

I stride at a fast pace and step in front of them. They come to an abrupt halt. Blondie's eyes widen, and Violet purses her lips even as she touches the tattoo on her wrist.

I've put her on edge. Good. She should never—and I mean *never*—feel safe around me.

She opens her mouth, but I speak first, in my most cordial tone. "There you are, sweetheart. I've been looking for you."

Her lips part, but before she can react, I pull her arm from his grip. She loses her balance and crashes against my chest.

I have to stop myself from closing my eyes and inhaling her deeply.

Like a fucking drug.

She smells like soft roses and bergamot—a breeze of calm amid maddening chaos.

And she *shouldn't* be what defines calm when she's part of the reason behind the fucking chaos.

My hand stretches across her lower back, and she vibrates against me, a blush creeping up her cheeks.

That wasn't there in her feeble attempts to flirt with Blondie.

Serves him right for coveting what belongs to me.

"Vee?" he asks like a goddamn idiot, staring at us with eyes so wide, they'd be comical under different circumstances.

She snaps out of it. Her body that was soft and pliant in my hold stiffens, her small hands fisting against my chest.

Violet tries to push me away as if that were even possible.

I lean down, speaking so low, so close to her ear that only she can hear me. "One wrong move, and I'll slice his throat open and fuck you in his goddamn blood."

Her eyes widen as I push back, her entire body going into shock.

Blondie doesn't step forward, just watches from a distance, like when I snatched her away from him. He doesn't attempt to protect her or take her back.

And this is her type? Like fuck he is.

"Who are you to Vee…?"

"Violet." I maneuver her to my side, my arm still on her lower back. "Her name is Violet. And she's mine; that's all you need to know."

I can feel her rigidity, but she won't fight it. She's that responsible and annoyingly cares about others, so she won't let herself be the reason for her little friend's death.

Though I wouldn't really kill him and just said that to keep her in line.

I'd still break his arm, though.

"Uh…" He rubs his nape, staring at the ground and then back at Violet. "You didn't mention you were going out with *the* Jude Callahan."

He knows who I am.

Even better.

"We're not going out…" She trails off when I tighten my grip on her waist, then sighs. "It's complicated."

"Oh, okay." He gives a small pout like a fucking child whose candy has been taken away, not even mad that his fuck mission for the night was aborted.

"I'm sorry, Toby." She tries to release herself from my grip to no avail. "You're a great guy. I don't want to put you in this mess."

Great guy?

Great fucking guy?

What bad taste in men.

"Nah, that's fine. You're kind of out of my league anyway. But…" He rubs his nape again. "Can I have your autograph, Callahan? I'm a huge fan. My friends will be mad jealous."

Violet goes lax in my grip, not even attempting to hide the look of disappointment on her face.

Her type was so ready to throw her away for an autograph.

I'm suppressing a smile as I nod. There's no pen or paper around, so Tobias—that's his name—asks Violet for her lipstick and tells me to sign the tank top beneath his shirt.

He barely even looks at her as he turns around and leaves with a bit of a spring in his step.

I mean, he *should* be happy, considering he left with an autograph instead of a broken arm.

Violet has already stepped away from me, clutching her wrist. No, the tattoo on her wrist.

The one that she uses to calm down or pull herself from whatever ledge her brain pushes her toward.

I roll the lipstick tube in my hand. "Want an autograph as well? Maybe somewhere bolder? Your tits, maybe."

She takes it from my grip and slides it into her bag. "No, thanks. I'm not a fan."

My jaw clenches. "You seem to be Davenport's fan, considering how you praise his play style more than the tabloid hacks paid by his dad."

She's still staring down, fiddling with the zipper of her bag, her hair that looks prettier than usual flying in the wind. "That's because he doesn't get high on violence, unlike a certain someone—"

I'm in her space now, which is why she jerks her head up so fast and cuts her words off. "So your type is nonviolent people like Tobias, who wouldn't even lift a finger if you were in danger."

She swallows but keeps her chin up. "You don't know that. People act unpredictably when faced with danger."

"Or maybe it's their true nature that shows. Here's the thing, Violet." I step closer and she stumbles in her attempts to escape me, but I wrap my arm around her waist, trapping her against my chest. "I don't give a fuck who your type is. From now on, I'm your *only* type."

She releases a long exhale. "Why are you doing this, Jude? Because you can? Because messing with an insignificant person's life brings you so much joy?"

"It does."

"You know what I think? I think you're only holding on to the remnants of your rage because without vengeance and killing and unleashing your monster side on others, you'd have to face the hollow emptiness lurking inside you." She taps my chest with her finger. "Right here."

I grab her hand and twist it away. "You're into psychoanalyzing now? Shouldn't you have used these abilities on your clusterfuck of a fragile mental state and mommy issues?"

"We both have mommy issues, it seems."

"One big difference. I wouldn't kill myself, and my mother loved me, unlike your waste-of-space mom."

Her lips tremble, and her eyes seem brighter under the glow of the streetlight. "Yes, we are different. Worlds apart, actually. Because I'd never knowingly hurt someone or throw a violent tantrum just because life screwed me over."

My jaw clenches, and I can feel it aching from how hard I'm grinding my teeth. What is it about this fucking girl that seems to push my fucking buttons?

"And yet you already did." I speak close to her lips. "Didn't you?"

"I did not. I'm really sorry about your mom, b-but... what did you expect a civilian like me to do? Run into the knife? Get killed as well?"

"If it would've kept her alive, yes."

"Right." She laughs, but it sounds heart-wrenching. "Because the lives of people like me mean nothing, so the rich should live while we rot away."

"It's not about rich or poor." I stop myself before I blurt out that it's about losing the one person who cared about me unconditionally in a heartless world.

Because why the fuck would I need to explain myself to Violet? She's the one who owes me, not the other way around.

"Then what's it about?" She's watching me now, closely, as if trying to sink beneath my skin and latch onto my bones.

"Nothing you should concern yourself with." I let her go and she steps back. "What you should worry about, however, is how you'll pay for the stunt you pulled tonight."

"Why should I pay? You're the one who ruined my date."

"I'll ruin as many dates as you're foolish enough to have. And you'll pay for not following simple instructions, Violet.

I clearly told you to thank him for the night and leave alone for home. What did you do?"

"I don't have to listen to this." Something flashes on her face, something dark and potent, matching the sparks that make my dick twitch on the regular whenever I'm around her.

She must also feel it, this dangerous attraction that shouldn't exist between predator and prey. This lawless, unhinged need to slam her against the goddamn wall and fuck her.

Because she turns around and walks away, her fingers sinking into her bag's strap as she quickens her footsteps.

She's running away. The only thing she knows how to do well.

But I catch up to her and grab her elbow. She gasps as I pull her into an alley that's far enough away from the main street.

I'm towering over her, again, and she's pressed up against the wall, *again*.

Trapped with me.

Her eyes glow in the near darkness as she licks her lips.

My gaze zeroes in on the motion, my cock growing thick and heavy in my jeans. "Are you seducing me, sweetheart?"

"I would never," she says, but then she's breathing heavily, and her voice is hoarse.

"But you were seducing Tobias earlier, weren't you? Falling against him. Giving him a view of these tits." I grab a handful of her breast, and she presses her lips together as if fighting, struggling to deny what's happening. "But these are *my* tits. I saw them first, touched them first, licked your favorite drink from all over your tight, little pink nipples first."

"S-stop talking like that."

"Why? Is it making you hot and bothered?" I slide my

other hand down her stomach, relishing the tremor that grips her even though I'm touching her through the camisole.

My fingers open the button of her pants.

She doesn't stop me, but she doesn't touch me either, her arms motionless on either side of her.

"If I reach inside your panties, will I find you dripping wet for me?"

She turns her face the other way, but I slide my hand from her breast to her jaw and turn it back toward me as I bite her lower lip and then kiss her.

Damn.

God fucking damn it.

I've been *craving* this.

A nip. A lick.

A *taste*.

The kiss is hot, quick, and absolutely maddening, like everything about her. Violet's tongue moves against mine tentatively, cautiously, as if she doesn't want to do this, but, like me, she can't deny it.

The pull.

The unhinged energy.

I glide my fingers inside her panties, and she jumps, releasing an unintelligible sound into my mouth.

"You *are* soaking wet, sweetheart." I pull out my fingers and hold them out in the light so she can see the stickiness. Then I thrust them into her mouth, making her swallow her taste.

Her glasses fog up with her quickening breaths, and she sucks my fingers, her eyes never leaving mine.

"Mmm. I'm going to need your lips around something bigger."

I pull out my fingers and push her down with a hand on top of her head.

Violet gets to her knees as I unbuckle my belt. She looks at my hand, then back to my face, her breathing shallow and her pupils dilated.

"I really hate you," she murmurs, almost as if trying to convince herself.

But I'm already pulling out my cock and placing it at her mouth. "Show me how much you hate me, sweetheart."

CHAPTER 16
Violet

I HATE HIM.

I truly, irrevocably, and without a shadow of a doubt despise Jude Callahan and everything he stands for.

But my feelings toward him don't seem to deflate my reaction when he's around. I'd never admit it out loud, but there's been an insatiable emptiness in my life lately. Something deep and ferocious and maddening, like an itch beneath the skin I can't reach.

However, that only lasted until he showed up tonight.

Threatening me and my date and announcing that we're together as if that will ever happen.

As if I'd ever be with someone like him who's hell-bent on killing me and making me pay just because he can.

We're impossible.

I know that.

He knows that.

But whatever spark that ignites whenever we're around each other doesn't give two damns about those simple facts, because it mounts with every encounter.

And God…the way he looks down at me with ravenous, lustful eyes is intoxicating.

There's rage there as well, harsh and red-hot. Probably

because his cock is already half erect right in front of my face, and he's angry that I make him hard. Or his obsession with me does.

I have no clue what the hell he's thinking when he corners me on the regular, inserting himself into my life like a damn parasite, but I'm growing dangerously used to this.

My whole life, I've been uncomfortable with the way men look at me, but I crave the way his pupils blow wide and how ravenous he looks when I'm in his sights.

The feeling that's been coursing through me since he trapped me in the bathroom rushes to the surface. The ache between my legs intensifies as I rub them together on the ground, needing some friction I never thought I'd ache for this much.

Jude taps the crown of his cock against my mouth. "Open."

I purse my lips, not because I don't want to, but because the idea I'd simply fall into this unorthodox encounter, like when he ate me out, is terrifying.

His cock's size is also making me self-conscious as hell, because it's not even fully erect and it's already this enormous.

Grabbing his cock in one hand, he squeezes my cheek with the other, making me look up at him. He's towering over me, like the horizon, and despite the public space, it feels... weirdly intimate.

As if we're the only people existing in the here and now.

"Be a good girl and take my cock in your hot little mouth, sweetheart."

I remind myself that it's not for him, but for me, to prove to myself that I still dislike oral so I'll finally stop having those disturbing dreams about a man with a helmet and leather gloves visiting me every night.

"Use your hands. Don't just leave them lying around," he orders in firm words that rush through my spine.

I wrap both hands around him and jerk him up and down, looking up to gauge his reaction. That's what I've learned about blowjobs—it's all about the man's reaction.

Jude's face remains impassive, but he's growing bigger in my hand, harder, and...*holy hell*. If I thought his cock was big when half erect, it's massive now, and the base of my stomach tingles with a weird sensation.

He slides his thumb over my mouth as I swallow hard, squeezing and feeling on edge just from his eyes. "You wore lipstick today. You never wear lipstick."

"It was a special occasion." *Why do I sound breathy?*

"Special occasion, huh?" His voice is huskier but darker. "From now on, you only wear lipstick for me."

"That's not—"

"Shh." He removes my glasses, and I can see him clearly now, probably because they've been gradually fogging up. "You shouldn't hide these eyes."

Something about the way he's watching me feels intrusive and frighteningly intimate because I love the way he looks at me.

As if I'm someone he can't explain.

Someone he can't help but want.

Jude slides the glasses in his back pocket and grabs my hands that are around his cock and guides it to my mouth. "Enough with the foreplay. Wrap these pink lips around my cock."

Still looking up at him, I pull him deep into my mouth, the smooth, velvety skin sliding all the way to my throat, and I still can't fit all of him.

I take a moment to fall into the choking sensation instead

of fighting it and then dart my tongue, licking the underside of his cock, bobbing up and down to use the inside of my mouth, my tongue, and my throat for friction.

"Mmm." He sinks his fingers into my hair, his jaw tight, betraying his usually unaffected expression. "Your little mouth is made to take cock, isn't it?"

I moan around him, using the spit and the salty precum as lube, working my mouth even if my jaw hurts. The obscene wet sound is so titillating, I'm rubbing my thighs together.

No clue why I'm getting hot and bothered by sucking his cock, but I can feel my panties getting soaking wet.

This is degeneracy.

"But not just any cock." He gathers my hair in a fist as he thrusts into my mouth. "*My* cock."

I groan, deep-throating him as far back as possible, remembering to breathe through my nose.

"From now on, this mouth won't be fucked by any other cock but mine." He drives deeper, holding his cock at the back of my throat. "These lips will only wear pink for me."

For a second, I can't breathe.

I'm choking and spluttering, slapping my hands against his muscular thighs, clawing at his jeans.

Then the strangest thing happens.

Pressure builds in my pussy, violent and sudden, as tears stream down my cheeks.

"Mmm. You look beautiful when broken." He pulls out his cock and I choke, coughing, the excessive saliva, precum, snot, and tears mixing in an unceremonious mess.

There's no way I look beautiful.

But as I stare at him, panting, I can see his wide chest heaving and his eyes darkening to two orbits of reckless desire.

"Open." He taps his wet crown against my mouth again, and I don't think twice, opening it wide as he thrusts all the way to the back of my throat.

I don't attempt to put in any effort. I just let him choke me—fuck my throat, actually, using his grip on my hair to guide my head whichever way he pleases.

"Damn. God fucking dammit." He's so high on lust, so hard and brutal, I'm gasping, and it's not in response to what he's doing.

My own thighs are shaking, rubbing, searching for something...*anything*.

"Why does your mouth feel so fucking good, Violet?" He's mad, and so close to coming, I can feel the anger and lust and hate emanating off him.

And I find solace in his anger because he wants me. But I'm mad at myself for finding his dark brutality so alluring right now.

The way he touches me, uses me, makes me feel as if he can't get enough of me, is turning me delirious.

"Why you, of all people?" He grunts, his every muscle tightening and coiling, and then he pauses because he notices.

Of course he notices.

His gaze slides to my thighs that are rubbing together, and I want to stop. I really do, but I just need something more.

"Jesus Christ. You got turned on being throat-fucked?"

I try to shake my head, but I feel him getting even harder in my mouth—which I would've thought was impossible—and something inside me brightens and explodes in a myriad of colors I've never experienced before.

A gasp leaves me when he pushes his boot between my legs and presses it against my core. Even with the jeans and my panties as a barrier, the pressure electrifies me, and I hum against his dick.

"Mmm. I love how red your face is." *Thrust.* "You're a natural at taking my cock, sweetheart."

"Mfff." I'm moaning, squeezing my thighs against his boot, needing the pressure and the fucked-up pleasure only this man can give me.

"Ride it." He slides his boot up and down my pussy. "Show me how much you want to come, Violet."

I don't even know what's happening to me, and I don't allow myself to think.

Holding on to his leg, I lift myself up and down against the tip of his boot. The pressure makes me lightheaded, or maybe it's his cock in my mouth or the lustful power he's looking at me with.

"Good girl." He holds his cock at the back of my throat, my face so close to his groin, but I don't stop moving.

Rubbing.

Grinding.

Moaning.

Falling.

I don't recognize myself anymore, but I don't have to, and I don't want to.

If anything, I stop thinking altogether when his rough voice cuts through my mind. "You're doing so well."

I kind of melt. I don't know how or why his praise affects me, but it does, and then I'm coming, the rush overtaking me like a storm. But I remember to open my mouth wider as I ride his boot, feeling my wetness dampening my jeans.

"Fuck, Violet. Fuuuck."

He cracks.

His dick swells and bursts, flooding the back of my throat.

I swallow it, and as I watch him, his face tight, his abs contracting beneath his shirt, another orgasm hits me like a tidal wave.

Rushing and pulling and turning me delirious. Knowing he came because of me.

I'm making *the* Jude Callahan, worshiped hockey god and unfeeling monster, come in pulses in *my* mouth.

Cum trickles on either side of my mouth despite my attempts to swallow as much as possible, and I'm flinching, too sensitive after the orgasm.

Jude pulls his cock from my mouth, and I kind of... suck around the crown, which makes him release a gruff sound.

I don't know why I do it, really. A thank-you? The need for this moment to stay a little longer before reality hits?

He seems to be as lost about the reason as I am, but he strokes his fingers along my jaw, gathering the cum and thrusting it back into my mouth.

I'm about to swallow, but he shakes his head and holds my mouth open, his thumb pressing on my lower teeth. "Open wider."

My jaw aches, but I try to open as wide as possible, and his eyes turn ravenous.

Insatiable.

Hell, I think his cock is twitching.

And it's because he's watching his cum pool on my tongue, I realize, my spine tingling in response.

He watches it for long moments, or maybe it just feels that way because I'm caught in his gaze, completely taken by the way he watches me as if I'm...what? Something precious.

Don't be an idiot.

He clamps my mouth shut. "Swallow every drop."

I do, accidentally licking around his thumb that's still there, and I think I feel him vibrate, but it only lasts a moment before he removes his finger and steps back.

The distance is small, but the sexual tension fades in the background of a bigger tension as reality sets in.

The 'we're not supposed to do this, let alone enjoy it' reality.

The 'this will end in a disaster' reality.

Jude tucks himself in, then buttons up his jeans as he glares at me.

There's a feeling of anger and hatred and even a hint of confusion.

And it's as if I'm being stabbed by it as I stand up. I run my fingers through my hair, willing it into submission, and dab the corners of my mouth.

I'm not sure if that will remove all traces of him when I can still taste him with every swallow, but the silence is deafening and I feel exposed and too self-conscious.

Especially when I notice Jude watching me with narrowed eyes.

"Where did you learn to suck cock like that?" he finally asks, offering me my glasses back.

I put them on, looking anywhere but at him, then let my lips pull in a sad smile. "Watching my mom give hundreds of blowjobs through the crack of the closet door during most of my childhood."

His eyes widen the slightest bit, but I turn and leave before I can see the pity in them.

Or worse. More hate.

———

"Vi! Oh my God, are you okay?"

I startle as blood drips from my finger, and I realize I sliced through it with a knife as Dahlia rushes toward me.

She holds my hand under the stream of the kitchen faucet, and I wince through the sting.

"Does it hurt a lot?" She checks my finger left and right. "Thank God it's not that deep, but it's not shallow either."

"It's fine." I try to go back to chopping the vegetables, but she turns off the stove and drags me to a stool so she can bandage my wound.

"It's *not* fine." She frowns as she retrieves her first aid kit and cleans my finger with antiseptic. "You've been zoning out as usual, probably overthinking."

"That obvious?" I grimace.

"You do that a lot anyway, but it's more serious lately."

By lately, she means ever since Jude came into my life. Even I can tell I'm on edge but also not on edge.

It's weird to describe, but one moment, I feel like I'm flying, and the next, I plummet, racing to the bottom of a cliff with my demons.

My mood is flaky even when I mask it and shove my emotions in the grave I made for my ten-year-old self.

And I don't know how to fix it half the time. The only solution I've found is to always be busy. Work, school, side activities. Even now after we're back at school, I try to work as many shifts as physically possible, both for the money and to avoid alone time with myself at night.

Because that time—nighttime—scares me and I've been waking up shaking and even crying from nightmares.

Sleep has always terrified me.

I've given up hope to ever enjoy it.

Dahlia's brow furrows, locks of her dark hair escaping her

messy bun as she wraps a Band-Aid around my finger, then sits across from me. "I feel like you're hiding something from me."

"Don't be silly, what could I hide?"

She narrows her eyes. "Are you sure?"

I nod.

"Hmm, I don't know about that." She tilts her head to the side, still watching me with suspicion.

"Enough about me." I rub her arm. "Tell me about your classes at Graystone University. Is it everything you wanted?"

"Hell yeah!" She punches the air. "I've been going through all the material, and their medical program is honestly one of the best! I feel so lucky to have been offered a scholarship there right before school started."

"It's hard work, not luck. Don't downplay how much time and effort you dedicate to your grades, Dahl."

"I know, but, like, it's super hard to get in. And since they rejected me three years ago, I never thought they'd open the doors for me again. Gah, I'm loving it so much!" Her smile falls. "I'm not loving that we're on different campuses, though. Maybe I shouldn't stay at the dorm and come home every day instead."

"Absolutely not. It's an hour's drive and you only have a bike, so that would take forever and cut into your study time. Just stay there and make new friends."

"Nah." She hugs me. "You're my only friend."

I hug her back. "We're meeting on weekends like this, and you can come home on holidays."

"Or maybe you can apply to GU?" She pulls back, her eyes sparking. "I know it's a long shot, but maybe…"

"I don't think that will ever be possible." I'd never study at the same campus as Jude. It's enough hassle that he comes all the way here.

Though he hasn't since I creeped him out with the reason behind my blowjob skills.

That was three weeks ago. Mario said he hasn't been around, because he has family obligations and has been busy with resuming training ahead of the start of the hockey season.

I feel like Mario is trying to console me or something.

But for some reason, I can *feel* Jude everywhere in this tiny place. Even when he's not there. Like a damn ghost.

I don't want to get in touch with him, especially now that I don't have to since he stopped bugging me to watch his hockey games.

But I can't help but be worried about the whole thing with Dahlia and GU.

It simply can't be a coincidence.

As she said, they rejected her application a few years ago, so it's unusual that they'd change their mind out of the blue right before the start of classes just because a previous scholarship student dropped out.

I mean, they could have, and Dahlia is seriously smart and hardworking, so they might have been dazzled by her grades, but still.

This entire situation is giving me a bad feeling.

Dahlia is humming as she goes to return the first aid kit. As I wait for the broth to finish cooking, I pull out my phone and stare at Jude's name, then at the counter where I keep seeing images I'd really like to forget.

It's been weeks, and yet those erotic dreams won't leave me alone. I swear I've used my vibrator the past couple of weeks more than I have in years.

Is this a sexual awakening or something equally ridiculous?

After much deliberation, I type out a text.

Me: Did you have something to do with Dahlia's
   acceptance into GU?

My heart jumps when I receive a reply right away.

Stalker: What happened to hello?
Me: Hello. Are you behind my sister's scholarship?
Stalker: If I wanted to offer someone a scholarship,
   wouldn't I have offered it to you instead of your
   sister?
Me: I don't know. Maybe you want to control me
   through her and make sure I always know you can
   get to her whenever you want.
Stalker: I can get to her whenever I want now. If I
   wanted to threaten her life, I don't need to offer her
   a scholarship.
Me: Is that supposed to make me feel better?
Stalker: Not sure. Did you text me to feel better?
   Or because you're now alone, with no support to
   distract you from yourself or me?

How does he even know that? How can he recognize
that I've been feeling low since Dahlia moved to the dorm
at GU two weeks ago? I try to put up a courageous front
so as not to spook her, but, truly, I miss her so much, but I
don't want to be selfish and sabotage her once-in-a-lifetime
chance just because I can't be a grown adult and simply exist
on my own.

Me: Good night.

Stalker: You can end the conversation, but you can't
   escape me, Violet.

Me: Haven't been trying to. You're the one who ran away.

I realize I've said too much even before his next text
appears.

Stalker: Miss me?

Me: No, I've never been more at ease. If you don't
   show up again, that would be great.

Stalker: Liar. You've been looking over your shoulder,
   searching for me everywhere you go.

Me: How do you know? Mario?

Stalker: Not important.

Me: Why do you even want to know all these things
   about me? Do I not creep you out?

Stalker: Creep me out? I thought I was the creep.

Me: Well, you are.

Stalker: Wow. Thanks.

Me: You're welcome.

Stalker: Very funny. Now, tell me. Why would you creep
   me out?

Me: It's nothing. Forget it.

Stalker: Tell me.

Me: No.

Stalker: Then I'll jump over your balcony and find out
   the answer in person.

Me: You can't. Mario said you're busy training.

Stalker: Bold of you to assume I won't leave. Be there
   in an hour.

Me: Fine. It's about what I said about my mom. Just
   forget it.

I wait and I wait, watching the dots appear and disappear. It feels like forever, but when his text appears, I have to hold on to the counter. Because he says the words no one has ever said to me.

> Stalker: It's not your fault your mother was a deplorable human being who didn't deserve to be a mother in the first place. She creeps me out, not you.

I'm still reading and rereading his words when my phone pings with another text. I think it's from Jude, but it's an unknown number.

> Unknown: Hello, Violet. Your life is in danger. It has to do with Jude. Please text me back so we can discuss this further.

CHAPTER 17

Jude

ANOTHER ONE BITES THE DUST.

Unceremoniously.

Scratch that. Preston kind of carved him the fuck up. He's a mess of cut flesh and rotten insides spilling out on the ground of the forest.

His face is disfigured, and a knife is lodged in his right eye while the other one hangs out of its socket, dangling against the exposed bone of his cheek.

"What a fucking mess." Kane looks at the body slumped on the ground as he sheaths his gun with a silencer in the holster strapped to his side.

The three of us are dressed in black, but Kane is the only one without any splashes of blood on his face or hands.

I'm wearing gloves, but I felt the warmth splattering my neck when I stabbed the scum earlier.

Preston kneels by his handiwork and pokes the corpse on the forehead as if checking for any sign of the life he snuffed out with his bare hands.

When the dead man doesn't even flinch, Preston grins maniacally, blood streaking his hair like red highlights, staining his teeth, forming rivulets down his face and dripping from his chin.

"You mean a masterpiece." He flicks the handle of his knife that's lodged in the man's eye, making it wobble, then taps his scraped cheek. "You were a good sport, number ten."

I cross my arms, standing beside Kane and looking down at him. "I remember telling you not to kill my targets, Pres."

"Finders killers."

"It's finders keepers."

"I meant it the other way. Shut it." He jumps up, stretching and cracking his neck, still wearing his manic expression like a second skin.

He's high.

While Preston does love the chase and the high of killing, he doesn't usually carve them the fuck up as if he has a personal issue with them.

The last time he did this was with that scum teacher we killed at twelve at the boarding school after Kane and I found him sexually assaulting Pres.

Kane punched the teacher, and I held him down, then gave Preston a knife to take his own revenge. He stabbed him in the eyes. Over and over again. Then in the throat.

It was a bloody mess and the three of us looked like extras in a cheap snuff film afterward.

However, the huge smile on Pres's face was worth it. Especially compared to the dead look in his eyes when we first found him.

Naturally, Kane and I got punished by our dads.

Preston, however, started his unconventional journey with mental illness diagnoses, ranging from antisocial personality disorder to bipolar, psychosis, and a basket full of issues in between.

He was ping-ponged between several clinical psychiatrists who worked for Vencor and was given several experimental medications, courtesy of my father and Julian, until he finally, only recently—and by recently, I mean since we started college—got himself under control for the most part.

I say *for the most part* because he relapses sometimes.

Kane and I always make sure he's not alone, because his depressive episodes are brutal, and the last time he went through one, the last year of high school, he threw himself off the roof of the Armstrong mansion and fractured multiple bones. He was lucky he didn't hit his head and die.

He also tends to be excessively violent and unpredictable, which is why I prefer he joins me on my personal vendetta hunts than go and stab a random person on the street just because they got in his way. Or supervise Vencor members on their missions, then become theatrical and put them and himself in danger.

It happened last week, when he chopped up the mayor's aide into tiny pieces, then sent them to the mayor. Yes, the aide did betray Vencor, but the mayor was the one who reported him.

In Preston's words, "He needs the visual so he doesn't think of doing anything funny."

He got punished for that by the organization by being whipped seventy-five times. Kane and I volunteered to take twenty-five each despite Pres's objections. Not only because he would have become a drama king during the recovery period, but, really, we needed to remind him of the consequences of his actions, because they truly seem to fly over his head most of the time.

Despite his constant threats to go find new friends, Kane and I know we're the most important people in Pres's life, and as his friends, we have to keep him in check. Which is why I've been shadowing him ever since that incident.

I still don't like that he kills my victims, but tonight's particular scum was an elementary school teacher who's facing allegations of sexually assaulting his students. And while nothing was official, the accusations were enough for Pres to go all out.

He wraps an arm around Kane's neck. "I'm hungry. Make me a mean meatball pasta with lots of carbs that has the potential to send me into a coma."

"I'm not your chef." Kane removes Preston's bloody hand. "And don't get that dirty blood on me."

Preston slides his fingers all over Kane's face, smirking. "There. Much better."

"You little—"

"Juude," Preston whines, running toward me, then hiding behind me.

"Just leave him alone," I tell Kane, resisting a smile at the view of the bloody marks on his face. "You look better like this anyway."

"Right?" Preston jumps to my side. "Less put together and more like us. I keep creating masterpieces today. Bow down to me, peasants, muahaha."

"Speaking of masterpieces," Kane says, tilting his head. "Are we not going to address the fact that one name is still missing from your list of targets, Jude?"

I tense up, but my expression remains neutral. "I told you that's none of your business."

"But I want to play." Preston punches his palm. "Hockey season is taking too long to start, and I'm bored."

I shove him away with an index finger to his forehead. "Go and participate in the murders with Vencor members. *Without* drawing attention."

"But that's boring! We can only torture for answers, and

we're not allowed to get gory, because it's too messy to clean up, and my family would be up in my business like bored housewives. My witch of a grandmother told my dad that I need to be admitted to the mental institution after my harmless fun last week. Apparently, I'm a liability to the Armstrong name. Did I mention I despise her? Anyway, I prefer this." He headlocks both of us. "The three musketeers doing their own thing, with me as the reigning god, of course."

I elbow his side and Kane punches his stomach at the same time. He wails dramatically as he releases us. "My talents are not appreciated in this toxic friendship. I need to find me a new gang and throw you all under a yacht."

"It's under a bus, Pres." I sigh.

"I mean a yacht, so you'd be chopped up by the propellers. And you're not changing the subject, Jude. What's come of this mystery number seven?"

I flick his forehead. "None of your concern."

"Suspicious."

"So are your recent frequent trips outside of town, but you don't see me commenting on that."

"I'm fucking my stepmom's friend!" He makes a motion of slapping the air. "Amazing ass. Gives great head and will give my stepmommy a stroke when she finds out."

"That's, like, the worst idea you've ever come up with," Kane says. "And most of your ideas are shit."

"Nah, this one will really get to her, I'm telling you." He bursts out laughing, clutching his stomach. "Oh my, fuck, I'm getting high just imagining the shock on her face." His excitement immediately dies down. "And the usual sighs from Dad. I think he doesn't care what the fuck I do anymore. I could be found rotting somewhere, and he'd just sigh. Maybe in relief this time."

"It's better that way." I slap his shoulder. "Regis is too involved in my business. Asshole locked me the fuck up in my room for a whole week, making me have dinner with him every night just because I ignored him for a while."

"The for a while being since your mom died." Kane sighs. "But yeah, Pres. Grant's idea of attention is making me hang from the ceiling for a whole night while dousing me with ice showers."

"I'd take the locking up and forced dinners over sighs." Preston lifts a shoulder, his expression aimed downward, but then he perks up. "Just kidding. Hate the guy more than his wife. Anyway, let's eat! Then how about some late-night training? That wasn't a question. You're coming. Let me get Hayes to clean up the mess." He jogs ahead, calling in a sing-song voice, "Haaayes, where are youuu? Show yourself, my miiiinion."

I watch him for a while and then turn to Kane, who also has his full attention on Preston.

"Fucking prick," I mutter. "Thought he was spiraling for a second."

"He was for a bit there, I think." Kane sighs again, dragging his gaze toward me. "Pretty sure he's either not taking his medication or not taking it properly."

"He is." I run a hand through my hair. "I make sure of it every day. It's just…"

Kane is facing me fully now, the frown appearing monstrous with the blood. "Just what?"

"It's not working anymore, or it's losing its effect. The psychiatrist doubled the dose, so we'll see how that works."

"Fuck."

Silence stretches between us for a bit, only punctuated by a distant owl's cry and the heaviness of the uncertainty of what will become of Preston. Kane and I have been his only non-enablers in his environment.

Which isn't comforting, considering we're not your average college kids.

If we hadn't always been keeping Pres busy and watching over him, he would've ended up in a grave a long time ago. And now that the meds are barely keeping him in check, it's a problem.

A *huge* problem.

And it's probably behind the tension lodged in my bones lately. Because I refuse to fail to protect Preston as well.

That just won't be fucking happening.

"Can your brother work on something innovative?" Kane breaks the silence. "He's been testing all these off-the-record drugs lately, surely he can tailor something for Pres that's better than what he's on."

"Eighty percent of his tests go sideways. He's been spending more time killing his test subjects than helping them. I wouldn't trust him with a psychiatric drug. Preston was already used as a test subject for my father and nearly died. That won't be fucking happening again."

"I suppose we have to wait and see if he can keep himself under control."

"He can. I'll make sure of it."

He squeezes my shoulder. "You don't have to put more responsibilities on yourself when you're already struggling with control."

"No, I'm not."

"Jude, you're stalking one of your targets and doing God knows what in between, and it's messing with your head. You might not notice it, but I do. You're on fucking edge and it shows."

I clench my fists and then unclench them but choose to keep my mouth shut because he's not entirely wrong.

"Listen up, I don't care what you think you should do with Violet, but keep Dahlia out of it. You don't go near her, okay?"

I narrow my eyes. Kane has never had this much interest in a girl he's never even talked to. He's worse than me in the opposite sex department and rarely hooks up.

However, ever since the first time he took me to that Stantonville shithole to show me where Violet lives, he's been enamored with Dahlia.

Not sure if that's the right word.

Intrigued? Impressed, maybe?

I was too busy recognizing Violet as the girl with the blue umbrella, but then I noticed the gleam in his eye when Dahlia used a gun—an unloaded one—to threaten the drunk who was harassing Violet.

Dahlia was firm and loud, unlike Violet, who remained in the background, then scolded Dahlia for having the gun.

That's what Violet does best—scolding instead of being grateful.

And now I'm thinking of her, and I refuse to think of her after my recent resolution.

At any rate, Kane told me to stay away from 'the sister' that very night, and he sometimes plugs in a reminder to not disturb her in any form.

I narrow my eyes on him. "What's with you and Dahlia? You arranged her scholarship, didn't you?"

"You stay out of my business, and I stay out of yours, yeah?"

He changes the subject, talking about how we can gain more power in Vencor. Something about turning as many

Seniors as possible to our side and subtly forcing our dads to relinquish power in our favor.

A sort of a coup d'état.

Kane has always had this ambition for us to become stronger and run Vencor however we please.

And I agree in principle, but I don't have time for it.

Or maybe I do because I promised to stay away from my recent fixation.

And I have.

For about four weeks now, since the night Violet sucked my soul through my cock.

I've never come that hard or wanted to come that badly down someone's throat. Or mess them up with my cum.

Or watch my cum on her tongue as she looked up at me with watery blue eyes that were so goddamn alive.

Passionate, even.

I'd never seen that look on her face—satisfaction mixed with a hint of submission. Not until I saw my cum on her tongue.

And for a moment, I had a raging possessive thought about locking her the fuck up somewhere only I had access to.

But then I was disturbed by that thought because I've never considered making a girl so wholly mine; she'd never look at anyone else, let alone go on dates or flirt with them.

And that girl won't be Violet Winters, number seven on my list, who'll meet an untimely end like all of them.

It's just a matter of time before I rip off the Band-Aid.

The thought didn't sit well with me, but I chose to stay away.

The first week was because Regis locked me up. Ever since I was released from the prison of my old room, I've only been going at night to read her journal while she's asleep.

Sometimes, she'll have these brutal nightmares, and I find myself sort of...placing my hand on her back, which surprisingly seems to calm her down. Especially if I pat her for a while.

I don't really know why the fuck I do that.

Maybe it's because she's going through a depressive episode, seeming to talk less and less in her journal. She doesn't write much about death, but I've learned from studying the patterns that she tends to be less creative and more one-sentency in her entries when she's off. Not to mention, she talks less about herself.

Laura is having a hard time. She was crying in the bathroom during break. I want to help, but I can't do much except take some of her shifts or look after Karly whenever possible.

Dahlia is so excited for GU, and I'm so proud of her. She's meant to go places, and I can't wait to see how far she reaches.

Karly is so cute. I want to protect her contagious smile.

Good weather. Black insides.

Finished an ugly stitch. Threw it away.

Learned a new recipe. I ruined it.

Went walking. Would've been hit by a car if it weren't for my guardian angel.

The sky is colorless even though it's beautiful outside.

The demon sitting on my chest is heavier lately.

Why couldn't Mama love me even a little? Just a tiny bit. Would I have been better if she hugged me and told me she loved me even once? Or am I grasping at straws and finding excuses?

Endure.

Endure.

Endure.

Endure.

Endure. Please.

Her last entries have been just that word, and it's starting to creep me the fuck out. Pres and Mom both tended to be self-destructive, and if their depressive episodes are any indication, Violet could be headed down that same path.

In Pres's case, he'll be too reckless, testing gravity and physics. Mom's episodes usually manifested when she stopped eating and withdrew into watching TV all day, looking straight through the screen. And attempting to take her own life…or someone else's.

But then again, Pres and Mom struggled with more issues aside from depression.

Violet's episodes are… I don't know what the fuck they are. Mario says she's acting normal, but I can tell something is off about her lately. Her nightmares are frequent, her embroidering is almost nonexistent, and her journaling isn't the same.

She doesn't reply to my texts either, having completely ignored the few I've sent since she asked about Dahlia's scholarship a week ago.

My mind races as Kane and I clean up in the old cottage tucked deep in the Armstrongs' forest. It's the same place where we used to hunt, the same one we were abandoned in as kids and told to "learn how to survive."

It's become one of our playgrounds of sorts. A place where we come to inflict the same pain that was once inflicted upon us.

I'm putting on my shirt when my phone rings.

Larson.

My shoulders tense at seeing his name. Why would Mario's aide of sorts call me?

I pick up, my voice already on edge. "What's wrong?"

"I can't reach Mario. Something is off."

"Off?"

"I'm afraid something might have happened to them."

What. The. Fuck?

CHAPTER 18
Violet

"HERE." I HAND MARIO A CUP OF COFFEE. "YOU'RE WORK-ing late because of me again."

He stares at me, then at the cup in my hand, frowning slightly. The night air feels heavier than usual, clinging to my skin with a disturbing eeriness.

My sneakers hit the pavement as I shove the cup into his hand. "Just take it."

"You don't have to do this." He taps the elbow of his jacket, where I embroidered a falcon patch to cover an area that was a bit worn out. I thought it was the least I could do after he lent it to me the other day because I was feeling cold. "Or this."

I smile as I fall in step beside him. "It looks good, though, and it's not that I *have* to do it, more like I want to."

Mario is kind of my companion, walking me to my shifts at the bar, my classes at college, or even my shopping at the grocery store.

Over the past few weeks, when my head has become foggy and my nightmares have gotten to be too much, I've found a bit of comfort in knowing I have Mario as a guardian of sorts.

I know he's a pseudo stalker, but I don't like to think of

him that way. Especially since he's never been malicious and even looks like he feels guilty at times.

And since he's mostly in his car, I give him coffee or even food. Poor guy doesn't get enough sleep, and I feel guilty, even if this whole thing is Jude's fault.

"You're not supposed to feed the man who works for your stalker," he says with a note of irritation. "Do you have *any* survival instinct?"

"I do, which is why I don't feel any danger from you." I point a finger at myself. "I'm a great judge of character."

"You're too nice for that."

"And you're grumpier than your boss." I sigh. "Has he ever mentioned how all of this will end? I mean, I know how, but has he ever talked about when he'll finally do it?"

"You believe he'd kill you?"

I nod sharply. "He's made that clear countless times. But it's been months since he promised that, and he still hasn't taken any steps, so it's making me a bit anxious. Okay, a lot. My depressive episodes are worse, and his lack of action makes me overthink… Forget it, I don't want to waste your time with that. Just…can you talk to him or something?"

"I'm telling you this once, so listen carefully, Violet." He throws me a look. "If he wanted to kill you, you'd be dead by now. He wouldn't be wasting his time and resources this way."

"W-what?"

Mario opens his mouth to say something else, but the quiet is shattered by a sudden screech of tires against pavement.

He stiffens, his hand reaching behind his back out of instinct. I turn just in time to see a van hurtling toward us, its headlights off, its engine snarling in the dark like a nocturnal beast.

Just like that day.

The day he was shot.

Oh my God.

The van barrels forward, cutting through the silence with its raw, hungry speed. My breath catches, lungs locked, heart thudding.

And for one terrible, disorienting moment, I just stand there.

Frozen.

Paralyzed.

My body refuses to move, as if it's still trying to understand whether this is real or another nightmare I haven't woken up from as I catch a glimpse of the driver.

A silver mask stares at me through the windshield. The glow from the streetlights catches on its edges, revealing serpentine details coiled along the surface, twisting and curling like it's coming alive.

The sight sends ice through my veins, my pulse slamming against my ribs and my hands shaking.

For someone who often thinks about death, actually facing it is making me jump out of my skin.

What about Dahlia…? You promised to never leave her alone in this world.

Move, Violet, move!

Before I can do so, Mario shoves me back, hard.

A gunshot rips through the night as he fires at the van, and it swerves, its tires screeching, but it keeps coming.

Mario fires again, aiming for the driver. Another crack of gunfire, but this one misses as well.

Then, from the side, a motorcycle comes out of nowhere.

I barely have time to register the gleam of metal before it slams into Mario at full speed.

His body snaps backward, legs twisting unnaturally as he crashes against the pavement.

No. No. No.

The wet, sickening thud sends a shock wave through me, and my stomach lurches at the sound of bone hitting concrete.

"Mario!" I lunge toward him.

"Run!" He groans from between clenched bloody teeth.

Before I can reach him, a fist grips my hair and yanks me back.

Pain explodes across my scalp, my neck snapping at the force. A hand clamps over my mouth, suffocating my scream. My vision blurs as I thrash, my nails digging into flesh and clawing, but another blow crashes against the side of my head.

White-hot agony splinters through my skull.

The world tilts violently, the pavement rising up to meet me as the edges of my vision darken.

Through the haze, I see Mario reaching out to me, and my fingers twitch, but I can't touch him.

"What about him?" one of the voices murmurs, gruff and low and seeming to reach me from underground.

"Collateral damage," another replies as my eyes roll back. "We need to take care of her. Now."

So this is it.

The end?

A tear slides down my cheek as I watch Mario's motionless body bleeding out on the pavement.

Then everything goes black.

———

Pain.

That's the first thing I register. A deep, dull throb in my

skull radiates behind my eyes, tightening with every sluggish beat of my pulse.

The room is too bright, sterile white walls stretching for as far as I can see, the steady *beep, beep, beep* of a heart monitor filling the silence.

I blink against the burn of artificial light, the effort sending another sting of pain through my head. My mouth is so dry that every breath feels like sandpaper at the back of my throat.

My limbs are heavy like I've been weighed down with something thick and invisible. The nightmare…?

No, it's dark in my nightmares, not this…white.

Where am I?

My body freezes when I turn my head and realize I'm not alone.

A man sits on a large leather chair beside my bed, his long fingers leisurely turning the pages of a book, the smooth rustle of paper the only sound slicing through the mechanical beeps of the machines.

He's well-dressed—tailored navy slacks and a crisp white shirt that looks too perfect for a hospital setting. Not a wrinkle, not a misplaced thread. His tie is loosened just enough to suggest comfort rather than carelessness, and his jacket is folded neatly and draped over the back of an empty chair.

His posture is relaxed, one ankle resting over his knee, but there's an unsettling precision in the way he holds himself, like he's used to being watched and controlling every movement he makes.

Who is he…?

My gaze drags up to his face, and my mouth hangs open.

His eyes.

Dark brown, deep, unreadable, and disturbingly familiar. The type that don't just look at you, but through you.

Jude's ruthless eyes.

But this man lacks the raw, untamed fire Jude carries in his stare. These are colder, more refined, sharpened into something surgical. His dark hair is neatly styled, not a strand out of place, and the faintest trace of expensive cologne lingers in the air.

Brother? Uncle?

He seems to be in his early thirties, not old enough to be Jude's dad.

I shift, wincing as a fresh wave of pain flares up in my head. The movement must catch his attention, because he turns the page with deliberate slowness before finally looking at me.

I don't know why, but my blood freezes.

There's no warmth in his expression. No concern. Just mild curiosity, as if I'm a puzzle piece he's studying, deciding where I fit.

My gaze flicks to the book in his hands.

The Antichrist by Friedrich Nietzsche.

My pulse jumps.

Is he reading Nietzsche in a hospital room?

Something about that feels so deeply wrong, but before I can process the thought, a polite but entirely insincere smile tilts his lips.

"Ah. You're finally awake."

The stranger sounds as elegant and put together as he looks. Where Jude speaks in deep, rough words, this man speaks in a deep, commanding tone.

"Do I…know you?" I say in a hoarse voice.

"No, but I know you." He pauses, running his gaze over

me. "My name is Julian Callahan, but I wouldn't say it's a pleasure to meet you, Violet."

I swallow. "Are you related to Jude?"

"I'm his older brother. Older half-brother, to be precise. Same father, different mothers. Mine wasn't the one you watched die." He flips the page even though he's not reading the book.

He's just...looking at me. No—staring. With no change in inflection or expression, even as he stabbed me with those words.

He seems mildly interested in watching me bleed, but apparently, not for too long, because he speaks again. "Aren't you going to ask why someone as poor as yourself is in a private suite in the hospital?"

"Why...?" I jerk up, ignoring the pain that throbs in my skull as memories pierce through me. "Mario! How is Mario? He was run over and bleeding—"

"Not important."

"What?"

"A foot soldier is not important."

Rage flares up inside me until I see red. This is what's always happened whenever anyone has threatened Dahlia, and apparently, I feel the same type of anger toward Mario.

Staring into Julian's dead eyes, I say in a clear voice, "I will not listen to whatever you have to say until you tell me what happened to Mario."

"You believe you have negotiating power?"

"Yes. You obviously want something, or you wouldn't have made the time in what I'm sure is a busy schedule to have a word with me."

He raises a brow, turns a page, then pauses. "He was badly hurt. The surgery was a success, but he hasn't woken up yet, and he possibly never will."

My eyes well up and I sink my nails into my thighs through the sheet.

It's because of me.

Mario was hurt and is facing death because of me.

Why did he have to protect me?

Would he still be okay if I hadn't been born like Mama often said? Because she's right, I seem to only bring misfortune to those around me.

"As for why you're here…" Julian's voice brings my attention back to the present as he flips another page. "Jude tried to kill you, but I saved you."

My lips tremble, my whole body going into shock. "W-what?"

"He was the one who sent the killers. They work for him—or, more accurately, follow his command in our organization hierarchy."

"Why would he do that to Mario?"

"Because Mario was overstepping in his duties. He got too close to the subject he was watching, and that's not how it works. He failed to do his job and, therefore, is considered collateral damage."

That's what the guy called Mario—*collateral damage*—right as he was bleeding out on the pavement.

As if he were an insect.

Because the lives of people like me and Mario don't matter to people like Jude and Julian.

And yet my chest hurts at the thought that Jude really stooped that low. That…he'd kill me and Mario in a heartbeat.

Over our last couple of encounters, I thought I was feeling some softness in him. Even his words about not blaming me but my mom soothed me, and I felt like…something was different.

Apparently, I was wrong and Mario was right—I'm a horrible judge of character.

"Do I not get a thank-you for saving your life, Violet?" He flips a page, then another and another. "It was a hassle to have my people kidnap you from your assailant and bring you to the hospital."

I wipe my eyes with the back of my hand. "You couldn't care less about my life. It's unimportant, just like Mario's. So, no, I won't be thanking you, because you had an ulterior motive behind your actions."

His lips curve in a smile. "I can see why Jude chose to play with you for a while before killing you. Despite the innocent appearance, you're smart, so I'd appreciate it if you keep the intelligence streak throughout this conversation. Let me ask you, Violet. What do you want?"

"You and your brother out of my life."

"You got it."

My lips part, but then I purse them again, holding on to the courage even if my hands shake.

He's messing with me. He *has* to be.

"Excuse me if I don't believe that. Jude said he wouldn't leave me alone until I died. Just because he failed once doesn't mean he won't try again or go back to watching my every move and threatening my sister so that I'll do his bidding."

"You're correct. He wouldn't. Unfortunately, Jude is... *persistent*, to put it mildly, and he'll find you even if you run. Lucky for you, I have a solution."

"What type of solution?"

"I'm not sure if you're aware, but I run the Callahan empire, which is the pioneer in the medical-industrial complex. The reason we made it this far isn't because of transparent and on-the-record testing, it's because we use unofficial methods as well. My scientists developed an interesting coma-inducing drug with little to negligible side effects. It'd revolutionize the industry; however, we know we won't get the approval to test it, considering its volatile key composition, but you see, I *need* to test it."

"You want *me* to test it? Is that it?"

"Yes. Your blood tests are extremely promising. You have the near-perfect genetic profile to test it."

"I refuse."

"Then you'll die by Jude's hands sooner or later or be driven to slit your wrists. That's not ideal, is it?" He leans over, still gripping the book. "Especially since Jude arranged for Dahlia's scholarship to GU, where he can hurt her anytime he wants just to get to you."

My spine jerks. "Jude said he didn't…"

"Convictions are more dangerous enemies of truth than lies." He closes the book and then taps it with a finger. "According to this clown."

I swipe my finger against my tattoo, back and forth. I don't care what Jude does to me, though I feel stupid for feeling a spark of something whenever he touched me or texted me, but I'll never allow something to happen to Dahlia because of me.

Never.

"For the record," Julian says, pulling out his phone and tapping a few times before angling the screen toward me. "This is how Jude takes care of his targets. You made a lucky escape."

My stomach twists before I even see it, and then bile surges up my throat.

On the screen is a grainy surveillance image—a man torn apart, his body sliced open with brutal precision. One eye is gouged out, the other still impaled with a knife that's buried to the hilt.

Standing in front of the scene is Jude.

I'd recognize that stance anywhere—rigid, menacing. His hand grips the blood-coated knife, his expression unreadable except for the fury burning in his eyes. Another man is beside him, turned away from the camera, but I barely notice him. All I see is Jude. And what he's capable of.

The room tilts. I turn my face sharply, swallowing down the nausea crawling up my throat.

I'm going to be sick.

"Listen, Violet." Julian pockets his phone. "You and your sister will never be safe as long as you're in Jude's orbit. If you help me test out this drug for three months, I'll effectively remove you from that orbit."

"Remove me how?"

"I'll arrange new identities for you and Dahlia, give you a house and a new life on the West Coast. I'll fund your education and your sister's at top universities and even pay you for the experiment. In the meantime, while you're in a coma, Jude won't have access to you, and I'll protect your sister until you wake up. How does that sound?"

"Too good to be true."

"Not really. You have to know that there's a 50 percent chance you'll never wake up from this coma. But even if you don't, I'll honor my promise about Dahlia and give her the life I just pledged."

"I'll need a contract and a financial advance so that your promises don't sound empty."

He smiles. "Fine."

"Can I talk to Dahlia?"

"No. She has to believe you were attacked and brought

to the hospital, which is the reason for the coma. Otherwise, this won't work."

God. She'll be so worried.

I don't want to stress her out when she just started her new journey at GU, but I also know that if I don't take care of the Jude problem, she and I will never be safe.

It's just for three months.

Three months, and then we'll reunite and have our new beginning.

My eyes stray to Julian, who's watching me intently. "Do you not care?"

"About?"

"Susie...your stepmother who I couldn't help?"

"Doesn't matter when you have the perfect profile to test my drugs." He stands up and places the book in my lap. "Besides, you wouldn't have been able to help Susie even if you had intervened."

CHAPTER 19

Jude

I FOUND VIOLET AT THE BOTTOM OF A BRIDGE.

Unconscious, but not dead.

The only reason I found her was because my hacker managed to install a tracking device on her phone.

She was bleeding from her head, rivulets of red trickling down her neck, and from rips all over her hoodie and jeans.

Her hair was tangled with leaves and debris from when she hit the ground and her lips were blue.

But what made me crouch and touch her face were the two dried streaks of tears running down her freckled cheeks.

She was crying.

Violet cried before whatever the fuck happened.

At first, I thought she'd finally given in to her demons and committed suicide. It got to be too much with all her depressive thoughts, her inferiority complex, and her inability to rise above everything her bitch mother said to cut her self-esteem to pieces.

Worse, as I was holding her frail body in my arms while one of my guards was speeding to the hospital, I thought she'd thrown herself off the bridge to escape me.

And that…cut me fucking open.

It made me tighten my grip on her arms, holding her

closer and breathing her in, and telling myself she wouldn't do that.

Violet's suicide method would be taking pills.

She hates anything gory, and even in death, she wouldn't want to hurt others by having to see her blood or disfigured body.

But there was still a chance, right?

I hid my face with my hoodie as I dropped her off at the closest hospital, which happened to be the shithole in Stantonville, then disappeared before anyone could start asking questions.

After that, I made calls to the Callahan empire's higher-ups and arranged for Violet to be taken to Graystone General Hospital's trauma center since it's better funded and has superior services to Stantonville.

But no genius medical crew or advanced equipment managed to fix her completely.

Her bruises are mild, but the head trauma sent her straight into a coma that the doctors aren't sure she'll be able to recover from.

And now I'm standing in the hospital room, staring at her.

I've never liked hospitals.

Despite the fact that my family owns them and profits from people's lives and deaths, these establishments have always been a manifestation of Mom's pain.

Her tears. Her screams. Her begging to 'bring her baby' back.

Within these white walls, my mother battled with miscarriages, depression, cancer.

Everything.

So being within their walls, inhaling the smell of

antiseptic and clinical coldness that sticks to my skin and clogs my throat makes me tense.

On edge.

Every muscle in my body is wound up as if I'm about to fight.

The machines beep in slow, mechanical intervals, a hollow, unnatural rhythm that doesn't belong to Violet. Just like it didn't belong to Mom.

But my mother is gone, and Violet is here.

And she will always be right *here*.

She looks small in the hospital bed. Too still.

Too fucking quiet.

Violet is never still. Always moving and forcing smiles and being a busybody. Even in slumber, she shifts, curls in on herself, and exhales little breaths that catch on the edge of her nightmares. She thrashes and cries and even mumbles in her sleep.

But now, there's nothing.

Her hair spills across the pillow, strands of copper and gold catching the light's soft glow slipping through the hospital window. Normally, her hair is a bit messy, tangled from restless movement, from fingers raking through it absently. Now, it's too smooth, too perfect, too untouched.

But what unsettles me the most is the absence of…her stare.

I reach out and pull her eyelid up, but distorted white greets me, her pupils unfocused, not really there.

There's no blue.

There's no hint of the quiet storm she directs at me when she's pissed or the icy stares she gives when she's guarded, or the deep ocean that's there at night when she's thinking too much.

I release her lid and her long lashes rest against her cheek. I've watched her sleep more times than I'll ever admit.

Back at the bar, when she'd finish a long shift and she'd sit in the back, massaging her shoulders with her fists, before her body would slump from exhaustion and her head would droop to the side. In that tiny living room, shaking, mumbling, her fingers twitching from nightmares she never spoke about.

But she's not sleeping right now.

She's not even here.

And I fucking hate it.

I hate how wrong it feels to see her lifeless, quiet, tethered.

I hate that I can't reach into her head and rip her out of whatever abyss she's stuck in.

But maybe she's there on purpose, to avoid being trapped in those paralyzing nightmares.

At least now, the demons in her head aren't eating her alive.

I step closer, my fingers itching to push her hair back, to prove to myself that she's still warm, still real, still Violet.

But I don't.

I just stand there, watching her, staring into something that's starting to swallow me whole.

Starting? Is that really the correct word to describe these feelings I've had since Violet disappeared without my permission?

My fist clenches. "I told you that your life is mine. How fucking dare you be in a coma?"

I know I should go, but I can't seem to swallow the rage that's been flowing in my veins since I found Violet a week ago. We have a game tonight, and if I check my phone, I'll find everyone screaming at me to get to the arena.

Besides, Dahlia, who left an hour ago, will probably be back soon.

She's barely left Violet's side since she was discharged from the ICU a couple of days ago, and she's spent entire nights crying and begging Violet not to leave her alone.

Dahlia is a problem like everyone in Violet's fucking life.

If she loves her so much, how could she not know her beloved sister is one big ball of depression wrapped around suicidal ideation?

But then again, Violet is a professional at hiding herself— even when writing in her journal. If I hadn't personally witnessed her countless nightmares and the way she was crying so bitterly in her sleep, it would've been hard to see any of the pain behind her constant wide smiles and soft-spoken platitudes.

In reality, Violet doesn't cry. Even when she's shocked, in pain, or downright terrified.

"Fucking liar," I mutter, staring at Mario's bed beside hers.

He's also in a goddamn coma, so I can't get anything from him either.

Only these two know what happened that day. Because, for some phantom reason—aka suspicious as fuck—all road surveillance footage for that day was wiped out.

It can't be a suicide attempt.

Evidence?

One, no security footage, which means someone was covering up a crime.

Two, Mario was run over or hit by something and had severe internal bleeding. Violet likes him—too much for my liking—so she would've definitely tried to help him.

Three, and most importantly, I found her far away from

Mario's location, which means she was transported, by force, because she'd never leave him bleeding out on the street.

Now, the only evidence we have—that Dahlia has been pestering the detective about nonstop—is the traces of human skin under her fingernails.

Because Violet fought. And there was blood, so she clawed, too.

I can only imagine how much she cried and screamed, wanting to save Mario and being helpless to do so.

Maybe that's why she cried. Or maybe it was because of something else. Something worse.

At any rate, I asked our head of staff, Lucia, to look into the DNA since the police are coming up empty. Lucia is Mario's mom, and even though she makes a show of being loyal to Regis and even Julian, she'd never forgive anyone who hurt her son.

Lucia's a wise, resourceful, and very detail-oriented woman. We struck a deal—she helps me solve this case, and I'll take revenge for Mario and make sure he's given the chance he deserves to climb the ranks once I become a Founder.

That is, if he ever wakes up.

I never told Lucia that I intended to give Mario his chance anyway. We kind of grew up together behind the Callahan prison bars. He's smart and attentive, which is why I trusted him with watching Violet.

A decision I regretted when I saw how effortlessly close they became. She kept giving him gifts and food—which I asked him to refuse, but the bastard just ignored me.

"What really happened, Mario? Who could hurt you this badly?"

Only the beeping machines are his response.

Mario has Special Forces training and quick reflexes.

Unless it was professionals like himself, he wouldn't be lying in a hospital bed right now.

"Jesus fucking Christ."

I tilt my head sideways as Kane, who just spoke, strolls into the room with Preston following behind, both of them dressed in blue Vipers sweats and varsity jackets.

"I knew you'd be here, watching two comatose people like a creep." Kane crosses his arms. "We have a game tonight, Jude. We're supposed to be at the arena by now."

"This is why I haven't seen much of you?" Preston stares between the two beds. "You replaced me with comatose people? My pride is so wounded, I'm gonna cry."

"What is he doing here?" I ask Kane.

"He tagged along. You know how persistent he gets."

"Poor Mario. So young and probably a virgin. We should've pressured him to fuck around..." He whistles upon seeing Violet. "And who is this beauty—Oww!"

I slap his hand away before he can touch Violet's face.

Preston shakes his hand. "The fuck was that for?"

"She's number seven," Kane says, leaning against the wall with his arms crossed. "The one he didn't kill, but she still got attacked and sent into a coma anyway."

"Oooh, so this is mystery number seven. She's hot!" Pres grins. "Still want to chop her head off, big man? Though, seriously, not the face, something about it feels like it'll be a waste for some reason."

"Stay the fuck away from her, Pres, I mean it."

He cocks his head to the side. "Consider me fucking intrigued. Who is this chick anyway?"

"Unfinished business," I say from between clenched teeth, then stare at Kane. "Lucia said you switched the DNA sample the police got a hold of. Why?"

"Until you figure out who's behind this, it's better not to have them in our business, even if they're on our payroll. Besides—" He jerks his chin toward Violet. "—her sister won't let this go. She'll come sniffing around, and when she does…" A rare smirk tilts his lips. "She's all mine."

I'm distracted by Preston, who's poking Violet's cheek, and I growl as I slap his hand away again.

"Hold on, there's something about her face." He tilts his head to the side. "Where have I seen it before? Hmm? Good skin, though. You didn't by any chance take note of her skincare routine during the stalking side gig, did you, big man?"

I punch him in the chest, and he groans, doubling down. "Fuck! Want to kill me or something? Kaaaane, if I'm not in my best form tonight, blame Jude."

"Don't ever touch her again." I shove him away.

"Fuck me!" He snaps his fingers. "It's the girl who told you that you're a disappointing fuck, isn't it?"

"Shut the fuck up."

"She is! Fucking hell, I'm disappointed I didn't meet her before the Sleeping Beauty phase. Hey! Wake up, Violetta! I wanna talk."

I grab him by the arm and start to pull him away.

"Wait! Hold up!!" He tries to fight me. "Let me try scaring her into waking up."

"Don't make me punch you again." I drag him down the hallway as Kane follows behind us with a sigh. "This time in the dick."

"Not my Armstrong lifeline. You're so cruel to my highness." He grins. "On second thought, do it. Curious if Dad will still sigh when his only son can't continue the family legacy."

"Just shut it, Pres." I toss him away because my phone is vibrating.

Lucia.

"Any progress?" I ask as soon as I pick up.

"Good news and bad news."

"Good news first."

"We found a DNA match."

"Who is it?"

"A Vencor Member who's a hit man of sorts."

Fuck.

Kane, who's being pestered by Preston, side-eyes me as I walk at a slower pace.

I clench my fist. "Is it one of Julian's men?"

I've had my suspicions about that motherfucker since he was giving me ultimatums about cutting out the 'childish, fruitless revenge.' I suspected he was the one who sent men to kill Violet or scare her that first time Mario got shot.

But there's one problem with that.

The whole thing is not his style. It's too showy and in-your-face. Julian doesn't leave evidence behind, and his hit men are doctors. Just a jab of medicine and people die of nervous system shock or heart attacks.

He prefers controlled and bloodless kills—unlike me and, to my dismay, Regis.

"Are you insulting my intelligence?" Julian looked down at me when I confronted him, throwing the tablet with the security footage to the side. "If I wanted her dead, I'd poison her drink. She'd die in her sleep, and I wouldn't have to deal with the hassle of security footage and witnesses. On the bright side, this shouldn't be hard if they're doing such a sloppy decapitation job."

That's what Julian called it. *Decapitation.*

Something we do in Vencor where we cut off the head of

the snake so the rest of the body—the organization, other members—will stay in line.

But Violet has nothing backing her.

She was born and has lived as a fucking nobody. When I asked Julian what he meant, he said it was merely a figure of speech.

My brother does not use words in vain. He reads just so he can piss off other people with his pretentious philosophical nonsense or just to call people who read certain thinkers clowns.

But as I've been watching Violet sleep whenever Dahlia doesn't get in the way, I've been thinking that if Julian had something to do with her attack and I didn't stop him... If I brought this upon her...

"He's not one of Julian's men," Lucia says. "As for the bad news, he's dead."

"What?"

"Saul was found dead in one of the containers heading to South America the day after the incident."

"He was rubbed out?"

"It seems so. There are clear signs of poisoning."

"Fuck!"

"And, Jude?"

"Juuuude." Preston pulls on my arm. "Kane said I'm annoying. Let's punch him."

"What now?" I ask Lucia, fighting Preston off.

Our head of staff speaks as I'm staring into Preston's grinning face. "Saul was a hit man on the Armstrongs' payroll."

CHAPTER 20
Jude

"IS SHE WITH YOU?" KANE'S TIRED VOICE FLOATS FROM the other end of the phone.

My gaze flits to Violet, who's sleeping on the bed, her fingers twitching, and her body—that's been sluggish for months—has been shifting, curling, like she does in her sleep.

Three months, to be precise.

It's been almost three months since Violet was put in a fucking coma.

A *false* coma.

A *drug-induced* coma caused by none other than that motherfucker Julian.

The only reason I found out is because I got her out of the hospital.

Kidnapped her—if we're being technical.

Over the past couple of months, as I was slashing and fucking up most of the targets on my list and ending a few players' hockey careers to blow off steam, I started to notice patterns.

Violet doesn't show the same signs as Mario. She has more 'involuntary' nervous system reflexes, and that struck me as weird despite the doctors' platitudes.

Once, I said, "You don't possibly think you can escape

me, do you?" And to my surprise, her eyelids twitched, and so did her fingers.

Mario has never shown any of those signs, but the doctors keep saying that different people have different ways of reacting when in a coma.

I should've known better than to trust Julian's doctors and establishments. *Everything* in the medical field is under his or Regis's thumb.

Including Violet's coma.

The final piece of information that confirmed my suspicion was Violet's disappearance from the hospital two days ago.

I remember the fucking tightness in my chest when I walked in like I usually do early in the morning—because Dahlia spends most nights by her side—and I didn't see her lying in bed.

There was no pale face or frail body or shell of a person. Only emptiness—and Mario sleeping peacefully.

The nurses mentioned a transfer to one of our headquarters, and I knew Julian must've been behind it. There's no way a meticulous, well-planned transfer would happen without his interference or approval.

Turns out that Julian and Grant—Kane's father—were using Violet's kidnapping to twist Dahlia's arm. Maybe hurt Kane through her. Maybe delete her and her annoying snooping habits from town.

I didn't give a fuck what the reason was. All I cared about was having Violet back exactly where she belonged—under my thumb.

So I barged into Julian's office and threatened to crush his skull if he didn't tell me where she was.

He merely ignored me, so Kane spoke to him, trying his

boring diplomatic shit that also failed, because Julian doesn't change his mind when it's set on something.

I searched all our safe houses, holding out hope that he'd be keeping her in one of them. Naturally, he's not that stupid, so I couldn't find a trace of her.

Today, however, Lucia managed to locate her in one of the unmapped hospitals.

Well, it's an illegal experimentation center window-dressed as a clinic on a small island right off the coast. I had no goddamn clue this shit existed in the Callahan empire, but then again, Regis has never considered me his actual heir, not when golden-boy Julian exists.

Seems Julian's tyranny and degeneracy run a lot deeper than I thought, because that goddamn place looked like an asylum. It was full of patients, many of whom I recognized as Vencor members who betrayed the organization and, therefore, were dead.

But apparently not, because Julian is using them as his lab rats.

Despite the high security, I managed to raid it with the help of Lucia—and my Callahan last name that made the guards hesitate to hurt me.

Point is, I got Violet out, kidnapping one of the doctors as well so he could look after her.

Under some torture, he mentioned a coma drug experimentation and swore he'd recently started working on the project and didn't know much.

He said Violet's vitals were pretty good throughout the period they were monitoring her and that if she didn't take her assigned daily dose of the drug, she'd start to wake up soon.

It's been almost twenty-four hours, and she still hasn't.

Maybe Julian's drugs messed with her indefinitely.

No—she's moving, her eyes fluttering and her body restless. She's no longer in a coma.

She has *never been* in a coma.

Why did Julian do that to her? If he'd wanted to hurt her, a simple injection or food poisoning would've done the trick. Or was she aware of what was happening? She wouldn't...do this willingly, right?

I have so many questions, but the most important thing is that she's here and safe.

"Yeah," I say to answer Kane's question.

A long sigh escapes him. "Is she waking up?"

"Slowly, as the doctor keeps saying."

"Good. Dahlia will want to see her."

"Fine." I tighten my grip around the phone. "And, Kane?"

"Yeah?"

"I'm sorry about your father."

"I told you I'd kill him one day for all he did to me." Another sigh, this one sounds too loaded. "That day came sooner than I expected. Hurting Dahlia was the final nail in the coffin."

"Is she okay?"

I couldn't care less about Dahlia, and I truly dislike her meddling ways ever since Violet's coma. Not only has she wormed her way into our lives, but she's also kind of got Kane wrapped around her little finger.

The past few months, I've had to watch with pure disdain as my friend, who I honestly thought lacked any form of illogical feelings, as he calls them, became too addicted and obsessed with that girl.

And that's bad news, because he's slipping and making mistakes he shouldn't.

But while I don't care about Dahlia, Violet does. She's her only family, and I'd rather she doesn't wake up to find her sister mutilated.

"She's fine. Just some cuts," Kane says. "I have to supervise getting rid of Grant's body. Check on Pres. I don't like his sharp manic episodes lately. Talk soon."

I hang up, stroll to Violet's side, and sit on the edge of the bed.

I don't touch her.

Ever since the time I tried to peel her eyelids open, I haven't laid a hand on her. There hasn't been a reason to.

She hasn't been agitated in her sleep and hasn't needed my hand on her back to calm her down.

Not when she's been so…still.

However, she's making slight movements now, no longer playing dead in a hospital bed.

I sit on the edge of the mattress and look at her soft face. "Wake up, Violet. We have a lot of shit to talk about."

She stirs but doesn't open her eyes.

And I wonder what she's dreaming about. Is it her mother again? Maybe Dahlia?

Would she ever dream of me?

Not that I want her to, especially since most of her dreams are nightmares.

My phone vibrates in my hand, showing the group chat, now named "The Vipers' Den."

Pres: Guess what I've done?
Pres: I'm glad you asked. Voilà!

Attached is a picture of a burning motorcycle.

Kane: JFC, what is that?

Pres: Marcus Osborn's ride. 😇

Kane: The fuck, Pres? I told you to figure out a way to
    keep him out of Vencor.

Pres: Eh, that's what I'm doing?

Kane: No, that's not what you're doing. You're
    deliberately provoking him. With all the shit you
    keep pulling, he might accept the Osborns' offer to
    officially join the family. We don't want that.

Pres: Nah, he would never join the family that slapped
    the bastard child tag on him and cut him and his
    mom off.

Kane: You're underestimating him. Stop messing with
    the prick just because he humiliated you in the last
    game, Pres.

Pres: He did NOT humiliate me. I was having an off
    day that had NOTHING to do with him. Besides,
    he's the one who fucked with me first. I'm petty,
    PETTY. Like the greatest petty any petty can ever
    pettily meet.

Kane: How the hell did he fuck with you?

Pres: Not important. He just did, and I burned his bike.
    @Jude doesn't this shit look hot as hell?

Me: Kane is right. Stop poking the bear, Pres.

Pres: You're supposed to say: Hell yeah, you're so
    fucking awesome, Pres! I feel privileged to have you
    in my life. Copy and paste, please.

Kane: You know Marcus will get his revenge for this,
    right? You burned his only mode of transportation.

Pres: That's the whole fucking point, man.

Me: Instead of these childish tantrums, how about
    you conserve that energy to train harder so you can

handle him on the ice next time we play against the
    Wolves?

Kane: What Jude said. He made a fool out of you the
    other time, Pres. It was embarrassing to watch.

Pres: Friendship revoked. You bitches can go die.

*Preston Armstrong removed Kane Davenport and Jude
Callahan from the chat.*

I shake my head. He'll add us back in when he has some
other shenanigans to report on.

Kane is right about Preston's episodes, but I have no fucking clue how to deal with the motherfucker, especially when
his brain decides to burn shit at three in the fucking morning.

I'm even considering talking to his dad, because things
are getting out of control fast. But then again, I know all
about the love-hate relationship they share, so I'm not sure
if that would help rein in Pres or make him spiral further out
of control—

Bang!

A sharp, metallic crash comes from somewhere outside
the room.

Instinct takes over as I pull a gun from my belt. The safety's off, so my body moves before my thoughts can catch up.

I stride toward the door, gripping the weapon firmly,
ready to fire if necessary—

My chest seizes.

A vicious, suffocating constriction wraps around my
lungs, like invisible hands digging in, squeezing the air from
me. My vision blurs at the edges, dark tendrils creeping in
like ink spreading through water.

What the fuck—

I stumble, my knees buckling before I can even reach the

door. My hand spasms, the gun slipping from my grip, clattering uselessly to the rug.

Gas.

Fucking *paralyzing* gas.

I've been trained for this—conditioned for it by my father to prepare me for Vencor. Poison, gas, and pain training are a must for all Founders' children, and I was no exception.

But this is different.

It's too strong.

I can't even twitch my fingers.

Because whoever did this knew the dosage it would take to bring me to my fucking knees.

And there's only one person who would keep that in mind, because he oversaw my training right alongside Regis.

Julian.

I don't have to look up to know it's him.

I hear the measured footsteps, the deliberate pace, and the effortless control.

"It's not good manners to steal from me, little bro." His smooth voice laced with amusement lands on my muddled brain like polished steel.

He steps into view, his dark-brown eyes gleaming under the sterile light, holding a mask to his nose and mouth. His suit is pristine, not a wrinkle in sight, his tie adjusted just enough to be casual but never careless.

Meanwhile, I'm on my fucking knees, my lungs burning, my muscles locking up, the weight of invisible chains dragging me down.

"Julian Callahan always collects his debts," he says, looming over me. "You knew that and still had the audacity to raid my establishment."

I glare at him, trying to clench my fist, but my muscles won't move.

"Don't give me that look. It's nothing personal. Just business." He strolls to Violet as a few men, also wearing masks, barge into the room with a stretcher. "I'll admit that you have more insiders in the Callahan compound than I gave you credit for. Consider me impressed."

I want to lunge and punch him and keep Violet where she belongs—under my thumb—but I can't move a muscle.

"Unfortunately, I'm not done with this one, brother dearest. I have a deal to complete." He checks the monitors and then sighs. "She's waking up before we're done. You truly are a *nuisance*, Jude. Your punch first, think later habits are a disgrace."

He motions at his aides, and they move her onto the stretcher. I groan, foaming at the mouth to fucking destroy Julian as he strolls to stand in front of me again. "I suggest you give up on her."

I snarl.

"Listen, I mean her no harm. If anything, I'm impressed by all the data we've gathered these past few months. Perfect test subject, if you ask me. Besides…" He tilts his head to the side. "The poor girl chose to undergo this, knowing there was a 50 percent chance she'd die, just so I'd help her escape you once she wakes up. Get a hint, little bro."

My eyes widen.

No.

That's not…

Violet wouldn't agree to this knowing she'd leave Dahlia behind. She just wouldn't—

"I'll keep my word and send her and her sister out of here. Somewhere you'll never find her. Besides, you also know

someone in Vencor wants her dead, right? The reason behind
her attack and Mario's coma is someone closer than you
think. Yes, my men saved her from them and had to abandon her down at the bottom of the bridge so you'd find her,
but I truly wasn't the one who hurt her. There was a third
party. You still can't find them and probably never will, so let
her escape alive." His eyes darken, a harsh emotion shining
through. "While you can."

How…?

Lucia wouldn't have told him we've been investigating
and coming up empty about the hit man's connection to
the Armstrongs. I even asked Preston to look around, but
he didn't find anything except that we should blame his dad
because he's an asshole.

The Armstrong family tree is huge, but only a few of
them live in the mansion. Preston's grandfather is frail and
an honorary chairman. His father, Lawrence, is a milder
version of mine but an autocrat through and through. His
grandmother is vicious, but I'm biased because she always
calls Preston names that correlate to his mental illnesses,
and his stepmother is a socialite who only cares about
image, power, and money. His sister is pretty young and
irrelevant.

That leaves two people. His uncle, Atlas—Julian's best
friend and, therefore, a secretive, cunning son of a bitch—
and Preston's late mother, who was absolutely crazy, to say
the least, and did a lot of questionable things to remain rele-
vant. But she died a long time ago.

That only leaves Atlas—who has no reason whatsoever
to kill Violet.

Zilch.

Like Julian, he's more interested in an internal war to

kick Preston's dad off the throne and take all the power he can get.

Atlas, Julian, Serena—Marcus's half-sister—and Kane's uncle Kayden have always been power-hungry assholes who'd kill and sabotage just so they can remain on top.

But there's no reason for Atlas to kill Violet. Her death wouldn't benefit him in the least.

Also, if he'd wanted to kill her, Julian would definitely not have intervened.

"It doesn't matter how much you search," my brother says. "You'll still come up empty."

Fuck you, I say with my eyes.

"Take my advice, let Violet go and focus on your role within the family." He pats my cheek. "Don't disappoint me or taint Susie's hard work, yes?"

And then they carry Violet out.

And I can only watch.

CHAPTER 21

Violet

MY EYELIDS FEEL HEAVY.

Tired.

Almost as if I haven't slept in ages.

I open them with agonizing difficulty, and all I see is…
white.

Too much white.

Clean.

Sterile.

The oppressive color coats the walls, the ceiling, and the
sheets tangled around my legs like restraints I don't remember getting trapped in.

My breathing is too shallow, too controlled, as if my
body is relearning how to function.

I try to blink away the fog, but my lashes are heavy, my
lids sluggish.

My muscles ache in places I don't even recognize, deep
inside my bones, like they've been frozen solid and only now
decided to thaw.

Where…am I?

My fingers twitch against the stiff sheets; my limbs feel
like two slabs of stone I can no longer control. I'm so disoriented, I feel disconnected from my own body, like I'm an

imposter in someone else's skin. The air smells like linen and faint cedar laced with emptiness and everything that's... wrong.

I try to sit up.

Pain punches through my ribs, the ache spreading to my shoulders, my legs, *everywhere*. My stomach clenches, nausea clawing at my throat with every sharp inhale.

Is this a nightmare?

A different type of nightmare?

My arms tremble as I push myself upright, breathing through the sharp, electric pulses overflowing my nerves.

I move like I haven't moved in a long time, and that's when the first spark of recognition hits me.

Memories of the attack, Julian, and his stupid Nietzsche book slam through me. That was hours ago, right?

Swinging my legs off the bed is an effort. Cold air bites at my bare feet and zaps through my bones, and I press a hand against the wall as I push myself up, my legs shaking like they might buckle at any second.

Like I'm learning how to walk all over again.

Still grabbing onto the wall, I walk out of the room, and the farther I go, the tighter my chest gets.

Everything about this place feels wrong.

The house is small, painfully neat, like a picture someone arranged for the sake of appearances. A single untouched gray couch sits in the living room. A fireplace stands cold and empty. Through the large glass window, the outside world is coated with snow, the sky a vast, unforgiving gray that stretches endlessly.

I swallow hard. My heartbeat pounds in an erratic, stuttering rhythm.

Snow?

It's…September. Why is there snow?

The outside world feels out of sync with my internal one. Like I'm playing catch-up with reality, but something isn't adding up.

I nearly fall, and I hold on to the sofa for balance. My gaze flicks to a small stack of newspapers on the sleek black coffee table.

I don't realize I'm reaching for them until my fingers skim the top one. The pages feel thin and strange under my fingertips, new, even—

My hand clenches around the paper when I read the date.

Late December.

No.

It was September. Fall.

It was just a few hours ago when Julian was sitting beside me, flipping through a book and watching me like I was nothing more than cattle lined up for slaughter.

But now…it's December?

Three months?

My stomach plunges.

The room sways and warps around me, and I collapse onto the sofa, my breath ragged and sharp, every inhale slicing through my ribs like shattered glass.

I've been gone for three whole months, but my brain refuses to recognize it.

A sharp, shrill ring shatters the silence, and even my jumpiness is sluggish as I see the phone that's sitting beside the newspapers.

My fingers shake as I pick it up, pressing it to my ear.

Silence.

Then a low, controlled voice fills my ears. "Welcome back to the world of the living, Violet."

Julian.

"Where am I?" My voice is hoarse, fractured, almost alien.

"Rhode Island. The start of the new life I promised. You need to lie low for a while as I arrange your transfer to Seattle."

"D-Dahlia. Where's Dahlia?"

A slow exhale filters through the receiver like he's indulging me with the bare minimum of patience. "She will join you shortly."

Oh, thank God.

She's okay.

And I'm alive.

Does this mean it's all over now? Am I allowed to breathe properly?

"Before then, you'll be visited by my doctors for a final checkup to assess your body's regenerative capabilities."

"What about Mario?"

"In a *real* coma. Will probably never wake up."

My throat closes.

I open my mouth, but no words come out.

God. What have I done to poor Mario?

My jumbled thoughts start to filter in. Memories? No—words. Dahlia's mostly, but also…

My heart thuds as fragments of dark promises and a deep voice I could never forget filter through.

Jude.

He was there somewhere.

My head hurts the longer I think about it. I think I woke up at some point, opening my eyes, even, but how long ago was it? I remember seeing the snow outside, the TV was on, and the Vipers were playing.

Jude slammed someone, and I wanted to close my eyes, but I couldn't. I was surrounded by people in white and…

"Her pulse is unsteady," one of them said mechanically.

And then Dahlia was kissing a player on TV—Number 19, Davenport.

Why was Dahlia kissing someone from the Vipers…?

The memory slips through my fingers as fast as it appeared, like sea foam, disintegrating with each of my breaths.

And then another grainy, distorted memory hits me—a large hand on my face, hot breaths skimming my lips, and unintelligible words.

I inhale and exhale harshly into the phone. "Was Jude by my side recently?"

"Yes. He kidnapped you, but I saved you in time. You owe me a considerable number of favors, Violet."

"Kidnapped me? Why?"

"You know exactly why."

To finish what he started and kill me.

But if he wanted to kill me, wouldn't he have had many chances to do that while I was sleeping?

Yes, Julian mentioned that Jude would have no access to me while I was in a coma, but knowing how resourceful Jude can be, he could have found me.

And why does my chest ache? Is it a side effect of the coma?

This feels the same as when I learned he sent those people to kill me and Mario.

Those emotions of betrayal I'd hoped to never experience again, because they're beyond stupid. I'm the one who chose to have naïve thoughts about Jude and his motives.

"Listen, Violet. I better not see you or your sister around

here again. Not in Stantonville and certainly not in Graystone Ridge." Julian's voice is still calm, but it's a threat wrapped in silk.

And then, like a knife pressed against my throat, the last words slide in. "For your own good."

The line goes dead.

I stay there, the phone still clutched in my trembling hand, the silence pressing in around me. The white walls. The untouched furniture. The frozen world outside.

I've been gone for three months.

Mario is in a coma because of me.

And Jude still wants to kill me.

Even though I woke up, I want to go back to the nothingness of whatever I was in.

————

Things didn't go as Julian planned.

And I'm not sure whether it's a blessing or a curse.

It's been over three weeks since I woke up from the coma, and I'm now living in Graystone Ridge.

It's due to many reasons.

For one, Dahlia is dating the Vipers' captain and Jude's best friend, Kane Davenport. They got together because she approached him to avenge me.

For Dahlia's sake, Kane offered Jude the rest of the folders containing names of the people who were present during Susie's death with the sole condition that he wouldn't hurt me.

Also, for Dahlia's sake, Kane somehow pulled strings to have me admitted to GU in the second semester and paid for it in full.

As if that weren't already too much, Kane bought us a

huge penthouse that I live in alone because, in reality, Dahlia lives with him now.

He also told me not to worry about Julian and that he has the situation "under control."

Kane wanted to pay for my expenses as well, but I drew a line at that. However, something tells me he's arranged for my acceptance into a well-paying part-time job at a youth charity, even though I have zero experience.

I'm deeply uncomfortable with him giving me things, even if it's for Dahlia. My sister, who's become even more overprotective since I woke up, told me to just take it.

"I know it's tough, and I also thought I shouldn't accept his money in the beginning, but, really, should we be so pressed about it? It's the first time we've had a chance to live a better life. After being in survival mode all these years, I think we deserve to stop struggling and just be happy."

I don't know about that, but what I know for certain is that Kane worships the ground she walks on. I've seen the way he looks at her when she's not paying attention and the constant smile he wears when she's talking nonstop.

He loves her deeply, and she's head over heels for him, which I never expected Dahlia to ever be.

She used to treat relationships like an afterthought, and she has worse trust issues than me. So seeing her this happy and in her element lately has warmed my heart—which is probably the only good result of my coma.

I still hate third-wheeling them, though, and I feel guilty when she comes to spend the night instead of being with her boyfriend because she's worried about me.

Or right now, because she ditched him and is walking with me from campus because it's our "movie night."

She's grinning at her phone, typing with super speed,

her cheeks slightly flushed, her lower lip trapped beneath her teeth.

God. She's glowing. Her light-green top and pale-beige jacket contrast against the tones of her olive skin, and she has the most beautiful complexion, especially lately since she's not stressing out.

"Oh," I say, pretending to scroll through my phone. "I have a mock test tomorrow."

Dahlia looks up and then narrows her eyes. "Don't you dare cancel our movie night."

"I'm sorry." I side-hug her. "You know I've been trying to catch up, especially with the new school and everything."

She pouts. "Are you sure you're not doing this because you don't want to spend time with me or something? You can tell me if I'm annoying, Vi."

"Never. You're my only friend and family, remember?" I smile and rub her arm. "Go have fun with Kane."

"Fiiine. Want to go watch the Vipers play this weekend? I have premium tickets. Perks of interning as a medical assistant and being the captain's girlfriend."

My chest constricts at the reminder of the one player I think of when that team is mentioned. I try to breathe normally, but my ribs ache even as I force a smile.

"You know I'm not a hockey fan."

"I wasn't either, but it's so much fun! Besides, Kane is a badass and an actual hockey god. The entire team is amazing, actually. If a skeptic like me can be converted, so can you."

"I'm good, thanks."

"All right. I'll take Megan, then. She'll be over the moon." She types into her phone, probably telling her friend and previous roommate about the tickets. "I'll call you later."

I nod and hug her as we separate.

I smile as I watch her walking in the opposite direction. At least one of us got her life together.

As a habit I can't get rid of, I check my surroundings, expecting to see a large man wearing a helmet and gloves and leaning against a bike.

Watching me with disapproving dark-brown eyes.

Eyes that visit me in my sleep on the regular now. In my dreams, they're harsh and unforgiving, always making me wake up in a cold sweat.

I have no idea why he won't leave my subconscious.

He's not there—no longer stalking or tormenting or threatening me. And Mario, whom I've been visiting regularly, is still in a coma.

Jude probably got bored, as I expected he would, and moved on to his other targets. Like Kane said, he won't hurt me.

I haven't even seen him on campus, and I'm thankful that my social studies building is far away from where he studies business.

And yet…I can't help but feel ill at ease.

Why, I don't know.

Theoretically, my life couldn't get any better than this. I live in a spacious penthouse, my studies are paid for in full, and I work fewer hours than before.

I have more free time that I use to embroider, mostly while visiting Mario. Dahlia told me she used to talk to him as well, so he wouldn't feel lonely, so now that I'm back, I go to the hospital on the regular, mostly to keep him company. But also because I don't like being alone. I talk to him sometimes, just to fill the silence.

Due to all that, I've ended up with too many handkerchiefs and patches, so I opened a little online shop to sell them, and I'm hoping that if sales are good, I might be able to volunteer at the charity and let someone else have the paid position.

Things have been better than I could ever dream.

Now, if my brain could catch up to those facts, that would be great.

"Hold up, it's you!"

I come to a halt, or more like I'm forced to stop walking, as a large man stops in front of me. He's surrounded by two leggy brunettes whose eyes throw daggers in my direction as if I wronged them in a past life.

The tall, muscular guy has styled blond hair, a square jaw, and disturbingly beautiful Caribbean-green eyes. He's prince-like in his beauty but also so broad and tall and… a Viper.

He's wearing the team's jacket, and I definitely recognize him. Number 13, Armstrong.

Now, I refuse to think that I recognize him because Jude always got into a fight whenever anyone came near Number 13.

I search my surroundings, thinking he's talking to someone else, but he comes closer, grinning, and, wow, he has deep dimples in his cheeks. They're adorable.

Though, that's an oxymoron because I don't think this guy is anywhere near adorable. He's dangerous just like all of them, but he somehow seems more approachable.

"Viola, right?" He stops in front of me, and the two girls follow suit, their smiles looking forced at best.

"Violet," I say. "Do I know you?"

"You haven't had the pleasure, but I'm Preston! Call me handsome for short." He shakes my hand even though I didn't offer it. "Dakota must've told you so much about me. I'm kind of a big deal."

"Who's Dakota?"

"Uh, your sister?"

"Her name is Dahlia, and she never mentioned you, actually."

He pauses, almost as if I slapped him, and one of the girls wraps an arm around his. "Come on, Pres. Why are you talking to a nerd?"

He places his index finger on her shoulder and pushes her away, then wipes his finger on her coat. "I told you not to touch me. Leave, now."

They both freeze, but when he gives them a poker-faced look, they hurry away, gulping, and one of them glares at me.

What did I do?

Preston grins as if he didn't look downright murderous not two seconds ago. "She must've spoken about me, but you forgot."

"I don't think so…?"

"I'm Kane's bestie. Of course she did. Anyway, you really have great skin. What's the skincare routine secret?"

"Excuse me?"

"Oh, right!" He snaps his fingers in front of my face, and I flinch, my shoulders tensing, but then he balls his hand into a fist and places it near his mouth. "Today, we have a one-of-a-kind witness to Jude's lackluster performance. We'll tell you all why you should vote Preston for the best dick around. Miss, can you tell us in detail why sex with Jude is disappointing?"

My mouth hangs open as he places the imaginary mic close to my face. Jude told him about the sex? Can those encounters even be considered sex?

I mean, they technically were, but still. Also, how much does this Preston know?

"Come on." He steps closer. "Just give me some ammo to crush that big man."

He's peering down at me, narrowing his eyes and kind of pushing into my space. My chest tightens and I step back. Pushy men, or those who don't respect space, hike up my anxiety and trigger memories I covered up and shoved into my metal box that I'm glad Dahlia kept with a few of my belongings.

Those memories start slow, like a spark of electricity through my brain. Preston's cologne asphyxiates me, and I can feel thick, meaty fingers trying to pull at my skirt, large hands landing on my shoulders, over my breasts.

Our last foster father tried to touch me any chance he got, and even though I pushed him—and got punched—I always feel his meaty hands on me whenever a man touches me threateningly.

Not with Jude, though. The irony.

My shoes catch on the concrete and the spark of discomfort grows and expands. My mouth fills with saliva, and I know I'll be sick soon.

A large body appears behind Preston.

My heart stutters.

And so does my breathing.

My shaky fingers latch onto my wrist as I stare into those dark eyes, the color of the night. Still as disapproving as ever, still as…hypnotizing.

It's been months since I last saw Jude Callahan in person.

But seeing him right now is like being hit by an arrow right in the heart. A rush of inexplicable emotions buzz through me, and my limbs are trembling.

Is it anger? Is it all the unsaid things I couldn't tell him?

Is it something else?

He looks as tall and muscular and intimidating as I remember him. A man who's able to snap someone in half if he wants to.

A monster.

The man who tried to kill me but changed his mind after he made a deal with Kane, and Mario became collateral damage in his games.

I don't know what I expect him to say or what I'd reply, but he says nothing.

Just stares.

And I stare back, hoping he sees how much I hate him. That I'll never forgive him for what he's done to Mario.

"Oh, big man. It's Sleeping Beauty, who's not asleep anymore," Preston says, completely oblivious to the tension thickening the air.

Jude wraps an arm around his neck from behind, head-locking him, and then drags Preston with him.

"Wait! I still haven't heard her answer about the disappointing sex. I was going to start a podcast!" Preston tries to fight, but Jude is already taking him away.

He doesn't look back.

Doesn't acknowledge me.

As if I'm back to being the wallflower he wouldn't have noticed if life hadn't shoved me right in his way.

CHAPTER 22
Violet

THE PLACE I LIVE IN IS AN OVERWHELMING EXTRAVA-
gance and bigger than anything I've ever stepped foot in, let
alone called mine.

Every inch of this penthouse screams wealth and power
and is way beyond my dreams, let alone reality.

The decor is a blend of beige, deep black-blue, and lay-
ered shades of blue, probably Dahlia's doing. She must've
told Kane that blue is my favorite color.

Despite my acting strong being on my own, like when I
abandoned our movie night the other day, I'd rather have her
than this place.

I don't know how to describe it, but when we used to live in
shabby, creaking houses with black mold and health hazards,
I was happy knowing she was sleeping under the same roof.

That I wasn't alone.

That, no matter how hard it gets, she's just there, trying
to make me laugh, and buying me ginger ale while tasting
the food I cook.

It's not that we don't have that anymore, and I can still
spend time with her, but she also has her own life and a dash-
ing boyfriend that I don't want to annoy, because he's only
treated me well.

But as I walk around the new home that doesn't feel like home, I just miss my sister.

The walls are smooth, the lighting soft, casting a moody, elegant glow over pristine floors that never creak and furniture that looks too expensive to touch.

The kitchen is a chef's wet dream, fitted with state-of-the-art appliances, glossy marble countertops, and large cabinets. The island is massive, a centerpiece of luxury, but it's cold because no one has ever leaned against it, laughed over coffee, or made a mess of flour and sugar.

Or ginger ale.

I close my eyes, refusing to get consumed by that memory.

It might seem ancient in real time, but the months I spent sleeping feel like a couple of hours in my brain. I still can't force myself to think of that time as months.

My feet are sluggish as I walk out of the en suite bathroom, draped in a towel. I throw one last admiring glance at the jacuzzi set against a backdrop of ivory marble, brushed gold faucets, and sleek glass panels that reflect too much of my unsightly body back at me.

The bedroom is even more extravagant, draped in soft, rich fabrics and subtle gold accents that glimmer under dim lighting.

Beyond the bedroom, the balcony stretches into a massive terrace, offering an uninterrupted view of Graystone Ridge's skyline.

From up here, the town is breathtaking—a sprawl of glittering lights, the sky vast and endless in a way I've never seen before.

It should feel freeing and beautiful.

But as I slip into the oversized bed, journal and pen in hand, all I feel is discomfort.

The sheets are too soft, the silence too heavy, the air too still.

Because, no matter how stunning this place is, I don't want to get used to it.

It's not mine.

And I'd trade it for my old life with Dahlia in a heartbeat.

My eyes skim over the lines I wrote a couple of days ago.

I saw him today. Jude.

It was the first time I've seen him since I woke up.

All this time, I've waited for him to barge in uninvited and I've been…on edge. No, I've been hopeful?

I don't know what I was expecting, but it certainly wasn't the way he completely ignored me.

It was the first time I've truly felt that I actually spent months sleeping.

The world moved on, and so did he. Which is good. Right?

I slam the journal closed, frowning. Why the hell would I be this bothered by that encounter?

The look in his eye.

The way he seemed mad?

I'm the one who's supposed to be mad, especially after the attempted murder thing. Well, I don't know about that, really. I never believed Julian 100 percent, because I feel like if Jude wanted to kill me, he'd make it personal.

I also like to think he wouldn't hurt Mario like that.

But then again, my name was on his damn list, so…

I open my journal again and scribble a few other notes about the strange erotic dreams I've been having since that encounter and how a part of me wants them to come true even if the other part is ashamed I'm even having these thoughts.

The man in my dreams has a name, but I don't write it.
I can't make it real.

After I finish scribbling down everything muddying my
brain, I pause upon seeing rivulets of water sliding down the
bedroom window.

I check the time and frown. The Vipers' game Dahlia
went to see is ending soon, and she didn't take an umbrella,
no matter how many times I've told her to.

With a sigh, I put the journal on the nightstand and put
on a hoodie and jeans, choosing to forgo the glasses because
they'd fog up.

Armed with two umbrellas, I take a taxi to Vipers Arena.

I arrive when the masses are exiting the arena. Crowds
of people head to their cars or run in the rain. Some have
umbrellas, but most of them hide by the building overlooking
the parking lot.

But apparently, the Vipers won, considering all the
excited commentary.

"Callahan was a beast."

"I swear I get so fucking excited whenever he checks
someone."

"And the way he fights? Fucking awesome!"

Callahan this and Callahan that.

Yes, some others praise Preston and Kane, but most
people seem to have a boner for Jude. I don't think I'll ever
be able to understand hockey, because why is a notoriously
violent player everyone's favorite?

It takes me a while to slip through all the fans and stand
on an empty corner, holding one of the umbrellas over my
head. I text Dahlia.

Me: You forgot your umbrella, Dahl. It's raining. I'm

in the arena's parking lot near Kane's car. Come
pick it up.

Dahlia: Aw, thanks, Vi. You didn't have to.

Me: Of course I did. I don't want you to catch a cold.

Dahlia: On my way.

The moment I look up, I nearly drop the phone.

I'm holding the umbrella so low, I can only see sneakers,
jeans, and the hem of a leather jacket. But I know it's him,
even before I tilt the umbrella up, watching the rain cascade
down.

Jude stands in front of me, fully drenched, absolutely
unconcerned about the rain that beats down on him. His hair
is glued to his temples and his face is tight.

Too tight.

"What are you doing here, Violet?"

I pause because his voice sounds rougher, deeper. I wish I
didn't recognize that, and I wish my heart wasn't beating so
damn loudly right now.

"That's none of your business." I turn and start walking.

I don't know where I'm going or why I'm running away
from him.

Maybe it's because a part of me felt a crushing weight lift
off my chest upon seeing him.

Maybe it's because, really, I knew Kane could have an
umbrella and Dahlia wouldn't have been walking in the rain,
but I still *chose* to come here anyway.

Whatever it is, I realize I don't truly want to face Jude
right now.

A large hand grasps my wrist and spins me around. The
umbrella falls from my grip and hits the ground as Jude slams
me against the wall.

I'm drenched within seconds, rain falling on my face and hair, gluing my clothes to my body, but I'm consumed by Jude.

He's so close, I can smell him, the scent of wood and leather provokes memories I wanted to ignore until the end of my days.

"Why is it yellow this time?" His gruff words slip beneath my skin, feeling too intimate, too raw.

"What?"

He doesn't speak, just watches me as if I'm not real. The place where he grips my wrist tingles and burns, not even the rain is able to douse it.

The silence stretches for long, suffocating moments, and the tension wraps around my throat like a noose.

I can't read his expression.

But I can feel the tightness in his emotions spreading from his hand to my wrist, to my soul.

"Why did you do that to Mario?" I ask. I don't blurt it out, don't shout, just ask in a low, steady voice.

"Do what?"

"Let him be collateral damage. I know you hate me and want to kill me, but Mario was following your orders; he didn't deserve to be hurt by you."

"Hurt by me?"

"Yes! He's in a coma because you sent people to attack us—"

Jude grips my chin, slamming his other hand on the wall above my head. "You believe that?"

"That's what Julian said."

"And you believe whatever the fuck Julian says?"

No. But if it's not Jude, who else would want to hurt me?

"Believe whatever you want, but, Violet..." He leans

down, his breaths skimming my skin. "I better not see you parading yourself around the team, looking for a boyfriend like your sister."

Slap.

I don't know how I do it, how I lift my hand and just slap him, but I do. Because how dare he insinuate anything about my sister? I'll stab him to death if he ever hurts her, even with words.

My breaths are heavy as I stare at him, expecting his usual anger, but I'm slammed with a smile.

Almost as if he's…proud of me? Why would he be proud?

I think he'll say something, but Dahlia runs in our direction and drags me to her side. "Go away, Jude!"

My heart thunders when he glares at her. I swear I'll turn into the most toxic person if he causes her harm.

And I tell him that with my eyes when he looks at me. *Touch her and I'll hurt you, Jude.*

I don't know how I'll do that, but I'll figure out a way.

Instead of using his fists or force like he usually does, Jude actually walks away, and I release a long, fractured breath.

———

I've been overthinking since last night.

Dahlia joined Kane and the others to celebrate the Vipers' win but then came straight here to spend the night with me. She was visibly concerned about the way Jude cornered me.

I told her not to worry and even said I'd be fine on my own today, catching up on orders and sleep.

And while it's true I need to fulfill the order for one of my favorite clients, UnderTheUmbrella, who keeps paying me more than I deserve, I don't like being alone.

"I should probably get up and change from the bathrobe

I threw on last night into my pj's, but I don't feel like it." I squeeze my eyes shut, trembling slightly, because the thought of sleep still terrifies me. I can feel the shadows lurking in the room, even though I keep the light on low.

Ever since Mama died, I've always had some form of light on when I go to sleep, having spent too much time in that oppressive closet. Pitch darkness sends a shiver of trepidation down my spine.

As I drift off, I keep picturing Jude's face from last night.

And as I fall into slumber, I feel big hands wrap around my waist.

He's always rough and impatient in these types of dreams, his massive body looming over me like a threat.

A promise.

A possibility.

And it makes me rub my thighs together, the friction doing nothing to scratch at the hidden ache.

The need for…something.

Hot breaths, warm skin, and that intoxicating cologne I can't help but sniff and breathe into my lungs.

God, he smells good.

Feels good.

And forbidden.

I shouldn't want a monster this deeply, shouldn't wish for him to visit me in my dreams instead of the ghost of my mother.

Because unlike her, he doesn't call me names, doesn't remind me that I'm back to being alone, that I'll die alone, that someone like me doesn't deserve any form of companionship or happiness.

No.

Not like that.

The Jude of my dreams touches me sensually, like right now, his hands running up and down my sides, his muscular body pressing into my softer one, his breaths skimming my skin in a low, intimate whisper.

I'll wake up and feel shame later.

I'll wake up and question my sanity and beat myself up.

But since this is a dream, I fall into his touch, feeling the pad of his fingers, his presence, letting him awaken that insatiable hunger that's chained in self-imposed shackles.

I truly thought I didn't care about sex, and I had extremely bad first impressions of it. Whether with my mom's job or with my bad choices of men.

And yet these dreams, coupled with the strange sensations I felt whenever Jude touched me, have awakened a beast inside me.

And I'm starting to accept this different part, even if it's only in my subconscious or I talk about it in my journal.

My hand slides down, parting the bathrobe, and I flinch when the pads of my fingers stroke my folds.

"Mmm…" My dream Jude's voice is all rough and deep, and I'm wet now, my fingers rubbing and circling my clit.

"Are you dripping for me, sweetheart?"

"Y-yes…" I say, falling into those dark eyes from memories, picturing him looking at me with intense lust.

I don't want to open my eyes, because the second I do, he disappears.

Or worse—the momentary bliss transforms into a nightmare.

"Open your legs wider, let me see how you touch that wet pink cunt."

Heat rises to my cheeks, but I do as he asks, stroking myself faster, the obscene noise of my horniness echoing in the air.

"Push a finger inside you. Fuck that tiny cunt for me like a very good girl." His voice is rougher now, more gruff, and I think I hear a choked breath as I thrust a finger inside me.

"Mff…" My lips part.

"Does it feel good?"

"Yeah…"

"Add another finger, sweetheart, we have to stretch that cunt so you can take my cock."

"Okay…"

The second finger makes me feel so full, and I arch my back, feeling my nipples rub against the bathrobe I'm wearing.

"You're dripping all over the place."

"C-can't help it. It feels good."

"It does?"

"Mmm."

"Why?"

"Because you're watching me. Your gaze makes me so turned on."

"Fuck, sweetheart."

He shifts above me, and I hear the sound of unbuttoning and can imagine him pulling out that huge cock of his or tugging down on it.

"Spread that cunt for me. How else will you be able to fit this big cock?"

"Fuck…"

"You will take my cock, Violet. You'll open and stretch and moan when I stick it in your soaking pussy, won't you?"

"Yeah."

"That's it," he rasps. "Fuck yourself for me like a very good girl."

"Mmm." I rub on my clit with my thumb, pressure building inside me faster and more persistent.

I'm going to come from these dreams again.

I'll feel shitty again.

But I can't seem to give a damn.

"Are you going to come for me, sweetheart?"

"Y-yes…"

"Because you love how I watch you?"

"Yes."

"You don't look like it, but you have fucked-up fetishes, don't you?"

"Mff, yes."

"You like being ambushed in the dark? Fucked while you sleep like a dirty little whore?"

It's screwed up, but it's my dream and I can be myself in my dream. I can let my subconscious roam free a la Freudian, so I nod, touching myself faster.

"I do."

"You like being fucked hard and deep until you're screaming?"

"Y-yeah…"

"Who do you think about when you're dreaming, when you're rubbing that clit and moaning?"

"Y-you…"

"Am I the one you write about in the journal? Your forbidden fantasy?"

"Yeah…mmm, please…keep coming over, okay?"

"Oh, I will, sweetheart. I fucking will." The rough edge of his voice makes me delirious. "Come for me. Let me watch how I make you feel."

Not sure if it's his dirty talk or the way I can smell the sex, too potent and more real than any other dream, but my orgasm is paralyzing.

It rushes through every inch of me, my belly and legs

going stiff, then erupting in tremors as the waves of pleasure roll through me.

I think of his face when he was eating me out on the kitchen counter. Of how I was reflected in his rich brown irises when he looked fucking gorgeous just staring up at me. Or how he grunted and moaned when I had his cock in my mouth and he made me come like I've never come before.

This time is similar.

"You look so beautiful when you break apart for me, sweetheart." His voice sounds closer, his breath sending goosebumps along my skin.

I know I shouldn't, I know I should hold on to this dream for a while longer, but I open my eyes.

And my heart stutters.

Because Jude doesn't disappear.

His massive body looks ethereal in the low glow of the light as his knees straddle my face, his jeans open, his cock so hard, the veins are bulging.

And his eyes.

God, his eyes are the most beautiful eyes I've ever seen. Like the night, with tiny flecks of bright gold.

I can see myself in them again as he jerks himself roughly. "Fucking Christ, you're addictive. I can't quit you." He places the tip at my mouth. "Open. Take my cum."

I let my lips part and he comes deep inside my mouth, his body tightening, and he releases gruff noises that make my spent pussy throb.

Cum trails on either side of my mouth as he pulls out and tucks himself in. I'm watching in pure bemusement as to why I can still see him in my dream when I already opened my eyes.

Not that I'm complaining.

This is not a bad development per se. And I certainly love this over the tension I sensed from him at the arena last night.

He gathers the cum and thrusts it back into my mouth, watching me suck his fingers clean with darkened eyes. "That's a good girl."

A noise of protest leaves me when he pulls out his fingers and stands up.

"I'll see you tomorrow, Violet."

And then he's out the door, and I close my eyes, a weird sensation wrapping around my throat like a noose as I drift off.

That was a dream...right?

CHAPTER 23

Violet

Dahlia: Viii! Lunch together?

Dahlia: Actually, no question mark. Lunch together. I'll ask Kane to eat with his friends, so it's only us.

Me: You don't have to do that.

Dahlia: I want to. See ya!

AS I'M ABOUT TO POCKET MY PHONE WHILE WALKING out of my building, it pings.

Unknown number: You should leave this town while you still have the chance.

I frown, my fingers gripping the phone tight.

This can't be…Julian, right? For some reason, this seems way beneath him. That man would threaten me face-to-face or on the phone without having to resort to these tricks.

Besides, Kane clearly said Julian is taken care of. Not sure how, but it's been a couple of weeks since I returned to Graystone Ridge with Dahlia, and I've had no contact with Julian, so I believe Kane.

From my understanding, and all the smart-looking people I saw surrounding Julian when I signed that contract, he's powerful enough to eliminate me without threatening me.

Unless there's a benefit in *not* eliminating me?

My head slams into a solid wall, and I recoil. "Sorry…"

The word bunches up in my throat when I look up from the phone and my eyes crash with the deep dark-browns from last night's erotic dream.

And it *was* a dream.

It could have *only* been a dream.

"Do you lack the ability to watch where you're going?"

The rumble of his voice drags over my skin like sandpaper and silk all at once. A shiver rushes through me, leaving goosebumps in its wake.

Jude's so tall, so broad, his presence consumes the space and air around us. The black leather jacket strains over his shoulders, stretched taut by muscle, the fabric creaking slightly as he shifts. The T-shirt beneath it does nothing to hide the sharp ridges of his torso and the way his barely contained biceps flex.

But it's his face that makes my pulse stutter and my fingers tremble at forbidden dreams I refuse to acknowledge.

He's a grumpy, good-looking mess of closed-off but dangerously captivating features. Sharp jaw, full lips pressed in a firm line, and dark brows drawn together in a look that hovers between annoyance and something I can't read.

The intensity of his dark gaze presses against my ribs, my skin, and even though we're fully clothed and in public, it's like he's stripping me bare.

Like last night.

No. Absolutely not.

I step back, hide my phone, and start to sidestep him. I'm

simply not getting myself into the Jude mess after I finally escaped him.

My stupid fantasies that would get me killed don't matter—

A strong hand wraps around my arm and drags me back. The air whooshes out of my lungs as I stand in front of him, swaying slightly before I ground myself again.

"Where do you think you're going?"

"Away from you." I twist my arm, trying to set myself free, but he only tightens his hold.

"You sure about that?" There's a glint in his usually closed-off features, a rush of brightness and intensity that puts me on edge.

I still lift my chin. "Yes. How about you continue to ignore me like you have so far?"

"How can I ignore you when we have so much *unfinished* business?"

My lips part at the way he grunts the word *unfinished*. He steps into my space now, and I inhale his cologne that sets my skin ablaze.

Like it did last night when I was touching myself as the dream version of him watched me.

The orgasm was real, but I refuse to believe anything else was. I just...*can't*.

"Kane said he gave you the list in exchange for removing me from it. You should've killed me that time when you put Mario in a coma."

His jaw clenches, the pads of his fingers tightening around my upper arm. "You still think I attacked you?"

My lips tremble because his rage is seeping into my bones. I shouldn't even *feel* his rage, let alone be affected by it, but I still lift a shoulder. "I told you. That's what Julian said."

He releases a humorless bark of laughter. "Julian said I attacked you and you believed him, then proceeded to become his fucking lab rat?"

"He said he'd give me and Dahlia a new start away from you."

"Is that new start anywhere to be seen? Because you just came back right into my claws, Violet. Three months of slumbering did you no favors."

"Well, they kept me away from you and your suffocating attention."

I realize I've spoken too much when he narrows his eyes to slits. "Right. Risking death is *definitely* worth escaping me."

"You would've killed me anyway."

"If I wanted to kill you, no one would've been able to stop me, Violet. Not Julian and not fucking Kane. The only reason you're not buried six feet under is because *I* chose not to put a bullet in your pretty little head. Are we clear?"

My lips part because he sounded...offended? Maybe I'm being naïve again, but I believe Jude over Julian. It's probably because Jude never lied to me, and he's too straightforward to play games.

I swallow. "Am...I still a target?"

"No."

For some reason, that doesn't send relief through me. "Then why are you here?"

He lifts a brow. "I told you I'd see you tomorrow last night, remember?"

My heart stutters, thudding harshly behind my rib cage.

No. No, no, no, no...

"That was not... It's not..." I stop talking because I'm sweating, my ears are heating, and my eyes are so wide, I think they'll bulge out.

"It's not what?" He cocks his head to the side. "You swallowed my cum like a good girl after you finger-fucked your tiny cunt for me—"

I place both hands on his mouth as I study my surroundings, and I feel his lips curving beneath my palms.

"Shut up." I drop my hands. "It was just a dream."

"Sure. Let's call it that when I shove my cock into your tiny cunt the next time."

"Stop that, Jude."

"Mmm." There's a glint. No, a smile. How the hell does this man even know how to smile?

He's done it twice now, and it's giving me an existential crisis.

"I like the sound of my name in your voice."

My lips part, but I clear my throat. "Just…forget what happened last night. I thought it was a dream."

"Do you dream about me a lot?"

I step back, or try to anyway, because his grip forbids me from creating any form of distance. He's so close, and his scent is so overwhelming; my body is reacting, and my brain is a jumbled mess.

"Tell me, Violet. Am I the fantasy man you write about and dream of?"

He read my journal.

Damn it, of course the freaking stalker would.

God. This is so embarrassing.

If the earth could split open and swallow me whole, that would be awesome. Thanks.

"Did you touch yourself to memories of me every night?" His low voice sends shivers through me.

Why the hell is it so hot in freaking February?

"Please. I don't even like you," I say in my calmest tone.

"Didn't stop you from shattering to pieces in front of me."

"I was thinking of someone else," I lie through my teeth.

Something curious happens then.

A flash.

A tightening of his jaw and a gradual darkening of his eyes. "Someone else?"

His voice sounds impossibly deep, like it's ringing from the wildest corner of hell.

"Yeah," I whisper.

"Who is this *someone else*?"

"No one you know."

"I know *everyone* in your fucking life, Violet."

"That's not something you should be proud of."

"Don't change the subject. Who is it?"

"Don't be desperate." I pause, biting my lower lip. "Just leave me alone."

"So you can keep picturing *someone else* while you touch yourself at night?"

"What if I do?"

His lips lift in a snarl. "There will be no one but me, Violet. Your life is mine, and so is your fucking body. You hear me?"

"Yeah, well, you can have neither my heart nor my soul."

He's angry.

No, he has that enraged expression he wears when he's about to beat someone up on the ice or snap a hockey stick in two.

Why the hell am I provoking him, really?

Because I'm embarrassed and he's pissing me off, that's why.

He leans down, his mouth so close to mine, I can feel his minty breath on my sensitive skin. "I will have your fucking everything, sweetheart."

"I'm not your sweetheart. I'm not your *anything*."

It's a challenge to keep looking him in the eye, but I do, refusing to let him stomp all over me again.

Maybe because I already faced death, but Jude will no longer stop me from living my life.

"We'll see about that." He drags me behind him to where he parked his huge bike.

"What are you doing?" I try to shake off his grip, but fighting Jude's strength is like going against a damn bull.

He offers me the helmet. "Hop on."

"No, I won't. I have school."

"I'll give you a ride."

"No, thanks."

"Hop the fuck on, Violet. Don't make me repeat myself."

"I won't—" My words end on a yelp when he grabs my hips and lifts me up, then sets me on the bike as if I'm a rag doll.

Before I can say anything, he shoves the helmet on my head and then puts on his own and drives off.

The distance to campus isn't that far since the place Kane bought for me is about a twenty-minute walk, but with the way Jude's speeding, I feel like I'm fighting for my life.

And I have to wrap my unsteady arms around his waist, or I'll fall.

The moment I try to loosen them, he speeds up.

We're in front of the human sciences building at GU in three minutes flat, and judging by the annoyed breath he releases, it seems he doesn't like the fact that we arrived in no time.

I'm ready to just disengage and disappear into school.

When I hop off on unsteady feet, I'm painfully aware of the multiple eyes flashing toward us. Whispers, stares, people stopping and looking, some getting their friends' attention.

Gossip.

Words.

Hate.

Shit. It's like Mama's death all over again. Being the center of bad attention, of malicious stares and whispered words.

It's excruciatingly painful for people who don't know you to assume and spout rumors about you just for their entertainment. Almost as if I'm no longer human and just an object in their eyes.

My fingers shake as I try to undo the strap of the helmet.

God damn it.

I forgot that Jude is kind of worshiped at GU and in this town as the hockey god and source of violent entertainment. They idolize him and the Vipers as if they're immortals amongst humans.

Since he showed up with a girl on his bike, it's naturally put me and my shabby hoodie and jeans under scrutiny.

I truly dislike having my body be the center of attention. It makes me feel on edge.

My nail catches on the strap and my hand slips off, but before I can try again, bigger, stronger hands wrap around mine, unclasp the strap, and he pulls the helmet over my head.

Jude's touch is disturbingly gentle as he removes the strands of hair that got stuck to my glasses and tucks them behind my ear.

"What are you doing?" I whisper, seeing some people pull out their phones. "They're watching."

"I don't give a fuck. From today on, you're mine to do with as I please, Violet."

"Do I get a say in this?"

"No. It's payback."

I let out a sigh. "You still didn't forget about revenge after all. Did you disappear after I woke up from the coma to give me a sense of safety before you barged back in? Am I a punching bag for your frustration and anger issues?"

"Think whatever the fuck you want. The only fact that remains is that I'm claiming you, and there will be no one else."

And then his lips crash against mine, devouring me. His hand rests possessively on my neck as he drags me out of my tiny bubble for the entire campus to see.

———

"Is it true?"

I wince as Dahlia pins me with a stare. We're at a local restaurant at her insistence, and, honestly, I'd rather just eat at the cafeteria, but all the stares were becoming unbearable.

Hell, I was even cornered by a few girls and guys who demanded to know my relationship status with Jude, but when I said there was no relationship, they didn't believe me.

The chatter around us heightens as Dahlia keeps staring at me.

"It's not what you think," I whisper after I swallow a mouthful of the falafel wrap I'm eating.

"Uh…then what is this?" She pulls out her phone and shows me a picture posted on some social media platform.

Of Jude kissing me.

Damn.

He has me by the throat, my glasses are hiked up my nose, and I have a hand on his chest because I was trying to push him, but that doesn't show in the photo.

It just seems that he's devouring me, plain and simple.

And he was. My lips were tingling the entire morning.

Damn him.

"Oh my God." Dahlia puts her phone away, her face paling. "Did he force you? Is he still threatening you? Because I'll have Kane—"

"It's not that. Don't make a big deal out of it, okay?"

"Considering he intended to kill you after he stalked you, yeah, I say I'll make the biggest deal out of it. So what if he's scary? I can be scary too or…like, Kane can be."

I smile and take a sip out of my ginger ale. "Don't be the one who comes between best friends, Dahl."

"Well, if his best friend is bothering my sister, I'll have words. Lots of them."

God, she's so fearless. I love that about her to bits.

But I'm also scared for her safety, and I definitely don't want her to be on Jude's shit list. Or for Kane and Jude to have a falling out because of me. It's why I refused to tell her what happened after I woke up from the coma, but truly, I dislike hiding things from Dahlia, and she's also persistent, so I ended up telling her about the stalking and why Jude came into my life.

In pure Dahlia fashion, she threatened to kill Jude, then she blamed herself for not noticing, which is the whole reason I didn't confide in her in the first place. I hate that she still blames herself for my coma no matter how many times I made it clear that it's not her fault.

I wish I was back to working long shifts at HAVEN and worrying about each month's bills.

Because Jude's attention is not only murdering my invisibility, but it's also provoking a side of me that terrifies me.

I know he'll keep his word.

And despite the fear, the trepidation, and everything in between, a part of me is looking forward to that.

"It's just complicated," I say truthfully.

Dahlia stops with a French fry halfway to her mouth. "What do you mean by complicated?"

"I don't think Jude would hurt me."

"But you were so scared at the mere mention of his name after you woke up."

"It's…because he puts me on edge, but it's not necessarily bad. I'll figure it out, okay? Just don't bring Kane into this."

"I still don't like him roaming around you. I went through hell during the time you were in a coma." Her lips tremble. "I don't ever want to lose you again, Vi."

"You won't." I stroke her hand. "I promise."

Being in that coma made me realize what really matters. It's not my fractured childhood or my shitty past. It's not the broken personality Mama gave me or my attempts to bury it all.

It's having the luck to meet Dahlia and becoming each other's family. It's helping people like Laura and Karly who I paid a visit to the other day. It's finding my wings through my small embroidered pieces that many people seem to love.

It's surviving one day at a time so I can see Dahlia smiling and happy.

I don't ever want to be the reason for her pain like when I was in the coma.

If it's for her, I think I can hold on a bit tighter and just stop being a burden so she doesn't overthink my safety or well-being.

"Why, if it isn't Dallas."

A large guy slides onto the chair next to my sister, throwing a hand over her shoulder. Preston.

He's dazzlingly handsome and seems to brighten up the

scene with his presence—nothing about his beauty is concealed or subtle or dark like Jude.

Stop thinking about him.

"It's Dahlia." She glares at him, but he's not looking at her as he steals one of her fries and smiles at me with those deep dimples creasing his cheeks.

For some reason, he looks so...familiar. Though I'm pretty sure I only saw him on TV before and only 'met' him the other day. "Hi, Violet. You still didn't give me an answer to my question."

"What question?" Dahlia stares between us. "And since when do you know Vi?"

"Since now. Listen..." He eats more of her fries as she tries and fails to push him off. "I'm like the prodigy child and totally the best catch when compared to Kane and Jude—and yes, that means you two obviously don't have taste. But even though I wasn't picked, I need to make sure no one is playing my friends. You know, some medieval code of honor or some shit. Point is, you need to have my approval, which you still didn't completely earn, by the way, Daniella."

"Well, let me just drop to my knees and beg real quick."

"That would be an ideal start." He takes her drink, and she grabs it, too.

"Just order your own!"

"But I want this."

"You don't always get what you want."

"Of course I do, Delilah." Some of the drink spills on his hand, and I push mine in his direction, removing the straw.

Dahlia loves her soft drink more than I do, so I'd rather he have mine.

"Aw, you're so nice, Vee. I can see why Callahan is obsessing." He grins, gulping half of it in one go. "He and I always had a soft spot for the kind ones. Comes with all the love we totally didn't receive as children. Oh, and the mommy issues. Big man and I share that in spades."

"Mommy issues?" I ask, leaning closer on my chair.

If I want to handle Jude better, I need to learn more about him, and there's no better source of information than Preston.

"I'm glad you asked." He places both elbows on the table. "He was the parent to his mom. She was a fucking mess, both mentally and physically, but the times she was all right, she showered him with love, and Jude chooses to completely erase the bad in his mind and only keep the soft, kind-natured version of her." He taps the side of his head. "If you look closely, there's a scar on the right side of his head. Because she tried to kill herself and he stopped her, so she hit him with a vase there. If it weren't for Julian, she might have killed him. Scary stuff, right?"

"That is scary," Dahlia whispers.

"Oh, you're still here, Dinah?" He sighs, then grins. "I was just kidding about everything I just told you."

Something tells me that's not the case.

He's not joking.

All this time, I thought Jude mourned his mother because she was his light in the darkness, but what Preston just revealed makes me question something.

Does he feel a toxic attachment to her like I do with Mama?

CHAPTER 24

Jude

I HAD EVERY INTENTION OF LETTING VIOLET GO.

Not because of Julian's or Kane's threats. I couldn't give two fucks about those, and they certainly don't influence my actions.

It's because of something deeper.

Because she chose death to fucking escape me.

Violet preferred to take an experimental drug that had a high percentage chance of killing her just so she could have another life away from me.

She didn't attempt suicide like I was led to believe that day she was attacked, but she still chose death over me.

A coma.

Leaving the one person she deeply cares about, Dahlia, and risking never opening her eyes again.

Just to escape me.

For that reason, I kept my distance after she woke up. I avoided her, even—which was difficult, considering we live in the same town and attend the same college.

During the time I stayed in the shadows, I indulged in my favorite habit.

Murder.

I killed more people in a couple of weeks than I normally

did in a month, enabling Preston's mania in the process. But then again, I couldn't control myself, let alone help rein him in.

We did it for Vencor instead of my vendetta because I'm trying to prolong it. I'm down to only three names on my list.

Three.

And then I'll have no purpose.

Mom will still be gone, and there'll be…nothing.

Maybe that's why I came back into Violet's life. Maybe it's because I saw her talking to Preston and having lunches with Kane and Dahlia and hated that my friends got her smile and I didn't.

Maybe it's because I saw her by the arena and was enraged that she might have her sights on someone on the team.

Not sure what the actual reason is, but I fell so easily back into old habits. It's almost as if I never stopped.

Like right now.

I put in the code to her penthouse and walk in.

And yes, I have the code. Of course I do.

She won't know how I have it, though.

So, yes, I'm back, even though I truly intended to let her go.

Just kidding.

I would've always only done that temporarily, but still, I was going to avoid contact with her for at least a month.

Just kidding again.

Because I was around. I couldn't have avoided her when I've been roaming in her environment. She just wasn't aware of me, because Violet has shit awareness of her surroundings.

Or I'm just that good at camouflaging my presence.

I was here when Dahlia and Kane first showed her this house. I was on the terrace, actually, watching through the window, just to see her reaction to all the blue.

Violet was half in awe, half uncomfortable because she

doesn't like to owe others and she feels like she's imposing on Kane.

I could read all of that on her face even when she was smiling, and it disturbed me because why the fuck am I that good at reading her?

After that, I didn't come around here as much. Until a week ago.

My steps are silent as I walk into the dimly lit space. There's always a light on here—*always*. She turns it on remotely about half an hour before she comes in.

Over the past few weeks, Violet has added a few personal touches to the place—some throws and embroideries on the pillowcases in the form of stars, half-moons, suns, and a tree of life. It's like the sketches she scribbles in her journal.

The same journal that shoved me back into her life at full speed.

I didn't mean to come in while she was working. I only ever wanted to…check on things. See if she's having any suicidal thoughts again.

And the best place to look into her thought process is her journal.

But instead of suicidal thoughts and her usual musings about why her mom didn't love her, I found something a lot more interesting.

Entries upon entries of sexual fantasies.

And not just any fantasies—Violet has a somnophilia fantasy. She wanted to be visited by the man of her dreams in the middle of the night and be ravaged whole.

Which I almost did when she was thrusting her fingers inside her cunt for me to see. The only reason I didn't fuck her was because I needed to talk to her about it first and I wouldn't have been able to stop.

It was pure fucking torture not to ram my hard cock into her wet, glistening cunt. But I did come down that pretty throat as she blinked up at me with lust and pure confusion.

I can still see her face flushing a deep shade of red and her eyes growing wide and glittery blue.

It's fruitless to wonder why the fuck Violet is the only woman who's had this effect on me. Fucking has always been an animalistic need for me, just like violence, so I couldn't care less about my sexual partners, and they couldn't care less about me either. It's always been physical and fleeting, where I fuck the girls, they have a good time, and then it's over.

This is the first time I've wanted to own someone, chain them to me, not allow them to leave my goddamn sight.

And that someone had to be *Violet*.

And Violet, thinking I no longer snoop in her journal, has been writing constantly about sex lately. She didn't even mention the time I ate her on the kitchen counter or how she rode my boot in that alley, but I now know it's because she didn't want me to see her thoughts.

She has lots of those—thoughts about sex and fantasies.

One of them is being ambushed. She mentioned that it happened in her dreams with her fucking fantasy man, who I'll find and maim to pieces.

Because she can't have anyone but me.

She *won't*.

Which is why I'm here again. To erase any motherfucker she has fantasies about.

I'll fulfill *all* of her fantasies, especially this ambushing one. My own demons roar at the thought of her trembling body beneath mine.

Her breaths stuttering like when I kissed her for the world to see this morning.

Her heart thundering like when she held on to me on the back of the bike.

Fuck.

I'm getting hard already.

My cock seems to have a mind of its own whenever Violet's involved.

I adjust my erection and grab her Kindle from the top of the coffee table. All her physical books are some self-help nonsense and human sciences garbage.

So I expect her Kindle to reflect that.

Wrong.

My brows arch when I find what seems to be romance books with skulls, snakes, or men on the covers.

Hmm.

I take a picture of what's in there, especially the ones she has in a 'Favorite' folder, so I can do better research.

I'm about to open one of the books when my phone dings.

Kane: What the hell is this, Callahan?

Attached is a picture of me kissing Violet.

I save it.

Preston: It's called kissing? Something you do a lot of with Daphne, remember?

Kane: You stay out of it.

Preston: No can do. I'm Jude's defender for life, and I like Vee.

Me: Her name is Violet.

Preston: Nah, too long. She's so adorable, BTW! Had lunch with her earlier, and she gave me her drink and even shared her food. I want her.

Me: You'll want your fucking grim reaper when I'm
done with you, Pres.

Preston: Jeez. I was just saying. Figuratively. Unless, it
becomes literally. You never know.

Me: Fuck around and find out.

Preston: It's not in your best interest to piss me off
when I can spill all your secrets, big man.

Kane: As I was saying, what the fuck were you doing,
Jude?

Me: I don't answer to you.

Preston: What Jude said.

Kane: You promised to stay the hell away from her
when I gave you the full list.

Me: I never mentioned how long I'd stay away. Also,
technically, I only promised not to kill her, which is a
promise I'm keeping.

Preston: I also vote don't kill her.

Kane: Dahlia is worried you'll pull some shit.

Me: I don't give a fuck about what Dahlia thinks.

Preston: Me, neither. *high five gif*

Kane: Well, I do. And I won't sit still if you hurt her only
family.

Me: Is that a threat?

Preston: I vote a threat. Let's fight.

Kane: It is whatever the fuck you see it as. I didn't
spend precious resources to keep Julian away so
you'd ruin it. If you're messing with Dahlia, you're
messing with me.

Preston: BRB, I'm gonna bring my favorite knife. This
will be epic.

Me: I told you this before and I'll say this again. Stay
the fuck out of my business, Kane.

Whatever I do with Violet is none of his or Dahlia's business.

Not even sure what the fuck I want to do with her in the first place.

Except stake a claim so no other assholes will come near her.

That one's for sure.

Everything else, however, is still wobbly and tentative. In a sense, it feels like the start of something new.

In the beginning, I approached Violet to torment and kill her, but now, I don't possess any trace of those thoughts.

Not sure when they completely disappeared, but it happened long before she was in a coma.

There's still anger, though. Or maybe it's tension. Aggression.

A need to fucking punish her for choosing to go into a coma.

My phone lights up with a text from Preston, who's been trolling this entire conversation, but I don't get to read it, because the sound of the door unlocking echoes in the penthouse.

I click on the app on my phone, turning the entire place pitch-black. The only light comes from the town seeping through the large window.

My vision instantly adjusts to my surroundings, courtesy of countless hunts in dark forests.

Violet, however, panics.

I can see the contours of her body as she freezes, her limbs locking before she fumbles in her pocket for her phone.

"Shit," she whispers, her voice trembling, her fingers unsteady.

She truly is afraid of the dark.

One more reason why this is the perfect setting for what I have planned.

"God." She taps fast, her movements chaotic, her breathing shallow.

The door closes behind her, and she visibly jumps, dropping the phone. As it clatters on the floor, light glows from the screen, and Violet starts to lower herself to pick it up.

But I'm already moving.

As if walking on nonexistent ground, I'm completely drawn to the girl I should've stayed away from but couldn't.

Not since the very first time I saw her.

Or the second.

Or the hundredth.

There's something about Violet Winters that calls to a strange side of me. It might have to do with the disturbing memories that plagued my sleep after Julian said she chose to be his lab rat and risk death just to escape me.

Or distant memories of soft hands that turned brutal or tears that couldn't be wiped away.

No matter how much I've tried to separate the two, Violet and my childhood memories seem to correlate.

A part of me is rebelling at that thought, writhing and falling and rolling and revolting at the very thought of those memories that I erased a long time ago.

The murmurs.

The screams.

The blood.

They're getting louder and more vicious, screeching and ripping at the bandages with bloodied fingers.

But the moment I touch Violet, they fade into the background, their slimy forms retreating and vanishing from sight.

She goes still, even as I push her against the wall, twisting and securing both her wrists behind her back with one hand.

Her body slowly relaxes as I lean into her, my cock raging hard against her ass and my mouth a few beats away from her cheek.

I'm breathing harshly and so is she, her inhales stuttering, her lips parting, begging to wrap around my goddamn cock.

But even with her erratic breathing, she's not stiff.

I know she recognizes me even before she whispers, "J-Jude?"

"Mmm." I nuzzle my nose in her hair and briefly close my eyes as the scent of her rose shampoo overloads my senses.

Why the fuck am I even sniffing her hair?

"What are you doing?" she asks in a small but clear voice.

I grab her jaw and speak so close to her lips, I touch them with every word. "Going through your list of fantasies one at a time. You wanted to be ambushed and used, remember?"

She trembles, but her body melts against mine, her fingers twitching. "That's not…"

"Blue," I say.

"What?"

"Say blue, and I'll stop."

Her breathing cracks, then her lips accidentally touch mine, and she purses them but doesn't say the word blue and, instead, nods.

Because she's defective just like me, my Violet.

I always thought we shared a fucked-up connection, and it's about time to see how fucked up it can be.

"This is about to get dirty. Buckle up, sweetheart."

CHAPTER 25
Violet

MY HEART IS ABOUT TO JUMP OUT OF MY THROAT.

It thumps faster, thudding against the walls of my rib cage, slipping through the bones, and cutting itself on the edges.

Because holy hell.

I knew Jude would come find me. He made it clear this morning after the very public display in front of the entire campus.

The moment he devoured me, I realized he isn't done with me.

In fact, he never was.

And now, he's breathing against my neck in the dark, his hot exhales making goosebumps erupt on my skin, rushing beneath the surface and stealing my own breath.

He looms over me, towering behind me taller and broader than the darkness.

And, for a moment, I forget my irrational fear of the dark.

I forget about how I squeezed my eyes shut and slammed both hands to my ears in a fruitless attempt to silence the darkness.

Because right now, I'm plagued by tremors and warmth.

And I can't chase away this reaction I have whenever Jude touches me. My brutal awareness of him is heightening, lengthening, and becoming so maddening that I find it hard to breathe.

His large hand slides around my spine, his fingers grazing my skin beneath the hoodie as he unbuttons my jeans.

My toes curl in my shoes, and a yelp rips out of me when he shoves the jeans down, a sound of tearing fabric echoing in the air.

"Mm." He grabs a handful of my ass, and even though it's over my panties, my heart throbs and so does my aching pussy.

Am I turned on by his manhandling?

How can I be this horny because he actually did ambush me, shove me against the wall, and is touching me this roughly?

Blue.

That's the word I need to say to stop this.

So why am I pressing my lips together, refusing to even think about it?

Slap.

I go up on my tiptoes as Jude kneads the ass cheek he just spanked, then he does it again. Slapping, then kneading, alternating between my ass cheeks.

And again.

And again.

Mixing pain with sensual pleasure.

I'm trembling all over, unshed tears blurring my vision, but they're more like pleasure tears, really, because I've never been this wet before.

"I want to make your skin red and fill it the fuck up with my bruises," he whispers in dark words near my ear. "I want to mark you so thoroughly that no one dares to fucking touch what's mine."

His words should appall me.

Disturb me.

This man is sick.

But apparently, so am I, because each of his words feels like a lick of heat against my most intimate part.

Jude releases my jaw and glides two fingers over my panties. "Fuck, sweetheart. You're soaking wet for me."

I drop my forehead on the wall, shame and humiliation ripping through me.

He squeezes my aching ass cheek as he slides his finger beneath the seam of my panties. "Do you like how I touch you, Violet? How I'll use this tight little cunt to get off?"

"Do you have to talk like that—"

My words end on a moan when he thrusts two fingers inside me. My body tightens and, to my horror, I can feel my pussy clenching around him.

"Yes. That's it." He spanks me again, and I whimper, tingles erupting over my skin and all my blood rushing to where he's touching me. "Your cunt is strangling me, sweetheart. God, you're so tight... How are you going to take my cock if you're struggling with my fingers, hmm?"

His thumb rubs my clit as he thrusts deeper, rougher, with a rhythm that commands and demands my entire attention.

"Oh God..." I mumble, the pleasure heightening and heightening until I'm panting, vibrating, completely taken in by the beautiful nightmare that is Jude Callahan.

"Shh..." He slaps my ass again, slowing his thrusts. "Don't rush into it. I need to stretch you out properly so I can stick my cock into this tiny cunt. You'll take me, won't you, sweetheart?"

He scissors his fingers inside me and flicks my clit at the same time. A spark of pleasure slithers through me, and my fingers curl against the wall, beads of sweat coating my temples.

Just when I'm about to fall apart, he slows down, his breath scorching hot against my cheek. "Answer me, Violet. You will take me like a very good girl, right?"

"Mmm."

"That's not an answer."

"Yes...please..."

"Fuck. I love it when you beg." He pounds into me. "Ask me to make you come on my fingers."

"I..."

"Say it, Violet."

"Please..."

"Full." *Slap.* "Sentence."

"Please let me come." I'm panting, my stomach tightening and my heart hammering so loud, I think it'll somehow combust.

I shouldn't be doing this.

He shouldn't be doing this.

We shouldn't be doing this.

And yet I'm falling with no landing in sight.

"I said." His hand lands on my ass in three consecutive slaps. "The full sentence."

"Please let me come on y-your fingers..." I'm sobbing now because the mixture of pleasure and pain is so intense, I can't see anything past them.

Not the fucked-up situation.

Not the man who's ripping this part out of me.

Not the fact that I'm *begging* him to use me.

Not even the darkness.

"That's a *good girl.*" His voice drops on the last two

words, all but growling in my ear. "Come for me, sweetheart. Show me how much you want to be used."

I don't know if it's that or the way he calls me sweetheart or how he expertly thrusts inside me or even the feel of the sting mixed with pleasure, but I'm falling.

My whole body goes still as the rush of pleasure vibrates through me. I'm trembling against him, my fingers slipping off the wall as the orgasm rips through me.

It's so intense, my knees buckle, and I would've fallen if it weren't for his grip on my ass holding me upright—and his fingers in my pussy.

"You made a fucking mess, sweetheart." There's a dark chuckle to his words as he pulls his fingers out, but before I can die of shame, he flips me around, and the world tilts from beneath my feet.

I gasp as he lifts me up so effortlessly and throws me over his shoulder with my head dangling against his back.

I, a full-grown woman, am on a man's shoulder.

But it's not just any man. It's Jude Callahan.

My stalker. The man who hates me.

The man I tried to avoid but couldn't.

And in hindsight, I don't think I ever would've.

He pulls down my jeans and panties fully, discarding them somewhere I can't see, and places a big, rough hand on my sore ass. I rub my thighs together at the sensation because, apparently, my body mistakes this for pleasure.

Because pain comes with blinding pleasure with this man.

It came with an orgasm so powerful, I'm actually a bit dizzy now.

Jude's steps are wide and controlled, his touch firm and nonnegotiable as he grips me tight.

Almost as if he never wants to let me go.

"W-what are you doing?" I whisper in the dark silence.

"Keeping up with the user manual you wrote."

"What...?"

I don't realize we're in the bedroom until he throws me on the bed and I bounce off the mattress.

"The next step after the ambushing." He grins, looking devilish. "Devouring."

There's a faint light here, and I can see in full detail how Jude lifts his shirt over his head.

I always knew he was muscular, big, and just packed, but actually seeing him half naked is an entirely different beast.

God, he's beautiful.

Toned and cut, and extremely well-proportioned, as if he's been sculpted by an artist.

But that's not what makes me stop and stare. It's the tattoos.

Many of them.

I've seen his full sleeves before, but now, they're everywhere. His arms, chest, ribs, and abs.

I can't stop staring at the one on his upper bicep that curls toward his chest. A shadowy black wolf with glowing red eyes, its head slightly tilted downward as if stalking its prey. The wolf's front paw is stepping over a field of broken skulls.

Or the one in the center of his abs. A detailed black raven in mid-flight, its wings spread as if caught between rising and falling. A dagger pierces its chest, and black ink drips from the wound like poisoned blood. The dagger's hilt has an intricate design, resembling a twisted crown or a snake curling around it.

They send a shiver through me.

A slight premonition that I shouldn't be allowing this man to touch me, let alone have this hold over me.

But then I see a different type of tattoo on the left side of his rib cage, stretching slightly toward his back.

There's a twisted barren tree with jagged, lifeless branches etched in deep black ink. Beneath the tree, a single closed umbrella rests against the roots.

I frown, but before I can study the rest, he pulls his jeans and boxers down his V line, revealing his hard cock. It bobs free, looking a bit purple with angry veins pulsing on the undersides and precum coating the crown.

My mouth waters because I truly love that I can turn him on this much, but a slither of apprehension goes through me.

It's been a long time since I saw his cock in the alley, but how come it looks bigger? I've never had someone as big as him, and I'm kind of losing confidence. What if he doesn't fit? What if I'm a disappointment again—

"You look so goddamn beautiful when you're ogling me, sweetheart."

He's the one who's ogling me now. His heated eyes feel like fingers on my naked flesh.

A part of me wants to hide.

The part that shrinks beneath oversized clothes and thick glasses.

The part that still believes I'm as ugly and worthless as Mama said.

The part that feels unsightly, unwanted.

But the way he looks at me forces those thoughts to scatter.

Because right now?

Right now, I feel alive.

I gulp, the sound echoing around us as he kneels between

my legs and then grips my hand and wraps it around his length. His cock grows bigger, pulsing like crazy in my palm.

"Mmm. Fuck. You feel what your touch does to me?"

I gape at him, my heart thundering so loudly, I'm sure he can hear it. He can hear how his words are doing the strangest shit to me.

Because I'm stroking him up and down, using his precum as lube, and my core is getting slicker and wetter with each of his grunts.

"You're making me nice and hard so I can fuck you?"

I bite my lower lip. "Why...do you want to fuck me, Jude?"

"Because you want to be ravaged, and no one but me can fuck you."

"Shouldn't you hate me?"

"I should." His voice is a soft grunt as he grabs my hand that's around his cock, squeezing slightly.

"Then why don't you leave me alone?" I'm murmuring low as he guides my hand and his cock to my entrance.

"I can't."

I watch with pure fascination as he slowly slides inside me.

He stuffs me full of him, making my heart beat in sync with his pulsing cock.

"God damn." He grunts, giving a harsh shove of his hips and burying himself deep in my pussy. "God fucking damn it, you're tight, sweetheart."

I'm soaking wet, like truly and utterly turned on by this monster of a man, but he's still huge, like really big, and he stretches me more than I've ever been stretched before.

Then he fills me up.

To the brim.

Until he's everything I can feel.

It hurts a bit, and a part of me believes I'm making a big mistake, but the other part—the part that scribbled and wrote all those fantasies in the journal, the part that had malevolent butterflies slaughtering each other when he kissed me in front of the world—is at peace.

I never thought I'd feel peace or even know the notion of it, but Jude sliding his hand to my throat and staying still, his face tight and his temples glistening with sweat because he's forcing himself not to move, is somehow…peaceful.

Comforting, too.

Because he's allowing me to adjust even though he's struggling with it.

"Fucking hell." He breathes harshly, squeezing my throat the slightest bit. "God damn…relax for me, beautiful."

He called me beautiful.

"Breathe, Violet." He strokes my pulse point back and forth.

"It's too big…" I strain.

"I know, but you're taking my cock like a very good girl. Relax…that's it." He moves a little. "You feel so good, beautiful."

"I…do?" I'm grabbing onto his arm because he's thrusting slowly, making me get used to the rhythm before he slams in.

"Your cunt is the best thing I've ever been in."

I know he probably says that to every girl he fucks, but that doesn't stop my heart from thudding or the butterflies in my stomach from multiplying.

My legs relax further as his thrusts grow more powerful, his grip on my neck grounding me and his eyes peering into mine.

I look to the side, my body tightening and clenching around him.

He's fucking me so hard and deep, the headboard slams into the wall with each thrust.

"Look at me," he orders with a slap to my pussy.

I squeal, my eyes flying to his, and what I see in his deep-brown ones holds me captive.

The lust, possessiveness, and even hatred swirl on his face and rush through me.

"Is this what you imagined when you were writing those fantasies? Your cunt being used so thoroughly you can hardly breathe?"

I can't focus, because he just thrust against a spot inside me I thought didn't exist, and my vision lines with stars.

"Answer me."

"Yes...yes..."

"You'll never let anyone else but me see you like this, Violet, are we clear?"

"Fuck...right there...please..."

"Tell me you're only mine."

"Yours...just..." I don't know what type of nonsense I'm blabbering as I shatter on his cock.

The orgasm hits me out of nowhere and is so overwhelming that I'm momentarily taken aback.

It doesn't matter that I just came, because my whole body erupts in spasms as I scream Jude's name.

"Fuck, you're beautiful." He grunts, slapping the side of my ass cheek, and it makes me come a bit more, my stomach tightening, and my hard nipples poking through my hoodie.

Jude thrusts deeper, using me as he promised, but it doesn't feel like it.

No, not in the least.

As he strokes and squeezes my neck, kneads my ass or sucks on my collarbone, I feel him growing bigger and harder.

Soon after, he grunts, the masculine sound making me wetter even though I just came.

"You going to take my cum deep in this cunt, sweetheart?"

I nod, staring at him.

"That's my fucking good girl."

I almost come again when he tenses and growls as his warmth spills inside me.

God, he looks so handsome when he comes. All cut lines and jagged edges.

I lift a hand and touch his forehead tentatively. He tenses, but he seems to be too busy orgasming to focus much on my touch.

That's when I see it.

Right on the left corner of his forehead, buried beneath the hair, is a long scar. The one Preston mentioned.

And now that he's so close, I can see all the other scars buried beneath his tattoos, and my chest squeezes.

Just…what type of horror did he have to go through?

When he breathes harshly, I drop my hand, not wanting to kill the mood.

I brace myself for when he'll fall on top of me like all guys do, crushing me in their post-orgasm halo. Jude is a heavy man, so hopefully, he doesn't stay like that for long—

Instead, he pulls me up by his hand beneath my back so that I'm sitting on his lap, one of his arms around my waist and the other deep in my hair.

"Stay with me, sweetheart."

"W-what?"

"We're not done. I've only just gotten started."

CHAPTER 26
Violet

"YOU THINK YOU DESERVE PEACE AFTER YOU RUINED MY life, you worthless piece of shit?"

I gasp awake, my throat closing and my limbs shaking uncontrollably.

It's over.

Mama's face with protruding cheekbones and flashing hatred in her eyes was just a dream.

And that dream is *over*.

I shift and pain explodes all over my body, but mostly my ass and sore pussy.

Memories from last night flash back in.

The ambushing, the spanking, and the fucking—a lot of fucking.

Pretty sure Jude kept at it for hours and probably only stopped when I kind of fell asleep in the shower.

He must've been the one who finished cleaning me up, dressed me in his shirt, and carried me to bed, because I don't remember leaving the bathroom, let alone going to bed.

The man is a machine. It seemed as if he couldn't get enough. As if he suffered from an acute thirst that couldn't be quenched, and it turned me on for some reason.

The whole thing did—from the way he couldn't stop and

was hard again so soon after he came, to how he wanted to fuck me in all positions possible while speaking dirty words in my ear and calling me a good girl.

His good girl.

The girl he couldn't get enough of.

No wonder I can barely walk. I even have to hold on to the nightstand for balance.

Damn.

I don't think I'll be able to go to class today. I'm so sore and achy all over. I pull open the bathrobe, and my body is full of dark-purple hickeys.

Usually, I don't like seeing my body naked, but I don't seem to mind when Jude's ripping my clothes off.

I stand in front of the full-length mirror and study the marks he left everywhere. My neck, collarbones, breasts, thighs, and ass are full of hickeys, handprints, and bite and finger marks.

Damn. I look abused, but I'm blushing.

Because every mark brings back memories of how he touched me. It was rough and unapologetic and out of control, but I felt...worshiped.

And he didn't really hurt me. He always slowed down when it started to be too much, and he could tell from just the look in my eyes.

As if he could read what I was feeling.

That's stupid.

Jude only sees me as a tool. Whether for revenge or sex— I'm still a tool.

He's nowhere in the bedroom, probably having left in the middle of the night like the other time.

I check my phone and there's nothing from him.

My shoulders hunch as I trudge to the bathroom. It's

not that I expected him to stay or text, but it still tightens my chest.

It shouldn't.

I've never expected anything from the men I've fucked and have always had zero expectations. In fact, I was glad some of them didn't get in touch again. Some of them told their friends I was like a dead fish and that a fuck doll had more emotions than me. One guy said fucking me was creepy as fuck because I had a poker face the whole time.

Maybe it was because I didn't feel anything.

I definitely didn't have a poker face last night. Not when Jude made me feel him instead of seeing him, talked dirty to me, praised me, and couldn't get enough of me.

Maybe that's why it feels like my chest will explode. The only man I've ever enjoyed sex with disappeared, and I'm...

I pause brushing my teeth, my eyes widening.

No. I can't be disappointed or hurt. I'd have to care in order to feel those emotions, and I'd *never* care about Jude Callahan. I shouldn't have even allowed him to fuck me, let alone enjoyed it.

But somehow, I forgot all about the safe word. Like, it completely slipped my mind.

It's probably some stupid hormones that are muddying my head. That's all.

After I finish freshening up and spend a long time putting on a hoodie and jeans, I grab my phone and pause as a text lights up my screen.

I rush to open it, but my heart falls when I don't see Jude's name.

Unknown number: Heeey! It's the one and only, the

man and the legend, Preston. Got your number
from Daisy. Just kidding, she said no, so I had my
methods. Anyway, want to hang out?

Me: Hi, Preston. I'm not sure why you'd want to hang
out with me.

Preston: Because I'm better company than Jude and
Dakota combined. And I'm definitely a better fuck.
Not that I'm saying we should fuck, but it's on the
table just in case.

Me: I'll politely decline. Thank you, though.

Preston: Aw, don't go hurting my feelings like that. Just
think about it. I'll see you around campus!

I'm staring at his text as I walk into the living area. Not
sure why Preston seems hell-bent on getting close to me, but
I'd rather stay away from anything related to Jude. Starting
with the man himself.

"Who are you texting?"

I bump against a wall. A warm, tall, and broad wall.

My eyes widen, the phone nearly falling from my grip, as
I stare at Jude. My neck hurts from how much I'm craning to
look at him as he grabs my elbow, steadying me.

He looks so beautiful in jeans, a black T-shirt, and his
full-sleeve tattoos that are on display.

"W-what are you doing here?" My mouth feels dry, and
my belly tightens as his intoxicating scent triggers memories
from last night.

"Brought some breakfast." He motions at the table
that's stacked full of pancakes, eggs, toast, and three types
of juices—orange, strawberry, and green. Who drinks three
types of juices in the morning?

Jude, apparently.

I ignore the flutter in my chest as I step back, then wince, because, really, I feel him inside me with every move. And the fact that he's actually standing in front of me fills me with flashes of warmth.

"Why did you bring breakfast?" I ask.

"Why not?" He glares at my phone. "And you're not changing the subject. Who are you texting?"

"So now I can't text anyone without telling you?"

He narrows his eyes the slightest bit. "Preferably."

"Don't be ridiculous." I walk past him, mainly to escape the trap of his intense gaze and the way my body is reacting to that gaze. "Shouldn't you be at practice?"

"You're following my hockey schedule?" There's slight amusement in his tone.

"I don't have to. You and the Vipers are kind of everywhere in this town."

"Apparently not everywhere, because you still haven't come to see me play live. You should do that sometime."

"And watch you beat up people up close and personal? No, thanks."

He narrows his eyes but says nothing.

I pull out a chair and even my arms hurt, probably from when he held them in a tight grip behind my back and fucked me on the edge of the bed. "This is too much food. I could've cooked instead."

Jude strides to the chair across from me, watching me with his head cocked to the side. "I figured you'd be too sore to move properly, let alone cook."

"That's not—" I wince when my ass meets the chair, and I have to hold on to the table for balance.

"You were saying?" Amusement laces his voice, and a small smile appears.

I feel spoiled by his smiles, and I can't help but think this will backfire exponentially.

"Whose fault is that?" I grumble. "You're the one who can't have sex like normal people."

"Neither of us are normal people, sweetheart. You know that, your body knows that, and even your journal knows that." He swallows half a boiled egg. "Will I find other fantasies after last night?"

My cheeks heat, but I spread butter on my toast, pretending I'm not actually dying of embarrassment. "No idea what you're talking about."

"The fantasies, Violet. The ones I'm putting so much effort into making come true. Shouldn't I get some recognition?"

"Why would you?"

He pauses with his coffee halfway to his mouth. "What?"

"Why would you put so much effort into making my fantasies come true?"

"Why? You'd rather it's the man you're fantasizing about?" His eyes darken to a frightening color, and I look down, scared he'll see my chaotic emotions written all over my face.

A hand shoots up in my direction, and I gulp as he stands and grabs my jaw. "I told you, didn't I? No one will satisfy that cunt aside from me. You're mine, so there will be no fantasy men or anything in fucking between."

The possessiveness rips through my flesh and flows into my blood, but I still whisper, "Why would you want me to be yours?"

He releases me and sits down. "As I mentioned. It's because your life is mine."

"I don't see the correlation." I take a bite of my toast. "My life being yours doesn't mean you'd want to fuck me."

"It does. Because I own every inch of you." He sips his coffee, then sets it back down. "Your fantasies included."

"Right." I let out a scoff. "Will you have someone following me again? Like Mario?"

My voice catches on his name, and I fill my mouth with toast to stop it from trembling.

"No." The word is firm, but I also sense something underneath. A tension of sorts, and now, I feel like shit.

I know I thought Jude attacked us, but that's obviously not true. Dahlia said he visits Mario regularly, and even now, I can tell he feels some form of guilt about him.

"I'm sorry about Mario," I whisper. "He's in a coma because he tried to protect me. It's all my fault."

"If we're playing a my-fault game, then it's mine. I'm his boss and the one who put him in that position."

"But it was because of me—"

"Enough, Violet." His voice booms in the silence. "Blaming yourself and being a martyr doesn't make you a saint or anything grandiose. It only allows predators to prey upon you."

"Predators like you?" I ask, then regret it immediately because why the hell am I saying what I'm thinking without a filter?

"Yes, predators like me." He doesn't seem offended, just…accepting, I suppose.

I clear my throat. "Do you think he'll ever wake up? Mario, I mean."

"I don't know."

"Can't you ask Julian for help? He seems to be way ahead in developing drugs for comas and stuff."

He narrows his eyes.

I gulp the bite of the most divine, fluffiest pancake I've ever had. "What?"

"Don't bring up Julian or praise him."

"I wasn't praising him. He just seemed to know what he's doing."

"Like when he told you I tried to kill you?"

I frown. "Why do you think he did that?"

"So you'd be more terrified of me and take the way out he was offering. He loves cornering people so they'll do his bidding."

"He's really cunning."

His eyes are still narrowed, but he says nothing.

I make him some toast with butter and jam, and he pauses before he takes it, almost as if he's never had someone make him some toast before.

I'm so used to making it for Dahlia, I didn't even think twice.

"Are you close to him? Julian, I mean."

"What do you think?"

"I don't know, which is why I'm asking."

"He's just a controlling pain in the ass."

"Do you…have other siblings?"

"No. My mother had too many miscarriages while I was growing up."

The words land like thunder on the table, and I gulp, afraid to breathe. "I'm sorry."

"It's not your fault. Why are you sorry?"

"I'm just… I know that must've been painful."

"Yeah. She was in pain for a long time, but she still did everything and went to all the doctors so she could conceive." He pauses, swallowing a mouthful of toast. "Thirteen."

"What?"

"The number of miscarriages she had."

"Oh. Were the pregnancies too close together?"

"Her entire life after me, really. She had some form of an autoimmune system deficiency. Had many failed IVF attempts and refused the notion of a surrogate. Apparently, she lost quite a few before I came along, too. After me, she had one stillborn. Three were lost in the second trimester. The rest were miscarried early on."

"Why did she keep doing that?"

"She wanted a girl so badly." His lips twitch a little. "Pres looked girly when he was growing up. Probably why she loved having him around. But..."

"But?" I lean forward in my chair, looking at his hair that's falling over his forehead, hiding the scar I know is there. The one his mom gave him.

"But it was hard on her body and mental state. Especially the stillborn and the second trimester losses. It didn't help that she'd try to conceive as soon as she could, despite the doctors' warnings that it was turning into an obsession."

"Your father didn't say anything?"

He lifts a shoulder. "I don't know. Julian said he tried to stop her, but that motherfucker is the source of all evil. If he hadn't married her, she would've had a perfectly normal life."

"But you don't know that." I speak softly. "She could've had the same problem with another man."

"Maybe, but he made everything worse." He pauses, runs a hand over his face, then looks away. "She had uterine cancer last year and needed a hysterectomy."

"Oh God."

"She...had a mental breakdown." Jude's voice becomes deeper as he stares at the toast in his hand. "I've never seen her so broken and frantic as when it was time for the surgery. She begged me to stop them, but I couldn't, because she would have died. That *fucking* father of mine made them sedate and operate on her. When she woke up, she kept touching her belly and crying. She didn't die of cancer, but three months later, she was stabbed to death in broad daylight."

"I'm sorry." I wipe the moisture that's gathered in my eyes. "I'm *so* sorry."

"Your apologies won't bring her back, Violet."

"I know. I'm just sorry because you had to go through that. It must've been so hard growing up dealing with the fallout of her miscarriages, then her cancer."

He pauses, looking at me as if he's never heard those words before.

Wait. He has, right? From Julian or his dad?

Hopefully, his mom?

She must've cherished the actual child who survived, right?

"Do you also tell yourself that?" he asks.

"Tell myself what?"

"That it was so hard growing up with a mother who only belittled you and made you feel worthless?"

"My mom was different." My fingers shake on the cup. "She was a gorgeous socialite, but pregnancy killed her life-style, and she had no one to rely on, so she had to sell her body to feed me."

"How is that any of your fault? Did you choose to be born? Because if you did, you sure as hell wouldn't have chosen to be a degenerate, narcissistic woman's daughter. Don't make excuses for her."

"I'm not. She did me wrong on too many levels that I'm slowly unpacking." *Like how sex is meaningless and I shouldn't get attached.*

Last night was the first time in my life I've enjoyed

penetrative sex and didn't have images of my mom lying like a lifeless doll as all sorts of men rammed inside her.

"But?" He tops off my orange juice glass.

"But she was my only family, so yeah, it kind of hurt not to be loved by your only family, you know." *God, why am I even telling him this?*

Maybe because he opened up about his own mother, and I got to see the human side of him in full-blown colors.

Maybe it's because this is the first time we've actually sat down and talked, and I feel oddly comfortable around him.

Jude rolls the black ring on his index finger and his next words hit me in the chest. "You don't need that type of love, even if it's from your only family."

CHAPTER 27
Jude

THE CROWD'S ROAR PIERCES MY EARS AS PRESTON SKATES toward me and hits me on the shoulder.

"Nice block, big man!"

Kane pats me on the helmet as I cross my stick with other players'.

Our crowd is going wild, cheering and banging on the boards. It's understandable, given the way we turned the game around. We were behind against the Knights, mostly because I was sent to the penalty box and they had an effective power play.

What? Number 16 hit Preston, so I had to break his legs. I didn't manage to actually do that and just flattened him against the ice, and so I found my way back to the annoying box.

Coach Slater was screaming his head off, but I don't really give a fuck about that, since the main reason I'm here is for the violence anyway.

Hockey has always tamed the raging demons inside me and given me a venting outlet. I've been into impact sports since I was young because I could feel the aggression fading away with each blow.

Crunching bones, delivering punches, and sporting bruises all over.

Violence.

A way to fucking feel.

Of all of the sports I tried, hockey is the one that came out on top, and it turns out that I have an innate talent, according to all the hotshot coaches I've had. They tried to tame that talent, sculpt it into some boring technical prowess like with Kane and Preston, who I dragged into this, but, really, my unhinged side is what makes Callahan #71.

The beast Callahan.

The 'watch out for your career if you're up against him' Callahan.

The league's raging bull Callahan.

A fireball. A violent monster.

A goddamn lunatic.

It doesn't matter what they call me, and it's not like I love the box. If anything, it irritates me to just sit still instead of being in the midst of the fast-paced action.

I usually get sent to the box multiple times during one game, and sometimes, the coach has to pull me off the rink so I don't risk misconduct.

This time around, though, I was only in the box once.

And it was due to a very specific reason.

While I was hydrating and looking at the screens showing some of the crowd, I caught a glimpse of someone I never thought I'd see at a hockey game, let alone a Vipers game.

Violet.

The camera was more focused on Dahlia since everyone and their uncle knows she's Kane's girl. She's wearing his jersey and has his number, 19, written on her cheek.

But it wasn't her that made me pause with the bottle halfway to my mouth. It was Violet standing beside her, looking a bit spooked by the chaos. She's wearing a Graystone Ridge sweatshirt that's not too tight but also not that loose either.

What is…Violet doing here?

I know she must've been dragged to the game by Dahlia, but I heard Dahlia ask her the other time, and she vehemently refused. She also refused when I asked her to come over a week ago.

What changed?

Violet shifted slightly, pushing her glasses up her nose, touching her wrist a bit as she watched the game.

No.

Violet wasn't really following the action like everyone else.

Was she looking at the penalty box?

The camera went back to the game before I could make sure, but I'm certain she wasn't focused on the team like the rest of the crowd.

I could be reading too much into it, but ever since I was released from the penalty box, I have never gone back in.

Because how the fuck could she watch me if I was stuck in a useless cage?

Not that I'm sure she came here to watch me per se.

I'm fully aware she despises the idea of sports or anything of the sort. But as I skate back to defense, cleanly checking the Knights' center, I can't help but think maybe Violet truly is here for me.

Even though it hasn't been long since the first time I fucked her, it feels like forever ago.

Like I've been fucking Violet my whole goddamn life. Like she fucking exists for me.

I've had my fair share of sex, but none of it compares to

the way my whole being resurrects the moment I touch Violet. It's damning and electrifying, and I didn't stop that first time.

Couldn't stop.

Maybe it's because I'd wanted to fuck her for a long time, maybe it's because I couldn't get enough of the throaty erotic noises she released or how she tentatively touched me.

Whatever the reason, I shouldn't have blurted everything out about my mother the next morning.

I still don't know why I did that.

It wasn't so she'd apologize or feel guilty. In reality, I don't think I ever meant to kill Violet Winters like I have the other targets.

Maybe I would've if I hadn't met her first and she hadn't given me her umbrella and a protein bar. Or maybe I would've still seen the true Violet and decided not to hurt her either way.

Sometimes, I think my rage toward her, my inability to stay away, and all the fucking bad habits I developed because of her are just my mind's way of rebelling against the logic that I should kill her for not saving Mom.

And maybe I should.

But I won't.

Not because I can't, but because I don't want to.

Not when I'm goddamn addicted to her.

Her rose scent, her abundant smiles, her beautiful grace, and her irrevocably kind nature.

But mostly, it's the way she submits to me, how she looks at me with hooded eyes, and how she traces her fingers along my tattoos as if she wants to memorize them.

Especially the barren tree tattoo. I'll catch her looking at it and my scars whenever I'm naked. Which is most of the time when I'm in her company.

Since the time I first fucked her, I've been doing it every day. Sneaking into her house—or kind of walking in, really—waiting for her to come home so I can snatch and fuck her against the door like a feral animal.

And Violet *loves* that. She's even started wearing sexy lingerie beneath her clothes for the daily fucking. Her favorite type of sex is when I wake her up with my mouth, fingers, or cock.

She truly loves somnophilia, my Violet, getting so wet and noisy and then coming for such a long time.

She doesn't tell me directly, but she writes her thoughts in her journal that she knows full well I read.

I loved last night so much. Not only was the sex so intense and amazing, but also waking up with his mouth on my pussy made me even more turned on. Next time, I want to be woken up with penetration. I know, I know. Something's wrong with me.

He listened. I want more, but I can't say it out loud, so I'm writing about it here.

I think I'm having too much mind-blowing sex lately. Is this normal?

It was a form of communication, I suppose. Even though I'd rather she ask for what she wants directly, but we'll get there.

Eventually.

I still don't know what *there* is or what the fuck we're even doing, but I refuse the very idea of not spending my nights in the penthouse, slipping into Violet's bed like a degenerate stalker and fucking her brains out.

It should be disturbing, the reason I even came into her life, but I couldn't care less.

Even as I'm playing right now, I lift my head and look at where she's standing.

Our eyes meet, and she pauses in the middle of whispering something to Dahlia.

She's in the front row, across from me, with only the glass separating us, and I can see a blush creeping up her neck and onto her face.

Fuck.

God fucking dammit.

Now, I can't stop picturing the red marks I left on her ass last night as I fucked her from behind or the throat hickeys she's covering with a turtleneck beneath the sweatshirt.

Violet bites her lower lip, and I'm hit with memories of my teeth sinking into those lips as I fucked and spanked her and made her scream—

Something hard slams into me, and I'm flattened against the boards.

A collective gasp echoes through the crowd, and Violet brings both hands to her mouth as I straighten and consider smashing the motherfucker who cut off my thoughts.

But then again, I decided not to make another trip to the box tonight.

I do check him for the rest of the game, cleanly but violently. I target the piece of shit so much, he starts to avoid me.

Good.

Next time, he'll learn not to fucking touch me.

We ended up winning after flipping the game's score in our favor.

The crowd's cheers of excitement pierce through my skin, yet all I can look for is Violet.

But she's already being dragged toward the exit by Dahlia.

She pauses for a bit, staring behind her, and when her

eyes meet mine, her lips twitch in a small smile, and she lifts a thumb up.

And then she's gone, mingling with the crowd.

For a long time after she's out of sight, I'm standing in the middle of the rink, gripping my stick so tight, I'm surprised it doesn't snap.

What the fuck?

Why is my heart beating so loudly that I feel like I need medical intervention?

It can't be because Violet smiled at me and gave me a thumbs-up, right?

No.

It must be the high of the game. It *has* to be.

I'm shoved by Preston, and I nearly lose my balance as he headlocks me. "You were fucking phenomenal, big man. But only right after me, because I'm obviously the motherfucking best."

"Phenomenal game." Kane fist-bumps me.

"Callahan!" Coach Slater shouts at me.

He's a veteran of the game, born and bred in Graystone Ridge. He was one of the hotshot players who told me about my innate talent, but he also truly and irrevocably hates my penchant for violence. But, mostly, he despises my wasted potential and my time spent in the penalty box.

"From now on, that's exactly how you play!" he tells me, giving me a fatherly pat on my shoulder.

I'm soon swept away to the locker room with teammates who are celebrating and being extra noisy.

As soon as I walk out of the shower and start putting on some clothes, I slide up beside Kane, who's already dressed and is stretching.

This guy finishes showering in a minute, I swear. But then

again, Kane's never liked displaying his scars or putting his unfortunate past on full display.

I throw a shirt over my head. "Is Dahlia coming to the club tonight?"

He lifts a brow as he presses on his leg. "Why?"

"For the celebration. She knows the regular place, no?"

"Yes, but what I'm asking about is why you would care whether or not my girlfriend is coming."

"Nobody gives a fuck about your girlfriend, Davenport." Preston slides in like a fucking hyena, wrapping both his arms around our necks. "Big man here wants to know whether or not Darcy would bring her sister like she dragged her to the game."

I flick him on the forehead. "How do you know there was dragging? Maybe she came voluntarily."

"To see me. Of course she would! No one hears about the legendary Preston Armstrong and misses the chance to see me in full-blown action. I'm God's gift to peasants."

"It's God's gift to women," I say.

"I meant peasants. Fuck off. Anyway, I bet money Vee will come along."

"Her name is Violet." I elbow him, and he grunts, releasing us.

"*Vee* will come." He makes a face at me, then tilts his head in Kane's direction. "Right?"

"Not sure, and I would rather you stay away from her, Jude. Dahlia doesn't like it, and I'm also not a fan."

"I don't give a fuck about your and Dahlia's likes and dislikes."

In fact, I still want to punch the motherfucker because Violet used to praise his style of playing. Pacifist, boring, technical powerhouse captain.

I'm the one who dragged him into hockey, so I should get the credit for any of the praise he gets.

"Callahan." The coach's voice cuts into the locker room like an arrow as he tilts his head to the side. "My office."

The guys hoot and give me shit as I trail behind him. "I thought I played well?"

"For once," he grumbles, and I shake my head.

Not sure why he's even singling me out instead of Kane, but I ignore that as I check my phone in case Violet texted me.

Over the past week, I've been the one who mostly texts, and she barely replies. And if she texts first, it's about food.

Do you have any allergies? Is there any type of food you don't like?

Negative on all accounts.

I told her not to cook and that I could get the best meals from my chef, but she always has something ready. I stopped asking her not to after I realized that she looks truly happy when she's cooking. She'll have a smile on her face and sway to songs on the radio.

And, really, knowing Violet only ever cooked for Dahlia makes me feel special. Not to mention that her cooking is better than five-star meals.

"There we are." Coach stops at the entrance to his office.

I lift my head, and my jaw locks when I see my father standing in the middle of the office, scrolling through Coach's notes.

He always has things to say to the coaches about my stats, my performance, and my ability to improve more.

I've only ever been a machine to this man.

Coach Slater can't even lift his head in front of Regis Callahan or argue, not when my father could have him black-listed not only from town, but also from hockey.

He slowly retreats and closes the door, leaving me alone with the one person I hate more than anything, despite his blood that flows through my veins.

My father lifts his head. "Almost perfect stats tonight."

Regis Callahan is a man carved out of marble and ice, untouched by time or weakness.

His posture is rigid, as if every movement is measured for maximum control. Silver streaks through his dark-brown hair, perfectly styled, not a strand out of place, a contrast to the harsh lines of his face.

Julian and I inherited some of his features. Sharp cheekbones, a straight nose, and eyes as dark brown as mine, but his gaze holds cold precision.

He's always in tailored suits, crisp and immaculate, not a wrinkle to be found, because disorder has no place in his world.

Which is why Mom's fits grated on his nerves. He was absent, uncaring, or downright ruthless with his doctors and institutes that he forced my mother into.

"If that's all…" I turn toward the door.

"I'm being civil by talking to you here instead of dragging you to the house. Don't make me lock you up, Jude."

I grind my teeth and face him, wearing the poker face he engraved into me one whip at a time. "If you have free time to come to a college hockey game, maybe you should spend it on your golden child, Julian."

He folds the book closed. "I choose to spend it watching my son play hockey. Is that an issue?"

"Not really, as long as I don't have to see you."

"Jude." His voice betrays the slightest hint of impatience. "You're pushing it."

"I thought I did that a long time ago."

He releases a long breath, his chest straining against his shirt. "How long will you be indulging in these self-destructive habits and cutting me out of your life?"

"Forever is a good start."

"You wish to follow the path your mother took, is that it?"

I stride toward him, then stop because I won't stoop as low as him. "*Took?* Are you wording it as if she had a choice? Is mental illness a fucking *choice*? You're the one who ruined her!"

He doesn't shift. Doesn't budge, just stares at me with unfeeling eyes. "Apparently, she ruined you, too."

"What—"

"Listen, Jude. I was ready to turn a blind eye to your impulsive, fruitless revenge as long as you kept yourself in check. I forbid Julian from interfering with your way of blowing off steam and even provided you with the manpower to do as you damn well pleased, but you need to stop being so obsessed with your mother and her disturbed mind."

"Did you just…call it disturbed mind?"

"It was. Deep down, even with all the coping mechanisms and memory-filtering you seem to do, you know she wasn't normal." He squeezes my shoulder. "Join me and Julian for dinner sometime and we can talk about it if you wish."

"No."

"Do so while I'm asking nicely, Jude."

He leaves, but I'm shaking with rage and the need to scream in his face.

Punch him.

Bash his fucking head in.

But I don't, because that would mean he's right, and he's getting in my head, and that's simply off the table.

Regis did manage to accomplish something tonight, though, agitate the fuck out of me.

I was in a good mood until he forced me to be in the same room with his repulsive presence.

So even when I make it to the club downtown that we usually go to after our wins, I'm feeling murderous.

The moment I pull into the parking lot, I see Violet.

But she's not alone.

And my vision is red.

CHAPTER 28
Violet

I SHOULDN'T HAVE LET DAHLIA TALK ME INTO JOINING her to celebrate.

I really, *really* shouldn't have.

Going to the game was already out of my comfort zone, but then again, I was the one who asked her if she still had that extra ticket and if I could join.

Not sure why I did it in the first place.

Well, I do. I wanted to see Jude play. Against my better judgment, I've been getting curious about him lately and wanted to learn more about his past and what made him who he is.

And hockey is a big part of who he is.

I could tell the sport held a special place in his life. Not only because of the violence but because when I watched him, it felt like it was the only time he could be free and be himself.

That knowledge made my chest hurt.

According to Dahlia, Jude—and Kane and Preston—had a very tough upbringing and have huge legacies to uphold, so they can't be themselves.

They couldn't even when they were young.

In reality, my chest shouldn't hurt for Jude. Even if he's the best fuck I've ever had, even if he often tells me these things that make me reconsider everything I took for granted about intimacy.

It doesn't change the fact that he was my stalker and the man who was bent on killing me.

But I seem to completely gloss over those tiny facts whenever I'm with him.

It's wrong and strange that I feel safe around him and that I leave him little notes in my journal because he religiously reads them.

The breach of privacy should be appalling, but for someone like me who struggles to communicate my needs, it's been a blessing.

Still, despite everything that's been going on, I shouldn't have come to the game or been kind of…mesmerized by him. His power, his control, the way he commands the ice. Even his bursts of violence didn't frighten me.

Not sure when I stopped being scared of Jude, but it just kind of happened, and now, I'm more in awe of his brute strength, even if I'm still slightly apprehensive.

The game and my confusing feelings aside, I should've gone home, not let Dahlia convince me to come to the club.

"It'll be so much fun!" she said. "If you're uncomfortable, you can leave at any time. No pressure, Vi."

So here I am, dressed in a denim jacket over a sleeveless black dress that reaches my knees, but I still find myself tugging it down, self-conscious that it'll be blown up by the wind and reveal things that shouldn't be exposed.

One of my foster parents called me a whore at eleven because my dress showed some of my thighs. Her husband looked at me creepily and even let his hand wander up my leg when she walked in, but *I* was the whore who should cover up.

Ever since then, I haven't been comfortable with dresses

and have done everything in my power to dress in a way that doesn't draw attention so that I'm not blamed for flaunting myself for the male gaze.

But, lately, I've been thinking about how that thought process is wrong. I've had a few online therapy sessions since I can afford them now, and I got a discount for a top therapist, Sloane Harriot, who's helped me tremendously in such a short time.

She made me realize that I blame myself too much for other people's actions.

I was eleven, literally a child, and shouldn't have been blamed for adults' actions when I did nothing wrong.

I was ten when Mama died, and I ran to the neighbors for help. The wife wasn't around, but the man hugged me and started touching me weirdly, his hand roaming down to my ass and inside my jeans. He only stopped when his son unexpectedly showed up.

I was fully dressed, and that didn't stop him.

So, it's never really about what I wear like my foster mother said. It's about the creeps in this world that I had the misfortune to meet.

It's because I grew up in a broken home, watching Mama being shoved around and treated horribly that I thought women were supposed to let men do whatever they wanted. That if I fought, I'd only get hit or yelled at.

That time, after that man copped a feel and pretended to console me when his son showed up, I ran away, wandering around in the rain and wondering, what's the point of life? I also ran away from that foster home about three years later with Dahlia. After I kneed our foster father in the balls because he snuck into my room and tried to rape me.

He punched me in the eye and it hurt, and I blamed

myself for being such 'a whore' like his wife called me. A little bitch, as Mama said again and again.

But now, I'm coming to the realizations that make me cry involuntarily.

Like my therapist said. *What if everything that happened in your life is not your fault, Violet?*

I still don't know the answer to that, but I'm starting to accept it's not my fault that they're creeps.

Maybe that's why I want to feel pretty lately and I convinced myself to wear this dress and even stopped wearing the glasses. I've been taking better care of myself and been seeing one of Dahlia's professors for my chronic back pain. The other day, we went shopping, and I bought a few pastel-colored clothes that represent the femininity I want to embody.

It feels good to get out of my shell.

Now, if I can be more comfortable in my skin, that would be great—

My whole body goes still as the sound of a motorcycle cuts into the silence.

I stop in the middle of the dim parking lot as blinding headlights flash in my face, and I squint, covering my eyes with the back of my hand as the engine revs again.

No, no. Not again.

I dart back, my legs shaking, and slip between two cars.

The motorcycle comes to a halt right in front of me, and the dark figure dressed in black clothes and a helmet pulls out a gun.

Oh God.

Oh God.

Is this the same guy who tried to kill me and Mario?

"Help!" I scream, my voice ringing around me.

I don't want to die.

Not now, just when I'm starting to figure out my life.

I really, really don't want to die.

My shaky legs barely carry me as I run around the car. I know I can't outrun a bullet, but I won't stand still while he kills me—

"Who the fuck are you?"

My head snaps to the side, where a luxury sports car rolls in. The man who just spoke from the window is none other than Preston, who's now racing forward, trying to hit the figure in the dark.

In a flash, the motorcycle revs again, and then it's out of view, disappearing in a cloud of smoke and speed.

I grab onto the car's trunk with trembling fingers, my limbs so unsteady, I can barely remain upright.

Memories of Mario bleeding on the sidewalk ripple through my head, and nausea spills into my mouth. I think I'm going to throw up—

"Hey."

I breathe harshly when I look up at Preston. I'm panting, really, my clammy fingers barely holding on to the car's cold metal.

"Why do you have a hit man on you, Vee?" He asks with a tilt of his head.

"I d-don't know."

"God, you're interesting. Something about you." He grins and offers me the glass bottle of water he has in his hand. "Heard this helps. Don't take my word for it, though. No clue why people shake and shit."

I take the bottle and swallow a few gulps, the feel of the cool liquid soothing my parched throat.

"Thanks." I exhale slowly. "For the water and coming along just now."

I think I'd be dead if he hadn't.

That thought makes my fingers tremble on the glass.

"Anytime." He ruffles my hair. "I'm a big, bad wolf everyone is scared of. Woo. Stay away if you don't have a death wish and a need for a few broken face bones."

"Are you guys all this violent?"

"Sometimes?" He forms a *V* at his chin with his fingers. "I'm still the prettiest, though."

I smile a bit, and he grins. "There. Made you smile."

My smile widens. Preston has been showing up around me out of the blue. He'll have lunch with me and Dahlia more often than not, and that usually makes Kane and Jude join. Then both of them—especially Jude—will glare at Preston or even elbow him or stomp on his foot.

That doesn't seem to deter Preston, though. He keeps coming back and texting me the most random things.

I reply, mostly because I feel some sense of…friendship, I guess. I've never really had friends aside from Dahlia, and Preston is friendly and extremely nice to me.

Dahlia said it's weird because he's been aggressive toward her, especially since he found out about the ex she dated for a couple of weeks, Marcus.

She always tells me to be careful with that 'snake Preston' since he's unpredictable, but I haven't sensed any bad vibes from him.

Besides, Preston is kind of my window into Jude. He answers any questions I throw at him and gives more info than I even ask for.

"What did you think of my game tonight?" he asks with the same grin, dimples still creasing his cheeks.

"You were great."

"More passion, Vee. I know you only came to watch

Jude, but give more importance to my godly energy on the ice." He narrows his eyes. "Are you one of those girls who gets blind to everyone but their boyfriend?"

I can feel the heat creeping up my cheeks. "Jude's not my boyfriend."

"Oh? Then what is he?"

"I'm not sure, to be honest."

"Want me to ask on your behalf? Tell him to fuck off while I'm at it?"

"You don't have to…"

"Well, fuck me all the way to Sunday. You like him that much?"

"I d-do not."

He hits my shoulder with his jokingly. "Is that why you look pretty tonight? Because you totally don't like him and didn't come to the game and club for him?"

"Just…" I push at his arm. "Stop teasing me."

He laughs, and something about it is so comforting. Preston is truly beautiful. I'd say he's way more beautiful than Jude if I weren't biased, but since I met him, I've felt that his arrogance about his looks is just a front.

I don't know how to explain it, but I see myself in him—someone who's struggling with his own perception of himself and doesn't want to let his true self loose.

So even when he smiles or laughs or is being mischievous, it all feels calculated, because it's his method of projecting himself onto the world.

But right now, as he laughs so genuinely, I can't help but smile.

"No clue what you see in the man. He barely knows how to talk to a girl. He's so closed off, he gives me a bad name."

"Were you also close with his previous girlfriends?"

"What girlfriends? He's never had one of those. Don't get me wrong, he's my best friend, but he's too brutish. If he gives you trouble, let me know."

"What will you do? Punch him for me?"

"Hell yeah. I'll be punched back ten times worse, but I'll survive. It'll be worth it for your beautiful smile."

"What would be worth it for her beautiful smile?"

We both freeze at the newcomer's voice. Or I do, because Preston's cheerful expression immediately darkens, and his upper lip lifts in a snarl.

At first, I can't make out the tall, broad guy who walks toward us with a slight smirk painting his lips.

Then I see his face under the dim light, and recognition sets in.

Marcus Osborn.

The Wolves' captain and center, as well as one of Dahlia's worst exes.

He has angular features and a scar that slices through his right eyebrow, giving him an unsettling presence. His dark-gray eyes look black in the lack of light as they flicker over me in a mechanical profiling.

It's almost like he's seizing merchandise.

I've never met Marcus before, only heard Dahlia curse him a thousand times over and had to listen to people idolize him in Stantonville.

"Go ahead." Marcus's eyes look void and creepily unsettling as he stares at me. "Show me the *beautiful* smile so I can decide what is worth it or if it's worth anything at all."

"The fuck are you doing here?" Preston nearly growls the words.

"Aw. Why so cold?" A spark lights up Marcus's previously

dead eyes as he smirks, cocking his head in Preston's direction. "Came to celebrate your win. Aren't I supportive?"

"You—" Preston cuts himself off, then grins. "Wrong timing. As you can see, I'm busy with Vee."

"*Vee.*" Marcus's smirk drops and I shiver as he directs a glare at me. "Why don't you smile for me, Vee? I'm trying to figure out if Armstrong has a fucking death wish on this fine night."

"Leave her the fuck alone." Preston punches him in the chest. "And you're the one who seems to have a goddamn death wish, Osborn."

I gasp when Marcus grabs Preston's fist that's on his chest.

Marcus's knuckles are covered in bruises, some of them busted, as if he's fresh out of a fight.

"My, oh my." Marcus grins, his eyes shining bright. "Are you angry, my prince?"

Preston shoves him away and smiles at me, but it's forced. He wraps an arm around my shoulders. "Let's go inside, Vee. Some fly is polluting my air with its constant buzzing."

"I haven't finished talking. Also, this needs to go." Marcus grabs Preston's wrist from my shoulder and twists so fast and powerfully that I think he'll break his arm.

Preston releases himself and kicks Marcus. In the stomach.

"Motherfucking bitch! You just never know when to back the fuck off." Preston kicks him again and again, but Marcus is just laughing.

The whole scene feels surreal to watch. As if I've been thrust into an alternative reality.

It's the first time I've seen Preston this worked up, and

I'm pretty sure that Marcus is normally the one doing the beating, not the other way around.

Preston stops kicking him, releasing a long breath and flashing him an entirely fake smile. "You got your five minutes of attention. Now, shoo and stop disturbing us."

I think I see a flash of rage in Marcus's eyes, but before I can focus on what's going on, a motorcycle stops beside us—or more like screeches to a halt.

Jude hops off the bike and removes his helmet, revealing hard features and a scowl that's worse than his permanent one.

It should be wrong that my chest flutters and my stomach tightens upon seeing him.

It should be illegal.

He wraps an arm around my waist and pulls me flush to his taut, muscular side.

He's not even touching me directly, but his grip starts a little riot on my starving flesh.

God, am I becoming a sex addict?

Because he didn't come over yesterday, and I couldn't help being a little disappointed. That's part of the reason why I joined Dahlia and Megan for the game in the first place.

"What's going on here?" he asks Preston and Marcus, who've stopped glaring at each other or whatever those two are doing.

Marcus smirks upon seeing Jude's arm around my waist. "Just a friendly drop-by."

"Nothing about your presence is friendly, Osborn," Jude says, tightening his grip on me.

"True." He taps his lip. "Is Vee your girl, Callahan?"

"Her name is Violet, and yes, she is. You have a problem with that?" Jude shifts slightly, so he's kind of shielding me.

But I'm just staring dumbfounded because, did he just call me his girl? I'm not. We're just...friends with benefits.

Okay, we're not friends, so it's just the benefits, I guess.

"No problem whatsoever." Marcus grins and then points a thumb at Preston. "Armstrong might, though, considering he was flirting with her. Keep a better eye on her, yeah? Wouldn't want her to end up in a freak accident."

Jude takes a step forward, but Preston is already wrapping an arm around Marcus's throat from behind, choking him. "Never mind us, big man. I'mma beat the crap out of this creep real quick."

"Question. What's with all the choking?" Marcus strains, tapping Preston's arm. "Is it a form of paraphilia up for exploring?"

"Just call someone to throw him out of town," Jude tells Preston. "And don't kill him."

"But why not?" Preston glares down at him. "He's obviously itching to meet his maker."

"If you're my grim reaper, why not? Yum."

"Fucking creep." Preston shoves him away. "Your face doesn't even give me the urge to kill. What a turn-off."

Jude narrows his eyes on both of them, then pins Preston with a look. "Call someone. Don't do anything alone."

Then he's dragging me to his motorcycle.

"Wait." I pull on his hand. "We're not going to the club?"

He pauses, pulling out the extra helmet. "Do you want to?"

"Not really."

"Then you won't have to." He slides the helmet on my head. "We're going on a ride."

CHAPTER 29
Violet

I DON'T KNOW WHAT I EXPECTED.

Maybe I thought Jude would take me home or, I don't know, just drive his bike around like he usually does in the morning—lingering on longer routes before we reach campus.

Instead, he stops at the top of a hill overlooking the town.

I'm slightly apprehensive about the whole night. Not only is this the first time I've worn a dress in over a decade, but we also left Preston with Marcus, who looked like he'd hurt him.

However, the strongest reason why I'm on edge is Jude.

He's been tense and silent the entire ride.

He kills the bike's engine with a flick of his wrist. The sudden heavy silence stretches wide over the cloudy night, broken only by the distant rustle of wind through the trees.

I hesitantly pull my hands from around his waist, and he hops off and walks to the edge of the hill.

Rubbing my arms, I do the same, my heart beating loudly. The chill stings, slipping under my clothes, biting at the skin of my exposed hands.

The earthy scent of winter is laced with the faintest trace of smoke from chimneys burning somewhere far below.

Graystone Ridge unfolds beneath us in a vast sprawl of

winding streets and towering buildings, their golden lights flickering like tiny stars trapped behind glass.

The town looks peaceful from this distance, softened by the night, but the view does nothing to calm the faint disturbance clinging to my bones.

Jude stares at the horizon, both hands in his jeans pockets. The wind tugs at the loose strands of his dark hair, and even as he fixates on the town, he doesn't look like he belongs to the world below. He belongs to the dark, deep, and mysterious night.

His shoulders are rigid, every line of him drawn with tension I don't understand the reason behind.

Well, I do.

I think he's mad that I was with Preston. I know he doesn't like that we've gotten close, but then again, he's never been like this whenever he joins us for lunch.

And I'm not supposed to feel this bad.

Don't blame yourself for others' actions or fluctuating emotions or what you can't control, right?

Yeah, I need time to apply that to my life, because I'm tugging at my dress, wishing I'd worn jeans instead. This whole thing was a huge mistake, it seems.

Standing a short distance away, I pretend to be mesmerized by the view. "You think Preston will be okay?"

I realize my mistake when Jude cocks his head in my direction, his eyes glinting like a feral beast's. When he speaks, his voice is calm but edgy. "Why are you asking?"

"I'm just worried about him. Marcus is bad news from what I've heard, and Preston seemed off."

That doesn't ease Jude's expression.

If anything, a deep line appears between his eyebrows, and his nostrils flare. "You're worried about him."

It's not a question, but I nod. "Aren't you worried about him, too? Surely, you know Marcus is violent. Have you seen his busted knuckles?"

"I'm violent, too. Does that make me a threat to Preston, whom you're so worried about?"

"You guys are best friends."

"Doesn't mean I wouldn't hurt him. After all, he was comfortable flirting with what's mine."

I bite the inside of my cheek and flick my thumb over my wrist. "So that's what you're mad about?"

"Mad? Try fucking enraged, Violet." He storms in my direction, and I gasp when he wraps a huge arm around my waist and pulls me flush against him. "I don't like others coveting what's fucking mine, especially when you look like this."

"You should've killed me, then." I look away, my stomach falling at his words.

Jude's rough gloved fingers grip my jaw and pull me back to face his furious eyes. "The fuck you just say?"

I lift my chin, staring him square in the face. "The only way to stop others from looking at me is if you kill me. I can't exactly be invisible or only exist for your eyes, you know."

He narrows his eyes, his gorgeous face not as closed off as earlier, and his huge body partially melts around mine—only partially, though. "That mouth of yours seems to talk back a lot when you're with me."

I pause.

I do.

I mean, it's been more frequent lately. In the beginning, I was too scared of him to dare talk back as often. Eventually, little by little, the fear disappeared, and I kind of…what? Felt comfortable enough to show my true self?

Somehow, I stopped worrying about disappointing him or being a burden or just annoying him.

Is it because he's never made me feel judged?

"Would you rather I didn't?" I whisper.

"You can talk back all you want, but don't flirt with other men."

"I wasn't. We were just talking. Besides, he saved me from a gunman."

His expression darkens, his arm around me tightening. "*What*?"

Placing a tentative hand on his chest, I tell him about the attack in the parking lot and that the man on the motorcycle looked exactly the same as the one who attacked Mario and me twice. The gunman who's the reason Mario is in a coma in the first place.

"So yeah," I finish. "If Preston hadn't come in time, I wouldn't be here."

"Jesus Christ." He slides his hand over his face. "I'll need to assign you security."

"You don't have to—"

"I want to. There's no way in fuck I'll let you roam around unprotected while some psycho is out to kill you." He releases a breath. "Until I find out who's behind these murder attempts, you'll have to put up with it."

I smile a little.

"What?" he asks, watching me closely.

"Nothing, it's just odd that you're protecting me when you wanted to kill me not too long ago."

"Odd," he repeats but says nothing else, seeming deep in thought.

I might have suspected it before, but I'm certain now. Julian was definitely lying about Jude trying to kill me.

Judging by his expression right now, he seems murderous that anyone would even try to hurt me.

It's strange and unorthodox, but Jude and I share a connection. Maybe it'll become destructive over time, but it's there all the same.

"Don't blame or hurt Preston, okay? We were just talking after what happened," I say in a pleading voice.

His eyes narrow to slits as he runs them over the length of me, and I have to physically stop myself from tugging on the dress.

"Did you also get dolled up just to talk to Pres?"

I stay silent, and his grip becomes firm on my chin. "Tell me, Violet. Who did you think of when you put on this sexy little dress and that shiny pink lipstick? Hmm?"

"Myself," I say clearly. "I wanted to feel pretty."

He pauses and his grip even loosens. "You did it for yourself?"

"Yeah. Is there a problem with that?"

"On the contrary." A flick of his finger, a tiny graze, and he's stroking my cheek. "I'm glad you're seeing yourself in a different light."

My lips part, and something inside me warms.

God. He sure knows the right things to say for a grumpy asshole/murderous stalker.

His hand falls from my face and moves under the hem of my dress, his gloves leaving goosebumps on my starved skin as he sensually slides it up while pushing me back.

"I still hate others' eyes on you. It makes me homicidal." He's speaking so close to my mouth, I can only breathe him, inhaling him with every drag.

"This." He slaps my ass beneath the dress, and I yelp. "Is mine, isn't it, sweetheart?"

I flinch when my lower back hits something, and I realize he's backed me up against the bike.

The leather creaks under our weight, and I slam both hands on his chest. "What are you doing?"

He grips my ass cheeks, then flips and pushes me so that I'm bent over the bike.

I'm still dizzy from the sudden jolt when he shoves my dress up to my waist. Cold air skims my bare skin and goose-bumps break out on my thighs.

The sound of his unbuckling belt echoes in the silence and rushes to a starved, feral side of me.

Oh God.

I grab onto the sides of the bike, my nails digging into the leather, and look behind me. For a moment, I'm frozen because goddamn it, he's hot.

The sexiest, most beautiful man I've ever seen.

His muscles swell and ripple with power beneath his jacket and his veins bulge, visible even underneath the gloves, as he pulls out his hard cock.

When did he even get that...hard?

My mouth waters, and my thighs clench. "We're in public, Jude."

"You think I give a fuck?" His voice is thick with lust as he strokes his cock and slides my underwear down my thighs. A soft growl spills out of him. "Seems you don't give a fuck either, considering how soaking wet these panties are."

"It's... It's..."

"Shh." His hard chest covers my back as he drops a kiss on the hollow of my neck, then sucks on the sensitive skin until I almost feel his tongue and lips on my dripping folds. "Don't offer excuses for how much you love this. Just feel, sweetheart."

My mouth is dry as he pulls away and grabs my waist, his cock aligning with my pussy.

I should probably fight more.

We're still in public and anyone could stumble in and see this tattooed dark, broody man fucking me against his bike.

But that image only causes my legs to shake.

Maybe I'm actually broken.

Jude has ruined my perception of normal until I'm even wiggling my ass at the feel of his crown at my entrance.

"I'm going to make this quick and raw, sweetheart." He nudges inside me and I clench. "Be a good girl and hold on to the handlebars for me."

As soon as my fingers wrap around the smooth metal, he thrusts inside me in one firm, delicious go.

I gasp, my body convulsing, all my blood rushing to where his body meets mine. My mouth waters and I'm panting, downright salivating at the way he fills me so thoroughly.

"Goddamn. Mmm." He grunts. "You're so fucking tight, sweetheart. You always take my cock so fucking well, you know that?"

My body slides back and forth on the seat as he pounds into me, going deep and slow one moment, then hard and shallow the next.

"Oh, Jude…"

"Mmm, yes, moan my name like that."

"Jude…that feels…"

"Good?"

"God, yes, harder."

"Fuck, sweetheart. Your body fits me like a fucking glove."

"Yes…yes!" Because, truly, when did a man ever fuck me so good, to the point I'm ready to orgasm just a few moments in?

Or maybe it's not about the man, but what I *feel* for the man.

No.

I don't really have feelings for Jude. This is strictly physical.

It *has* to be.

Slap.

I moan as his gloved hand meets my ass while he's thrusting into me raw and so good.

The sound of our arousal echoes in the air. It's sticky and loud and obscene, but I don't care. My hands hold on to the handlebars for dear life as he fucks me into the bike.

"You look so beautiful, sweetheart." His chest covers my back again as he pulls my hair from my face and grabs my jaw. "It's not the dress, it's the confidence that comes with the dress. I'm so fucking proud of you."

I stutter, my vision becoming blurry as I try to lift my face.

There's this undeniable urge flooding inside me—the *need* to kiss him. However, his grip doesn't allow me any movement and I can only *feel* as he told me that.

Jumbled emotions I never wanted, let alone asked for, fill me up as fast as his hard cock.

"I'm proud of the way you played tonight, too," I murmur. "You looked so cool, Jude."

"Don't flirt."

"I thought we were already past the flirting stage." I chuckle, but it ends on a moan because he's hitting that spot inside me, and I can barely see him through my hazy vision.

"God damn it, fuck." He grunts, his grip loosening around my jaw, and then my lips meet his.

I don't know if his mouth fell to mine or I reached for

his or we just met somewhere in between, but he's kissing me senseless.

Like he can't get enough of me.

Jude has been fucking me every day, multiple times a day, religiously, and he still feels like he can't get enough of me.

Like he can't touch me deep enough or fuck me hard enough.

And I fall for it every time.

So the moment he kisses me while pounding that spot inside me, I'm coming.

The orgasm is long and paralyzing, but I still try to kiss him back, still try to have as much of him as possible.

Because maybe I can't get enough either.

"You're milking my cock, sweetheart," he growls against my mouth as warm liquid fills my insides, drips down my thighs, and makes a complete mess.

"Take my cum." He grunts, his lips touching mine. "Mmm. Such a good girl."

My pussy throbs and I'm close to coming again just from his praise.

Who would've thought I'd be so feral for praise from Jude, of all people?

I'm dizzy, and my hands grow lax on the handlebars. I don't think about how I just had one of the best sexual encounters of my life in a public place or that anyone could've seen us.

Jude wipes me with a tissue and puts me together again, smoothing my clothes, wiping my face, and even taming my hair into submission like he always does after sex.

I sway in his arms, still in awe of how a massive grumpy man like him can be so gentle after sex. I thought men didn't care once they blew their load, but apparently, they do. Or

Jude does, at least, because he's never walked away from me after he's done.

Never.

As I stare into his dark eyes, my lips part. It's like I'm being sucked into an orbit I can't escape.

Because I believe what I thought when he was fucking my brains out is true.

The reason I enjoy sex with Jude so much isn't only because of the little fantasies or that he truly knows how to fuck me.

It's because my feelings for him are entirely different from the feelings I've had for any other man.

I think I'm falling for my stalker.

CHAPTER 30

Jude

"IF YOU HURT VI, I'M GOING TO FIGHT YOU."

I raise a brow at Dahlia. Her hand shakes a bit as she hikes it on her hip, but she still doesn't break eye contact.

She has balls—I'll give her that. She wouldn't have caught Kane's attention if she didn't.

But she'll accidentally get herself killed if she doesn't watch it. The only reason I never officially put her on my shit list is because Violet considers this girl her only family.

"Am I supposed to be scared now?" I ask.

"Yeah, because—"

"She has me." Kane wraps an arm around her shoulders, pressing her to his side.

She grins, lifting her chin. "Yeah, him. He can definitely fight on my behalf."

"What is this? The Middle Ages?" I hold his gaze. "Besides, you have way too much trust in someone who wouldn't beat me in a lifetime."

"Want to bet?" Kane squares his shoulders, preening like a fucking peacock in front of his girlfriend.

It's foolishly working, because Dahlia won't stop smiling, seeming completely taken with his "protective ways."

Honestly, Dahlia isn't *that* bad—she's loyal and

protective, and she was the one who fought for Violet when I wasn't around.

My gaze strays to Violet, who's putting the dishes on the table in her apartment with Preston's help. Or more like— he's eating from all the plates like a fucking rat, but Violet isn't angry or disapproving, for that matter. If anything, she just smiles at him and shakes her head.

I don't think she even smiles at *me* that freely. And if she does, it's few and far between.

Unlike Dahlia, who's currently sucking Kane's face, Violet isn't comfortable with PDA, and if I force her into it, she just retreats into her shell, so I stopped doing it.

She's been making so much progress in therapy, and I don't want to be a negative influence.

I also stopped trying to separate her from the pest that is Preston, because it's extremely rare for her to be this relaxed around anyone but Dahlia.

I still walk up to him and hit him upside the head, though, and he nearly chokes on a bite of cucumber.

"The fuck was that for?" He tries to kick me, but I dodge it at the last second.

"Stop being a nuisance." I grab him by the nape. "She spent the whole afternoon cooking, so the least you can do is wait until dinner is served."

"Well, I was helping!" Preston objects.

"By being a pain in the ass?"

"Veee." Preston shrugs me off and walks to her side. "Jude is being mean."

She smiles, but it falters when her eyes meet mine, the blue deepening until it resembles an ocean before she looks away.

My fist clenches.

Ever since I fucked her on the hill last week, she's been...
guarded?

No, she's always been guarded around me. But this is
different, taking it a step further.

As if she's hiding something.

Which is ridiculous. I like to think that I know Violet
inside out, but she often proves that she runs deeper than I
think.

"I helped, didn't I?" Preston asks while removing invisible
dust from the table. "All this food couldn't have been made
without my good vibes."

"I'm the one who actually helped," Kane interjects as he
and Dahlia bring more dishes to the table.

"Fuck off. No one asked you." He grins down at Violet.
"Right, Vee? Without me, this dinner wouldn't happen."

"True," she says. "You suggested that I should host."

"I brought it up, too." Dahlia wraps her arms around
Violet. "I'm jealous someone other than me will get to taste
your food."

"Hmph. You're not that special, Diana." Pres flicks her
on the forehead, and Kane twists his arm.

Preston yells and protests while Dahlia waggles her brows
at him.

As the three of them bicker, Violet walks up to me with
a smile.

She doesn't have the glasses on, her face looking brighter,
more glowy, and her eyes spark gently.

And today, she's dressed in a soft-blue cardigan and a
light-blue knit skirt that stops just beneath her knees. I've
noticed she's more comfortable wearing skirts and dresses
lately.

While jeans and oversized hoodies are still her go-to, she

sometimes dresses like this, and I love the light in her eyes when she does.

The confidence.

The way she's growing into herself after over a decade of believing she's worthless.

Even her journals are now more positive, filled with notes from her sessions with her therapist that she "loves to death" and "feels lucky to have."

She also includes childhood memories that she reflects on differently, having stopped the blame shifting and now trying to heal through finding closure.

She's been…a force of nature lately. The fucking sun I'm orbiting around whether I like it or not.

Violet stops in front of me, her hand extending toward me before she lets it fall back down. "Are you still mad about this dinner idea?"

"I'm not mad. But as you can see, it's a shitshow." I wrap an arm around her waist because, apparently, I *have* to touch her.

I can't be near her without this overwhelming need to keep her close. Shield her.

Make sure no one messes with her.

Not even me.

And even that is…not plausible. Since when did I stop *wanting* to mess with her?

I have no clue about the reasons, and I've stopped trying to figure it out.

Lucia hates me because I've been overworking her ever since Violet was attacked in the parking lot. We have little to no evidence to go on, and the surveillance cameras didn't provide us with any clues except that the assailant was on a motorcycle.

I've spent hours watching that footage—mainly because I couldn't get Violet's frightened expression out of my head, and I hated that I couldn't be there for her.

For hours on end, I keep watching the way she was shaking while escaping between the cars or the frightened expression on her face when he pointed the gun at her.

She didn't want to die.

For someone with a shit ton of suicidal ideations, she truly didn't want to die from the moment she had a gun pointed at her head.

I don't know who the fuck wants her dead, but they'll pay for making her feel that way.

Even if it's Julian or Regis.

Especially if it's Regis—I've been itching to bring down that man all these years.

"I've always wanted to cook for this many people. It brings me joy." Violet pauses. "I made you lasagna, too."

I narrow my eyes. "Is it only for me, though?"

"Come on, don't make that face. You look so handsome when you smile instead. Besides, this is so much fun." Violet's hand lands on my chest, and I can't resist the hum that ripples through me.

Jesus fuck.

Her softness has always been my undoing.

She touches me so gently that I'm ready to murder my entire bloodline for her.

This ailment needs to be studied.

"Preston's antics are anything but fun," I grunt out in my usual closed-off tone.

"I heard that." He pauses his bickering with Dahlia. "And stop being jealous. Doesn't look good on you, big man."

Violet vibrates with laughter in my arms.

I lift a brow. "He's not *that* funny."

"I just find it endearing."

"You find what endearing?"

"The relationship between you guys." She lifts her hand to my face, then drops it back down, still seeming to think twice about her actions around me. "Even though we come from different worlds, I feel like you guys bonded over harsh circumstances just like Dahlia and I did."

"Dahlia doesn't push her luck like that little motherfucker Preston."

"Heard that, too! Want a fight, big man?"

I'm about to pummel him against the wall, but Violet clenches her fingers in my T-shirt, her manicured nails digging into my muscles. "Please don't fight."

My eyes narrow. "That's what I do, though. Fight. Punch. Kill. You *know* that. If you have any fantasies about fixing me, it's better to abandon them."

Her smile falters a bit. "It's not that…"

She trails off as Dahlia approaches to interrupt the moment, dragging Violet to the table.

All of them are a damn nuisance tonight.

I'd prefer it be just the two of us watching some TV or talking about school. But no, Violet wanted to invite 'the important people in our lives' on this fine Sunday.

Dinner is loud and obnoxious, mostly due to Preston and Dahlia—who refuses to let him have the last say in anything.

My mood is split between being annoyed at all of these people stealing Violet's attention from me and being apprehensive at Preston's state.

He seems hyper and cheerful, but he also has a bruise the size of fucking Texas on his side. I saw it earlier when he was changing in the guest room. He said he got it in practice, but no puck would form that kind of bruise.

He's lying.

Preston *never* lies to me.

The fact that he did is the reddest flag of all flags.

I need to get to the bottom of this before he does something stupid. He's been whining more and more about his dad lately, which is bothersome in and of itself because he does dangerous shit to get his dad's attention.

"This is truly amazing, Violet," Kane says after sipping the soup.

"Aw, thanks." She blushes. She fucking *blushes* at Kane's remark?

What. The. Fuck?

Kane smiles. "I mean it. I need the recipe."

"See?" Dahlia says smugly, pausing her nonsensical fight with Preston. "I told you Vi was the best cook ever."

Kane raises a brow. "I thought *I* was the best cook ever."

She keeps her thumb and forefinger slightly apart. "You're just a teeny-tiny bit behind her."

"Now, I'm offended."

Dahlia strokes his cheek, and Violet smiles at the cheesy-as-fuck scene as I stab my fork into the lasagna.

Her gaze slides toward me…expectantly? No, it's something else.

"What do you think?" she asks in a small voice.

"It's amazing!" Preston cuts me off before I can even say anything. "I'll be having dinner here regularly."

"I'll cut your throat," I warn.

"Boo. Who will you bond with over mommy issues once I'm gone?"

I narrow my eyes, and he just grins.

I think I catch a glimpse of Violet studying me intently.

No fucking clue what Preston has been telling her about me, but I often catch her watching me with this sympathetic edge.

And it pisses me off.

I don't need her to feel sorry for me.

My phone vibrates on the table before I get a chance to read her expression further.

Julian: You're not here. Father is livid.
Me: Couldn't care less.
Julian: You promised to make it to dinner tonight.
Me: I just said that so he'd shut up.
Julian: He says if you don't make it in the next thirty
    minutes, he'll lock you up.

Typical fucking Regis.

Resorting to threats when things don't go his way is his modus operandi.

Me: He wouldn't do that during the hockey season and
    jeopardize my nearly perfect stats that he loves so
    much.
Julian: He would, judging by his expression as I read
    that text. He said: I'll also erase that girl you've been
    roaming around lately, not knowing what's good for
    you.
Me: You told him about Violet?
Julian: I didn't need to. You seem to forget he's still the
    head of the Callahan family, and considering you're
    the apple of his eye, he's bound to survey you.

Apple of his eye, my ass. Julian always says that, probably so I won't feel bad that he's Regis's favorite, but it's getting tedious and old.

Julian: Twenty-eight minutes, Jude, or tonight will be
    the last night you see Violet breathing.

I stand up, my grip tightening on the phone. "I'm leaving."

"Whaat?" Preston stands, too. "But I still didn't beat your ass in all the board games Dakota brought."

"It's Dahlia," she grumbles.

"Sorry. Dallas," Preston says with a grin.

"You didn't finish your dinner," Violet says with a wounded expression that stabs me in the chest.

Fuck. Since when do I care about her moods? And why does she even look so disappointed?

Kane abandons his fork on his plate. "Where are you going?"

"Regis," I say, then face Violet. "It's my father. He asked for me urgently."

She doesn't show much of a reaction as I step past her and toward the door.

My brain is full of ways to make the night insufferable for both Regis and Julian so they'll regret ever dragging me back.

Just when I'm mounting my bike, Violet hurries outside wearing a jacket and a scarf. Her cheeks are flushed by the cold as she approaches me.

Something about this girl looks otherworldly. It's not only the blue-teal color of her eyes or the delicate features on her face.

It's everything—from the way she carries herself to the way she looks at me.

It's been even more prominent lately, and I can't keep my eyes off of her.

"What?" I ask. "Did I forget something?"

She hesitates, her lips parting. "No, I just…"

"What?"

"I thought you looked odd, especially while you were typing on your phone, so I wanted to make sure you're okay," she blurts out, staring down at her feet as she finishes.

Fuck.

Fucking hell.

When has anyone ever wanted to make sure I was okay? Even my mother didn't do that, let alone Regis.

This girl is demolishing me, piece by each agonizing piece, and I can't seem to fight it.

Maybe I don't want to fight it.

"What if I weren't?" I ask like a dick. "Is there anything you could do about it?"

"I could try to cheer you up."

"And how would you do that?"

"Give you a blowjob?" she whispers.

"Fucking hell, sweetheart. You're trying to get me hard as I'm about to make the most annoying journey of my life?"

"No. Just trying to help."

"Thanks."

She blushes, and the view makes me glare. "Why were you shy when Kane praised your food?"

"I wasn't shy. I was just happy." She touches her wrist. "It really felt nice to have a proper dinner with so many people I care about."

"Right. Including Pres and Kane."

"They're your best friends last I checked." She narrows her eyes. "You're kind of over-the-top possessive."

"Am I?"

She chuckles. "You totally are."

I stroke her cheek, and she leans into my touch. "It's because of you, sweetheart. What the fuck are you doing to me?"

"I don't know, but I like it." She pauses. "Despite everything."

"Everything?"

"Mmm," she whispers, "do you have to go? I made the cookies you loved the other time."

"Just make sure Pres doesn't eat them all."

She laughs. "Will you be okay? I know you're not on the best terms with your father."

"Julian and his wife serve as a buffer."

"Are you sure?"

"If I'm not, will you join me?"

She flinches a bit, and I curse myself for bringing up something that makes her uncomfortable. "If you...want."

"I was just kidding."

She lifts her chin. "I meant it."

"You don't have to put yourself through this. My family is kind of fucked up."

"So is mine." She grabs the extra helmet. "People like us need to stick together."

"What about the party you're hosting?"

"Ah." She pulls out her phone and types something, then grins. "Dahlia will take care of it. Besides, I wouldn't enjoy it without you there anyway."

"Hard to believe with all the Preston entertaining you did."

"That's because…he's easy to talk to."

"And I'm not?"

"Sometimes? But truly, I did everything so you could officially meet Dahlia and we could have a get-together, but if you hate it…"

"I only hate your attention on someone other than me." I shove the helmet on her head and reach under the visor to touch the freckles that are visible through it.

God, she's beautiful.

A part of me knows I shouldn't drag Violet into my family drama, but as she hops on and wraps her arms around my waist, I feel a sense of peace.

Strength.

And I know that I can handle anything as long as she's by my side.

My demons included.

CHAPTER 31
Violet

THIS WASN'T MY BRIGHTEST IDEA.

Not sure what I was thinking when I offered to accompany Jude here, but he seemed to be on edge, and I wanted to soothe that somehow.

That's how I find myself walking beside Jude to the entrance. He's silent, but his shoulders are bunched, and his brows are knit together.

I want to reach out and do something—not sure what, as long as it helps with the tension.

It's probably foolish, but ever since I figured out that my feelings for Jude run beyond the physical, I can't stop myself from trying to be there for him.

In the beginning, I thought it was my bad habit of caring for people too much. But then I mulled it over and decided this is different.

In reality, Jude cares about me, too. Not only does he have a bodyguard following me everywhere, which I think is a bit excessive, but he also buys me my favorite ginger ale, embroidery supplies, and tons of books that are…uh, a bit embarrassing because I tend to read unconventional romance. I just hope he never reads them and judges me, because these books are my comfort reads, and they mean so much to me in my self-acceptance journey.

Besides that, Jude's been there for me. All the time. Even when we're sitting together and I embroider while he watches hockey on TV, when we eat together, when I fall asleep reading and he carries me to bed. It feels…peaceful.

And that scares me.

Because I've never had this type of peace before, and I feel like something will happen and I'll lose it all. I talked to my therapist about it, and apparently, it's because I've conditioned my brain to always be in survival mode.

A fight, flight, or freeze response.

It's because I'm expecting the worst-case scenario even when nothing indicates that things will get worse.

Childhood abuse and lack of parental love have altered my brain and shaped my life in a manner I can't control.

Or couldn't.

Now, I've become more aware of my reactions and my self-deprecating habits.

I'm learning to remember all the good things happening in my life lately. How Dahlia is happy, how we don't have to suffer or worry about money. I remember that I'm having fewer nightmares and doing better in school. I remember that I'm making some people's lives better at the charity and with my embroidering.

I'm living. Breathing. I don't think about death anymore.

I don't feel lonely or scared or unsure or like I'm trapped in a black hole.

It's largely due to my own self-acceptance and finally seeing my self-worth, but a part of it is because I have Jude.

It's not that he made me find myself, I had to go through a coma and a life-changing experience to realize I wanted to live, but he always encouraged me to stand up for myself, even if it was against him.

In the beginning, I was always tight, waiting for when he'd lash at me, call me names that were entrenched in my psyche for life.

Stupid. Worthless. Ugly. A nuisance.

Not only has he never said those, but he's always called me beautiful and looked at me like I was the most precious person in the world. I *feel* beautiful in his arms—something I never felt before.

Being with him helps me ground myself and dig deeper into the knots of trauma I kept in the dark my whole life.

Now, I focus on the fact that he's right *here*, currently walking beside me, and my anxiety subsides a bit.

My gaze flits to the looming Callahan house.

No. Mansion.

From the outside, it's a fortress of dark stone and towering windows that feel more like creepy, watchful eyes than anything meant to let light in.

The entrance is lined with massive iron doors, their intricate medieval carvings swallowing up the faint glow of the lamps that line the path. As we approach, a woman in a pristine skirt suit pulls the door open.

Streaks of white hair line the sides of her face, and I pause upon seeing her familiar features.

"Lucia." Jude acknowledges her with a nod. "Is dinner over yet?"

Lucia slides a mechanical gaze over me, then focuses back on Jude. "We just served the second course."

"Awesome." He lets out a frustrated breath as he shrugs off his jacket and gives it to Lucia.

She waits for me to do the same, so I remove mine and thank her.

As we resume walking, I steal one last glimpse at Lucia, who's standing in an erect position by the door.

"Is that…?" I ask, my voice low in the silence.

"Mario's mother, yes. She's our chief of staff." Jude glances at me. "She's helping me find who was behind the attack that pushed her son into a coma and you under Julian's claws."

I hang my head, the reminder of Mario and what he's going through because of me tightening my stomach. I wouldn't blame Lucia if she hates me.

The air inside the house is colder and heavier, laced with the faint scent of polished wood and something ominous.

The foyer is too large, too pristine, with high ceilings that stretch into shadows and floors of black marble so polished, I can see my reflection looking back at me. A crystal chandelier hangs above, glittering but cold, its light casting sharp patterns across the walls.

Everything feels meticulously placed—not a single chair is out of line, not a speck of dust on the sleek furniture.

The deeper we walk inside, the quieter it gets.

A long hallway stretches out before us, lined with gold-framed portraits of men who share Jude's features—the same sharp cheekbones, the same calculating brown gaze, all frozen in time.

Just beneath the scent of fresh polish and old wealth, the smell of faint smoke, whiskey, and leather linger in my lungs, suffocating me.

Jude moves through it all like none of it touches him.

But to me, it feels off. Like a legacy built on expectations, silence, and ghosts that refuse to leave.

But then again, that seems to be the case for all of this town's founding families—almost as if they're trapped in place, unable to ever leave.

We approach large double doors that two well-groomed staff members open, and then we're in a giant dining room with glittering candelabras and shiny plates.

"You're late," an authoritative older voice rumbles from the head of the table.

Regis Callahan.

Jude's father looks like an older version of him, his features harsh and unforgiving, and his facial expression is as cold as ice.

"You didn't mention bringing company," Julian says, seeming more menacing in his natural habitat, his gaze pinning me in place.

"I never said I wouldn't." Jude wraps an arm around my waist, pulling me close to his side. "Violet, meet Annalise, my sister-in-law."

The woman in question, an ethereal beauty with soft features and a gentle smile, gets up from Julian's side and gives me a hug, which is awkward because Jude barely releases me. "Hi, Violet. It's lovely of you to join us. Jude's never brought a girl home before."

I stare at him, but he seems preoccupied, glaring at his father even as his grip tightens around me.

"You're not going to introduce me?" the father asks.

"Certainly," Jude grunts out a reply. "Violet, meet the sperm donor, Regis."

"Enough," Julian says with an edge, and his wife gulps a mouthful of wine.

Regis's face reddens, his fingers clenching around a napkin, and I tense, thinking he'll assault Jude or something.

"Sit down." His voice booms in the hall like thunder.

I can feel Jude's arm tensing before he releases my waist,

takes my hand, and goes to sit on his father's left. I hesitate before I settle in beside him.

The staff members quickly place dishes in front of us. The lobster smells amazing and looks to be high quality, but my stomach is so tight, I have no appetite.

I prefer the easygoing atmosphere we left at the penthouse instead of this suffocating tension that could be cut with a knife.

"How is school? Hockey?" Annalise asks in a careful tone.

"Good." Jude grunts, smearing his fork all over the dish, but he's not eating. Usually, he'd devour anything I cook for him.

"That's great," she pipes up. "I'm glad you're doing well. It feels like forever since I last saw you."

"That's because he's an ungrateful cretin who has no notion of family ties whatsoever," Regis says, then takes a sip of his wine.

I touch Jude's hand under the table. It's balled in a tight fist on his lap as if he's enduring something. It relaxes a bit beneath my touch, but he doesn't uncurl it.

"What can I say?" Jude's lips pull in a mocking smirk. "I learned from the best."

"What on earth is wrong with you tonight?" Julian's harsh voice echoes with a warning. "Have you left your manners at the door? Or do you believe Violet's presence will shield you from consequences?"

"No, leave him, Julian," Regis says. "He seems to have a lot to say for once. Let's hear it."

Jude barks out a humorless chuckle. "So you can lock me up in the basement for your entertainment?"

He…locks his son up in the basement?

I mean, after I woke up from the coma, Dahlia told me many things about Vencor and how cruel these families can get, but isn't Jude doing well? He's a star athlete and, according to Dahlia, a very successful member of the organization.

Thinking that Jude comes with all of these labels attached makes my head whirl.

Lately, I seem to gloss over the fact that Jude is a killer. He's ended many people's lives, and he'll continue to. But right now, as I look at his father, I blame him for bringing Jude into this world.

Jude had no choice but to fit the mold he was shaped in.

"I won't. You have my word." Regis swirls the wine in his glass. "So go ahead."

"Father, this is not the right time—"

"Silence, Julian. Stop speaking on his behalf and cleaning up his messes. Let him voice all his complaints."

"Complaints. Sure, let's call you murdering my mother a fucking *complaint*, Father."

Silence falls like doom on the table. Annalise winces, putting her fork down, seeming to have lost her appetite. Julian glares at Jude, but Regis is staring at his younger son with an unchanged expression.

"Your mother was murdered in broad daylight by a mentally unstable person. You know that, considering all the killings you've indulged in since then to avenge her. If anything, the girl sitting by your side witnessed the murder in full detail, no? Tell me, young lady, did you see me murdering that woman?"

I swallow hard, my hand trembling on top of Jude's, and he flips his over, uncurls it, and holds my fingers tightly. "Violet has nothing to do with this."

"Nonsense," Julian interjects. "The sole reason she's

even sitting next to you is because you targeted her due to Susie's death."

Annalise's face blanches, and she gives me a sympathetic look and a little pained smile. I try to smile back, but I'm so agitated, I'm not sure if it reaches my lips.

"See?" Regis says. "I didn't murder your dear mother, Jude."

"Just because you didn't stab her physically doesn't mean you didn't kill her a thousand times over the past twenty years." Jude's panting, his hand gripping me so powerfully, it hurts a bit, but I still stroke the back of it with my thumb, trying to ease some of what's paining him.

"She killed herself," Regis says.

"Father!" Julian shakes his head.

"What the fuck did you just say?" Jude asks.

"Enough is enough. Julian said you didn't have the mental capacity to accept or even face Susie's true image and that if we let you play the role of slasher for a while, you'd come back to your senses, but that obviously didn't work. Killing all those people only made you feel hollow and brought no sense of peace whatsoever. And for whom? A woman who attempted to kill you?"

"Shut up." Jude's whispering now.

"Why? Because you don't want to recall the times she held you underwater in the tub when you were six years old? When the bubbles escaped your mouth and you thrashed and screamed, but she didn't let go? Or when she held a pillow to your face, trying to smother you when you were eight? Or the fact that she tried to kill you several times after birth when you couldn't have remembered? Because I do. If Julian, Lucia, or I hadn't gotten there in time, I'd be one son down."

"Shut the fuck up."

"Your mother was mentally unwell, Jude. Just because you refuse to acknowledge it doesn't mean it wasn't true. Sure, she loved and doted on you when she was in her normal phases, but she also seemed to have a strange contempt for you on her off days. If you hadn't gone on a hunger strike and nearly died at six after I locked her up in a mental institute where she belonged, I would've never allowed her back in. I only did so because she promised to medicate, but how often did she flush her medication down the toilet? How often did she play the victim just to make you defend her and prevent me from forcibly admitting her again?"

"That's not true." Jude's shaking his head, his eyes glassy. "Even if it were, she only became mentally unwell because she married you."

"It's the other way around." Regis releases a long sigh. "Marrying that woman was my tragedy."

"Then why didn't you let her go?"

"She wouldn't leave no matter what I offered and even threatened that if I kicked her out, she'd devise a way to take you with her and never let me see you again." Regis lets out a low chuckle. "You probably don't know this, but she's the one who came on to me, not the other way around."

"Liar."

"It's true." Julian swirls his glass of wine. "She stalked him for years while he was married. I saw her in all the places we went to, even when I was young. She used her family's power and influence to get close to Father until she eventually had her way. I recently found out she was the reason behind my mother's suicide, though unintentionally. My poor mother was led to believe Father was cheating on her again, and she couldn't handle it, so she overdosed on pills, paving the way for Susie to walk right in."

"You're fucking lying." Jude's speaking so gutturally, it makes my chest hurt. "Mom would never—"

"Because she was so sweet and caring?" Julian laughs. "I fell for that, too, but that woman was very mentally disturbed."

Annalise flinches at his words, but I can't focus on her, because Jude's face is pale, his grip growing lax.

"And while we're at it, all those babies she was so obsessed with having?" Regis says. "Most of them happened because she'd take my sperm to clinics for in vitro fertilization, Mr. Sperm Donor's son."

"Enough!" Jude stands up. "I won't sit here and listen to you slander my dead fucking mother just because you can't take accountability for your actions."

"I admit I was wrong," Regis says. "I should've freed you from her claws before she converted you with her propaganda."

"If you think I believe either of you, then you must be out of your mind."

"Believe your memories, then." Regis rises and motions at Lucia, who's standing by the door. "Do you ever recall the dark side or are you too far gone and they're always roses and sunshine?"

Jude's shoulders are so crowded with tension, I'm afraid they'll snap.

"I'm happy for you to consider me the devil, but your mother was no saint." Regis grabs the envelope from Lucia. "Julian said it's better we spare you the disappointment since she was the only light in your life, but your constant worship of her is starting to grate on my nerves. Either hate us both or stop with the high-and-mighty speech."

"Father..." Julian starts to stand, but Regis holds up a hand.

He offers the letter to Jude. "Read the last thing she wrote in the handwriting you love so much. I've been hiding it so it doesn't shatter your illusions, but you deserve to read the suicide note she left for Julian."

"Mom didn't commit suicide. She was murdered." Jude snatches it from his father's fingers, and I think he'll rip it, but he opens it.

I stand up, getting close to him, not sure why it feels imperative to be by his side right now.

From my position, I can make out the words written in a mixture of cursive and print letters.

Julian,

When this letter reaches you, I'll be dead.
Don't be alarmed. I've been planning it for a while now, paid one of the other patients I met in the mental institute to kill me in broad daylight and make it look like murder. I'm writing this so you'll kill him afterward. I don't want Jude to find out I've been plotting my suicide. It'll hurt him if he thinks I wanted to leave of my own volition, so maybe murder will hurt less.
Truth is, I can't live a life without purpose, and that purpose left me with my hysterectomy. I always wanted so many children from Regis, a football team of them, actually, but my body was uncooperative. How sad.
Sometimes, I hate Jude for being the only one who survived. The voices tell me he cursed my body and that if I kill him, I'll get all the kids I want.
But I don't want to do that, truly, Julian. Please believe me. I love Jude, he's my little miracle, and the reason I con-

tinue to breathe. But sometimes, I get intrusive thoughts about him. I also don't like that Regis is only keeping me around for Jude's sake. He loves him more than me, and I think I'm a bit hurt.

But I still love my son and I'm lucky I have him. I'm just scared I'll hurt him. Or kill him.

That said, I hope Regis is pained by my death. If he hadn't shoved me in all those mental institutes and pumped me full of stupid antipsychotic drugs, I would've given birth to many children, and he would've loved me.

But now, I can't do that, so I guess there's no reason for me to stick around. I'll haunt Regis if he marries someone after me, though, so maybe don't let him.

Take care of Jude for me, Julian, okay? He's your only brother and he does look up to you, even if he doesn't show it, so don't leave him to the vultures out there. Tell him I loved him so much and that I'm sorry I couldn't love him the way he deserves. I failed him as a mom, and I'm truly, truly sorry.

I hope he lives a happier life than I did.

Love,
Susie Callahan

CHAPTER 32

Jude

I THROW MY HELMET AGAINST THE BENCH AND FALL onto the seat that has seen me more often than not during this game.

One more penalty, and the coach will bench me.

He's been yelling at me nonstop, his face red, sweat trickling down his temples despite the ice cold. Chances are, I'll give him a stroke.

Fuck him.

And the referee.

And this entire goddamn game.

I chug a whole bottle of water, breathing heavily, my heart nearly dislodging itself from its confinement.

I despise the penalty box. Fucking hate it.

I should be out there crushing bones and breaking some unfortunate souls beneath my skates. But here I am, motionless like a caged animal.

Without purpose.

And all I can do is watch the guys try to keep up with the Warriors' brutal power play.

Preston speeds to the attack, his agile movements eradicating the defense.

Thud.

I jump up, banging on the barrier as Preston hits the ice.

The crowd erupts in a loud "Ahhh" as Preston remains down after being checked violently by Number 25—the one I beat the crap out of earlier because he keeps fucking targeting Preston.

Yeah, I'm sure Pres said some shit to provoke him at the start of the game, but he's been a raging fucking bitch who needs to be put in his place.

I'm going to twist his motherfucking neck before I'm benched for good in this clusterfuck game.

Preston stands up with the help of Kane and a couple others, but he removes his helmet and has to be checked by the doctor. Blood trails down the corner of his mouth, and he grins at me, holding two thumbs-up, because Number 25 got five minutes in the box.

Fucking prick seems to be suicidal lately.

I hate that he's willing to get hurt just to gain a power play or to send someone on the opposing team to the box whenever I'm there.

I don't know what the fuck is going on with Pres, and I don't have the capacity to check on him as often as I should, considering my own goddamn fucked-up situation.

Ever since that nightmarish dinner a few days ago, I've been spiraling. I know I have, because no amount of violence, various Vencor missions, or even killing on behalf of the Members has managed to fill this black hole inside me.

If anything, it's been widening and deepening at an alarming rate. The demons have gotten louder, demanding more blood, more crushed bones, and more empty eyes.

Just *more*.

Hockey used to be enough to calm this rage that's been consuming me since I was young, but now it's just a scratch on the surface of madness.

A drop of water after years of thirst.

And it's fucking with my head, because I don't know how to end it.

I considered killing Regis and even Julian. It'd do the world good if I wiped them both from the face of the earth so they'd stop talking nonsense about my mother.

But then Lucia gave me a flash drive after being instructed by Regis.

My father wanted me to watch memories of what my mother did to me, and I chose to erase them from my head.

Ignore them.

The attempted drowning. The attempted suffocation. The attempted poisoning—that I didn't even know about.

Regis documented the security footage in full detail, forcing me to see the empty look in Mom's eyes when she did all of that to me.

He forced me to see him, and sometimes Julian, come to the rescue every single time, because, according to Lucia, Regis always watched her or had someone watch on his behalf.

Apparently, he didn't trust that Mom wouldn't hurt me.

Fuck Regis. Fuck him and the letter.

For a while, I was in denial and convinced myself that he'd faked it.

Every single goddamn word in it.

That's not a stretch.

It wouldn't have been hard for him or Julian to have one of their close-knit bands of 'experts' fake my mother's handwriting.

But the more I read it, the weaker my convictions got.

Unlike what I told Violet that day as we left that horror house.

"It's not true. They're both lying," I said as we stopped by my bike.

She hugged me, her arms unsteady, her body trembling slightly against me, her breathing heavy on my chest.

And I couldn't hug her back.

Because why the fuck would she feel sorry for me?

It was rage, I suppose. Not only at myself, but at her for whispering, "It's okay if it hurts. I'm here for you."

No one's ever been *there* for me.

Not even the one person who I thought loved me unconditionally.

Definitely not Regis, despite his warped sense of grandiosity about saving me.

He still tortured me for Vencor, still was absent and had not one ounce of fatherly affection for me. My mother might have been mentally unwell, but she loved me and doted on me when she was herself.

Regis can say whatever the fuck he wants, but I've always been the spare to Julian's genius—and a family like ours need spares.

So Violet saying those words while hugging me grated on my last nerve.

I pushed her away and shook her by the shoulders. "How long are you going to continue being naïve, Violet? You're supposed to be enraged and feel wronged that I targeted you and made your life fucking hell for witnessing a murder that turned out to be a suicide. You're supposed to slap and punch me and call me a fucking piece of shit."

She had tears in her eyes, shiny droplets that shimmered under the driveway's lights. When she opened her mouth, a low whisper escaped her. "I don't want that."

"Then what the fuck do you want?"

"For you to process your pain, Jude. I've been learning a lot about unprocessed trauma lately, and while I don't claim to be an expert, I know the first step to dealing with it is accepting it."

"Shut the fuck up." I sidestepped her. "You know nothing about my life, so don't bring your hopeless idealism into this equation just because you learned some fancy psychological garbage."

"That's not—"

I drove away before she could finish her sentence. Seeing her gentle expression and feeling how goddamn forgiving she is made me even more enraged at myself.

Because that made me think I could've met her under different circumstances. Like after that time she gave me her blue umbrella and protein bar, whispering, "Stay strong."

But we didn't start like that.

I *stalked* her.

Invaded her privacy.

I killed a man right before her eyes to terrorize her.

I pushed her far enough that she chose a coma and the possibility of death instead of me.

And no matter how much I've liked to gloss over those facts these last couple of weeks, nothing can erase them.

And now, I've found out the reason I did all of that was a lie all this time.

Violet didn't ask for any of this.

And yet she got me as her fucking grim reaper.

I lift my head to the stands, searching for her fiery hair and bright-blue eyes, but I only see Dahlia and her former roommate. Both are wearing Vipers jerseys and cheering the team on.

Not sure why I was expecting to see Violet up there when this is the fifth time I've checked.

Fine. Tenth.

Why would she even come to watch the game when I've ghosted her since that night?

Yes, I made sure her bodyguard escorted her home safely, and he's always keeping an eye on her, but I haven't dropped by the penthouse since.

I've been busy slashing faces open and pretending they're Regis's.

The first few days, Violet texted me.

Are you okay?

You probably need time to deal with this, so I shouldn't bother you, but I wanted to check in just in case you need someone to talk to.

It doesn't have to be me. Kane and Preston would also listen, right?

I'm sorry you had to find out about your mother's suicide that way. I know it must've hurt, but it's not your fault.

Isn't it strange that you used to tell me that about my own mother, and now I'm saying it to you? I guess we're really alike in that regard. Preston said the three of us should form the Mommy Issues Club. *smiling emoji*

Jokes aside, I'm starting to unravel my past now that I've accepted that it's not my fault. Sometimes, it's hard, and Mama still appears in my nightmares, calling me names, but it's better than before I met you. In a sense, your telling me it's not my fault or I'm not my mom helped open my perspective, and it's part of the reason why I'm in therapy. Aside from being able to afford it now, of course. *laughing

emoji* So I'm truly thankful for that, Jude. I know
we haven't known each other for a long time, and
what we have is just physical, so I'm probably
overstepping, but I wanted to say that your mother's
illness or choices are not your fault. They're not hers
either, because she was obviously struggling and
battling her own head, but that doesn't change the
fact that you're the victim.

Can you text me back to say that you're okay? I
promise I'll stop bothering you. Preston says you're
living your best life, but I feel like he jokes about
everything.

All right, then. I guess this is it.

She sent that last text three days ago.

Then she completely stopped contacting me. Not that
I wanted her to, but the last text's tone keeps bugging me.

What does 'this is it' mean? Does she think I'll ever let
her go?

Fuck that.

It doesn't matter what I unveil about my past or the lies
I painted for myself; Violet will certainly not stop being a
part of my life.

I just need to stay away from her while I'm in this enraged
murderous mood. I like to think I wouldn't hurt her, but I've
also never felt this fucking attached to a person before.

So goddamn gone that the past week felt like fucking
torture.

It's part of the reason why I'm slipping back into old
habits with this game and embracing aimless fucking
violence.

The moment I'm unleashed from the box, I go back to

hitting people and picking fights, pumped by the crowd buzzing and the shouts and bangs that echo in the rink.

It's like a hit of a potent drug. The only problem is that the high only lasts a few minutes.

Seconds, even.

And then I'm back to that fucking itch of wanting more and more.

Fucking *more*.

I end up committing another penalty, and the coach benches me while cursing and shouting.

We end up losing.

Despite Kane's, Preston's, and the rest of the team's efforts to hold the fort, I fucked it up to a degree of epic proportions, and now everyone else has to suffer the same prickly mood I'm in.

Coach Slater pulls me aside to give me a piece of his mind and reminds me that my father won't be pleased by what he calls "the worst game of your entire career."

Fuck my father.

If he wanted the perfect hockey season and all the bragging rights that come with it, maybe he shouldn't have shown me the letter or the security footage.

He should've pulled a Julian and left me ignorant for the rest of my life. It would've been convenient for him, me, and the whole world.

But no, he had to make me doubt my relationship with my mom.

Julian said that all these years, Regis has really loathed that I've held her on a pedestal while he's been labeled as Lucifer in my head.

So if I can never develop any affection for my father, then he'd rather taint any affection I had for my mother, too.

He's always been the cruelest motherfucker.

Whenever I liked something or got attached to someone, he'd show me the hard way that people like us don't get attached. Everything is a transaction, including interpersonal relationships.

He only approves of Kane and Preston because they're part of our world and understand the meaning of the legacy we need to uphold.

After I listen to the coach blabbering about how I'm actually a superb player but let violence take over and I should be more mindful of the team I dragged down with me tonight, I leave the arena, my phone in hand.

> Me: Where is she?
> Larson: At home.
> Me: When did she get there?
> Larson: A few hours ago. After dropping by
>   Stantonville.

Larson said that Violet went to HAVEN, probably to check on Laura and her kid, because Violet doesn't forget about people. For instance, she still visits Mario all the time and even talks to him. According to her, "You never know. He could be listening. I want to keep him company."

One time, she said her online embroidery sales were doing well, but instead of spending that money on herself, she bought a shit ton of stuff for Laura's daughter.

Even with Larson around, I still don't like her going to that grimy place.

A weight slams against my back, and I grunt, losing my balance.

Preston jumps in front of me, grinning. "Drive me home."

"I'm not your fucking chauffeur."

"You should be whatever the fuck I want, considering you screwed us up tonight, and now we're behind the Wolves."

"Do I play hockey just to beat the Wolves?"

"Why else would you? They're the most annoying motherfuckers and need to go down." He smiles again. "Anyway, I'm coming with you."

He walks beside me, completely ignoring my attempts to push him away.

"What a fucking shame that despite my sacrifices and my busted lip and provocations that will add more enemies to my bucket list, your lousy penalties axed us."

"Stop being dramatic." I shove him toward his car. "You would've been provocative anyway."

"True, but I wouldn't do this." He taps the corner of his lip. "My precious looks are stained because of you, so you better make it up to me by telling me what the fuck got your panties in a twist, big man."

"Just get out of my sight, Pres."

"Nah." He steps into my space. "You haven't been yourself, and Vee keeps asking if you're okay. And you're totally avoiding her. What have you done?"

"Why do you think I did something?"

"Because she's kind and sweet and would never hurt a fly. Can't say the same thing about you."

"Whose friend are you?"

"Yours, of course, which is why I call you out on your bullshit." He grins. "Come on, tell me about it all over a drink?"

I don't want to.

But I do need to talk to someone, though Preston is not the best choice. He'll clown around and say 'Called it' about my mom being off and my whole obsession with revenge being weird.

"I have a better idea!" Preston taps me on the shoulder. "We cockblock Kane and make him cook us something, and then you can at least receive the sane bullshit advice. Deal? I'm glad you agree, deal!"

I shake my head, but I slide into his car's driver seat as he blasts some godawful loud music and starts singing off-key.

What a nuisance.

But at least maybe after I talk to the guys, I'll be able to face Violet properly.

CHAPTER 33
Violet

"WHAT ARE YOU EVEN DOING HERE?" DAHLIA ASKS WITH a hand hitched on her hip while glaring down at Preston.

He merely picks up a few grapes and stuffs his face full of them, then searches his surroundings. "You talking to me, Dakota?"

"It's Dahlia! You're obviously doing this on purpose, prick! And scoot away. This was supposed to be a cute little picnic for Vi and me."

"Nah, it's me and Vee. You go climb Kane as if he's a tree."

Her face reddens, but she attempts to kick him, and he rolls away on the blanket after snatching a sandwich. I don't think it's okay or even easy to eat while rolling, but Preston seems to do it completely fine.

"She's my sister, and I have priority," Dahlia mutters, flopping down beside me.

"Finders keepers, ya know." He rolls back close to us, propping himself up on his elbows and grinning.

He looks a bit different today, though I can't quite place why. He's dressed in jeans, a white shirt, and his Vipers jacket. His hair is more floppy, but his eyes are a bit dimmed.

Dahlia and I opted to have a picnic in the local park,

considering the beautiful weather, and Preston decided to join as usual. It's still a bit cold, though, so we'll probably have to pack up and leave in a while.

Since it's the weekend, the place is full of people walking, running, or playing tennis on the courts down the hill.

But from our position, we get a nice view of the town center and its centuries-old institutions.

The beauty of the setting and the pretty food I made for this picnic doesn't seem to ease the tightening in my chest.

It's been a week and a half since I last saw Jude in person.

I know I should take the ghosting as a sign. I've experienced that before with some guys, and it never bothered me. If anything, I was glad I didn't have to talk to them and was relieved they chose to leave me alone.

So why the hell are those emotions completely absent now?

"You're such a parasite," Dahlia tells Preston as he munches on a piece of mango.

He narrows his eyes. "You seem to have stopped being scared of me, Delilah. Want a reminder that I can crush you?"

She gulps as if recalling something, and I stare at him. "Don't threaten her again, Preston. I don't like it."

His serious expression morphs into a grin. "Okay! But she should stop talking shit if she can't take it. Just saying!"

"That's because you're a—"

"Dahlia," I say pleadingly. "Can you just stop fighting?"

"Fiiine, but he shouldn't be here like an intruder."

"I'm here for Vee, not you. Look." He points at the patch on his jacket with his number, 13, and last name on it. "She made this for me and didn't make anything for you."

"Did too. Vi's made me countless embroideries. Who do you think she gave her first piece to?" Dahlia points at herself smugly. "That's right, me."

His lips lift in a snarl, but then he smiles again. "Anyway, can you come to the next game, Vee? I'm pretty sure we lost the other day because you weren't there. The jinx is real."

My fingers tighten around the sandwich, and I audibly swallow the contents in my mouth. "I'm sure you'll do great whether or not I'm there."

"Nonsense. Jude was like a rogue wild beast."

"Right!" Dahlia snaps her fingers. "He spent more time in the penalty box than on the rink. Kane doesn't like to talk shit about him, but he's totally the reason the Vipers got knocked to second place in the league."

"The tragedy." Preston bangs his fist on the blanket. "My ego is so wounded, I could die."

"Well, the first loss of the season was because of you, so you're both bringing Kane down," Dahlia says, slurping from her can of Dr. Pepper.

Preston's expression darkens in an instant. "You have a death wish or something, Dorothy?"

"Everyone loses at some point. Don't take it to heart," I say in an attempt to relieve the tension, even though I know quite well that the last game was Jude's worst game of the season.

It's not that I meant to watch it or anything, but I wanted to take a sneak peek and see how he was doing. Consider it nosiness or curiosity.

But at any rate, I ended up watching the whole thing.

Because even through the screen, I could see how perturbed he was, how he looked to be on edge, how he got too aggressive for no reason.

And even though I didn't know what he was thinking, I could feel his pain and I knew he probably still hadn't processed everything from that dinner.

I've wanted to reach out and help him, but he made it clear that he wanted nothing to do with me, and I have my pride, so I stopped sending unanswered texts and have stayed away from him.

My therapist made me realize it's in my nature to empathize with others' pain. It's a way for me to accept my own pain and find solace in the fact that I'm not the only one who's had to deal with shitty circumstances. I find comfort in knowing that people from all walks of life have had their share of misery as well—oftentimes worse than mine.

It's why I go out of my way to volunteer or help those in need, even though I'm not better off. It's why I stood by Laura and did my best, hoping she would win the custody battle—which she did while I was sleeping, by the way.

And while that's good in theory, I have to set boundaries. I have to also prioritize my own well-being so that I don't absorb others' pain as if it's my own.

It's not.

I reached out to Jude and offered him emotional support, but he obviously doesn't care for that. If anything, the steps I took to bring us closer were met with his complete retreat.

Apparently, I'm the only one who was thinking that what we had was something deeper, and his ghosting was the wake-up call I needed.

No matter how bad I feel for him, I deserve better than Jude's cold shoulder and fluctuating interest.

Now, if I could stop thinking about him, that would be amazing.

"Everyone isn't me," Preston replies to my earlier statement. "I'm the god of this game."

"Nah, that would be Kane," Dahlia says with a note of pride.

"You're biased, so your opinion doesn't count." He nudges me. "Who do you think is the best, Vee? And for everything that's unholy, don't say Jude."

"I'm not an expert." I smile.

"Don't try to evade the subject. Wait a minute…you're saying that so you won't have to say Jude is the best, aren't you?"

"I…don't care about him."

Dahlia strokes my shoulder, giving me an encouraging smile. She was the one who listened to me a few days after that dinner. I told her about how he was avoiding me, and she offered to teach him a lesson in pure Dahlia fashion.

"Yeah, he's such a loser anyway," she says. "Don't know why everyone loves him so much when the dude clearly has anger issues."

"Hey!" Preston sits up. "Don't go talking about shit you don't understand. His issues have explanations."

Dahlia crosses her arms and lifts her nose in the air. "Whatever those explanations are, they don't give him carte blanche to unleash his rage on others."

"I don't agree, but he totally messed up when it comes to you, Vee." Preston lifts a shoulder. "You should've been the exception."

"I'm fine, seriously. That's life, right?"

"No, it's not." Dahlia breathes harshly. "He already stalked you and pushed you into a coma, so the least he can do is treat you right and grovel for the rest of his life. That fucking brute is hopeless. Don't worry, Vi, I'll find you someone better."

"Me!" Preston raises a hand. "Over here. Me, Vee! Come on, don't friend-zone me. Let me tell you something, the rumors about my dick size and performance are absolutely true. Free trial included."

"Oh, hell no." Dahlia throws a napkin at him.

"Shut up, Dina. This isn't about you."

"Well, I'm making it about me. You think Jude will be okay with it if she switches to you?"

"Hmm. Good point." He scratches his chin. "I suppose he won't, but then again, that's the whole idea!"

He takes my hand in his and interlinks our fingers, and before I can figure out what's going on, he snaps a picture. Then starts to type on his phone.

"See!"

He shows us his phone. Preston has sent the picture to a group chat called The Vipers' Den.

> Preston: Congratulate me, motherfuckers. I have a girlfriend!
> Kane: I won't believe it until I see it with my own eyes. Meeting in fifteen, don't be late.
> Jude: Preston Aaron Armstrong! Why the fuck are you holding Violet's hand?

My chest squeezes as I read his text a few times just to make sure I'm not seeing things. How did he even know it's my hand when it's not fully visible?

More importantly, why is he this attuned to me if he refuses to talk to me?

Preston types some more and Dahlia giggles, seeming to enjoy this as much as he is.

"Stop that, Pres," I say pleadingly. "I don't like playing these games."

"Well, I do!" He waggles his brows, then shows us his texts again.

Preston: Why else? Because Vee is my girlfriend now.
Finally! *confetti emoji*

Jude: I'm going to break your fucking neck if you don't
stay away from her.

Preston: Nah. Finders keepers, am I right? Of course I
am. No need to answer that.

Kane: Great. He just arrived and now he took off.
Count your days, Pres.

"Can't say it was lovely knowing you, but RIP, Preston."
Dahlia laughs, clutching her stomach. "Serves that prick
right. We should've done this before."

"I know, right? I'm such an adorable Cupid." Preston
chuckles maniacally. "Let's take one more picture just for
fun, Vee."

He grabs my hand, and I try to pull it away.

He pauses and pushes my cardigan up my wrist, his play-
ful green eyes whirling with a cloud of confusion, then menace
as he cocks his head to the side. "Why...do you have this?"

He lifts my bracelet with his index finger, his eyes hardening when they slide back to my face.

Dahlia has always told me that Preston is dangerous, but
I've found that hard to believe since he's only ever been cheerful to me and easily befriended me. This is the first time I've
seen the version she's talking about.

Unpredictable, unhinged, and...disturbing, even.

"It's my mother's," I whisper and attempt to pull my
hand back, but he keeps it in a firm grip.

"Did your mother steal it?" He frowns. "No, that's
impossible. Who gave it to her?"

"I don't know. She just told me to keep it... Pres, you're
hurting me."

He releases me, his jaw tightening. "Remove it."

"What?"

"Remove it, Violet. I need to check something."

"Hey, why are you being a dick all of a sudden?" Dahlia moves on her knees a bit in front of me. "It's progress she's even wearing it after she buried it in a box her entire life. It's a family heirloom."

"I said. Remove it before I rip it from your wrist."

I flinch.

"Hey!" Dahlia's shoulders square, but I pat her arm.

"It's okay. I don't like it that much anyway." I unclasp it and hand it to Preston.

He flips it and rotates something that holds the plate at the back, and just like that, the plate opens.

I watch in bewilderment as the two plates laid side by side reveal a crescent moon and a sun. The same symbol Preston has on the black ring he's wearing on his index finger.

He aligns them. My eyes widen because the ring and the bracelet have the exact identical symbol.

Preston's fingers trace the initials carved by the symbol. W.J.A.

"Jesus fucking Christ." He lets out in a breath. "What the fuck is this?"

"I don't know," I whisper. "This is the first time I've seen that. I…didn't even know it could be opened."

"This explains a lot of shit." He watches me for a few beats, his eyes seeming to peer into mine. Then he stands up all of a sudden, clutching the bracelet between his fingers. "I have to go."

"Wait." I stand, too, and Dahlia follows, her brows knitting as she watches Preston carefully.

"I'll give it back later." He pauses. "If I can."

"It's not that." I step in front of him. "Is that symbol common? If it's really valuable, maybe Mom stole it…"

"She would've never been able to steal my grandfather's bracelet. So that means he willingly gave it to her."

"G-grandfather?"

"Yes, Winston James Armstrong. This belonged to him at some point and has his initials. My father and uncle have similar ones. They're usually offered by the father to his off-spring, so I'm supposed to get one after graduating. Grandpa said he lost his a long time ago, but that doesn't seem to be the case—"

"Vi, watch out!" Dahlia's scream punctures my ears as the loud revving of an engine and a popping sound echo in the air.

My first instinct is to push Preston, but as I do so, he swings us around so fast, I'm disoriented and lose my footing.

Dahlia screams again when I crash to the ground, and I think I've been hit.

But a heavy body is on me as a few other gunshots are exchanged. I catch a glimpse of Larson running with his gun out. Dahlia's sobbing, and a very familiar warmth is enveloping me.

Jude.

I tap his shoulder. "J-Jude… I think…I think Pres…"

He gathers me in his arms, shielding me completely, but from over his shoulder, I can see a motionless body lying on top of the blanket, blood soaking his jacket and the grass.

And he's not moving.

Preston is *not* moving.

Dahlia's shaking, running toward me, but I push at Jude, and I run toward Preston on unsteady feet.

Because he's bleeding out and not moving.

"No…no…no… Pres, please…no!"

Strong arms try to pull me back, but I'm screaming so loud, I can't hear anything else.

This is a nightmare, right?

Please tell me I'll wake up soon.

Please.

CHAPTER 34
Violet

SKELETAL FINGERS WRAP AROUND MY THROAT, THE bones squeezing so tight, I'm wheezing.

Her amber eyes are dead, looking through me as two streaks of blood trickle down either side of her mouth.

She's sitting on my chest again, crushing my rib cage and stabbing my heart.

"Ma...ma..." I strain, my breath leaving my lungs in short gasps.

"You know." She adds another hand around my throat. "You're a curse, Violet. Not only did you ruin my life, but you're also destroying everyone else's around you like a useless whore."

"N-no...that's not..."

"I told you, didn't I?" She smiles, her canines looking like sharp fangs in the darkness. "You'll be the downfall of anyone who cares about you."

"No..."

"Didn't Mario like you? Where is he now?"

"That's...that's..."

"How about Preston? You killed him in his prime."

"No!"

I gasp awake, tears streaming down my cheeks and into

my mouth. The salty taste explodes on my tongue as I pant, my whole body trembling.

"Vi!"

I startle at Dahlia's voice, then release a long breath. It… was a nightmare.

The whole thing was a nightmare.

Dahlia, Preston, and I didn't go to the park. He didn't get shot.

All of it is…not real.

And yet the weight crushing my chest remains there, heavy and obstructive, and I'm sucking air into my burning lungs with short pants.

I focus on my sister and pause. She's wearing an oversized jacket—probably Kane's—and her eyes are red.

Why does she look as if she's been crying?

Dahlia doesn't cry. She's the strongest woman I know.

"Are you okay?" She sits on the bed, taking my hand in hers. "The doctor said it's just a graze, but…"

Her voice breaks, her hand shaking uncontrollably around mine. And that's when I notice that my upper arm is bandaged.

"Hey…" I don't recognize my hoarse voice. "It's okay. I'm fine."

"I know…I know that, but all I keep thinking about is when you were in a coma, and I guess I thought you'd be gone again. I'm terrified of losing you, Vi."

"You won't." I pull her in for a hug. "I'm right here."

She buries her face in my neck, sniffling softly, and I pat her back, my fingers trembling due to the pulsing pain in my arm.

Then I realize the room we're in smells of very familiar antiseptic.

The type of smell I was surrounded with for months and could breathe even when I was in a coma.

The hospital.

"Dahlia," I whisper, my voice catching.

"Yeah?" She pulls away, wiping at her puffy eyes.

My gaze strays to the blotch of blood on her sweater, visible beneath the jacket, and my heart burns. "Were you hurt?"

"Oh, no, no." She touches the dried blood. "This is because I was dragging you away from Preston."

"So…it's true?"

Images of Preston lying on the grass assault me. A large spot of blood drenched the center of his jacket, and his usually mischievous eyes were closed.

His lips were already turning blue.

"Where is Preston…?" I stumble from the bed, and Dahlia catches me before I fall.

I'm standing on unsteady feet as my sister hesitates.

"Tell me, Dahl, please."

"He's in surgery." She bites her lower lip. "I think it's bad, Vi."

A doom-like feeling tears through my chest as I grab onto both of Dahlia's arms for balance. "Take me there."

"It's better if you rest…" She trails off, probably at seeing my shaky lips and the horrified look in my eyes, and releases a resigned breath. "Fine."

We walk together down the hall, but everything is blurry—the patients, the walls, and the staff.

It's like I'm not here.

"Do you know who it was?" Dahlia asks, interlinking her arm with mine.

"What?"

"I heard Jude tell Kane that this has happened before."

She rubs my arm. "I thought the guard who was following you around recently was Jude being overprotective, but apparently, you were in danger. Is that true?"

"I…received a couple of texts asking me to leave and was attacked a few times, yes."

"Was one of those times before you were in a coma?"

All this time, I've tried to shield Dahlia from this mess, but she ended up right in the middle of it anyway. She deserves to know the truth.

"Mario saved me back then, and he ended up in a coma." I choke on my words as she pushes the elevator button. "Preston saved me, too. Twice. And now… Oh my God—Jude! He shielded me, didn't he? Did something happen to him… Is he…?"

I'm panting, my chest squeezing so tightly, I think I'm having a panic attack.

"No, no." She strokes my back, ushering me into the elevator. "He did injure his arm, but I think it's only a graze, just like yours. He's been in front of the OR with Kane ever since we got to the hospital."

A long breath rushes out of me, but the weight of dread still sits on my chest like doomsday.

The elevator doors open, and we walk to the OR's waiting area. My steps are lethargic at best, my energy waning, but I put an effort into placing one foot in front of the other.

The gloomy energy hits us as soon as we arrive.

But then yelling follows.

"Get the fuck out of here, Marcus."

It's Jude's rough and furious voice.

I hear him before I see him. Then he comes into view, slamming Marcus against the wall with one hand twisted in his collar, his muscles tight with unrestrained rage.

A thick bandage wraps his arm, already soaked through, and blood clings to his T-shirt and is smeared across his ink and his knuckles like war paint.

Marcus looks even worse; his jacket is covered in blood, and the same red stains his fingers and streaks across his face, making him look like a demon dragged out of hell. His usually mocking features are blank now, drained of expression, like whatever was inside him just...switched off.

"What is Marcus doing here?" I whisper to Dahlia.

"He came during the chaos," she murmurs back. "He showed up out of nowhere, almost as if he was hiding in the trees the whole time or something, the creep."

"I said. I'm not going anywhere." Marcus's eyes spark with something violent. "If anything, you're the one who needs to scram for failing to save him."

"The fuck you just say?" Jude snarls in his face.

"Want me to spell it out for you?" Marcus's tone is mocking, but his body is tight.

"Go fight outside." An authoritative voice echoes around the room.

The man is sitting on one of the leather-padded chairs, his fingers forming a steeple at his chin. He's a striking older version of Preston, but his presence resembles the deep ocean—calm on the outside but with a turbulent energy on the inside.

"Lawrence. He's Preston's dad." Dahlia tells me in a low voice, confirming my suspicions.

Marcus's glare slides to Lawrence, even though Jude is still strangling him by the collar.

I've never seen Marcus this...mad. No. Enraged is an accurate description. Granted, I don't know him personally, but I've seen him all over the place, and he's usually more unruffled than a monk. Even that time he showed up in the club's parking lot, he was the one provoking Preston, not the other way around.

Right now, however, he looks at Lawrence as if he's slaughtered his entire bloodline. "Is that all you have to say when your fucking son is facing death? *Go fight outside*? You have no other goddamn reaction?" He laughs, the sound unhinged. "God, you're all the same. Every single corner of your fucking empire is rotten to the core."

Lawrence doesn't react, doesn't even look at Marcus, his full attention remaining square on the door.

"That's enough." Kane's firm voice slices through the tension as he stops pacing. "Leave before I have someone escort you out using unpleasant methods, Marcus."

"And let you big shots handle everything, right?" He laughs in Jude's face, clutching him by the collar. "Like you got him shot, right, Callahan? Useless piece of shit."

"You fucking—" Jude slams him against the wall, the thud echoing loudly, but Marcus just laughs harder like a maniac.

"What? You're going to stand there and tell me you didn't, in fact, invite death upon your supposed best friend?"

"It's not his fault." I rush toward them, my voice and body shaking.

Both Jude's and Marcus's attention swings to me, and my trembling gets worse at Jude's stare. It feels like it's been ages since I saw him, and I almost forgot how brutally beautiful he is.

Like a rush of darkness in the light.

An anchor in the wild sea.

His brown eyes flicker over the length of me, observing, assessing, as if he needs to make sure I'm in one piece.

"It's my fault," I whisper to Marcus. "Preston did that to protect me—"

"That's right. It should've been you." Marcus barks, and Jude punches him in the face. Blood trickles down his nose and the corner of his lip.

"Shut the fuck up, Osborn!"

"But I'm right. She should be the one in that room right now—"

Jude punches him again, the sound echoing in the air as more blood drenches Marcus's face.

And then they're punching each other, the anger and absolute madness in their violence echoing in thwacks and grunts.

I try to intervene, but Dahlia pulls me away and toward Kane, who's on the phone, calling someone to come escort 'a raging bull' out.

"Jude says this is yours."

I look up at the sound of Lawrence's voice, momentarily distracted from the fight.

He seemed completely disinterested in his surroundings earlier, but he's standing now, and he's so tall, with a presence that grabs you by the throat.

Lawrence's hair is styled, his expression lined with years of experience and the look of a man who's seen it all but wasn't impressed. His eyes are a curious shade of blue and green—a familiar color I swear I've seen before.

But where?

He shows me his palm, where he's holding the bloodied bracelet I gave Preston.

My lips tremble, but I shake my head and don't reach out for it. "Pres…Preston said it's an important family heirloom, so I must've had it by mistake. Mom probably stole it or something…"

"But Preston said that's impossible," Dahlia interjects, then bites her lower lip. "Sorry, Vi. I told Jude and Kane that Preston lost his cool about the bracelet and seemed to have come to a realization."

"He did." Lawrence's voice is cool and collected but has an underlying tension. "I believe I'm coming to the same realization."

He's watching me closely, his eyes skimming over my face the same way Preston's did that first time I met him and he did an imaginary interview.

Ever since then, Preston's been treating me warmly, completely negating the rumors that he's malicious and never stays in anyone's company for more than a few days. That, aside from Jude and Kane, he distrusts and downright loathes everyone else.

That hasn't been my experience.

If anything, he's been so welcoming and has always made me laugh and tried to cheer me up. He made my move to Graystone Ridge such a breeze, as if I was always meant to be here and restart my life.

And all he got in return was being shot on my behalf.

Just like Mama said, I'm bound to hurt everyone who gets close.

"Do you mind if I keep this?" Lawrence strokes the bloodied bracelet.

"Not at all."

"Can you also do me a favor and not discuss any of this with outsiders?" He pauses. "I believe it'll help me pin down the culprit who put a bullet in my son."

"Absolutely," I say.

"Okay," Dahlia says, sounding suspicious. "But can you tell Vi why her mother had your father's important bracelet?"

"I need to verify a few things first. I'll ask for your cooperation in due time." His gaze flits to Jude, who's still trying to fight Marcus as a couple of men pull them apart. "From the little research I've managed to gather, you were Julian's test subject?"

My spine jerks. Julian is the last person I want to talk about right now, but I still nod. "Yes."

His lips purse, but he sets them back in a disinterested line.

I'm about to ask what that has to do with anything, but the door of the operating room area slides open.

Everyone comes to a halt, as if no air exists and we can no longer breathe.

Marcus, who was fighting off the men, grows still. Jude and Kane rush to the doctor, who removes his cap, revealing damp gray hair.

"How is he?" Jude asks, his voice thick with a tension that matches the knot in my stomach.

The doctor looks at Lawrence, who stops behind the other two and bows his head. "We tried our best, but he lost a lot of blood. My condolences, sir."

I fall onto the floor, bringing Dahlia with me as she tries to keep me upright. I choke on my tears, my fingers digging into my sister's arm as a wave of nausea rolls through me.

"What the fuck!" Jude grabs the doctor by the collar. "What do you mean by condolences? Go in there and bring him the fuck back!"

"You're lying." Marcus is breathing harshly, like an injured animal, fighting against the men who are trying to drag him away. "This is a fucking lie!"

His roars reverberate in the space as two more men approach, and they finally escort him out.

Kane tries to pull Jude away from the doctor to no avail. Jude's rage palpitates like a red cloud, engulfing everyone and everything inside it.

As he's about to punch the doctor, Kane wraps both arms around his shoulders from behind. "Ground yourself."

Jude remains still for a moment, and the doctor manages to escape.

"I want to see my son." Lawrence follows the doctor, his expression unchanged, as if he didn't just hear the news of his son's death.

Death.

Death?

A fresh wave of pain squeezes my chest, and I tap it a few times, but it only gets worse.

More painful.

"Fuck no!" Jude screams, shoving Kane aside and pulling out his phone. "I refuse to believe this."

A faint ripple of tremors passes through his fingers as he puts the phone to his ear and speaks, his voice raw with emotion. "Regis… *Father*. I'll do whatever you want. I'll be *whatever* the fuck you want me to be, and I'll forgive you for *everything* if you make Julian bring Preston back. You must have something for this in your experimentation centers. We're a medical empire, so we can do this much… I'm begging you. Do *something…anything…* Just bring back him back."

Jude's face pales as he listens to the voice on the other end and then lets his hand fall to his side, the phone cluttering to the ground, the screen smashing into a spider's web.

"Jude…?" Kane asks, his words strained and pained, as if his throat is suffocated.

Jude looks at him with a dark face, his fists trembling.

"He said no medical empire can bring back the dead. If it could, he would've gotten his first wife back or brought me back my mother."

As Kane clasps Jude's shoulder and Dahlia hugs me as I sob, I know—I just know—that this will break me beyond repair.

———

Grief is a strange notion.

I grieved a lot when my mother died, but I think I grieved my tarnished future more than her death. I grieved my loneliness that loomed once my only family was cremated.

That's what she wanted. Cremation. For her soul to be scattered on the ocean.

Pretty sure the charity that took care of the whole process just discarded her in a nearby lake.

I didn't understand grief when my mother died. I was sad, lost, and in pain, but it was all abstract.

This time, grief hit me like an intense earthquake—tangible and inescapable.

I'm barely standing, swaying in the black dress and flats I threw on without thinking. My eyes—hidden behind sunglasses—are puffy and bloodshot from crying every day since Preston died four days ago.

We're at his funeral now.

A ceremony that's somehow become a spectacle of wealth and grief, wrapped in black silk and gold-trimmed sorrow.

The Armstrong estate looms in the background, its towering columns casting long shadows over the sea of mourners dressed in tailored suits and designer mourning attire.

The sky is an endless stretch of gray, suffocating in its

vastness. Drizzle lands softly, silently, some of it sliding on my nose.

A polished black mahogany casket rests at the front, adorned with stark white lilies. The flowers look wrong, too delicate for someone like Preston, who oozed power and playfulness.

The metallic glint of the engraved Armstrong crest catches the light, a reminder that even in death, he belongs to something larger, something that probably demanded too much from him.

I stand in the back, my fingers curled into fists inside my coat pockets, trying to hold myself together when everything inside me is falling apart.

"You should get something to eat," Kane's soft voice speaks to Dahlia, who hasn't left my side, curling her arm around me as if I'll break if she stops touching me.

And maybe I would. She's the only reason I haven't surrendered myself to the shadows in the past couple of days.

Kane's dressed in a black tuxedo, with a lily in his breast pocket. He looks tired and distraught, and I know he needs Dahlia more than I do. That's why I pretend to be asleep, so she can spend more time with him.

He's the one who lost his best friend, whom he knew practically his entire life. I just came into Preston's life recently and managed to end it.

"It's okay, I'm not hungry." Dahlia strokes his cheek. "Have you eaten, though?"

"I have no appetite." He pulls her toward him in a hug and whispers something in her ear, and she wraps her arms around him, her eyes shining with tears.

"I'm sorry," she murmurs again and again. "I'm so sorry you have to go through this."

I use the chance and slip through the crowd, hearing the murmured sympathies mostly directed at Lawrence. His wife stands by his side, looking like she's straight out of a *Vogue* magazine in her tulle black dress and sheer black mourning veil draped from her pillbox hat.

In the front row, people bow down to shake the hand of Preston's grandfather, who's holding a cane, his face ashen. His wife, Preston's grandmother, sits beside him, accepting handshakes and saying nothing, looking stern and emotionless as if this isn't her grandson's funeral.

Another notable family member, according to Dahlia, is Preston's paternal uncle, who's more interested in talking to Julian and a smartly dressed woman at the perimeter.

And then there's a little girl with curly blonde hair, wearing a black lace dress, who won't stop hugging the casket and crying—Preston's sister.

She's the only one in Preston's entourage who's genuinely showing her emotions. But that doesn't last long. Her mother chastises her in words I can't hear, then sends her inside with one of the staff members, effectively killing any semblance of actual grief in the Armstrong family.

The only ones who are grieving are Kane, Jude, and Marcus, who seems unaffected while standing in the corner but actually looks like he hasn't slept a wink in the past few days.

Pretty sure there was a fight when he demanded to be here, and the only reason he got in is because his biological father—and the head of the Osborn family—got involved.

Dragging my gaze from Marcus, I get on my tiptoes to look for Jude in the first row, where Regis and Annalise are sitting, but I can't see him.

The priest's voice drifts through the cold air, speaking of redemption, peace, a life taken too soon.

It all sits wrong with me. Preston never wanted redemption. Never wanted peace. He wanted war, chaos, and to have fun.

He wanted to live his youth to the fullest and didn't deserve for it to be interrupted right when it was getting started.

My breath comes in short, sharp bursts, the cold slicing through my lungs, but it's not the air that's suffocating me. It's the truth. The ugly, inescapable truth that I should be the one in that casket.

A sudden gust of wind cuts through the crowd, sending the flower arrangement flying, their fragile petals trembling but refusing to drop. For a moment, I let myself believe it was him. That if I close my eyes, I'll hear his voice, his sharp wit, the mocking lilt of a man who pretended he felt nothing but burned with too much inside.

But there's only silence.

And the crushing realization that Preston Armstrong is gone.

I walk for as long as my legs can carry me, suffocated by the lack of love from people who are supposed to be closest to Preston.

My feet come to a halt by a tree at a side garden away from the funeral.

Jude.

He's standing by the trunk, stroking the surface over and over again.

He turns around, and my heart jolts because his cheeks have sunken, and he doesn't fill out the black shirt and pants like he usually does. His eyes have lost their light, and his shoulders are crowded with tension.

"You should get some rest, Violet. You haven't slept properly in days."

"How do you know? Unless you've been there?"

He was.

I could feel his warmth beside me on the bed every night. I pretended to be asleep as he pulled me to his hard chest, then let out a sigh as if he needed something to hold on to.

I did, too, which is why I pretended not to notice. I was scared that if I opened my eyes, he would disappear.

"I don't know what you're talking about." He faces the tree again, staring at a mark.

"So you're fine coming to my room every night but not fine with admitting it?" I storm toward him, then stop. "Forget it. I don't know why I even care. You'll do whatever you want anyway, and I'm done making excuses for you."

I'm about to leave, but his rough voice echoes in the air. "I needed you."

I start to look back at him, but big arms wrap around my waist from behind, and he buries his face in my hair. "Your warmth, your smell, even the sound of your breathing calms me, sweetheart."

My thumb strokes my wrist. "Then why did you have to do it in secret?"

"Because you're mad at me, and I can't handle your rejection. Not now, when my world is falling apart."

"Jude…"

"Preston was…*is* my brother, more than Julian ever has been." His voice is thick with pain. "Julian and I have a generational gap, and he was already a snake while I was growing up and rarely treated me like a brother. When I was young, I wanted to be close to him, but he was in college and plagued with power, so it was impossible. When I told Pres, he said, 'No worries, my dude, you have me! I'm the best and the most reliable and charming brother anyone could have. The

last one in stock. Better snag me now before I'm snatched up
by someone else. Also, let's be friends. No one likes me.'"
Jude chuckles humorlessly. "He said that while his face was
bruised because some kids beat him up after he talked shit
about them and I saved him. We shook our bloodied hands
as a blood pact and said we'd always have each other's backs.
We even engraved it in this tree over ten years ago. The mark
is starting to fade, and I can't fix it. Because he's gone now,
and I can't bring him back, no matter how many things or
people I punch."

My fingers stroke over his busted knuckles, tears streaming down my cheeks and slipping into my mouth, down my
chin and onto the collar of my dress. "I'm sorry. It should've
been me."

"Violet!" He whirls me around so fast that I almost fall
until he grabs my shoulders with both hands. "Don't you
fucking say that."

"But it's because of me that he's…he's…" I choke on my
words, my mouth flooding with saliva and pain.

"Then you better live for him." His eyes bore into mine,
his voice growing steady and resolute. "I know you're thinking you've cursed both Mario and Preston, so you believe the
world would be a better place without you."

"How…"

"You're obvious. It's why Dahlia and I have been keeping
an eye on you in case you do something stupid." He shakes
my shoulders. "I'm telling you, Violet. Your death wouldn't
bring back Preston or Mario. It'll only make their sacrifices
die in vain. Do you hear me? Live for them if you can't live for
yourself. You owe them that much."

A new wave of tears stream down my face, clinging to
the sunglasses.

"Live for me," he whispers, his head tilting down, and when his lips capture mine, all I can do is kiss him through the tears.

CHAPTER 35

Jude

I COULDN'T SAY GOODBYE.

Not when everyone else was.

Not even when Kane spoke about Preston, fighting emotions that were ripped out of us at a young age to tell the audience, that only came for the Armstrong name, how amazing Preston was.

How he was more than just Preston Armstrong.

How, despite his selfish speech and the grandiose way he talked about himself, he was actually the most selfless person on earth.

Only Kane and I knew the true Preston, but only one of us got up there and spoke about him as if he were listening. I was just trying not to punch everyone in sight.

All the fucking people—his parents, grandparents, and uncle, who seemed more interested in striking deals and turning his funeral into a show of wealth and extravagance.

The only reason I didn't act on my thoughts was because Violet held my hand through the whole thing, not complaining or wincing whenever I tightened my grip. She even stroked the back of it with her thumb as if she could feel I was spiraling.

Despite my stone-cold face and lack of emotions, Violet could tell that I wasn't all right.

That I won't be for a long time.

I don't know what state I'd be in if she hadn't been by my side these past couple of days. Even when she was sleeping, the fact that she was there, breathing softly against my face while I held her hand, was enough.

Her hand in mine earlier was enough.

But I sent her with Kane and Dahlia. She hesitated to leave me, but she finally agreed when I told her I needed to be alone.

Now, after everyone has evacuated the cemetery, I'm on my own, staring at the soil that's damp with drizzle.

To say goodbye.

I don't want to say goodbye.

The cemetery feels too quiet now that everyone's gone.

The mourners left in sleek black cars, the sound of their hushed voices swallowed by the hum of expensive engines and crunching gravel. The Vipers team was the last to go. Some of the guys shed tears as they spoke after Kane about how Preston was the life of the team.

But they'll all forget about him soon enough.

He's just returned to dust, as the priest said, praying for forgiveness from a God Pres never believed in. A God who'd fucked him over since he was a kid, then took his life too soon. As a last fuck-you of sorts.

Now that the whole charade is over, it's just me, Preston's grave, and the light, steady rain soaking into the earth like the sky itself is grieving.

The gray clouds hang low and swollen, pressing against the horizon, stretching over the rows of headstones like a heavy, unbroken shroud.

I release a long, fractured exhale as the wind moves through the towering oaks, rustling the dead leaves that cling stubbornly to the branches. Every so often, a gust sends them spiraling down, landing in damp piles that reek of decay.

I shove my hands into my pockets, and my fingers curl into fists. Cold seeps into my skin, settling deep in my bones, but that's nothing compared to the hollow space inside me. The one Preston used to fill with his sharp tongue and that smirk that made me want to either punch him or laugh along.

I stare down at the headstone.

It's polished, expensive, a witness of the Armstrong wealth carved into stone. The inscription 'Preston Armstrong' is neat but impersonal. Pretty sure Lawrence approved it without a second thought as if it were a business deal. It doesn't say anything about who he really was, what he really meant.

Just a name. Just dates.

Like he was just another goddamn statistic.

First, it was my mom. Now, it's Preston.

And I couldn't stop either from leaving.

I exhale slowly, my breath curling into the damp air, mixing with the faint scent of wet earth and rotting leaves. It feels wrong to say anything.

But I do.

"You went out like a fucking idiot," I mutter, my voice rough, cutting through the thick silence. "Pres...I don't think I'll be able to forgive myself for not being there in time, so while you saved Violet, I would've been able to save you. Or better yet, I would've saved her, and you'd be standing here instead."

The words hit the empty air, disappearing into the mist that clings to the ground like ghosts waiting for company.

A raindrop slips down the edge of the stone, trailing like a tear.

I rake a hand through my damp hair, my jaw tightening.

"You were supposed to outlive us all, not go out like this."
My voice drops lower, almost drowned out by the whispering
wind. "You said we'd be stuck together for life when we were
in that godforsaken boarding school, so how *the fuck*—" I
choke on my words, then whisper, "Why did you have to go so
soon? Who the hell is going to join me on my revenge murder
sprees to bring you justice now? You're well aware Kane can
be boring, and truly, you're the glue that held the three of us
together. Just seeing his face reminds me of you, of all the
times the three of us spent together, and it feels…feels like
I'm *suffocating* without you."

The drizzle thickens, soaking into my jacket, dripping
off the leaves, tapping against the marble like a quiet funeral
drum. The wind shifts, carrying the faint scent of laughter,
whiskey, and blood—memories of late nights, bad decisions,
and an unorthodox friendship that just worked.

Until it suddenly ended.

"Thank you, Pres. For being there for me, for saving
Violet even though you barely know her." I let out a breath.
"I promise I'll rip out the heart of whoever killed you with
my bare hands."

———

I don't know how long I remain at the cemetery, but it's long
enough that I'm soaked and the day turns into night.

No matter how long I talked to Preston, I felt like he
couldn't hear me. That, somehow, he's in a different space
than me, and I can't reach him.

So I went for a ride on my bike, letting the wind con-
sume me, but even that did little for my jumbled thoughts
and feelings.

Which is why I find myself in Violet's apartment again.

I remove my shoes and jacket and even my damp pants and shirt, remaining in my boxer briefs as I step into the darkness. I don't need lights to know my way around her place. I've been here countless times, waiting to ambush her, surprise her, listen to that delicious yelp she releases whenever she sees me.

Once I reach her bedroom, I hesitate, then slide the door open and walk in.

Violet is lying on her side, covered with the sheet to her chin. I approach her, not making a sound.

The light from the atmospheric crescent lamp she always keeps on at night shines on her peaceful features.

I lie down on my side, facing her, my hand resting on hers, and my mind calms slightly, my breathing almost shattering just at the feel of her.

While I have no clue what angels look like, Violet is my version of a goddamn angel. No idea what the fuck I've done to deserve someone like her in my life, but I'll do everything in my power to ensure that she stays right here.

Being mine.

She gave me time alone in the cemetery earlier upon my insistence and probably because she felt I needed it. I now know why she's so attuned to people and how she can determine their needs even before they voice them.

She's a healer, my Violet.

And someone like her, someone who feels too much and can be easily taken advantage of, needs a motherfucker like me to keep all the vultures at bay.

I slide my fingers along the tear streaks on her cheeks. She's been crying herself to sleep since Preston's death, and I know she blames herself for it, no matter what Dahlia and I say, but I won't allow her to self-destruct.

If I have to be her watchdog twenty-four seven, so be it.

Her eyes slowly blink open, the blue swirling in a pit of confusion before a small smile tilts her lips. "You're here."

"I'm here," I whisper.

She grabs onto my hand that's resting on her cheek and stares at me for a beat too long. "I'm so sorry, Jude."

"For what?"

"Everything that's happening to you lately. First, you find out about your mom and then…" She gulps, her lips wobbling.

Her words feel too raw, too intimate, and like me, she probably still can't believe what happened to Preston. My chest feels like it'll explode when I think about the fact that I'll never see him again.

Part of me refuses to come to that conclusion.

"My mom never meant to die that violently," I say, addressing Violet's first statement just so I won't have to talk about my best friend that I left six feet under this afternoon.

"No?"

"No. According to Julian, who questioned the murderer before he killed him, Mom asked him to make it look like theft gone wrong and instructed that she'd only be stabbed once or twice fatally. But apparently, that man took it as carte blanche to enact his disturbed fantasies."

"That makes sense."

"Makes sense how?"

"She obviously didn't want to hurt you, even if her mental illness pushed her to do things she would've never done if she'd been well."

"Yeah. I'm learning to accept that."

"Good." She rubs my hand back and forth. "You deserve to keep whatever image of your mother you wish to, Jude.

You're lucky to have received motherly love, even if it wasn't perfect, and I don't believe you have to demonize her to accept the truth."

"I won't, no matter what Regis tries to say."

"I love that you think that way." She smiles softly.

I stroke her cheek. "You also deserve motherly love, and just because you didn't receive it doesn't mean you're not whole."

She gulps audibly, a shine appearing in her eyes. "I wish one of the adults had told me that at the time. Maybe if they had, I wouldn't have felt like it was normal, that it was my duty to make myself as small as possible in front of her, or that women are meant to be used by men. It screwed up my whole perception, you know."

"Screwed up your perception how?"

"I thought it was okay for one of her clients to rub my thigh or stroke my face, even if it made me uncomfortable. Afterward, I thought it was my fault that my foster father kept looking at my growing breasts, being touchy-feely with me, or attempted to rape me, because I wasn't covering up enough and was tempting him. I thought unsatisfactory and emotionally hurtful sex was the norm. That women aren't supposed to enjoy it because Mom never looked like she did. But it turns out, I got everything wrong. It was painful to realize that I was let down by all the adults in my life, that most of the men in my life preyed on me since I was young, and that sex *should* only feel good. Sometimes, I'm happy I'm making these realizations so I can fix my mindset, but other times, I'm just sad that I missed out on so much."

Hot fire burns through my chest, but I continue to rub her skin, trying as hard as possible not to let anger get a hold of me.

"Sorry for the trauma dumping." She smiles awkwardly. "I swear I don't do this all the time. I guess… I really love talking to you about everything because you've always given me a safe space."

"And I always will. Don't be sorry for finally using your voice, Violet. I'm here for you."

"I'm also here for you. Whether you want to talk about your mom, your dad, Vencor. All of it."

"What do you know about Vencor?"

"The basics, I suppose."

I lift a brow. "Dahlia, I presume?"

She nods.

"I don't know what she told you, but Vencor doesn't mean much to me. It means a lot to my father and Julian for sure because they're power-hungry, but not me."

"You don't care about power?"

"I did while my mother was alive."

"But not anymore."

It's not a question, but I nod. Though I don't tell Violet that I'll have to start caring again. Aside from Regis and Julian, Kane also cares, and he's deeply entrenched in the organization after taking the reins of the Davenport family.

"You can't protect Violet if you remain on the sidelines while Regis and Julian confiscate the limelight, Jude."

That's what he told me the other day. He's always firmly believed that we need to be at the top to shield who and what we care for, and he's right. I need to become deeply involved again.

Not only for power, but also to be a thorn in Julian's fucking side.

I still haven't forgiven him for the coma fiasco, and I'll make sure to spend the rest of my life making him pay for it.

Violet sighs. "I'm so glad you came over tonight."

"I thought you didn't like my stalkerish tendencies."

She lifts a shoulder. "I think we're past that phase."

"I made your life hell and threatened to kill you. How can you so easily get past it?"

"I don't like holding grudges." She chuckles a bit. "Dahlia tells me I'm too nice and I need to be meaner, but I just can't. It's not in my nature to actively hurt others, and I know that's frowned upon in today's world, but I like to hold on to who I am. I'm learning to set boundaries and stuff, but I can't become mean just because my life sucked. I don't believe those who aren't involved should pay for my pain."

"But *I* am involved."

"As long as you don't hurt me anymore, I can forgive and forget. But don't ice me out again."

"I won't. I'm sorry, sweetheart. I was having a hard time and didn't want to burden you with it or take it out on you."

"That's the point of having each other, Jude."

"Okay."

"I mean it. If you stop communicating, I'll do the same. I'm no longer someone others can stomp on while I lie there and take it."

"Good girl." I stroke beneath her eyes, and she shivers. "I'm proud of you."

"You…are?"

"Hm. You've come a long way from being a scaredy-cat who used to run away from any form of confrontation, sweetheart."

"Speaking of confrontation." A line appears between her brows. "Do you know why I need to be present when Preston's personal will is going to be read?"

A sharp sting of pain cuts through me, and Violet must

see the change on my face, because she tightens her grip on my hand, leaving it square on her face.

I know why Lawrence asked Violet to be present—because of the bracelet that's an Armstrong heirloom.

While I'm not sure what that entails, I'm certain it'll explain something about her mother's disgusting behavior. Violet tends to close off whenever her mother is in the picture, so I mull over my words to avoid scaring her off.

"He probably mentioned you." I frown. "Though I find it hard to believe that he kept his personal will up-to-date. Maybe Lawrence made him update it regularly."

"He seemed off," she whispers, her words faltering for a bit. "Lawrence, I mean. It was as if he was conflicted."

"Mm. He had a strange relationship with Pres. Not as weird as the one Pres had with his mom, though."

"At least he looked like he was a bit in pain, which can't be said about the rest of the Armstrong family." She sounds angry for Preston.

One thing Violet will do is get extremely offended on behalf of the people she cares about.

"I'm kind of apprehensive about going to the Armstrong house again," she continues. "The grandparents and the step-mom have an odd vibe. I can't put my finger on it."

"You're just a natural at reading people. It's better to stay away from those three, but you don't have to worry…" I pull her closer. "I'll be right by your side."

Violet wraps her arms around me, her voice sounding muffled against my chest. "Thank you. I needed that."

"I thought you only needed Dahlia."

She pulls her head back, tracing both her hands along my chest tattoos, lingering on the barren tree. "Are you jealous of my sister?"

"Only sometimes. Will I have to see her all over you in the morning?"

"No, she's spending the night with Kane. He needs her more than I do."

"You don't need anyone when you have me."

She smiles slightly, her eyes still so fucking sad, but she's trying her hardest to cheer me up. "Okay, Mr. Petty. Don't put my sister on your shit list."

"Hmm. Depends." I kiss her throat, breathing her in and releasing a long fucking grunt at the taste of her.

Goddammit, she's like a rush of blood to the head.

"O-on what?" Violet tilts her neck, giving me access as I pepper kisses down her throat to her collarbone and pull out a breast from her nightgown, sucking hard on the nipple until she moans.

Her hands grip my shoulders for balance, her back arching, pushing more of her breast into my mouth.

"On whether or not I'm important to you, sweetheart," I speak against her nipple, feeling her shiver, and then drag the gown over her head until she's lying naked in my arms.

A blush covers her skin, and her pussy glistens, making me grunt. I love how she goes to sleep without any underwear since I started visiting her at night on the regular.

"You are…" Her voice is husky, slightly broken because I'm sucking on her nipple again as I thrust two fingers inside her.

Violet's hips roll, almost grinding against me, provoking my cock into a full-blown erection.

"How important?" I scissor my fingers inside her, alternating to the other nipple, sucking, biting, making her writhe on the mattress.

My cock is aching to be inside her, absolutely fucking

ravenous for this woman. I don't even know when she became my one and only, but she has.

I've never looked at another woman since she came into my life. And even before her, I barely paid them any attention.

Violet changed my entire fucking perception.

She's the light in an otherwise gloomy world.

She's the peace not even hockey is able to provide me.

"*Very* important." She moans, grabbing onto my boxer briefs. "F-fuck me, Jude."

"Jesus Christ. Say that again, sweetheart."

"Fuck me." She wraps her trembling hands around my neck, her eyes glistening. "I need you."

My cock is rock fucking hard as I tug the boxer briefs off and throw them aside.

Then I'm on top of her, my cock nudging inside her as I tighten my grip on her throat. "I'm the one who needs you, Violet."

Her short nails scrape against my back, her heels digging into my ass. "Go harder, Jude. Mess me up."

"Mmm." I thrust inside her in one ruthless go, and she hums in my arms. "When you talk like that, you make me feral."

"More…"

"Fuck." I pull out, then push in until her head rolls back and her noises of pleasure fill the room.

"Yes…right there…please…"

"You're taking my cock like a very good girl, Violet." *Pull out. Thrust.* "I'm the only one who's allowed to ravage this little cunt, aren't I?"

"Yes, yes…oh God."

I slap the side of her ass cheek three consecutive times. "I can be your god, Violet. I'll be your fucking everything."

Thrust. Slap.

She shudders, her body molding to mine, her noises ricocheting in the silence of the night. I love the look on her face when she comes, how her lips form in an O, and she has this otherworldly look in her eye.

I love how she's comfortable holding me close as her pussy clenches around my cock.

Every time she does that, I want to frame it so I can look at her beautiful form.

As she's coming, I release her throat, pull open the side drawer, and retrieve some lube.

Violet is still trembling when I squirt the gel on my fingers and part her legs. "Be good and hold these for me."

She blinks, then grips her legs, staring up at me in her post-orgasm haze.

I get on my knees, still moving inside her as I slide a finger into her back hole.

She blushes, sinking her teeth into her lower lip. "Are you still shy about me touching this tight little hole, Violet?"

"A bit—" She moans when I add another finger, her pussy clenching around my cock.

"You've taken three of my fingers before, sweetheart. You have to fit my fingers properly to take my cock. Relax for me."

She bites her lip again but nods. "You're stretching me out."

"That's the plan." I drop a kiss on her nose, and she relaxes. "Well done. Good fucking girl."

That makes her relax further, and I thrust another lubed finger. She tenses at first, but then mimics my breathing, her pussy clenching around me as I thrust in a deep, long rhythm. I can feel the thin layer separating my cock from my fingers and it makes me hum.

"Oh God…if you do that while fucking me, I'm gonna… I'm gonna come…"

"Not yet." I pull out from her pussy, and even though my cock is glistening with her juices, I lube myself up. "You'll come with my cock in your ass."

As I drench my fingers, she moans, watching me expectantly.

"You'll take my cock in this tiny hole so that I own every inch of you, won't you, sweetheart?"

She nods, and I grunt as I flip her so that she's on her elbows and knees, then slide a pillow beneath her stomach. "Ass in the air, Violet. Show me my ass."

Her limbs shake a bit as she lifts it higher, sinking further into the bed.

"God fucking dammit, you're beautiful." I position myself behind her. "The most beautiful fucking person on earth."

Her head on the mattress, she shifts slightly to the side so that her eyes meet mine. "I am?"

"You are." I slap her ass. "Don't question it."

"It's not that…"

"Then what is it?" I start pushing into her ass, and her muscles tighten. "Don't let your body fight me…focus on breathing and talk to me."

"It's that…" She wiggles her ass, relaxing further, taking more of me. "I love being called beautiful by you."

Fucking Christ. I can't come when I'm barely inside her ass.

I can't come yet.

Not yet.

"I only call you what you are, sweetheart… Mmm. That's it. Take this cock deeper. Can you feel your ass stretching for me?"

A slight noise is the only answer she gives.

"Does it hurt?" I slap her a few times, admiring how fast my handprints appear on her pale flesh.

"Yeah, but I like it." She moans. "More…please."

"Fuck, Violet. You're turning me into a madman."

She chuckles slightly. "One would argue you've always been one."

"Was that sarcasm?"

She hides her face in the mattress so I don't see her smiling.

Fuck.

She's adorable.

And genuine.

And so goddamn sweet.

Grabbing her hip, I pepper kisses on her back, on the tiny scars that tell the story of her tough childhood and life. On every blemish and freckle and mole.

All the while I massage her clit.

"J-Jude…what are you doing?"

"Worshiping you."

Unlike how I fucked her pussy hard and fast just now, this time, I go slower, deeper, until she feels every inch of me.

"Fuck, you feel so goddamn good, you know that? I could be inside you all day, sweetheart."

She moans, her ass pushing against me, demanding, wanting, making my cock weep in agony.

I release her hip and grab her hair, pulling her up until I'm breathing her air. Her eyes are shining with tears, but that's because she gets so fucking emotional, even when she's horny, my Violet.

"You're mine."

"Yours." She gasps, and I grow bigger inside her.

Can't help it. This girl speaks, and I'm a goddamn animal.

"Are you also mine, Jude?" she asks in a voice that's trapped between a moan and groan.

"Always."

She's kissing me then as she shatters against me, her noises and groans spilling into my mouth like an aphrodisiac.

I kiss her deeper, faster, matching my tongue to my cock's rhythm until I'm grunting and spilling inside her in long fucking spurts.

I come like I've never come before.

Like the world is ending, and Violet is my sanctuary.

And when she holds on to me like I'm her lifeline, I promise that I'll protect her till the end of my days.

However long that might be.

CHAPTER 36
Violet

I'M NERVOUS.

Anxious, even.

It's like I'm back in that tiny place I used to share with my mother, waking up in the morning with dread about what type of mood swings she'd have that day.

Times when I made myself smaller, quieter, and tried to breathe as little as possible just so she wouldn't notice me and take out her aggression and grievances on me.

Though she's no longer here, the bracelet she left has put me in this predicament. A bracelet that belongs to a family I'm now sitting amongst.

A *different* kind of family.

Unlike my mother and me, they have all the money, prestige, and shadowy power, but they still can't mourn Preston properly.

Maybe I'm biased, but I hold a grudge against them, except for the little girl who's not present today.

We're at a grand office with a leather sitting area surrounded by large bookshelves full of leather-bound books. Across from us, there's a mahogany desk against which Lawrence and his younger brother, Atlas, are leaning, both crossing their feet at the ankles. Atlas seems more preoccupied with his phone while Lawrence's arms are folded, and a frown is etched deep between his brows.

Winston and Marguerite Armstrong, respectively the patriarch and matriarch of the family, are occupying the large sofa.

The grandfather has a death grip on his cane, his expression solemn and unreadable. His black clothes scream wealth and stature, but his complexion is sickly pale, his eyes an eerie mix of blue and green.

His wife is wearing a dark-blue tailored dress and a neat bun, her blonde strands shining in the light. Elegant pearls decorate her neck and ears as she stares down her nose at the room, her thin red lips set in a line.

Beside her sits Preston's stepmom, Lilith, wearing a floral dress as if this is some form of celebration. In fact, her face looks radiant, her smile genuinely glowing, as if she's reveling in Preston's death. Her posture is as upright as her mother-in-law's, legs tucked to the side, revealing diamond-studded shoes.

Jude, Kane, and I are on the other sofa. Even though I wore a beautiful knitted dress that Dahlia bought me, I feel severely underdressed in the company of elegant gowns and tailored suits.

A hand strokes my shoulder, then rests on my thigh. A rush of warmth seeps into me, and I stare at Jude, who gives me a smile.

It's small and definitely out of character for someone like him, but it's comforting. Especially knowing that he goes out of his way to make me feel better.

This morning, after I woke up in a blissful achy haze, the happiness only lasted a while before the doomsday-like feeling rushed back in.

Jude had to talk me out of not coming here today.

"You have me, and if shit hits the fan, there's also Kane. We can fight our way out of there... I think."

It made me laugh as he intended, which is why I'm here.

"I still don't understand why Preston would leave a personal will," Lilith says, studying her French-manicured nails. "Everything he owned would revert back to the family anyway."

"You'd be surprised what that menace has to say." Atlas lifts his head, finally acknowledging the scene. He's dashingly handsome with a square jawline and bright eyes, but it's a sinister beauty—the type you'd run away from if you met him in an alley.

Just like Julian's.

"Can we get this over with so the strangers can leave my house?" Lilith offers a fake smile. "I'm not talking about you, Kane and Jude, darlings."

"You're certainly not talking about Violet either." Jude takes my hand in his, placing it on his lap. "Because you're more of a stranger to Preston than she ever was."

She opens her mouth to say something, but Lawrence pulls out a black envelope and flips it open. "Everyone present was specifically mentioned in Preston's personal will that I confiscated from the family attorney as I have no time for official nonsense. Now, then, I'll start reading."

Jude's hand tightens around mine and I stroke it, gulping.

"If you're reading this, then I'm dead. What a fucking shame. This better happen when I'm eighty or something or I'll cut a bitch. And no, lawyer, you can't take that out." Lawrence pauses and sighs.

Kane, Jude, and I smile because that sounds exactly like something Preston would write.

"First things first," Lawrence continues. "I want to announce from the podium of my ashes that Satan's lover, also known as Lilith Armstrong, with Satan being my dad— if you know, you know—is a terrible mother and stepmother and should totally be burned at the stake. But that's my two cents. If I turn into a ghost, you better count your days."

Lilith's cheeks turn red, her hands balled into fists.

Jude smiles and whispers, "He always calls her Satan's lover, never by her name."

Oh.

"Moving on." Another sigh from Lawrence. "Jude and Kane are my bros and the only family I have. Sorry, not sorry if the Armstrong clan is listening; I just didn't say that before because I didn't want to be cut out of the will. Well, now, I'm leaving everything in my name to them. Live and drink and, most importantly, slash the fuck out of shit for me. Hey, Jude. Kill one or two people on my death anniversary so I can have some toys in hell, would you?"

Jude's smile is sad, and I hold on to him tighter.

"There's a lot of Preston's shenanigans that are not meant for polite company," Lawrence says with yet another sigh.

"No, come on." Atlas tries to peek. "What did that little shit say about me? More importantly, what did he say about *you*? It must be scathing. I want to hear."

"That's not important." Lawrence cuts him off with a glare, flipping to the last page. "What is important, however, is this."

He stands straight, throws a fleeting glance at his mother, and then reads on, "Oh, I have an interesting anecdote. A while ago, I met the girl Jude's been obsessing over, but he can't just admit he likes her, so his best option was to stalk

her. Not that I'm judging my bro. Anyway, her name is Violet
Winters, and ever since I saw her at the hospital, I felt something strange about her. Time went by, and she abandoned
her Sleeping Beauty era and even came to study at GU! And
color me surprised when that strange feeling grew instead of
diminishing. She's sitting there, right? By the way, hi, Violet.
If Jude doesn't treat you right, I'll haunt him. Anyway, everyone. Look at her freaking eyes! You can't tell me they don't
seem familiar."

Everyone in the room directs their attention to me, and
I think I see disdain in Marguerite's and Lilith's gazes, while
Atlas narrows his eyes on me and Winston stares, unblinking.

"She's one of us, isn't she?" Lawrence reads on. "She has
part of Grandpa's heterochromia that his descendants share.
Uncle Atlas and I have the green. Dad, Miley, and Violet…you
guessed it—they have the blue. Though Dad has some green.
Anyway, I have no evidence, but I'm sure she might have some
relation to us. Now, who of you could have possibly spawned
her? Is she my sister, my cousin, or…my aunt—"

"This is complete and utter nonsense." Marguerite
stands up, making Lawrence halt.

"Sit down, Mother," Atlas says with no change of expression. "Lawrence is not done."

"I will not sit here and listen to some unfounded specu-
lations about a rat from the streets."

Jude's about to stand up, but I hold on to his hand and
say in a clear voice, "I'm not a rat from the streets. I'd appreciate it if you don't call me names just because you can."

Jude caresses my shoulder, giving me a soft look as if he's
proud of me. In reality, I'm not sure if I'd have this courage
if he weren't right by my side.

A cane bangs against the carpet. Winston doesn't have

to say anything. Just the crack of his cane, and his wife sits down, touching her pearls, then says, "This is entirely absurd."

Lawrence tilts his head to the side. "How so, Mother?"

"How so? You can't just believe your deranged son's rhetoric. That boy was mentally unwell, and we all knew it. Why are you even considering his ramblings?"

"Because I did a DNA test." Lawrence drags a black leather folder from the top of the desk and places it on the coffee table in front of us. "First, Violet and me. As you can see, we share approximately 25 percent of our DNA, meaning we share a close familial relationship. Half-sibling, to be more specific. Then I performed another DNA test that shows Violet shares 50 percent of her DNA with Father, and there's a 99.9 percent chance of him being her biological father."

The first to reach for the tests are Lilith and Jude. Marguerite looks away, her face scrunched in a dark frown. Winston's face pales further, but he doesn't move, doesn't even look at me. Kane and Atlas lean down to study the tests, but I'm just staring dumbfounded at Lawrence.

"How...?"

"You have to forgive me, Violet. I might have collected your DNA without your consent, but I needed to confirm a few things first. Such as..." Lawrence pulls out the bracelet. The one that was bloody is now shiny new. "You gave this to Savannah Winters in case she needed it to reach you, didn't you, Father?"

Winston looks at me for the first time, and I can't unsee it. My eyes are in his frail ones. The color blue that's bordering on teal is so unique and strikingly the same. "Where is she? Savannah?"

"She died about twelve years ago." I choke on my words. "Drug overdose."

He nods once, and I think I see a sliver of pain pass through him.

I want to ask him many things, but he speaks again, looking out into the distance. "She was a star ballerina. A beautiful swan that I trapped. I didn't know she was pregnant, though."

"Because Mother made sure of it," Lawrence says, looking at Marguerite. "According to the former head of staff you sent to the Caribbean with enough fortune to keep her mouth shut, Savannah came here to ask for money for her and the baby in her belly. You told her if she didn't abort it, you'd kill them both. You gave her some pocket change to disappear, but apparently, Savannah just put on the show of having an abortion and bribed the doctor to let her keep the baby. Then she moved a couple of states down and started from scratch in the worst circumstances imaginable. Maybe she thought there would be a day where she'd show up in front of my father again and use Violet for money. Maybe she died before she could ever do that."

My heart thumps so loudly, I can barely hear anything beyond my own heartbeat.

All this time, I thought I was the daughter of one of my mother's clients, but she was a ballerina? I thought she was just a socialite before she fell from grace.

No wonder she used to hate any *Nutcracker* holiday season shows, but sometimes, when she was drunk, she'd be whirling and dancing and then crying.

Turns out, I really did kill her career.

"Don't be ridiculous, Lawrence." Marguerite huffs. "You can't accuse me without proof."

"Oh, I have proof. Aside from the former head of staff's testimony, I have records of when you sold some of your properties via an agent around the time you had to pay the former head of staff and Savannah from your own money. I also have records of Swiss bank transactions to one of our former guards that you've been paying to assassinate Violet for a few months now—including the time when my son got shot."

Atlas whistles. "Wow. You've been quite busy, Mother."

"All this time…" Jude stands up. "It's been you?"

Marguerite cowers in her seat. "I was just protecting my family. That leech, Savannah, was trouble. I could see all her gold-digging ploys in her beady eyes. I should've killed her when she first showed up at my door, that greedy whore! I thought we were done with her nonsense, but then I spotted this little gremlin on Jude's bike in front of the house up the hill. I had my suspicions she was that bitch's daughter since she looks so much like her and confirmed it with a little background check, so of course I had to eliminate her. I couldn't let her continue her mother's cursed legacy and become a parasite to my family!"

"I never wanted to be part of your family!" I scream back. "I don't care about any of your wealth or a father I've never met. I lived my entire life believing I was fatherless, and this changes nothing."

"You say that now, but then you'll have your greedy hands all over my family."

"Don't be a hypocrite, Mother," Lawrence says. "If you cared about family so much, you wouldn't have killed your own grandson just to get rid of Violet."

"He got in the way like an idiot."

"You killed my son!" Lawrence yells, losing his cool for

the first time. "You put a bullet in *my*. Fucking. Son, Mother! So don't you dare sit there and try to play the role of a victim."

Winston stands up, banging his cane on the floor. The whole room falls silent as Marguerite grabs onto his hand. "Honey, you know I did this for us, for *our* family."

"There's no us or family when you attempted to kill my daughter and murdered my grandson. Pack your things and leave by tomorrow morning." His expression is cool and unperturbed as he pulls his hand free. "Lawrence, Atlas. Strip this woman of every last dime to her name."

Lawrence nods.

Atlas salutes. "I'll invest your money well, Mother."

"Winston!" she cries, her voice cracking. "You can't do this to me."

He stops by the door and glances at me. "I'm sorry, child."

And then he exits the room.

And I'm shaking in Jude's arms.

I found my family, but family isn't something you can choose.

Or just belong to.

I ruined my mother's life, and she certainly ruined mine.

CHAPTER 37

Jude

"THIS IS GOING TO BACKFIRE."

I dismount from my bike, ignoring Kane's words. The last thing I need is his nagging, and the fact that I don't have Preston to tell him off on my behalf intensifies the burn beneath my skin.

"Are you suggesting we don't do this?" I flip my gaze toward him. "If you want out, all you have to do is leave. I have Lucia on standby to clean up the scene anyway."

"Like fuck I will." He cracks his knuckles. "I'm just stating the simple fact that even though Marguerite was dropped by the Armstrongs, Winston, Lawrence, and especially Atlas will take issue with us touching their own."

"You're currently the head of your family and, therefore, can hold your own. I also talked to Regis and made him agree to take care of the fallout if anything goes south."

A gust of air ruffles Kane's hair as he lifts both brows. "You talk to your old man now?"

I tighten my jaw because it's true. I don't want to talk to that man, let alone ask for his help in anything.

"You know how he's always in my business. I just decided to use him for protection."

"Hmm."

I ignore Kane's knowing hum and the look he gives me, focusing on our surroundings.

The neighborhood is quiet, the streetlights casting a weak, flickering glow over the pavement, stretching long shadows across the neatly trimmed lawns and pristine sidewalks.

Marguerite's escape house sits proudly in New York's suburbs, a place that's meant to feel safe and untouchable—the American dream wrapped in white picket fences and security alarms.

But tonight, it's just another hunting ground.

The air is thick with the smell of damp asphalt, the pavement still slick from an earlier drizzle. A dog barks somewhere in the distance, but no lights turn on, and no curtains shift.

As if no one cares to look.

Kane and I stake out Marguerite Armstrong's house from across the street. The windows are dark, the curtains drawn tight, but she's in there.

We both know it.

I had Lucia disable her security system as well as the surrounding houses' security cameras.

"How do you want to do this?" Kane asks. "Offing an old woman is different from slicing up her goons."

"I don't give a fuck about that. She should've considered her age when she attempted to kill Violet multiple times and actually murdered Pres."

"Fair." Kane lifts a shoulder. "Who do you think took out the gunman who shot Preston? Lawrence?"

I frown. Ever since the reading of Preston's will a couple of days ago, Kane and I have hunted down the men who worked for Marguerite with the help of Lucia and Kane's expanding intel.

Since we knew they were connected to Marguerite, we managed to locate them in record time.

We only found two of them.

The third, the actual gunman who was on the motorcycle and was the one that killed Preston, was already dead.

And it wasn't a normal death.

We found him in a barren field, crucified to a tree near a hideout. His face was carved out, and his features were unrecognizable.

He had some unintelligible bloody letters etched on his chest and some candy scattered all over him.

"Lawrence would've just erased him from existence. That was too theatrical for him or anyone in the Armstrong family," I say.

"True. Hmm. It's not Vencor's modus operandi either, considering its attention-seeking nature and the absence of the cleanup process."

"Or maybe it was a form of mourning." I let out a breath. "Different people deal with grief in different ways."

Our way is definitely slashing people the fuck up.

After Violet falls asleep curled in my arms each night, I cover her up and go out to seek vengeance.

First, my vengeance-seeking avalanche was for my mom. Now, it's for Violet and Preston.

Seems I can't live without the constant need to maim people.

"How is Violet?" Kane asks.

I run a hand over my face. "She's struggling."

"Obviously. She had too many bombs dropped on her the other day."

"Yeah, but she'll eventually accept it." I clench my gloved hands, watching Marguerite's windows. "Winston wants to add her name to the Armstrong family registry. Lawrence and Atlas agree."

"But she doesn't?"

"I don't think so. She told Dahlia the other day that she misses their simple life in the slums." *Away from me.*

From whatever the fuck we have.

My jaw tightens until I'm sure I'll dislocate it.

I don't give a fuck what she thinks. She's staying right next to me.

"Yeah, that's not good." Kane releases a sigh. "Maybe you should make her feel safer in her current environment instead of going on these killing sprees?"

"I'll get to that after Marguerite's dead."

"All right, then. Let's get this over with."

He walks toward the house, his movements calm and deliberate, the streetlight catching on the engraving of his signet ring as he flexes his fingers.

I roll my tense shoulders as I step onto the pavement, the cold seeping into my skin through the leather of my jacket.

We manage to open the door using the code Lucia gave us, and then we walk into the darkness, our steps silent, like the prime hunters we were raised to be.

Kane is covering my back as I go up the stairs, two steps at a time, then stop when we see dim light coming from the last bedroom to the right.

Someone else is here.

We share a look, then move in that direction.

A distinctive noise reaches our ears first.

The wet, rhythmic sound of a blade sinking into flesh.

It grows louder by the second.

Slash.

Slash.

Slash.

The gurgle of blood echoes in the air as I bang the door open, pointing my gun ahead.

The scent of thick, metallic blood is the first thing that hits me. It clings to the air, coats the walls, and seeps into the floorboards.

Someone beat us to Marguerite and is currently straddling her on the huge bed.

His shoulders hunch and straighten with each brutal thrust of the knife, the blade flashing before disappearing again, buried deep in what was once Marguerite Armstrong.

Her face is disfigured, and her once blonde hair is soaked in red.

It's everywhere.

The blood.

The bed, the sheets, the floor, and even on the man who's performing what looks like a creepy stabbing ritual, completely controlled and unbothered.

Through the bloody haze, Kane and I see him clearly.

Marcus.

The man who's turned Marguerite into a canvas of slaughter.

He doesn't stop stabbing her.

Not when we enter, not when the door groans under Kane's push. Almost as if he's disconnected from reality.

"The fuck are you doing here?" I growl, pure rage rippling into my tone because he took away my revenge.

For Violet.

For Preston.

This motherfucker confiscated my last string of vengeance.

Marcus's head jerks up as if pulled from a trance, and for

a split second, his expression is full of pure, raw bloodlust. His eyes are wide, dilated, a feverish glow sparking behind them, something wild and feral.

He looks no different than an animal after a kill. His mouth is slightly parted, breaths coming in uneven gasps.

His entire body is drenched in red.

It drips down his arms, is smeared across his face in rivulets, and his clothes are soaked through.

The blade gleams, slick and wet, his fingers gripping it so tight, the tendons in his wrist stand out, stark against the carnage staining his skin.

Then slowly—too slowly—he tilts his head, a grin cutting across his bloody face, marring his teeth in red. "Took you long enough. I got a little...impatient."

His voice is hoarse, low, like he's been whispering to himself between every stab.

The body beneath him is barely recognizable, a ruin of torn flesh and shattered bone, her chest a hollowed-out mess of rage and violence.

"Get the fuck out of here, Osborn." Kane steps in front of me.

"Bring cleaners? Of course you did." Marcus chuckles as he stumbles off the bed and loses his footing. "I'll leave it to you, rich kids."

I grab him by the collar. "You think you can ruin my fucking revenge and then leave?"

"That's the plan, Callahan." He's speaking, but his gaze is lost somewhere I can't see.

I breathe harshly. "I should maim you instead."

Kane pulls me away. "Let him go."

"But this motherfucker—"

Kane shakes his head. "Pres wouldn't like it."

I think I imagine it, but Marcus flinches when Kane says Preston's name.

I didn't know the bastard *could* flinch.

As I release him, he reaches into his pocket, pulls out a candy, and throws it into his mouth as he walks out, swaying as if he's drunk, leaving bloody footprints in his wake.

"Why the fuck did you stop me, Kane?" I snap when he's gone. "And what's with Pres not liking it? He hated that motherfucker more than I did."

"Maybe, but it was complicated." Kane grabs one of the bloody candy wrappers that Marguerite's body is surrounded with. "He killed her and the gunman because they took Preston from him. He made it personal. Too personal, actually. We all know, aside from dealing with his family, Marcus never makes *anything* personal. And you know what?"

"What?"

Kane smiles sadly, knowingly. "If the roles were reversed, I believe Pres would've done the same."

———

When I walk into Violet's place, it's still.

Too still.

And I know part of it is because of the fucking emptiness gnawing at my insides.

I can't get past the fact that Marguerite is gone, and so is my revenge.

And now, I have to crash back into the reality of grief.

Of accepting that my best fucking friend is gone, and no amount of killing can resurrect him.

Kane suggested we go for a late-night skate after we left Lucia and her men to deal with the mess Marcus created. I could tell he wanted to go back to Dahlia, but he offered that just to rein me in.

To ground me.

He's worried about losing me to bloodlust.

However, I don't even know how the fuck I'll be able to play hockey without Preston around. I missed the last two games because I just couldn't do it without him there. He's the one who encouraged me when we were young and said he'd join because I loved it so much.

"Do you even like hockey?" I asked.

He grins, looking comical with his missing tooth. "Nah, but I can learn to! I'll keep you company. That's what bros are for."

But he bailed out too soon, and now, I don't even want to touch a stick. The whole game seems revolting without him.

And, really, I don't want to practice—I just want Violet in my arms.

I need to ensure she's doing well mentally. I don't like how she's been distracted lately or that she looks horrified whenever one of her 'new' family members gets in touch.

Knowing the Armstrongs, they'll force her into their midst whether she likes it or not, but I'll make sure no one makes her do anything she's uncomfortable with.

Even if I have to become best friends with my father for it.

I'd do anything to guarantee they don't destroy her like they did Preston.

Deep inside, I know Violet wants to belong to a family, but I'm sure she doesn't want it to be one of our families.

Which is fair, to be honest. I wouldn't wish this life on my worst enemy, let alone someone as pure and kind as Violet.

The bedroom door is ajar, and I frown.

She doesn't usually leave it open.

My chest falls when I walk in and I don't see her curled on her side in bed.

It's three in the fucking morning. I left her asleep around ten.

"Violet?" I call, walking to the bathroom, but she's not there.

My fist clenches as I go back to the bedroom and pause. It smells of her, but the mattress is cold.

My gaze flits to a folded piece of paper on the nightstand.

Dread gnaws at my insides as I grab it, and I have to sit down as I read.

Jude,

I'm sorry I couldn't say goodbye in person.

You wouldn't have let me go if I had.

I know you go out at night to kill the people who hurt me and Preston. You come back after showering, but I can still smell the blood when you wrap your arms around me to sleep.

And I can't help thinking that you're killing because of me, going on sprees to protect or avenge me. But that's a weight I can't carry. I just can't.

I know how much you suffered because of your mom, and I don't want to become another version of her. I don't think I could survive that. Just knowing I'm the reason for someone else's pain makes me feel hollow.

From the beginning, I should've known we were from different worlds. Yours is full of shadows. Mine is trying to find the light.

Being the illegitimate child of the Armstrongs means nothing to me. Blood doesn't make someone family.

Preston was the closest thing I had to a biological family member, but he's gone. I can never take his place in that family, and I don't want to try.

Don't worry. I won't kill myself or hurt Dahlia irreversibly. Like you said, I'll live for Mario and Preston and for the lives they couldn't have because of me.

So I'm starting over somewhere new. A place where no one knows my name. I'll never forget these months I spent with you.

I'll treat our time together like a dream I was never meant to have.

I know you'll be angry that I'm leaving, but truly, Jude, you can have anyone you want.

Hurting you is the last thing I want, especially with everything that's going on, but I don't want to add to your burden or cause you harm.

Mom said I'm a curse who's meant to hurt everyone around her, and as much as I'm trying not to think that way, I believe I truly am. First, it was Mario, then Preston, and maybe the next time, it'll be you.

I don't think I'll be able to live if you get hurt because of me, Jude. I just can't.

Consider me a coward who ran away.

I hope you will respect my wishes.

Don't look for me.

Please let me go.

Blue

CHAPTER 38
Violet

THE CRUNCH OF GRAVEL REACHES ME FIRST, AND MY FIN-gers pause around the embroidery before I let it drop on the small couch.

I pull the curtain back and look out the window and see Dahlia hopping out of the car, juggling a box.

Two distinct emotions go through me: bitter relief and crushing disappointment.

I'm the one who ran away a week ago, but every time Dahlia comes over—three times in a week because she worries too much—I'm hit with a sense of paralyzing anticipation and dread.

The hope that it might be someone else.

Even after I wrote the safe word and had to wipe my tears so he wouldn't see them on the paper.

God, I miss him. So much.

I feel hollow without him.

I stand up and head to the door.

The place I asked Lawrence to get for me is one of his unmapped safe houses and is only an hour away from Graystone Ridge in a forgotten, less affluent town.

According to Lawrence, Jude won't search for me this close and will assume I've changed coasts.

The wood creaks under my steps as I walk to the door, and the scent of stale wood and untouched air fills the space. Everything here is still, and the deep quiet presses against my ears. The walls are a soft, muted gray, and it should feel welcoming, but it doesn't.

The living room is sparsely furnished—a beige couch, a wooden coffee table, and a lamp I barely turn on. The hardwood floor is cool under my socked feet as I move through the space, taking in the kitchen's untouched countertops, the fridge stocked with food that I forget to eat, the sink that's empty because I don't make meals worth dirtying dishes for.

I've lost the will to cook when there's no one to enjoy those meals with me.

As I open the door, I can see the lingering remnants of winter clinging to the world, patches of old snow melting into the damp earth, the trees still skeletal, waiting for spring to bring them back to life.

Everything is waiting.

Maybe including me.

"Viii!" Dahlia drops the box on the porch and hugs me. "Ugh, I've missed you so much."

"You were here two days ago."

"I still miss you." She pouts. "This sucks. I suggested we ban Jude instead of you, and Kane just gave me a very unamused look."

My heart thuds at the mention of his name, but I swallow. "No one banned me. I just chose to leave, Dahl."

"I know, I know." She pulls away and grabs the box of my stuff that I asked her to bring me.

When I try to help, she jokingly kicks me before she steps inside and puts it on the counter.

Before I close the door, I cast a glance in the distance as

if expecting—or maybe hoping—to see the familiar black motorcycle I've been seeing in my dreams lately.

Or, more accurately, nightmares. Ones that end with Jude's blood all over that motorcycle.

For the first time, I wish for Mama's demon back on my chest. Anything is better than those ominous images.

I make Dahlia some coffee, and we sink into the couch. Neither of us is comfortable. This house doesn't feel like home.

It doesn't feel like anything at all.

"Are you lonely, Vi?" she asks softly.

"I'm fine. I might have to repeat this year at the new college I'll enroll in, but I've been having so much fun with embroidering."

"Liar. You've been working on that piece for the whole week. And you're not eating properly. Don't think I didn't see all the food you didn't touch in the fridge. You can't survive on just ginger ale."

"I'll take that as a challenge." I grin, trying to ease the mood.

"I'm not joking." She frowns. "I'm truly worried about you. I don't know what the hell you saw in that brute Jude, but I prefer the constant smile on your face when you were with him to these sad smiles."

My lips press into a line. "That's not possible."

"Why not? You're the one who left, so you can come back. Besides, he's been going berserk this past week. Honestly, Vi. Kane said losing you and Preston is messing Jude up big time."

"I'm the reason he lost Preston."

"Oh my God. Is that why you left?"

"He was going on killing sprees again because of me."

I touch my tattoo. "I've seen him murderous to avenge his mother, and I know it killed something inside him. I don't... want to be Susie Callahan 2.0. I don't want to be the reason for his eventual decimation down the road of no return."

"Okay, I get it. But those guys have been killing since they were young and will probably continue to do so for the rest of their lives. Do you think I like that Kane does it? Of course not. And I was a bit apprehensive at the start, but that's just a part of who he is that I have to compromise with. Because I love him, and I know he loves me and would kill to protect me. Already has, actually. Maybe Jude feels the same. Killing to protect you could be his love language. Do you think you'll never get past that?"

"It's not really that." I release a long exhale, my chest aching. "It's that I was the reason he lost both Mario and Preston. What if next time, he's the one getting killed?"

"Oh, Vi." Dahlia takes my hand in hers, and I realize a tear has fallen down my cheek.

I wipe it with the back of my arm. "I'm being ridiculous."

"No, you're not. Your feelings are valid. But you shouldn't feel guilty that you survived, Vi. You've always been a survivor and the strongest woman I know."

"Please. That's you."

"No. It's *you*. I had loving parents, but you didn't, and you didn't let that bring you down. You silently picked yourself up and moved forward. Whenever things got too hard, you didn't just lie down and take it. You always got up and found a solution to move past the hurdle and even tried to find solutions to other people's problems, too. You inspired me to be better and improve every day, and I'm telling you right now, I wouldn't have become the person I am today if you weren't in my life, Vi. The same applies to Laura and everyone in the communities we used to live in. So don't ever think your life is worth less than anyone else's, or I'll be super mad."

I laugh to hide the tears welling in my eyes. "You made me emotional."

"Good. You deserve a reality check." She grins. "Also, I know the whole Armstrong thing is making you uncomfortable, but I heard Jude tell Kane he'll never allow them to force you into the family."

"He...did?"

"Yup. I think he even asked his dad for help."

"Impossible. He hates his dad."

"Well, he obviously put that hatred aside for you." She bites her lower lip. "I really don't want to paint him in a good light, considering the stalking and the coma, but I found out a few things from Kane yesterday. He probably wanted me to influence you to come back. No, he was clearly aiming for that."

I sit up straighter. "What things?"

She releases a long sigh and takes a sip of her coffee. "Apparently, Jude is the one who bought you the apartment and paid for your college tuition. He asked Kane to take credit because you wouldn't have taken them if you knew they were from him. But if they were camouflaged as something Kane did for his girlfriend's sister, then you were more likely to accept them."

"He did that?"

"Yeah, annoying, I know. He's also the one who found you the therapist, because she's a big shot and doesn't take on just anyone, and he procured the apartment we 'accidentally' found in Stantonville for a bargain price. Apparently, he didn't like us—or, more accurately, you—living in that creepy guy's attic, so he had to make up the whole business about an old person dying. He actually offered the guy a price that was higher than the market price just so he'd move out immediately. Kane was onboard with the plan, obviously." She rolls her eyes. "Also, Jude is the biggest buyer from your online shop. The one who tips a lot?"

"UnderTheUmbrella?"

"Yeah, that one. Kane said he did that because you have too much pride and wouldn't have accepted his money outright."

"What an idiot," I whisper through a scoff.

Bastard.

He did all of that while he was ignoring me after the coma—when I thought he was finally done tormenting me.

In reality, Jude saw how I lived, hated it, and decided to give me a new life.

A new start.

A way to accept myself, even if the methods were sketchy as hell.

And now, I don't know what to do with all of this information.

———

After Dahlia leaves, I'm still snuggled on the couch, going through all of Jude's purchases in my online shop, particularly the custom pieces he paid a lot of money for.

A blue umbrella patch, another one embroidered on a shirt, and a third on a pillowcase.

I read through our conversation after he sent me a thank-you tip upon receiving the pillowcase.

Me: Thank you so much for all your generosity. I don't know if my embroidery deserves this much.

UnderTheUmbrella: It does. Don't underestimate your
    work and your passion.

Me: I needed that, truly. Don't hesitate to contact me if
    you need any other custom pieces.

UnderTheUmbrella: What else can a blue umbrella
    embroidery be put on?

Me: Tablecloths, napkins, jackets, tote bags, etc. The
    options are endless.

UnderTheUmbrella: We'll do those, then, and anything
    else you can think of.

Me: Oh, absolutely, and thank you! The umbrella must
    mean so much to you.

UnderTheUmbrella: It does.

A knock comes at the door, and I startle, letting my
phone fall to the couch. Then I go to open it. "Did you forget
something, Dahl—"

My words get stuck in my throat when I lay eyes on a tall
man blocking my entrance who's definitely not Dahlia.

Jude.

I almost don't recognize him at first.

His broad frame casts a shadow over the dim porch light.
He looks different—rougher, more worn down—but the
same dangerous gleam lurks in his demeanor.

There's a tension in the way he holds himself, shoulders
bunched, muscles tight beneath his black leather jacket, as
if he's carrying something heavy and refusing to let it show.

His face is sharper than I remember, like the sole week
we've spent apart has chiseled away anything soft, leaving
only hard edges and quiet violence.

There are faint dark circles beneath his eyes, like sleep
has been a stranger he doesn't bother chasing. There's also

scruff along his jaw, a shadow of neglect rather than intention, making him look even more untamed, more like something barely held together.

His cutting rich-brown eyes pin me in place, raking over me like he's trying to find something he lost.

The wind shifts, sending the scent of rain-soaked leather, cold air, and something unmistakably Jude curling around me.

My fingers twitch at my sides, resisting the urge to reach out, to trace the tension in his arms, to see if he's as solid as he looks or if, this time, he's just another figment of my imagination.

Instead, I swallow, then speak, my voice barely stronger than the wind howling between us. "How did you find me?"

"I followed Dahlia." His voice sounds deeper, a bit hoarser. "She was probably in a hurry today, so she didn't bother to lead me around in circles."

Or maybe she did it on purpose.

"Didn't you read the letter?" My voice breaks, and I swallow. "I asked you to let me go."

He grabs my shoulders, and I gasp as he pushes me back, kicks the door closed, and slams me against it. "And I'm saying no, Violet. You can run to the ends of the earth, and I'll find you."

"Why? Because you can't lose your toys?"

"Because I can't lose you!" He breathes harshly, dropping his forehead to mine, his pants mingling with my fractured ones.

"I can't lose you," he repeats softly, as soft as Jude can speak. "Don't make me lose you, too, sweetheart. Even if it's just out of pity, stay with me. Don't push me away."

"It was never pity. I…"

"You what?"

He's searching my eyes, but he's peeking into my soul, and I can't find the will to close the door in his face.

I'm tired.

Of hiding.

Of pining.

Of choosing everyone else's good before my own.

"Is this because of the killing?" He leans away slowly. "I'll always kill anyone who hurts you, Violet. *Always*. But I'll try to limit it, to make sure it doesn't cause you pain—"

"It's not that. I just…don't want you to get hurt because of me. I can't live with that."

He pauses, his brow furrowing, and then the light slowly returns. "Your leaving hurt me more than any imaginary scenarios you have in your head."

"But—"

"No buts, Violet. If you were so scared about my safety, you should've talked to me, and I would've told you my father has assigned shadow guards on me since I was a kid. No one would be able to hurt me, you understand?" He releases a sigh. "No one but you and the letter you signed with your safe word."

"I'm sorry." I reach a tentative hand to his cheek, and he briefly closes his eyes, leaning into my touch. "I didn't want to hurt you, but I truly thought you'd be better off without me."

"Do I look better off?"

"You look like hell."

His lips twitch in not quite a smile, but something similar. "It's all your fault, sweetheart."

"Mine?"

"You're the one who made yourself a nook in my life, heart, and soul and made me feel emotions I thought were impossible. You made me yours in every sense of the word, and I love you, Violet. I'm so far gone for you, I'd rather elope to the ends of the earth with you than live with all the riches and power without you. I know I'm not the easiest man to be around, and we started on the wrong foot, but if you let me, I'll make you my goddess."

"Oh, Jude." My heart is so full, I think it'll burst. "Why would you love someone as broken as me?"

"I'm broken, too. We can fit our pieces together until we make something whole."

"I have so many scars."

"I'll kiss each and every one of them until you love them as much as I do. Besides." He kisses the top of my nose. "I have many scars, too. The worst was covered by you."

"Me?"

He lifts his shirt, showing me the barren tree and the umbrella. "You don't remember it, but the first time we met, you gave me a blue umbrella and a protein bar. Even after I yelled at you to fuck off. I was bloodied and had a long gash here that I covered with this tattoo."

"Oh. That's why you ordered all those embroideries with the blue umbrella." I pause. "Dahlia told me."

"Yeah. I still have that umbrella and protein bar."

"Oh my God. That's so precious." I smile, my heart overflowing with emotions. "I wouldn't have guessed that stranger was you."

"Am I that forgettable?"

"No." I smile. "I just have fuzzy memories of it. I don't think I looked at your face properly back then. You know, because I'm a scaredy-cat and was truly terrified of all the blood."

"But you still helped."

"I can't stop myself from doing that—helping others in need, I mean."

"You don't have to. You can heal others, and I'll protect you, sweetheart."

"Jude…"

"Yes?"

"I don't know what I've done to deserve you."

"Allowing me to stalk you, maybe?"

I chuckle. "I liked it sometimes. Knowing you couldn't stay away."

"Mmm. Seems like we need to explore that in further detail."

I grin, then wrap my arm around his waist. "You're the only person I ever wanted all for myself. The first man who made me feel special just the way I am. I love you so much more than I could admit. I'd rather be with you despite all the drama and danger than live a boring, peaceful life without you."

"You'll be mine for life, sweetheart?"

"Mm. Will you also be mine, Jude?"

"Always."

And then he's kissing me, and I'm smiling through the tears.

Some need to change to find love.

I just needed to find myself with the help of the love of my life.

Violet

A week later

I'M STARTING TO DOUBT MY DECISION TO CATER AN after-practice party to boost the Vipers' morale.

Ever since Preston passed away, everyone has been down. They lost two consecutive games, and team spirit has been so low, Dahlia has been worrying nonstop.

But more importantly, Jude doesn't seem like he wants to touch a stick anymore.

It's not good.

Hockey isn't only his venting outlet, but it's also the one thing he picked for himself outside of his familial obligations.

He's never been in his element more than when he's on the ice, crushing the opposing team's defense. But during the last game, he kept looking around as if searching for Preston's ghost.

Yes, he smiled upon seeing me in the stands, even released a heavy breath. But my presence and Preston's aren't interchangeable.

The wound he left behind is still agape, and it hurts when I see all the team players in their Vipers jackets and he's not amongst them, throwing out a random joke, bickering with Jude, or annoying Kane just because he can.

I think Jude and Kane feel it, too, because even Dahlia thinks they have to force themselves to be on a team that's full of Preston's memories but without him there.

"Do you think I'm making it worse?" I whisper to Dahlia as she swallows the mouthful of roast chicken.

We're standing by the buffet table set up in the campus's conference hall with the words 'Go Vipers!' embroidered on a banner I personally made.

The space is big, but it's crowded with large hockey players who make it feel small.

The managing team is gathered in the corner, eating and chatting, while a few volunteering GU students—who helped Dahlia and me organize all this—mingle nearby. But most of the help came from Jude's men.

The bodyguards are also surrounding the arena. They're everywhere now—both from Jude's father and my biological father. Despite my making it clear that I have no plans to change my life or fit into the Armstrong family.

Winston and Lawrence didn't like that, but as Jude promised, they're leaving me alone.

At least, for now.

I truly don't like the family that didn't really mourn Preston and moved on with their lives as if he never existed.

But he did.

Sometimes, I can see his ghost amongst us, and it squeezes my chest.

Even though I only knew Preston briefly, I don't think I'll ever forget him.

I can only imagine how it feels for Jude and Kane, who knew him their entire lives.

"No, it's really good." Dahlia grins. "They needed this after the game two days ago."

I take a sip of water. "I don't think Jude and Kane look any better."

"I don't think they will for a long time. Preston was like their brother, you know." She rubs my shoulders. "But at least they have us, right?"

I nod.

She places the plate on the table and squeezes me in an aggressive hug. "Ugh! I'm so glad you're back!"

"Me, too." I pat her shoulder, smiling.

A strong arm wraps around my waist, pulling me away, and my heart does that squeezing thing that happens whenever Jude is near.

I used to think this sensation was an anomaly that would eventually fizzle out, but I'm becoming more obsessed with this man, more attuned to him, and addicted to the way he worships me with every touch.

Every word.

Even right now, I love how his usually harsh eyes soften upon seeing me as his thumb draws circles on my hip.

God, he's beautiful and—this might come as a surprise—charming.

Yes, he's rough around the edges and will never be *that* soft, but I love the peaceful look on his handsome face when he's with me.

I love that he releases a sigh of relief upon seeing me.

And I melt inside upon seeing him. Seems I'm truly head over heels for my former stalker.

The other day, I talked in therapy about how I seem to crave love from my abusers—my mom, mostly—and the doctor asked me if I think that's the case with Jude.

I smiled as I shook my head. Jude might have stalked me, and we may have started off on the wrong foot, but he never abused me, neither emotionally nor physically. If anything, he empowers me and offers me a safe space to be both vulnerable and myself.

He plays an important role in my healing journey, and I don't crave his love because he's my abuser.

I crave his love because he makes me a better person, and I like to think I bring out the best in him, too.

"Why the hell are you taking my Vi?" Dahlia protests.

"She's my Vi. Go to Kane."

My sister scoffs and then mouths to me, "What do you even see in this brute?"

"The same thing you see in Kane," he replies, obviously having heard her.

"Dahlia," I whisper-yell.

"Fine." She kisses me on the cheek and waggles her brows at Jude before she dashes in Kane's direction.

I smile up at him. "Don't mind her. She can be a bit petty."

He lowers his head and kisses me on the same cheek, lingering there longer than needed.

Heat creeps up my neck, and I swallow, his hot lips sending tingles up my spine.

"There. Much better."

I clear my throat because he kind of ignited my whole body with just a kiss on the cheek. "Wow. You're as petty as Dahlia."

"Damn straight." He strokes my cheek. "Thank you for putting all of this together. You didn't have to."

"I wanted to. Besides, your men did most of the work anyway."

"What did I say about not taking credit for what you do,

sweetheart? You're the one who came up with the idea and even cooked some dishes."

"I only did that to make you feel better, but I don't think it's working."

"It is." He pulls me into a tight embrace, his muscular arms wrapping around me like a protective cocoon. "I don't know what I would've done if you weren't by my side."

I sink my nails into his jacket. "I'll always be here, Jude. You won't get rid of me that easily."

"Joke's on you."

We remain like that for a few moments.

We often do this now—just hugging to recharge. To feel the other's breath and know we have each other no matter what.

It makes me feel safe.

It makes me think of something more than pain.

I know I still have a long way to go before I can kick the ghost of Mama from my mind and finally accept myself the way I am, but I know it'll be easier with this stupidly big man by my side.

"The audacity to throw a party and not invite my highness."

The entire place goes silent. No more chattering or clattering of utensils or even…breathing.

I reluctantly pull away from Jude, and we both stare at the doorway where the very familiar voice just came from.

Everyone is looking in that direction.

At the ghost of Preston Armstrong standing there with his usual grin, paired with deep dimples in his cheeks and a gleam in his light eyes.

He's wearing jeans and a white jacket with the Vipers' blue logo on his chest.

I blink twice, but he's still there.

In person.

Everyone else is seeing him, too, judging by the wide, unblinking eyes.

He cocks his head to the side. "Miss me?"

"P-Preston?" one of the guys stutters.

"Drayton! You *can* see me?" Preston mock gasps. "Just kidding. I'm not a ghost. Said every ghost ever! Muahaha!"

When no one reacts, too in shock to even speak, he releases an exasperated sigh. "This surprise drop is flopping so hard. Anyway, you can kiss the hand one at a time, peasants. Heard you bitches are ruining our championship." Another sigh. "Things just don't work out without Preston. I'm telling you—"

Jude jogs toward him.

"Hey, big man! You missed me, didn't you? Life sucked without me, didn't it?"

Jude grabs him by the collar, shaking him. "You motherfucking—"

"Ow, ow." Preston taps his hand. "I was shot, you Neanderthal. It still hurts."

Jude reluctantly releases him as Kane and all of us form a small circle around Preston.

He's here.

He...apparently came back from the dead.

"What the fuck happened?" Kane's voice is a bit tight, but I can hear the relief beneath it. "We buried you with our own hands."

"Did I look hot dead?"

"Preston," Jude warns.

"Boo, what a killjoy." Preston sighs. "I was in a medically induced coma."

"But the doctor said…" Kane trails off.

"Dad's idea. Don't look at me." Preston's eyes light up. "Did he cry when I was shot?"

"No," Jude tells him.

"Did he just sigh, then? Ugh, the unoriginality is killing me." Preston's shoulders hunch, then he perks up again. "Heard Granny's gone. Yay! Never liked that old woman. She called me crazy all the time, then shot me! Or tried to shoot Vee. Oh, hi, Vee! Heard you're my auntie. Can I not call you that, though? Pretty sure I'm older than you."

My lips tremble as I step toward him and hug him. "I'm so sorry, Pres. I'm sorry you went through that because of me."

"Nah, don't go emo on me! Juuude, how do I deal with this?"

When I ease away, Preston is grinning as he ruffles my hair. "Actually, Auntie Vee is growing on me after all."

After the team and the managers welcome Preston back, we go for drinks at my and Jude's place.

Just the five of us.

The whole drive back, Preston is joking and mixing all sorts of music, but the rest of us are still in shock.

"Stop looking at me as if I'm a ghost." Preston punches Kane in the stomach before he flops down beside me on the sofa. "See? You can feel that, so I'm as real as it gets."

"I just don't understand why you faked your own death," Kane says.

"I told you, it was Dad." Preston takes a sip of his beer. "He wanted to smoke out dear Granny and have you kill her because it seems he drew a line at killing his own blood. But, hey, I came back as soon as I was conscious. I'm still in pain, so all of you better nurse me back to health."

"We thought you were dead." Jude's standing, having refused to sit down since we got here. "Violet thought she was the reason you were dead."

"Sorry." Preston grimaces. "Blame your brother, or half-brother or whatever. He's kind of a stone, though, so good luck getting to him. Also, if it makes you feel better, I wouldn't be here if you hadn't already tested the experimental coma drug for Julian, Vee. He managed to develop and enhance it, which made my recovery so much faster. But Daddy dearest was mad, like, I'm talking livid, almost punching Julian and stuff. Because it appears the only reason Julian insisted you become a test subject is because of your DNA, meaning he knew you were an Armstrong and kept it to himself, then even tried to make you leave the area so Dad and Uncle Atlas wouldn't come at him for trying to decode our DNA. Which is, apparently, on Julian's power-mongering checklist—to know all about the founding families' DNA. For what reason? No clue, but Dad didn't like it one bit. Callahans and Armstrongs are fighting, FYI."

"Julian knew you were alive?" Jude barks.

"Yup, and so did Dad and Uncle Atlas."

"This feels so surreal," Dahlia says, leaning her head on Kane's shoulder.

"I know, right? Unlocked superpower: coming back from the dead." Preston rubs his hands together. "Anyway, tell me all about how you made Granny scream."

Kane frowns. "We didn't kill your grandma, Pres."

"Of course you did. Dad used you to get rid of her, remember? I almost shed a few tears knowing you avenged my wrongful early exit."

"It was Marcus," Jude says.

Preston's humor disappears. "*What?*"

"Marcus beat us to it," Kane says. "He also beat us to killing the hit man who shot you. Osborn crucified him in a gory scene. Your grandma was nearly sliced the fuck up. Both had unrecognizable faces and took a long time to clean up. We only witnessed him killing your grandma, and he looked fucking unhinged while doing it."

Preston bursts out laughing. It doesn't sound happy or mocking; if anything, there's a manic edge to it.

Kane and Jude share a look but say nothing. Preston finishes his beer in one go and tells us all about his 'adventures' in the hospital and his 'Sleeping Beauty days,' as he calls them.

I'm just glad the results from my coma helped get Preston back. It was all worth it.

Maybe Julian will develop it further, and one day, Mario will also wake up.

While I don't really like Julian, and I feel he's a manipulative snake, I respect that he would protect Jude and his friends. I just feel bad for his wife, Annalise. She seems like a genuinely nice person caught in an evil man's trap.

Not that I know anything about them or have the right to judge. Anyone looking at me and Jude could say the same, but no one sees him the way I do.

Jude walks out to the terraced balcony, and I follow suit, bringing an umbrella along.

I have to raise my hand up to cover him. "Are you okay?"

He looks down at me, takes the umbrella, and tilts it so that it's covering me, too, raindrops clinging to his jacket, then sliding down the fabric. "Go back inside. It's cold."

"Not without you and not before making sure you're okay." I plant a palm on his cheek. "I know this is a shock, but at least he's alive, right?"

"Right." He pulls me toward him by my waist. "I'm just not sure for how long before he defies all norms and actually gets himself killed."

"What do you mean?"

"I learned something from Kane, and I'm worried about Preston's future within Vencor."

"Is it that bad?"

"Possibly. The organization doesn't like rule breakers and Preston seems to be caught in what is considered a taboo within Vencor. But this time, I'll do everything in my might to make sure no one touches him."

"Me, too." I stroke his cheek. "I'll be with you every step of the way, Jude. Just like you're there for me as I slowly find myself."

"Always, sweetheart."

And then he's kissing me.

Under the blue umbrella.

For the rest of our lives.

EPILOGUE 2
Jude

Six months later

I TIGHTEN MY GRIP ON VIOLET'S HANDS THAT ARE wrapped around my waist. "Are you sure you want to do this?"

Her fingers are unsteady as I bring the bike to a halt, but she nods against my back. "I need to."

She hesitantly releases me, her body seeming weightless when she hops off the bike. Her hands still tremble when she tries to remove the helmet, so I do it for her, then push a rebellious copper strand from her glittery, expectant eyes.

Violet has been glowing lately. Partly because she's taking control of her life and learning self-love step by step, but also because Mario is showing signs of waking up after Julian decided to test the new variation of his drug on him.

By *decided,* I mean that he only agreed to help because it serves his goals. My brother is the most annoying person on earth, but I have to spend some dinners in his company because Violet has become close friends with Annalise for some reason.

Anyway, the most important thing is that Mario will get back to the world of the living soon, and Violet has been over the moon about the news. She's been preparing him gifts and doing research about how to help with comatose patients' rehabilitation, and while I don't like that—yes, I'm jealous of a comatose man, sue me—I love how radiant she looks.

I'd say that's the reason I'm in a constant state of arousal around her, but the reality is that I'm always ravenous for this woman, no matter what.

She could be sick and 'feel gross,' as she tells me, but she'd still be the most beautiful woman on earth for me. With her little smiles, hearty laughter, and that goddamn pure soul that I'll protect at any cost.

By protect, I mean kill for. You guessed it. I located the foster father who tried to rape her and stabbed him in the crotch, then cut his dick off and shoved it in his mouth. I'm on a mission to find every single person who wronged her and make them pay. Even if it was a random patron at HAVEN who thought it was an awesome idea to cop a feel.

But I won't tell Violet so she doesn't feel guilty since she can't help being such an empathetic soul.

Even though she was jaded and had to suffer her entire life, she still feels for others.

And yes, she was lost, but she's found her worth, and no one will hurt her now that I've come along.

Now that I've decided she'll be mine for eternity.

And because she's kind and doesn't like conflict, Violet's been slowly allowing her father's side of the family in, but really, she only likes Preston and maybe Lawrence. She made it clear that she wanted nothing to do with their money—not that Winston would listen.

But she doesn't need their fortune in the first place.

She's working toward becoming a therapist or a social worker to help those like her and Dahlia, but she's also been thriving in her online shop. She had to hire a couple of people to keep up with demand and even gifted me some free embroidery.

She told me that I've paid her enough for a lifetime, but the joke's on her.

I still create other accounts and buy all the shit I'll be decorating our family home with.

And yes, I know it's too soon, especially since she's slowly getting mentally better and embracing her younger self. It took her a while to realize that she had nothing to do with her mother's misfortune.

But whether or not it's too soon, Violet is the only one I'd start a family with.

And I know she wants that—a family. I can see it in her eyes when she stops to help a kid or when she affectionately smiles at them.

One day, I'll give her as many kids as she wants. A hockey team's worth of them if that's what it takes.

And truly, like Violet, I didn't have a traditional family. My mother loved me, but not enough to give up on her obsession or to get help, and my father was thoroughly absent.

My relationship with Regis is currently in that complicated phase where I want to keep my distance from him and only use him when I need help.

What?

Most of my life, he's only ever considered me a tool, too, so I see nothing wrong with doing the same thing.

Besides, I don't give a fuck about his sob stories and whatever happened between him and my mother. He still tortured me and gave me scars I can never erase. He's lucky I still talk to him.

Even Violet, who sees the good in everyone, doesn't

comment on my choices or ask me to spend more time with him. She just says to do what feels right, and that she'll always be there for me.

Which is why I'm also here for her.

Her eyes dart around as she touches her wrist. I can't see it well since it's half covered, but she changed her tattoo a couple of months ago.

From "Endure" to "I've Endured Enough."

And I couldn't be prouder of her.

My hand finds her waist, and I draw her against me. "Is it around here?"

"It should be, but…" She searches the area, the morning light casting a glow on her face, turning her eyes liquid blue.

"But?" I stroke her hip beneath her shirt, gentle and slow, and she relaxes. Violet craves all these little touches, and it also happens that I do, too.

I love how she melts in my arms and flashes me a small smile or even hums gently.

"Everything's changed," she whispers, still caught up in the unremarkable neighborhood we're visiting.

Her old neighborhood.

Violet chose to come here as part of her healing journey. An exercise about facing the past and letting it go.

And to finally bury the mother she couldn't for over a decade.

"The whole neighborhood was redone. Our house has been turned into a grocery store." She releases a humorless laugh. "Not that it was *our* house."

I tighten my grip on her waist. "Does that make you feel bad?"

She shakes her head. "I'm glad it's gone. Everything, including the closet and the room that smelled of black mold.

If anything, I like that it was all demolished and changed shape. I won't feel anything if I go into that grocery store."

"So that's a good thing?"

"Yeah. I can finally let go of this rotten limb that used to drag me down. My mother was dealt a bad hand, but it's not my fault."

"Good girl."

She bites her lower lip. "Don't call me that in public."

"Why?" I lower my voice, speaking against her earlobe. "Does it get you hot and bothered?"

She smacks my chest teasingly, laughing. "Jude!"

"What? I'm giving you different memories in the place that tried to break you but failed."

She faces me, wrapping both her arms around my waist. The way she looks up at me with that trust and love and complete adoration makes me want to shield her from the world.

To go back to the past and slay all her demons. To reach into her nightmares and kill the monsters that make her grow smaller.

She doesn't have them as often now, and she's no longer self-conscious about me seeing her in the throes of one. If anything, she wants me to hold her after them, burying her head in my chest and falling back asleep like that.

Violet has the type of soft, kind, and sometimes fiery personality that keeps me on my toes. I honestly refuse to remember my life before her and can't imagine it without her.

"Thank you." She smiles. "I'm glad I don't have to face that closet. Saved you a panic attack."

"Don't say that. I don't only love you on your good days, sweetheart. I love you more when you feel safe to be vulnerable with me."

"Who are you, and what have you done with my stalker who used to hate me to bits?"

"You turned that hate into love, sweetheart."

"I did?"

"Yes. You seem to have a lot of power over me."

"Do you hate that?"

"Not if it's you, no."

"Good. Because you have power over me, too, so we're equal."

"God, I love you." I stroke her cheek. "I don't know in which ditch I'd be in if you weren't in my life."

"I don't know if I'd still be alive if you weren't in mine, Jude." She gets on her tiptoes and kisses my cheek. "I loved you when I thought people like me don't deserve love."

"I'll spend the rest of my life showing you how much you of all people deserve that love."

And then I'm kissing her. Because I can't stop kissing her.

Looks like I need to marry her soon.

Make her my wife.

My partner.

And the light in my otherwise dark world.

THE END

Read on for a sneak peek at
Kiss the Villain,
a dark MM mafia romance

CHAPTER 1
Gareth

TONIGHT, I'M GOING TO HURT SOMEONE.

I don't care who as long as they wiggle and writhe like worms beneath my shoes.

Or, more accurately, a snake.

Just kidding. I do care who.

It can't be just *anyone*. The target of my night of mayhem needs to be a miscreant who's as bad as me.

Or worse.

On paper, *everyone* is worse than me, though, so there's that, I guess.

No one would expect The King's U—or TKU—college's resident genius law student to infiltrate the Serpents' mansion during one of their grand parties.

Or to target none other than the head of the Serpents, Yulian Dimitriev.

The son of the leader of the Chicago Bratva.

But I've always been up for a little challenge.

So here I am, walking amid the overflowing extravagance of their lively mansion, sliding between hot, drugged, and drunk bodies. Despite being a Heathen—the other secret club on King's U's grounds and the Serpents' deadly rival.

We've been at each other's throats since the start of school on this godforsaken island on the coast of the dreary, dark, and depressing United Kingdom.

And while we love causing trouble, the one who actually started the war was Yulian, who was just itching to have his head bashed in and splintered to pieces.

Obviously, we returned the initial blow, and ever since then, it's been a struggle to determine who holds more power.

Just kidding again. We're unrivaled.

However, the Serpents are up there as well. Especially Yulian.

Our fights are always the talk of the campus, and the underground fights draw more crowds than intended.

Truth is, everyone loves a bit of anarchy.

A touch of chaos and violence.

A drip of blood here. A crack of bones there.

The crazier the better. The more unhinged the scene, the more entertaining it is to the audience.

But that audience is appalled about the idea of getting close, throwing a punch, tasting that blood, or touching that broken bone.

It's shockingly disgusting.

Severely deviant.

Outrageously inhumane.

Vile.

Atrocious.

Horrifying.

I chant the same mantra in public—even among my friends. They know me as Gareth 'The Fixer.' Gareth, who makes sure no one gets killed and that the police are taken care of.

Golden-boy Gareth with the highest GPA, who had Ivy League colleges foaming at the mouth to have him join their ranks.

Gareth, who possesses the cleanest reputation and a future lined with open doors.

No one suspects that when they think I'm closed off in my room studying, I'm actually here, roaming behind enemy lines with the Serpents.

Doing what none of them, not even my brother, Killian, would ever do.

And I've been so meticulous about it, too. First, I needed to receive an invitation, and those are only issued by the upper echelon, i.e., Yulian and his gang of useless followers. But they also allow their invitees to bring plus-ones.

So I seduced one of the girls Yulian's been flirting with, pretending the book she was reading was interesting—it wasn't, just another piece of mind-numbing analytical bullshit written by a self-righteous idiot—and it got the convo going.

I was pretty sure she was Yulian's girlfriend since she was always hanging on to his arm and deep-throating him with her tongue around campus, but she sure didn't look like it when she had her foot on my crotch under the table in the library— disgusting, by the way, don't ever put your dirty shoes anywhere near me.

One incinerated pair of jeans later, I had the invitation I'd endured the urge to slit her throat for.

I've totally ignored her since I got here, though. The mask helps in keeping my preferred identity tucked away.

Invisible.

I adjust my white skeleton mask that has two large, black-painted holes where my eyes are—the Serpents' version of our neon stitch masks. While ours are differentiated by color, theirs can be distinguished by the symbols engraved on them.

Normal members, like who I'm pretending to be, wear a simple white skeleton mask.

The leaders wear black skeleton masks.

Yulian, whose movements I've been following from across the room, is also wearing a black skeleton mask, but his has engraved golden serpents shooting out from where his eyes are.

No surprise there, as he always loves standing out. The freakier the better.

His mansion is everything one would expect, though. An overwhelming display of power, wealth, and control. The grand hall stretches out before me in cold, decadent shades of ivory.

The chandeliers hang from the ceiling, dripping with crystals, emitting a dim, ethereal glow over the marble floors that shine like glass. Velvet drapes line the walls, their deep-red swaths casting a crimson hue on TKU's students.

Noisy chatter and loud music fill the air, but it all feels distant, muffled, because I'm standing on the outside of something I don't care to be part of.

I move through the crowd with ease, a faceless figure among the Serpents, blending in with the rest of them. My posture straight and movements confident, I slip further between them, unnoticed.

That's what I've always been.

Invisible.

Unremarkable.

Since I grew up in the overpowering shadow of my younger brother, I automatically became smaller.

Barely discernible next to him.

Completely overshadowed by his attention-seeking habits.

You're such a good boy, Gaz.

I never have to worry about you.

I'm so glad you're this dependable, son.

Responsible.

Reliable.

Perfect.

Perfect.

P. E. R. F. E. C. T.

Those are the words I grew up hearing from my parents, my grandpa, my teachers, and my entire entourage, really.

And I *love* it.

I like that none of them caught a whiff of this side of me.

The side riddled with urges and voids, and a thirst so deep, Kill would look like a saint if they realized.

Except for Grandpa.

Grandpa is different.

So back to those urges—the reason I'm wasting my time with these people. The air is thick with perfume, alcohol, and something else, something darker, like desperation and pain. It wraps around my throat like a noose, and I suck it deep into my lungs.

Like a hit of the strongest shit on the market.

Shit I slipped into Yulian's drink earlier when I casually passed by him while he was talking to one of his goons.

I made sure to be facing away from the camera so that if they checked the security footage later, they wouldn't find anything. Sure, they could track my movements throughout the evening, but I'm a step ahead on that front as well.

Not only did I make sure to avoid all cameras, but I also wore brown contacts, so even if they managed to get a picture of my eyes, it'd be misleading.

Yulian stumbles and grabs onto the staircase for balance. None of the other drunk fools pay him any attention.

My lips pull in a smirk behind the mask.

The drug is kicking in.

Soon, he'll be losing all his strength.

Don't misunderstand. I might want to ruin the Serpents' leader, but I'm not foolish enough to think I can handle him.

Not only is he big—almost as large and tall as my cousin Nikolai—but he's also cunning and surrounded by his people and guards who'll maim me on the spot.

I had to be smart about this.

I was never that good with my fists, which is why I learned archery and use arrows to shoot people at our initiations.

Pity I couldn't slip my bow in here.

He'd look cute with an arrow between his eyes and blood dripping down his face.

What a missed opportunity.

But my plans are more wicked. I'll humiliate him in a way that will get him blacklisted, not only on the island, but even back home.

His dad might put a bullet in his head. That would be fun.

My smile widens at the thought.

With Yulian gone, the Serpents will be over. Unlike us, who have a more balanced power structure, Yulian has been carrying this entire clusterfuck on his back this whole time.

Sure enough, Yulian trudges up the stairs slowly, holding on to the railing.

I wish I had a camera to record this scene.

The guys' minds would be blown if they knew what I've done and what I'll be doing.

But then again, they won't.

No one will.

Unlike my brother, I don't like showing off my masterpieces.

I blend in with a group that's heading upstairs and then break away and slide through other partygoers who are searching for a room where they can fuck the horniness out of each other.

It's beyond me how people can be such…animals. Letting their urges get the better of them, succumbing to dumb decisions and lackluster fucks they'll definitely regret come morning.

Don't get me wrong. Fucking is good, but only when I decide it's time to. I only get in the mood when I make the conscious decision to fuck, and never due to external stimuli.

Mostly, I love the power, the choking, seeing them writhe beneath me. I love it more when they have this little pained look in their eyes when it gets to be too much, and I wish I could keep hurting them. Turn their skin red. See their fucking tears. Blood. Their goddamn insides.

But alas, I can't have rumors that I'm a sadist going around. I'm known to be a good fuck with a huge dick who eats girls out until they come. I make sure they always come first, too. I also set the mood and ensure they stay hydrated and sleep well.

I'm the best fuck any girl can have, and I come with a ten out of ten recommendation rate.

So to keep that image, I can't exactly act on instinct.

Doesn't bother me, though. I've mastered the act of wearing a mask at all times—sex included.

Even with the people closest to me.

There's an external persona and an internal one.

The main version is the genius, well-mannered Gareth who's loved by everyone and would make a perfect politician.

The secondary version, coincidentally my true self, is Gareth, who I only let loose when the void gets too wide and I need to purge some dark energy.

Yulian happens to be the fortunate scapegoat.

Or unfortunate, depending on how you look at it.

I follow from afar and watch as he stumbles into a room. Whether or not it's his, I don't know.

Doesn't matter either.

I remain still near the corner for a few minutes.

Invisible.

It's a superpower I lost over the years as I grew up and became noticeable, mostly due to my looks. An accidental thing that happened because two good-looking people fell into something called love and decided to spawn some clones.

The clones were me and my brother—definitely not what my parents wanted.

They think Killian is the only anomaly with the Carson name, but that's only because they never *met* me.

Not really.

When I saw how they both freaked out about Kill's stupid harmless fun with killing mice, I stood around the corner and listened.

I listened to Dad blame himself, his genes, and that person who should not be named. I heard Mom cry and beg him to stop.

I heard the mess.

The desperation.

The impression that their perfect little family was shattered.

And I decided I wouldn't be like Kill.

I wouldn't flaunt my demons or publicize my emptiness. I wouldn't even let them figure out something was wrong or, worse, get so concerned that they'd take me to a doctor and have me diagnosed like they did with that idiot brother of mine.

I decided to be their unblemished boy. The picture-perfect son they actually never had and never will.

A spotless, unparalleled emulation of what I imagine a younger version of my dad would've been like.

Because that's who I would've turned out like if I hadn't been born me.

After a quick glance at my surroundings to make sure no one is paying attention, I walk to the room Yulian went into. My fingers are steady as I turn the doorknob, do a quick once-over to make sure no one is inside, and then go inside. With a small smile, I flatten my back against the door and lock it.

That was so easy, I'm slightly offended, but that doesn't stop my blood from roaring in my veins, a thunderous surge that resurrects me.

I've always loved the hunt, the way the creatures scurry in the shadows, the thrill of the unknown creeping in with every breath.

My heart booms and my demons claw at their chains, their rage spilling from the depths of the void, their bloodlust painting the room in my mind red.

My favorite color.

Yulian's room of choice is dim, the air thick with a stale, artificial chill. The walls are lined with dark wood paneling, casting shadows that stretch into the corners, making the space feel smaller than it is.

As I move closer, I catch a glimpse of a desk and shelves filled with books and knickknacks. But the only real thing that stands out is the black leather sofa in the center of the room, on top of which Yulian is sprawled. The sorry fuck probably couldn't make it to a room with a bed, too drugged out of his goddamn mind.

A mask still covering his face, he's dressed in black slacks and a long-sleeved shirt. My eyes flit to his pulse point—the first thing I notice about people.

It's beating steadily, the point throbbing against the skin in a hypnotizing view. It's silent, but I can hear the deep, rhythmic pulsating.

Thump.

Thump.

Thump.

And I want to cut it off.

To slice my knife through it and watch as it grows quiet.

Motionless.

Nonexistent.

I flick my thumb at the edge of my upper lip but quickly drop my hand before I can bite the skin and draw my own blood.

It's been a while since I got rid of that habit and I certainly won't let it rush back in now that I'm in full control of my being.

As much as I want to kill Yulian, I won't.

The one rule I have for myself is no killing.

It's not out of any moral code I mentally don't possess. In fact, I believe it'd do the human race good to get rid of the stupid wastes of space that keep diluting the average IQ.

It's the knowledge that I won't be able to stop and will eventually get caught.

Yes, I could avoid prison for a while. Not only am I a first-year law student who's studying law to manipulate it, but also, my dad's side of the family owns one of the largest and most successful law firms in the States, Carson & Carson.

My grandfather loves me more than his own son and would get me a 'not guilty' verdict no matter how many shady methods he had to use.

But how long would that last?

I'd still kill.

It would be impossible not to.

Especially after...*him.*

I know because bloodlust is the only urge I can't fully control. I watch people's pulse points and I wish I could turn them red. To see them choke on their own blood and let it fill the void inside me. I look into their eyes and I want them empty. I fantasize about dead eyes looking at me, knowing I'm the god who ended their lives.

It happens a lot during sex as they're moaning while I wrap my hand around their throats, and I want to squeeze that pulse point to nothingness.

I want their pleasure to turn into death. It'd be poetic, really. To end their lives in their happiest moment.

Unfortunately, that would ruin this whole image I've spent my entire life curating, and I do care about my image more than my need to see people die.

So, sadly, I can't kill Yulian.

I pause as I run my gaze over him again, the music thumping from downstairs barely audible.

Was he always this tall? I know he's big like that brute Nikolai, and they often go at each other in the fight club, but I thought he was closer to my six foot three than Nikolai's six foot four.

And he's not standing, so he shouldn't look *this* tall.

With a mental shrug, I stroll toward him and pull a knife from my calf sheath.

Step one: Undress him.

But I won't be undressing a guy personally—I don't even like undressing girls—which is why I brought the knife to cut his clothes off.

Step two: Empty the vial containing lube that looks and feels like semen over him.

Step three: Take a picture of my cock in my hand as if I just came on him.

Step four: Blast it all over the internet with his face on full display.

Step five: Retreat to my public persona, knowing I'm the one who brought his ruin.

Might punch and kick him a few times after, just to release this aggression that's been bubbling in my veins lately.

I pull on the hem of his shirt with a finger, not wanting to touch his skin. Preferably at all. Begrudgingly, once or twice for necessity.

The sharp knife cuts through the fabric and I pause as the two pieces of the torn shirt fall to either side of him, revealing a muscular chest, an eight-pack, and a very *wrong* tattoo.

Due to all the fighting he participates in, I've often seen Yulian half naked. While his back is tattooed with all sorts of shit, he only has one small tattoo on his chest—a line of scripture in Russian.

That's not what I see right now.

The guy lying in front of me, his chest exposed, has a massive 3D black snake coiling across his abs, its scales rising and twisting like they're alive, winding down to his side with menacing grace. Its mouth is open, fangs bared, inches from his heart like it's ready to sink in and tear into him.

I take a step back.

Unless Yulian got a new tattoo in the last forty-eight hours, this isn't him.

My mind races. How?

I clearly heard his voice when I slipped him the drug, and I kept my eyes on him from then on.

Except for when he went up the stairs first.

Fuck.

If this is a trap, I'm not waiting around to find out. My legs carry me toward the door in quick, silent steps.

The moment I grab the knob, a metal barrel is placed against my temple, and a gun clicks.

A deep, unfamiliar voice whispers in my ear, "It's bad form to get a man excited and then leave. How about we fix that?".

What's Next?

Thank you so much for reading *Sweet Venom*! If you liked it, please leave a review.

Your support means the world to me.

If you're thirsty for more discussions with other readers of the series, you can join the Facebook group *Rina Kent's Spoilers Room*.

The series continues with *Tempting Venom*, featuring Preston and Marcus.

About the Author

Rina Kent is a *New York Times*, *USA Today*, and #1 bestselling author of all things dark romance.

Better known for writing unapologetic anti-heroes and villains, Rina weaves tales of characters you shouldn't fall for but inevitably do. Her stories are laced with a touch of darkness, a splash of angst, and just the right amount of unhealthy intensity.

When she's not busy plotting mayhem for her ever-expanding *Rinaverse*, she leads a private life in London, travels, and pampers her cats in true Cat Lady fashion.